Micah Carlsen grew up on the Gower Peninsula, west of Swansea and was then educated at Cheltenham College. The university took him to the West Country, where he studied at Exeter and Plymouth. He has worked variously as a labourer, English and guitar tutor. Micah was a probation officer in the Devon cluster of prisons. He has lived in Swansea for the last five years with his Jack Russell and has enjoyed the support of the creative writing department at Swansea University.

For all those who have put up with me in the West Country and Swansea.

Micah Carlsen

DEAD MAN WALKING

Quarry Falls

AUSTIN MACAULEY PUBLISHERS™

LONDON * CAMBRIDGE * NEW YORK * SHARJAH

A CIP catalogue record for this title is available from the British Library.

ISBN 9781035824809 (Paperback)
ISBN 9781035824816 (ePub e-book)

www.austinmacauley.com

First Published 2024
Austin Macauley Publishers Ltd®
1 Canada Square
Canary Wharf
London
E14 5AA

To my family and friends and staff at the Humanities department at Swansea University with special thanks to Steve BDO for specialised advice and Kiwis Lulu and Jen for all their support and encouragement over the internet.

Prologue Part 1
Sapper Mike Lapin at Home: 1995

'What was he like then, Mikey?' His mother asked as she folded the red and white tea towel over the cooker handle to dry off. She turned to make eye contact with her son who was leaning against the door frame of the kitchen, replete after the Sunday roast.

Sapper Mike Lapin loved coming home for the weekend, back to Saltash, across the water from Plymouth. He'd been in the Royal Engineers for a year now and, at nineteen, it had been the making of him. Before that, having left school, he'd been listless and vulnerable. Apprenticed to his dad as a carpenter, Mikey had an aptitude for the work, but father and son had wound each other up and decided to part company after six months. It had upset the pair of them, but both knew it was for the best.

Then Mikey had been on the boats, scallop and regular trawlers, for the best part of a year, working alongside his cousins and uncles, but he couldn't get on with the lifestyle. Ten days at sea, four days home on the sauce and then back out on the salt again—it just wasn't for him. He'd given it his best, thinking he'd found his niche, and he'd stuck it longer than perhaps he should have. He'd persevered for nearly a year for fear of failure after not making it work with his father. But his mother had spotted early on that he was putting a brave face on it and that it wasn't for him. The life just didn't suit, he'd never found his sea legs and the uncles and cousins were a bit much. A rum, noisy crew they were. Sea Pikes, his father had always called them. Mikey didn't know why.

No, the Lapins, the three of them, were a different proposition altogether from the seafaring side of the family. They were quiet people who were self-contained and liked their own company. Some thought them aloof but they weren't. Being in any sort of limelight was just anathema to them. They were quiet and preferred to do their works in the shadows. Quick-witted, sensitive and blessed with a keen eye, the Lapins were sharp people. Just quiet.

Jenny Lapin had had an inkling that her son might join the army. He'd always had more than a touch of wanderlust about him, a sense of independence and adventure that had marked him out as an outsider at school, although there was no doubting he was a team player given his prowess at any team sport he cared to turn his hand or quick legs to. Yes, the army ticked all the right boxes. Mikey liked his boundaries and structure and he had a natural respect for his elders when they were consistent (unlike the Sea Pikes).

So, the Royal Engineers was a good fit as he'd always tinkered with bikes, scooters, outboards, anything with moving parts. But why bomb disposal, for goodness sake? His announcement eighteen months ago had made Jenny and Jack Lapin collapse down on the sofa in dumb silence. It wasn't the reaction Mikey had been looking for, but he supposed he understood it. He'd stuck to his guns and looked straight ahead as he delivered his news, his life intention. There was no way he could make eye contact. He would have crumbled, that much he knew, and his mother observing this knew then that she'd lost her 'little man'. What mother would like the idea of her son in harm's way like that?

Neither parent had challenged him after the initial protestations, such was their recognition of the resolve they noted fixed in his faraway eyes. They'd just got on with it and gone about their business quietly and had talked about anything but. Still waters run deep, as they say. That night at tea, the cutlery had been louder than ever.

Jenny Lapin noticed her son folding his arms as he shifted, as if on sea legs, in the kitchen door of their two up, two down fisherman's cottage in Saltash after their Sunday lunch, his first home leave since it had happened. He can't have been comfortable with the question, she thought, but she asked it again nevertheless, keen as she was to understand. Captain William Collins had been her son's senior commanding officer, mentor, father figure and friend for the best part of a year, his first year as a Sapper with the Royal Engineers as a Bomb Disposal Officer. Now that he was gone, she could see the sense of loss her son felt and she wanted him to talk about the Captain so that they all might better understand the man that had been such an influential figure in her son's life.

'Well, what was he really like?' Jenny Lapin repeated. This time she noted Mikey swallow as his glance flicked around the modest kitchen, searchingly.

'What can I say, mum? The longest serving bomb disposal officer in the history of the service. And one of the best, by all accounts. Constantly adapting...'

'For Pete's sake, Mikey, you know what I mean!'

There was a pause while Mikey searched his memories and then he began.

'He always wore a poppy fashioned out of a brass 18lb shell fired at Passchendaele and the swagger stick presented to him after thirty years of service was made of the wood of the mast from HMS Victory. That just about sums him up, Ma. Cut him in half and you would thought he'd've bled green blood. Well, I did until Portland...' Mikey peered at his feet.

Delicately now: 'Mikey, I kind of meant more of what he was like as a person.'

'I know what you meant, I just...' his eyes roved the room seeking words or inspiration. Exasperated, he blurted, 'I dunno what to say. He wanted to keep a few greyhounds when he retired. Called them gypsy shot guns. Said they were the most extraordinary feats of biological engineering in the canine world. He had a thing about whales too, and made Chinese puzzle boxes.'

It wasn't the answer to the question and certainly not what Jenny Lapin had had in mind. But she understood that that was all she was going to get for the time being and there was no point getting him all wound up. He was clearly frustrated with baffle. Continuing might just have closed the box on him *permanently. No, time would tell and he would too when he was ready. She'd sown the seeds for the next conversation and that was good enough for now.*

The Captain had made a powerful impression on her son and she wanted to get more of a sense of him but Mikey had never been much of a talker, particularly about feelings. And there was a lot of that going on there. She knew full well that those quiet waters ran deep and potentially turbulent in him, too.

Prologue Part 2

Oh, my days! When I told a mate that I was writing this book and outlined the idea for him, he beamed back at me. *A cracker*, he reckoned, *it could be*. And chuffed I was to hear him say it, I'm not ashamed to say! A bit of buoying up, I needed, when it came to the nitty gritty of sitting down to write this tale and most don't feel inclined to give the encouragement. Especially if they've heard those fabled words *I'm writing a book* before.

A lot of people react funny to that sort of statement too and it's not long before you see the usual ideas pass behind the eyes. *Oh, get a load of him, who does he think he is? 'I might write a book'. Everyone's got a book in them.* And then, *I'm not sure if I'm bright enough to write a book. All that stuff.* Someone actually said that to me. And he was a Tornado jet engineer too! One of the cleverest guys I've ever met. Can fix anything, build a house, do anything, run twenty miles straight if you asked him to, you name it! But he said that.

It's funny what goes on behind all that bravado and posturing. Scratch and tap the surface of a 'big-I-am' and you'll probably squint to hear an echoey, hollow sound. I reckon it's just an act, a mantle that covers the fissures in the confidence. It's something the successful learn to do early on. And it's a close cousin of the 'admit nothing and deny all' philosophy. How very, very British.

Anyways, back to those book-writing conversations. It's about then, just after you've admitted trying to write a novel, that the conversation dies. As soon as it's started, to be fair. And then you do a lot of smiling and nodding while you search for some conversational terra firma. It comes across as a strange mixture of envy and mistrustful respect. Not what you want to feel! So, when another mate didn't pause for thought and offered up his genuine encouragement, I thought, 'Oh my Lord, here we go!' And I gave him a rundown of the outline of the plot. He nodded and smiled a lot, asked questions and said all the right things. He'd taken the bait, got himself snagged on all the hooks I'd hoped he would. All the things I needed to hear, God bless him. We had a good slurp of tea and then went quiet for a bit as the contentment settled, as happens with close friends. No need for words sometimes. Quite the opposite of a book, I suppose.

But then his eyes clouded over with a question and I wondered if I hadn't been too hasty in my assessment. 'Trouble is,' he pondered, 'do people, young or old, know anything about Portland particularly? Like where it is, what it's like? And why should anyone care?'

Oh crap, I thought. Nearly on the rocks and I hadn't even made it out of port.

'So,' he said, 'tell me about the place and why I'd find it interesting as a setting for a story. What's it got to do with me?' He wasn't going to let me get away with it that easily and reply with a statement like, 'Interesting!' which people usually say when they've nothing to say. I inhaled deeply, nostrils flaring, while I thought of how to answer. So, here goes:

Portland is an island off the South Coast of England. If you travel due south across the Channel, you're in France and from there you can get to mainland, continental Europe. You can even get as far as Goa in the South of India if you're really determined! By sailing down the Channel, you can reach any ocean in the world; the Atlantic across to the Americas on the Trade Winds then around Cape Horn to the Indian Ocean, or alternatively there's the old Spice Route to the Indian Ocean around the Cape of Good Hope. You can reach Africa via the Med, or voyage in the opposite direction, up the Channel to the North Sea.

With a bit of imagination, Portland could be the starting point of a journey to anywhere in the world. And that's why the Admiralty, the British Navy, set up there. That and the fact it's one of the deepest natural harbours there is and it's a perfect point from which to defend the mainland from attack from any dastardly European invader. Hence, Portland and its environs are peppered with castles and citadels.

Henry VIII got all excited about it and built the castles around the same time that he got a fluster on about the Mary Rose. Unlike the Mary Rose, the castles are still there and didn't go belly-up *tout suite*. That's another, separate story for you to stick in your search engine though.

About a thousand years before Old Henry got in a lather about Portland, the Romans did too. Interestingly, and pertinent to our story, it was the Romans who introduced rabbits to our fair island, Britain. They weren't always here. Just think of it, there wasn't a single rabbit on the British isles until the Romans came. Brought them for food and clothing, no doubt. How did the rabbits get on to Portland before the Causeway was built, back when it truly was an island?

Well, the Romans took a shine to Portland. Called it Vindelis and after them, the Vikings got cosy in 789. The local tax collector tried to charge them for landing on the King's soil. The Vikings, however, were never ones to suffer a fool gladly, promptly did what Vikings do best—murdered the lot of them and rowed on for the next bit of savagery, probably to discover America some 500 years before Christopher Columbus and Vespucci Amerigo took all the credit for it. You could say, *how very American!* But I'd prefer to say, *You gotta love a Viking!*

Anyway, anyway (I can be a talker when I get going, you can tell)! Back to Portland where our tale is located. Technically, Portland is an island not even two miles square, famous for its white limestone from which a whole load of the nation's capital is built. Lots of London landmarks, starting with St Paul's Cathedral and the Cenotaph, are made up of huge slabs of the white stone, quarried on Portland and transported on barges up the Channel to the Thames. Whole heaps of Great British history began both on the isle and inside the hallowed buildings of the Capitol made of its stone. And that makes it significant.

Portland sits sentinel at the eastern tip of Chesil Beach, an eighteen mile pebble spit that runs part way along the Western Dorset coast. These days a modern Causeway links it to the mainland at Weymouth but historically, Portland was always an island.

It is thought that Portlanders of old, taking advantage of their geographical location, were pirates and wreckers. Shining lanterns from isolated coves, they drew the storm-battered, the weary and the unsuspecting towards the treacherous rocks and reefs. After splintering their hulls, their ship and hopes sinking, the sailors would have to head for safety and land on the pebbles of Chesil. There they'd be met by a baying band of islanders, Portlanders, who'd deport them of any last vestiges of hope out as they dashed out their brains, so as to plunder the cargo of their sinking ships.

Just think, how much desperation, hope, cunning and planning must it take to trick a listing ship to treachery and then to murder its crew to plunder their holds? Getting an impression? Nice! Well, now we're getting closer to an understanding of the character of the Portlander of old. Or not so old. It's why there is a graveyard on the isle known as 'The Pirates' Graveyard'; full of gravestones, a homage to the islanders of old, but without a single name inscribed so as to protect the families involved in their bloodthirsty heritage. Instead, carved into the slab of stone of each grave is the legendary symbol of piracy: the skull and crossbones. I kid you not. Go take a looksee.

So, what's it like, this tiny little island that's got such a stake in our country's history? Well, just like a person, it has many faces, facets, moods and dispositions. Catch it on a sunny day in summer, when the sea shimmers, the salt burns happily on your lips from the wind and the sky is cloudless, and it couldn't be more inviting. But when that sky darkens with angry squalls and the white water of the waves growls and vaults up venting its wrath over the cliffs, thirsty to drag back the unsuspecting, you see a different, other side of the isle. More than that, you can *feel* it, as the wind and rain and waves wash away its seaside welcome of sand castles and brightly coloured windmills to reveal something older, brooding, haunted.

Something that seems to want to get into the very bones of you, making you feel all unravelling and vulnerable, the same way you feel when you catch something out of the corner of your eye that vanishes when you turn towards it. Or, when a series of events is set in motion that you don't seem to have control of, which in the re-telling causes people to look at you funny, quizzical with disbelief, not a little bit afraid and reluctant for any of your ill luck to rub off on them. People make their excuses to hear no more and beat a hasty retreat as if they might suffer some aural contagion if they stay any longer in your company.

You think I'm being a bit over the top? Well, it might seem that way. But you ask your oldies about a place, an event, a feeling or set of goings-on that shouldn't really have happened and they'll tell a similar tale and describe that same tremor of *dis-ease*. That *someone's just walked over my grave* shiver. It's the same the world over. And so it should be, as it's a part of us, what makes us human animals. It's a part of our intuition that we're so busily trying to banish. But more of that later.

So, what on earth am I on about? That feeling … Kids have it in bucketloads. It's how they survive. That's why they are susceptible to seeing and feeling what adults have forgotten how to. (Though, the older they get and nearer the end, the more they remember it. Full circle, and not so strange when you think about it, after all.) Back to children, they don't know enough about life yet to make any other judgement than an instinctive one. *They always know when something's wrong.* It's instinct and it's what keeps us alive.

It's been in the developing since the beginning of human time and what's kept us alive. Stone Age man didn't go into the forest on a stormy night with the wind warping and screaming through the trees, not because he could see the wolves but because he knew in his gut, in his mind's eye, in his heart, in his whatever that to venture into that forest meant danger of death. He didn't think it, he *knew* it.

You still get this sense in old places of isolation where the spirits aren't drowned out by the electrical thrum of our modern life; no Wi-Fi, phones, laptops or screens to distract us from what we actually feel right down in our guts. Take all that away and we're left feeling a bit exposed with the distinct possibility of going to pieces. Our instinct is very, very old and is a close cousin of a lot that we have forgotten in our hurry to have the most modern and ultimate (*I hate that word*) in all things.

Instinct is also the plane on which the ghosts and spirits of our ancestors live and our old places are closest to that instinct. Talk to anyone who has been to an ancient place left untouched and they'll all describe the same feeling; that the rocks and the stones of the place seem to seep with its history. And that's what Portland feels on a squally day when the light changes at four o'clock in the evening in October and we're somewhere between light and dark and nothing looks quite like it should do. Or least how it did five minutes ago.

And Portland is steeped in it, in history, way back before French invading forces or the Spanish Armadas or Henry VIII, before all the piracy, right back to when man was no more than a clever monkey. There are Stone Age settlements on the isle and they've left behind something of themselves in the Rock. Ancient man must have felt its magic and noted its strengths as a strategic place of safety away from marauding peoples or creatures from the mainland. They could defend the island by hurling rocks down on their enemies.

Another storyteller named Portlanders 'the Slingers' because of their charming habit of flinging rocks and boulders at visitors from the mainland, England, such was the Portlanders' love of the mainlander. And that 'love' was reciprocated too. The mainlanders laid siege to them, or simply wouldn't let them land to barter for supplies when the catch wasn't aplenty and the crops failed. It works both ways living on an island, you see. And doesn't it make you think: if people separated by a few hundred metres of water can't get along…?

Back on track, back on track, I'm prone to rambling off on tangents and just about any crooked path. So, up until not so long ago, there were said to be only five families of Portland before they built the Causeway. There were others. But they were outsiders living on the isle. The Bartholomews, Combens, Moores,

Stones and the Scrivens were the principle five families. I say families but I think clans is probably a better word. I wonder how far back those clans can be traced? Right back to when mammoths and woolly rhinoceroses roamed those environs? The genetic codes could probably be traced. I don't know, but I do wonder. Tall, strong and dark, they were different-looking from the mainlanders who seemed to be of a shorter, stockier breed. I wonder how the mainlanders, looking out across the water at Portland with its tall, dark, strange inhabitants, felt about them?

Weather-hardened, quiet and insular are Portlanders. Not ones for a lot of chat for the most part, by all accounts. And sometimes when there's a lack of communication, tensions rise. Another bit of local folklore is that the clans were often divided against one another by bitter feuds; vendettas that spanned generations. And there's more than a few tales there, no doubt. But what brought them together was their common distrust of the mainlander and their acute sense of superstition.

Whereas the mainlanders weren't governed in the same way by their beliefs in otherworldly powers, the islanders were and still are sure to spot omens, augurs and the hand of the devil in all manner of everyday things. Quick shifts in the weather, a strange fish in the catch, the passing of dancing shadows in the firelight. All sorts. And it's still the same today. Whether this is linked to their history, the ancientness of the place and my theory of intuition, I couldn't say. But superstitious? They are with bells on. Maybe that's why they seem such an odd people. Can you say 'odd'? Dunno, but I just did. Perhaps better change that to 'different'. Whatever! Those Portlanders, they know it too, that they're odd! You could even go as far as saying that they're proud of their history of differentness, for around the time of the 2012 Olympics they came up with the bumper sticker legend: *Keep Portland Weird*. Seems they are proud of it.

That sense of foreboding, of other-worldliness, of superstition, is nowhere more manifest than in their feelings about rabbits. I kid you not! Rabbits, for goodness sake! But, a cardinal sin it is to mention these furry creatures on the island. The Sheriff of Portland once told me, 'If the word 'rabbit' is used in company in Portland, there is generally a bit of a hush. In the olden days,' he said, 'when quarrying was done by hand, if one of these animals was seen in the area, the quarryman would pack up and go home for the day until the safety of the area had been reconnoitred. It is an unwritten rule in Portland that you do not use the 'R' word.'

I could go on about this more. But I just want to give you a flavour of where our story takes place and the kinds of things our main character would have known and grown up with. Setting the scene, that's what I'm up to. Putting a bit of back ground in there so you don't think it's me who's completely potty. Or, where the heck is this going? Because most of the story, save for a bit of licence, is true. As is the fact that the appearance of spectral prisoners and officers trapped between the ominous, impenetrable grey stone walls of the island's prisons, plural (for that is where the majority of the quarrymen went to work when the need for stone slowed) is normal and no cause for alarm. It's just one of those things that happens on Portland. All in a Portlanders' day's work.

The sceptics will be thinking, 'he's making it up!' But I'm not. The screams of men crushed to death in quarry falls of two hundred years ago is pretty much a regular thing too. What's normal for some is just *bona fide* frightening for others, for the rest of us.

But don't get me wrong. I love Portland. Every year for yonks, I've been spending a two-week summer holiday there in our hut. It's cosy and simple; one bedroom with two bunks and all the seats double up as beds. Ours is one of about twenty in that field. The huts line the perimeter with the water butt in the middle. That was always the kids' first job—to fill up four gallon drums and lug 'em back to fill up the boiler. Or, we'd have to get on up to the post office shop for milk and bread. Everyone has to muck in, everyone their jobs. It's what gives the day its shape.

After the water was done, we'd arse around in the field or go off exploring. Daytimes were spent on the beaches and bluffs, climbing the rocks, or off fishing for Wrasse to bait up the lobster pots. All good stuff. At night we went searching for fireflies, illuminous green crescents nestling in the grass. Or hide and seek in the quarries and castles. Always on our own too, not an adult in sight! They'd be sunning themselves by day and reading or playing cards in the evenings. That's the rule on Portland. You've got to make your fun. Gosh, to think of the freedom we had back then, in those days before screens. The parents didn't ask us what we were doing and we didn't tell 'em. Just perfect! So much has changed in a generation.

Yairs, there's no doubt. Portland has a warm place in my draughty old heart. It's the place of a thousand happy memories; memories of freedom set against the backdrop dazzle of a restless July sea and an endless curve-blue horizon; of a field of fire flies mirroring the star-scape above; the reassuring sweep of the light house beam on dark, starless nights, scanning the surroundings and keeping an eye on us all; of being cooched up, snug in the hut as the wind and rain hammered the windows and pulled at the roof tiles, causing the hut to shift on its stumps, cantankerous-like. Happy fright!

That's the other, beautiful side of Portland, of the setting of this story. For me, it will always be the stage of my carefree, outdoor childhood. So, there's always another side to a story. More than one, if we really get into, it's just that sunshine and frolics are not the backdrop of *this* story.

But enough of all that though, before I start waffling on again. Let's get on with our story.

Chapter 1
Portland 1944

It was a week before it happened that Billy first spotted them. Those dark, sleek, flickering shapes that seemed to be moving much too quickly across the water. About two mile out, he guessed. Menacing, dark shadows, much quicker than anything he'd ever spotted before. And hadn't he seen some strange old things! Couldn't be whales, surely? Could they? Quicker than anything he was used to seeing, anyhow. Billy scrunched his eyes up further behind his field glasses, conscious that the wet grass beneath him had seeped right through his fisherman's tunic now as he watched them. Blumin' cold he was, teeth beginning to chatter ever-so-slightly, intermittently.

But he ignored the discomfort, gripping the glasses tighter still. He was made of sterner stuff than to be bothered by the cold, he told himself. And no-one else was around on a cliff-top on Portland at 3 am on a full moon 21 April 1944 to listen to his moans. If there was summat to be done, he'd be doing it, he told himself. But would they believe him? His confidence waned a little as cloud passed across the face of the moon, making its gaze quizzical. With the glimpsing of the light, Billy lost track of the shapes. Damn and blast, he was annoyed. What could he tell anyone now? That he'd seen some quick, dark shapes about two miles out? It just sounded silly. No-one would take him seriously and he'd be a laughingstock again or worse, if Mr Scriven got wind of it. He closed his eyes and made a rumbling 'no' sound in the back of his throat. Some of the other kids already called him 'Creepy Collins' and some, 'Cry Wolf Collins'. He didn't need be fuelling their fantasy anymore, he counselled himself.

Deflated, Billy put the field glasses down in the mossy grass and rubbed his eyes and then placed his palms on his cheeks, looking out over the water, hundreds of feet below. Ten years old and alone on a limestone cliff top wondering what to do next. After a few moments of enjoying the salt winds buffet him, eyes watering, fringe flipping, he pushed himself to his feet and carefully put his binoculars back in their leather case, having given the lenses a cursory clean with his shirt tail. Standing there, he felt proud that his grandfather had given him them. So immensely proud, as a matter of fact. And what a tale to go with them even if they made him as unpopular as Grandfather John in the trenches of World War I *and* then back home on the island to boot!

Billy'd never forget the night Grandfather John had died at home, not up in his room, but in the front room downstairs in Old Sea Dog Cottage. He involuntarily conjured the scene as he hurried home now. He didn't want Granny and Ma to find him gone. That sort of thing just freaked 'em out. Especially now as he was man of the house. They were all in the school house learning some geography or other about the British Empire. He remembered that Britain was pink and so were all the countries it owned which'd seemed odd as it was the smallest country of them all by a long short.

Even Mr Scriven's vaguely threatening, flat monotone had trailed off when they first felt and then heard the rumble and thunder of a large rock fall from up in the quarry. The rumbling went on for longer than it should. That was what really stilled them. With each over-extended second of rumble, the wider the children's eyes set. Billy and his class mates furtively keened and lowered their heads to the window to see and hear more. Then there'd been a deafening quiet, a terrible few moments of registration and think-time that seemed to go on for an eternity before Billy's class and Scriven had watched as people vaulted hedges and walls, and bounded across fields to the wide road up towards the quarries in a desperate hurry to help.

Portland came together at times of strife, Grandfather said. Old rivalries and new bickerings all dissolved when a boat was lost in a storm or when there was a rock fall at the quarry. And it was then, in that moment, in Scriven's stuffy classroom (why couldn't he open a window?), as he came to mind, that Billy'd realised something had happened to Grandfather John. Billy could see him wrapped in a red canvas sail, like the ones on the fishing boats on down on the harbour. It was a puzzling image.

Mum said it was gift, his second sight. Billy just said it made him feel sick. Like seasickness, but much worse. He'd feel white-hot across the shoulders and his vision would blur and he'd see what was to come or something that'd happened to someone close to the family either like a snapshot or a few seconds of film in slow motion. What was weird about it was that time seemed to stretch and a few seconds seemed like hours. But whichever way he looked at it, he knew that his Grandfather John was in proper trouble.

And why'd it have to be rock falls, drownings, beatings—none of it ever happy—that was the thing! Why couldn't he see the nice things before they happened? It wasn't as if he could keep it to himself either. He looked weird when it happened. No two ways about that. When he froze in a trance, only his real friends, Maggie Golding and Petey Carter, ever stayed with him. The other kids scattered like marbles. It'd only happened a few times. But that was enough for them. It was only Mags and Petey that looked out for him. The other kids just got silly or hysterical at worst, and that was what birthed his nickname, 'Creepy Collins'.

There was more to it than this as Maggie's mum had explained to him, 'They're just a bit ignorant on the island and is scared of what they don't unnerstand.' Billy took comfort from this as he did from anything Maggie's mum said. She was such a warm soul. But he hated being the outsider and had vowed to leave the island as soon as he was old enough. He'd said as much to Maggie and Petey and they were so dismayed that he'd never said it again. And that made him feel even further out of the loop of things.

The rock fall must have been about two in the afternoon, on Wednesday, a blistering end-of-July day. There was only the suggestion of a breeze, but the sharp, cloying scent of limestone dust had quickly reached them, inveigling itself with sea salt and the sweet, yellow scent of spring gorse. Scriven had kept the kids a half hour after school finish time for reasons known only to himself and so it wasn't until gone four that he got home to see the ashen, drawn faces of his mum and Grandmother. It just confirmed what he already knew.

By tea time, an hour later, Grandfather John had been carried down from the quarry on a stretcher that was two wooden poles with red sail-canvass stretched between them. He had a sheet over him too. Billy was in the back kitchen. The latch hadn't settled properly and the door had opened a few inches again after mum had quickly shut it behind her while drying her hands on her apron. That was when she'd heard the quarry men calling for her from the front door.

'Now stay put, Billy, 'til I've had chance to see if Grandfather's alright for you to speak to him,' she'd implored with her eyes. He couldn't say why she'd have said this, but he thought it might have something to do with the browning rose blooms that were showing through the sheet that had been draped over

Grandfather. There was a lot of shuffling, scrapes of boots on the slate floor as the two men carried Grandfather into Sea Dog Cottage.

His grandfather's eyes were closed; his lips pursed dry; his face a colourless, limestone grey and grubby with dust with clear rivulets on his temples where the sweat had cut through. He had some sort of cloth hat on that Billy'd never seen him wearing before. Billy remembered the two quarry men, one of them being Peter's father, the other with a beard, he didn't recognise. Both were panting and rasping for breath, sweating—it was a long way down from the quarry, but they complained not and communicated with grunts, intakes of breath, and juts of the chin.

They'd taken their time manoeuvring him through the stable front door into the narrow hall and into the front room. A bed had been set up for him in there as the staircase was too narrow and rickety to get him upstairs to his own room. Someone must have sent word ahead. Billy heard Grandfather gasp with pain. They must have set him down.

Billy had been staring out the window at the sea as a South Westerly had begun to give it a bit of froth and chop. As he tuned back into his immediate surroundings, he turned to see Petey's father with his kindly smile and the other grimmer-looking fellow declining the offer of some tea and bread and fish.

'More to be done, now,' Petey's father said meaningfully before turning about to trudge back up to the quarry. Billy's mum watched them to the gate and the other gave her a curt nod as he shut the gate behind him. She stood stock still and knotted her apron. Then she shut the door quickly and bustled into the kitchen. She'd lost that faraway look and was all business now.

'Doctor'll be here shortly. Boil up the copper now, Bill! Grandfather needs some warm water. And heat up the soup. *Maybe if I could try to get him to eat?*' she queried herself.

Billy set to it quick smart. Whatever needed to be done. Anything! Even these new and unusual requests. He'd not tended the stove before. Something had shifted. And Billy wondered why his mum'd called him 'Bill'. She'd never called him that before. He'd always been Billy, as long as he could ever remember. Not William, not Bill. Always Billy. But from that moment on, he was 'Bill' at home.

Time passed slowly in spite of his mother's quick deliberate movements. Neither spoke. She served up a bowl of soup for him and set one on a tray for his grandfather. She also laid out a bowl of warm water and a cloth. That hadn't happened before either. Then she said that she wanted to have 'a few minutes, just her and Grandfather' before the doctor arrived and that she'd call him in when she was ready. Ready for what?

The light in the kitchen dimmed as scudding cloud obscured the sun as it dipped to the horizon in the west. It took the sheen and colour out things the same way mackerel bellies lose their rainbows when they stop twitching. Open mouth, grey. Billy stopped spooning up his soup and looked to his mum, hoping for some sort of explanation. They both heard the gate go, then the crunch of boots on the crushed shells on the path, then more definite up the steps. 'Doctor,' she said. She dropped her eyes, took up the tray and left the kitchen.

Billy was about to get up from the table and follow her, help out or something, when he heard her sharply pull the door to and the latch click. He turned to look out of the kitchen window. The light was grey and the wind must have dropped to less than a murmur.

Billy folded the thick soup, toying with the chunks of hake and conger in his bowl, making them appear and disappear. At first a little made it as far as his mouth and then as time passed none at all until finally he licked the spoon and set it on the table. Usually fidgety and full of taps and ticks, he was now immobilised by the quiet and the hushed voices from the next room. This way he sat prone until the latch scraped back and Mum said Grandfather wanted to speak to him.

Billy nodded almost imperceptibly, aware of his breathing. The hush thickened so that everything else—a chair scraping back, the front door latch or the wind in the eaves—grated. In the sitting room, all was still, save for Grandfather's eyes which were open now though the rest of him moved not a jot as he scanned Billy up and down from the door way. Those rose blooms on the sheet were larger now and had darkened. They made him want to step back. Billy thought of the wooden bottom of his boat. And then the room rocked the way a boat did on a surge of swell.

'Come 'ere, Billy-bub, son,' whispered his grandfather, beckoning with the eyes, then pausing to catch his breath. 'You know you're a good boy, son. You're sharp and clever. Quick with your hands. Have only ever had to show you what to do and you can do whatever it is you need to do. Not many's like that.' He paused while he closed his eyes and the air rasped as it passed his lips. Someone in the room made a sucking, clicking, swallowing in the back of their throat noise that made Billy's stomach turn over like he was seasick, all giddy and shuffling.

The lines around his grandfather's eyes creased deeply as his focus sharpened and his voice lost some of its gentleness. 'Come sit, Billy. Sit!' he said and then, with a grip that still belonged to a much younger man, he took Billy's hand. Again his grandfather repeated, 'You are a good boy, Billy. Don't let anyone ever tell you otherwise. But you are different from the others. Perhaps not Maggie. But she hides it well. From the others, yes. And you wear your heart on your sleeve. That'll give you trouble if you can't learn to conceal it a bit more. On this island and at school at any rate.'

Billy winced, not from the painful grip of his grandfather, more from the fact he was foxed by these riddles. Grandfather was usually so clear. And then another sharp rattle of breath.

'Soon you'll be man of the house now. And I know you'll do a good job. I've got all my trust and confidence in you. Look after the boat (skiff). It's that that'll feed you and your mother. Do as you're told when you're told 'til you know there's a better way to go about it. Then be polite. Never belittle anyone, never corner a rat, give him every chance to get away 'cause if you corner him, he will bite and jump, he can too.' He paused and Billy's mum put a sip of water to his lips.

Billy noticed that the bread was still there and the spoon lay clean beside the soup bowl. A squeeze of the hand drew Billy's attention back. 'Now finish your schooling. I know the books is hard for you. But listen to what Mr Scriven has to say. We have our differences, but that doesn't stop him being a clever man.'

'Ah, Grandfather!' Billy complained, trying to pull away. Grandfather knew he hated Mr Scriven. They all did. Why were they talking about that hateful man now?

Wide-eyed with a ferocity that took the room off-guard, 'Do as I bloody say, now, boy! Listen to Scriven. You make money with your brains, not your brawn. Finish your schooling and do something that'll take you off Portland. Something that'll take you over the horizon. It's no good to stay put here all your life. It's familiar alright. But that breeds contempt. And you got something about you.'

His grandfather said a lot more about taking care of Billy's mum and being ever watchful, alert when he was out on the water. What he wasn't ready for was Grandfather telling him where his German World War 1 field glasses were and that now they were his. Another confusing switch.

Then it dawned on Billy what was happening, the summing up. And then out of nowhere, but back to a gentle caring tone, 'And tell them about the rabbits,

Billy-bub. And set 'em straight on that for me, will ya? They're helping, not hindering. If I'd have paid more attention to them, we wouldn't be having this conversation now.' His voice trailed. The grip slackened.

That was that for Billy's grandfather. He was buried up in the cemetery on a nondescript, grey day. Billy remembered little of it. Sounds and impressions. The clomp of boots as they entered the church. Then that dusty, morbid, shuffling as people manoeuvred into the rigid pews. Awkward sounds. Whispers, coughs. Stolen looks to see who was there. The vicar, who had a mouth that always made him look like he was having a nasty shock, was more ill at ease than usual as the congregation peered at him, clearly puzzled by his words, their antipathy barely concealed. Outside the light was listless and crows and gulls pulled at the wind. Some way off, something had irritated Scriven's dog. And Billy was cold from all the standing around. Couldn't wait to put the body in the ground and get out on the water.

Years later, Billy older, then older still, wondered why he couldn't remember more of that day. It was an important day. He loved his grandfather. His own father he couldn't remember at all and everything he knew had come from his grandfather or mum. Of course, it was because he was young. But when he learned the ways of his job, he learned to turn off his emotions and he noted that the clarity of his memory of events became crystalline. He wondered if strong emotions clouded the memory.

What he did remember as he ran back to Old Sea Dog Cottage that day to change out of his scratchy Sunday clothes, while he ran to the beach and prepared the skiff to go out to fish (and why shouldn't he fish the day of his grandfather's funeral?) was why all the talk of rabbits that last day? Even saying the word 'rabbit' was said to bring bad luck down on you. As a family, they didn't hold with superstitions about them the same way the other islanders did. Wary of them, maybe; fearful of them, no.

For the islanders, even the thought of them could bring down a hail of bad luck. Whether that meant a quarry fall or a boat capsized, it was bound to be bad. Strangely, even killing rabbits was forbidden too. 'Rabbits was taboo,' as his mother said. To have anything to do with them was enough to have the other islanders have nothing to do with you. Billy wondered if it was to do with that, that the Collinses were shunned by some. Why the ignorant like Scriven made life difficult for them, particularly Billy. It was an open secret that his grandfather trapped rabbits, had taught Billy to do it too. The family would have starved when the fishing was lean if it weren't for the rabbits.

And now, in the times of rationing, when ninety-nine per cent of the catch went to the war effort, when there was the stink of fish but little else, what were they going to do? Go hungry and watch all that meat hopping about? Don't be bloody daft! But that opinion, he'd learned to keep to himself.

The fact that his grandfather made winter hats for them all out of their pelts probably hadn't helped matters either. Just another reason for people to think they weren't like the other islanders. Perhaps that was why his grandfather was talking about Billy being different on that last day. Why he said, 'Take the field-glasses and watch the rabbits and tell the islanders what's what and not to be afraid. They're not bad omens. Far from it. Make them understand, Billy-bub. Make them understand. There was rabbits this afternoon, but no-one made tell of it. If they had, I wouldn't be lying here now, all broken up. Bloody stupid!'

He'd coughed angrily, 'It wouldn't be my turn to go!' The anger had taken the last out of him then. Shortly after, Billy'd been ushered out of the room, trying to put the three things together: his differentness, the rabbits, the field glasses. What did it mean? Why were those Grandfather's last words to him?

Chapter 2
Central London 1994

Since he'd received the call only an hour or so previous, Captain Collins had been assailed by memories. Memories locked away in the back of his mind for nigh on a half century, though as clear yesterday as they represented themselves to him. He marvelled in spite of the discomfort of the accompanying surges of adrenalin. It made him, at the age of fifty-nine, feel like he was ten years old again.

Over thirty years in the job as a Bomb Disposal Officer, a BDO in modern acronymic speak, which required him to be in complete command of himself at all times, focussed on the here and now. Not the sort of job where you could lose yourself in memory or emotion, not when you had to concentrate on making safe an IED or a World War Two bomb that could flatten a city block in an instant. That was the man he'd been for thirty years or more. But one phone call and the making of him had vanished. He stared at the tremor in his hands then clenched it away in disgust, closing his eyes.

Captain Collins had left, or rather had been made to leave, Portland when he was 13 years old and had never been back. He had been overseas when his mother had passed away. He had missed that funeral and after that had not felt any want to return to Portland. Quite the opposite, in fact. The closest he came to understanding the feeling was when BDO Collins, Service number 390778, understood that he and Portland were like two positively charged magnets that repelled each other. Until the call, that was what it had always been like. Try and put them together and an invisible force kept them apart. As a BDO, he understood the science of the magnets, at least. But all that was about to change.

At fifty-nine, Captain Collins was way beyond retirement age. A 'living fossil' to ignorant new recruits who only saw the old duffer until they understood 'the job' and their irreverence soon gave way to awe when they realised what and how much he had survived and achieved, including a George Cross. The stats on life expectancy came at the beginning of the training. Put that together with his age and you have the beginning of the legend. 'Living fossil, am I? That means I've been around a while and may know a thing or two,' he'd cajoled more than once. He could have put his feet up on a full pension after his twenty-five years as a public servant at forty-five. But no matter how much his senior officers tried to persuade him otherwise, they couldn't overcome his stubborn, rigid intent to carry on.

'Just getting into my stride,' he was famous for saying. 'Like a diesel engine. Only run in after a hundred thousand miles!' He'd beam. That was him all over. And physically? Fit as a butcher's dog, as they say. So, to be caught wide-eyed and a bit breathless from fifty-year-old memories was not something Captain Bill Collins was at all comfortable with.

The week before, he had decided on an uncharacteristic whim that the next job, whatever it was, maritime or on land, wherever, would be his last. Quite that, it wasn't. But more of that shortly. It wasn't that he felt his luck was running thin ('I've had seventeen of my nine lives. Must be past all that!') or that he was tired of the job. No chance, he loved it. He loved the life and the challenges it presented to him. Simply, he'd woken up, gone through his morning routine and while stirring his tea, the idea had come to him. It had taken him the time it took to drain the mug to know that was how it was to be. That, in itself, should have been warning enough.

When a man whose every move is considered suddenly acts on impulse, alarm bells should ring, surely? But we've all got our moveable blind spots. That day, that was his. And that was why the fact that his last job, the one to end his career, would have him return to Portland, the place where life began was daunting to him, left him breathless when he put the phone down. More than that, it was creepy. And Captain William Collins did not *do* creepy.

True enough, it was his job to diffuse bombs. And he'd been all over the world doing it: Belfast, the Falklands, Kosovo, Iraq, Afghanistan. So, they could have found one anywhere. Christ, there are at least 40,000 *known* unexploded World War II bombs still *in situ* in London alone! Why couldn't he have been called to one in Streatham or Dalston or Westminster or Wood Green? Why'd he have to go home for his last one? HE wasn't about to do that!

To plan and broadcast you were doing your last job was like *asking for it*, inviting bad luck. And you can't beat your luck, he thought. It seemed to Bill and his colleagues that if you told people you were doing your last job, you were asking for a 'really bad day at the office' as one of his team had put it about a colleague who had announced his last job. And they'd not found enough of him to fill a plastic bag, let alone a coffin.

So, a return to Portland for his final piece of work felt about as inviting as a sleeping bag full of snakes. There was a dreadful circularity to it, a neatness that had pulsed up, making his palms uncharacteristically wet as he gripped the steering wheel of the Red Wing Land Rover. He'd spent years getting passed the superstitions he'd picked up on the island as a kid. They nipped and tweaked him over the years for sure. But he'd put great store in being methodical, sorting out one thing at a time, not letting himself be rushed by anything or anyone. That was what the army, 'the job', had taught him. And great comfort it was too.

Captain Bill's focus and concentration was legendary. Meticulous, precise, unhurried and measured in all things. That was him. That was his rep. 'Can you be anything else sat on top of a 2500 kilo bomb with inner London sat on your shoulder hoping you don't muck it up?' he'd say, palms up querying. To interpret that as cocky would be wrong. Matter-of-fact, confident, is closer.

Another thing that set him apart was his openness to being proved wrong. 'No shame in being wrong as long as it's before the event,' he'd quip. 'How do you learn if you always think you're right? What if you've missed something? It's not as if it's just a cake collapsing if it all goes wrong! I'd rather be wrong and alive than deluded the moment before I'm dead.' Down to earth was what he was. 'Proper earthed,' as Sapper Mike described him to his father.

With an energetic, fluid movement that Captain Bill registered as a memory, Sapper Mike hopped into the passenger seat of the Red Wing, one leg out of the open door.

'That's all the gear now, sir! Double, triple-checked, too!' Mike smiled.

The Captain appraised his apprentice, the moment a tad too long.

'Everything all right, sir?'

Captain Collins took his time and then slowly nodded the affirmative. As honest as he was, he wasn't about to divulge. Couldn't. Just wouldn't do. All these memories of Portland that he'd buried (or not) when he'd left, returning like the screaming furies or, more to his way of thinking, those eerie car tyres buried in the earth that have a habit of rising to the surface after so many years. Captain Bill exhaled, shaking away the image, back to business, addressing the junior rank hovering at the vehicle door.

'Good, man, good! Paintbrushes in?'

'I'm not about to forget those. Most important bit of kit, sir!' replied the young man repeating his mentor's mantra verbatim.

'Right you are, Sapper!' These lines were well rehearsed, comfortable.

'Hop in then. I'm driving today. Good job on those wings, too. Shined up apple red, beautiful!' The faintest, closed-mouth smile of pride flickered about the young man's mouth. Red wings on an army Land Rover might have just looked like fancy military epaulettes but to those in the know, it meant that there was unexploded ordinance in the vicinity, take it steady. Vibration could set it off, be the death of all.

'Yes, sir! Did you say you were driving?'

'A bit less chat and a lot more do is what we need. So, in you get lad, there's a job to be done! And no blue light today. I'm not racing to this one,' Captain Bill slammed the Red Wing door emphatically and leant forward to find the ignition.

'No blue light, sir? It's nearly rush hour,' added the junior officer.

Captain Collins paused, stalled over the steering wheel. An inexplicable anger had swept over the Captain and he was puce. 'I said no blue light, Sapper! Know your bloody place!' The words were out before he'd registered them. It was difficult to know who was more shocked, the seasoned veteran who spoke them or the bemused young dog who received them. The Captain glared a moment longer until his composure returned, leaving his eyes watery, rheumy. He couldn't order his words into an explanation—required though it clearly was. Sapper Mike's mouthed dried like a low-tide rock pool, leaving him slaked and swallowing.

'Uh, right you are, sir.' Eyes down, pensive.

Captain Collins' bellowed outburst had stilled activity in the compound. Heads had raised and turned in unison at the sound like something from a wild life programme. The whole unit had stopped their preparations to take in the goings-on, some for the promise of entertainment, some assessing the potential need to intervene. Captain Bill's eyes and nostrils flared as he felt the eyes on him as he got out of the Red Wing to address the compound as a whole.

'Has anyone got a problem with that? Well? No. Thought not. Now sort your bloody selves out sharpish!' Perplexed eyes widened then silent shoulders shrugged in question. Captain Collins never lorded his seniority over his crew. His word and experience was law and he'd only ever ask quietly for action to be taken. His style made a change. It was part and parcel of who he was. Suddenly gripped with self-awareness, a giddy sort of vertigo made him grasp the door handle to steady himself and he got back into the Red Wing, this time closing the door with care. A brief glance confirmed that the young man hadn't moved and was having trouble processing. With a pang of guilt, the old man fired up the Land Rover to gee him along.

Gathered, Sapper Mike rounded the Red Wing and got in. He had trouble coupling the seatbelt. When he was set, Captain Collins found reverse then made for the compound security that had buzzed open passed the straight mouthed, straight backed, expressionless armed guards. The gates closed behind the last vehicle with inches to spare. At the junction, Captain Collins edged forward, indicating, unlikely to make an impression in the Central London dense traffic— no blue light. Just didn't make sense, particularly so close to Westminster. But it seemed the Captain wasn't about to reverse his decision. That didn't make sense either, though Sapper Mike wasn't about to put another query to him in a hurry. Nope.

Eventually, after an age of stop-start, stop-start through the traffic and the mandatory park up on the M25, they got onto the 303 bound for Dorset. Sapper Mike could see the Captain was just being stubborn about the blue light, saving face. He could have used this to describe any number of adults he'd grown up with: uncles, aunts and all sorts. Captain Collins was usually anything but. That's what made him refreshing and it wasn't something he wasn't aware of. 'Only a fool has to be right all the time. How can you be open to learn if you always think you're right? No shame in saying I don't know. Shows you're engaged and want to learn. I've got time for that, not for a smart ass!' He was fond of opening talks and lectures on BDO methods with this line to set the tone.

He liked the one about God giving you two ears and one mouth, too. So, why be an old boot now? Sapper Mike silently brooded on this one. And he missed the excitement, truth be known. But he'd learned to keep that under his hat too, he thought, trying to conceal his sigh.

And what was with the silent treatment? Captain Collins set a passenger at ease right away with his easy chat. He smiled a lot and liked to find the humour even in the most tricky situations, his way of circumventing frustration. Made him a popular old fella in the barracks and if there was an uproar of laughter in the Mess, you could be sure he wasn't far away. None of that today, though. No good. The radio was off too which didn't help matters. After these thoughts dissipated and with a bit of blood back in his face, confidence regained, Sapper Mike decided to break the silence.

'Where'd they find the bomb, Cap?'

'Up near where the old quarry was. Middle of a public amenity now, it seems,' Bill replied without turning his head, eyes fixed on the road ahead, deadpan, remembering how he had poured over the OS map of Portland, remarking on the changes of fifty years. Unrecognisable almost, save for the coastline and a few field demarcations. Then, what hasn't changed over the course of two generations?

'What is it, d'you reckon? A Herman or a Satan?'

'Hard to say.'

'What's your guess?'

'I don't make guesses. You should know that by now. Ordinance Disposal is not a game for guessing, Sapper,' Captain Bill, replied, eyes front. No thaw there, then. Diplomatic silence in order, then.

'Don't think, know, Sapper,' replied Captain Bill, turning with a glare. Mike felt proper uncomfortable and not a little hurt either. For the life of him, he couldn't work out what this was about. Everything had been normal, pretty much.

'Yes, sir!' he replied, trying to force a 'business as usual tone' that wouldn't have fooled anyone listening in. He'd only been in the army six months and was enjoying it immensely. Being away from home, from Mum and Dad, was tough but Captain Collins had been so avuncular and decent that he hadn't felt it as much as he thought he would have. But, by God, was he feeling it now. First time since week one. Homesick? It was going to be a long ride down to Portland with these thoughts buzzing around at this rate.

A Few Hours Earlier

The last couple of weeks, a change had come upon Captain Collins. He'd noticed he'd slowed, though no-one had made mention of it. The pressure had dropped in the barometer. Squalls of fast-moving memory from the back of his mind scudded across his concentration, darkening the light around him, often making him involuntarily turn and squint at the sky as if appraising the weather for his safety as he had done as a lad out in his skiff while fishing or setting pots. Or he'd find himself shivering away that sense that someone had walked over his grave.

He could be sitting pretty on his pension, puffing on his pipe, listening to the radio in the kitchen of his little flat or up the allotment putting in spuds and onions. The allotment was a full time job in itself as he well knew. His three rods were immaculate. Not a weed in sight, not a stone to show. Everything straight, regular and pristine like the shed he'd built himself from scratch—all squeaking dove tails that didn't really need glue. Like all the furniture he'd made for his flat for that matter. But his pride in his work was of little comfort and the flat just seemed empty these last weeks. Not like a home, but a place to camp for the night.

If the truth be known, it just made him claustrophobic and he couldn't wait to get out in the morning to do a couple of hours at the allotment at first light in spring and Summer before work. What he'd got around to admitting was that the bustle, movement and business of the city that he'd found an awesome distraction, well now the fumes and the blare of traffic just made him nauseous. Exhausting sensory overload. And then he was day-dreaming of the sea. He wanted the open space and of the coast, the open. Nocturnally, he dreamt of his life as a boy, running the bluffs of Portland or out alone in the Channel in his little red-sailed skiff. He was distracted, but only the astute would have noticed that as he'd always deftly concealed with an overdrive of method and calm.

Sapper Mike and a few other lads in the squad had noticed his unusual breaks in concentration, an over extended pause in chat, the occasional tremor in his hands although, none was about to say as much and question a senior officer. 'The old boy's alright. Strong as an ox,' was as far as the consensus generally went. No point speculating on what you can't know.

Enter Colonel Wildblood

Mike had only known the Captain for six or so months, had only just begun his army life and some of his civilian ways remained still. Something was definitely wrong though and he felt he had to step up and stop being a spectator. Besides, it felt like he had known the Captain a lot longer than just six months as it does sometimes when you click with someone. And click, they had. Almost father and son. And so, with this thought in mind, Mike found himself self-conscious on the parquet floor on 'Seniors Corridor' on his way to see Captain Collins's Commanding Officer.

Colonel Julian Wildblood's secretary, a pretty brunette with sparkly eyes that smiled and made him feel a bit odd, had waved him through, hadn't even made him sit and wait and toy with his beret to compose himself as he'd hoped. Though he had his doubts, he couldn't sit without fidgeting with her around. 'Just go ahead and knock,' the secretary had instructed as if it as a piece of cake. Sapper Mike, wide-eyed, timid and quaking, tapped on the Colonel's office door.

'Enter!' Colonel Wildblood brayed from the other side of the three-inch thick oak panelled door, though it might have been paper for all the difference it made.

Peering over the top of his glasses in mild surprise, the Colonel acknowledged the Sapper Mike. 'Ah, the Captain's apprentice,' he said and removed his glasses. In the moment of silence that ensued, he replaced the lid on his Schaffer fountain pen before appraising the newest recruit to the unit of the Royal Engineer's bomb disposal unit, running back his last conversation about him with the Captain. As the young man didn't appear to be about to speak, the Colonel took up the initiative and further asserted himself, 'Cat got your tongue, Sapper? Now, what's on your mind?'

'No, sir! I've come to you about the Captain, sir.'

The Colonel's eyes widened and creased in scrutiny. 'Yairs, continue.'

'I'm, err, well…'

'Haven't got all day, lad. Spit it out!'

Now or never… 'I'm a bit concerned … Not been himself the last couple of weeks,' Mike replied, having coughed away a tremble of nerves. He squared his shoulders and let his gaze fall on a space just above the Colonel, not ready for eye contact as yet, awaiting his next cue to speak.

Had he been the 'spluttering with anger type', the Colonel might have covered the junior officer in spittle for insubordination at this point. But he didn't. Beguiling was what he was. 'What concern of yours would be a senior officer's attitudes and behaviour?' offered the Colonel with a mild, even delivery. The subtle barb caught and quietened the young man. Having let the silence hang long enough and satisfied, the Colonel loosened and his eyes and tone softened, 'Yes, young man. And what is it that you've noticed?'

'He, err, um, mutters to himself, sir! And then he catches himself and some sort of anger rises up behind the eyes when he's noticed that I've noticed. If you see what I mean, Colonel?'

'I think I do, Sapper. I think I do,' replied the Colonel reflectively and then he was quiet as he processed this information. When he returned his attention to the new recruit before him, he started off on a new tangent that befuddled the already nervous Sapper.

'Takes a bit of nerve to come here and say what you've done today. Nerve and brains. I do believe the Captain was right about you, my boy. He thinks a lot of you. And he's not a man to be won over easily in spite of what people might think. There's a lot about that man you'll never know.'

The change of tack totally foxed Sapper Mike. How had the Colonel turned the meeting away from the Captain and focussed on him? And, more to the point, why? People talking personally about him and to him made him feel uncomfortable. He was much more at ease talking about things and ideas rather than himself. So, the next question put him further on edge.

'Are you still hand-writing those letters home?' Bewildered wasn't the word. What had his letters home to his folks got to do with the Captain? And then, absentmindedly the Colonel added, as if to himself, 'Yes, he always said that the most capable of men can come in unusual packaging.'

Sapper Mike decided to just go with it. What alternative was there but to answer the Colonel's questions? Best let it be. So, he squared his shoulders and puffed out his chest—all ten and a half stone of him. He raised up his chin too and addressed his reply to somewhere a bit further above the Colonel who'd sat back in his chair and was thoughtfully chewing the end of a draughtsman's pencil he'd picked up. He also had a disconcerting, wry sparkle of amusement in his eye.

'Yes, sir. I'm writing home weekly.' And then, 'With respect, sir. What's my letters home got to do with the Captain?' It was out before he knew it. Rule #1: don't question a senior officer. Damn it!

The Colonel chuckled, 'And candid too. Just like Captain Collins said.'

Sapper Mike felt a tick of embarrassment (or was it anger?) in his shoulder blades and the prickle of hot blood in his temples.

'Don't understand, sir.'

'No, you're doing very well, young man. Once a week did you say?'

Sapper Mike replied with a curt nod.

'None of the other lads write home. They're on their phones. Why aren't you? Bit old-fashioned to be writing letters, don't you think?'

'Not at all, sir! Not a lot but bad news comes through your letter these days as my father says. They look forward to my letters and do I theirs. I like to hear the everyday stuff that happens: about the dog, the unusual stuff that turns up in Dad's fishing nets, mum's visits to the aunties. And they like to hear what I'm up to and learning. Gives me time to have proper think about what I've been doing. Is there something wrong with that, sir?'

'Yes, he said you write it out rough. Then do a neat version,' replied the Colonel, nodding in affirmation. His tone had softened again too.

It was beginning to feel like a subtle torture, divulging all this personal information. Letters were private and you could say the stuff that was hard to speak out loud and so he was having serious second thoughts about being bold enough to further express his concerns about the Captain to the Colonel. And to cap it all, the more Sapper Mike felt like he was being insubordinate, the more the Colonel appeared to be enjoying the proceedings. But, if there was no malice in it, what did it also feel uncomfortably like a trap?

After another of his purgatorial, mirthful pauses, the Colonel repeated in *that* reassuring tone, 'You're doing very well, young man. Continue.' Was the savage old brute enjoying this? Mike would have preferred the strips torn off him. Calm, he told himself, getting a reign on his composure. He's your CO. Just answer his questions.

'Just once a week I write home, sir. Before tea on a Saturday night. Dad says it takes some of his Wednesday gloom away when they're having their tea and toast.' Inwardly, he winced for giving away this homely detail. And his sense of discomfort was compounded by the widening grin on the old sod's face. There was no disputing it. He was enjoying himself. Sapper Mike's teeth set.

'Excellent! Good man, good man!' boomed the Colonel, rising from his seat. 'Just as your visit here today confirms, your awareness of your colleagues *could* make you an excellent officer!' *Could?* Sapper Mike was utterly baffled, but his shoulders relaxed. The interview seemed to be over.

'Err, thank you, sir!' he replied definitely.

'Off you go!'

'But, Captain Collins…' Sapper Mike interjected, suddenly remembering purpose of his visit.

'Dismissed! And worry not about the Captain. I'll have a word with him before departure at six.' The Colonel had rounded his desk and had briskly moved to open the door to facilitate the Sapper's leaving. He gave him a curt nod of dismissal as he shut the heavy, tall oak door behind the young man. And that was the end of the exchange, save for the very definite chuckle he caught from the other side of the door.

Sapper Mike shook his puzzled head and looked up to notice the pretty secretary taking him in, shuffling some papers square to the desk like a summarising news reader. 'Good morning!' he choked and stalked off, attempting to muster all the sense of purpose he could. His mortification was complete.

Chapter 3
An Hour before Departure

By the time Sapper Michael Lapin reached the compound courtyard, his eyes had adjusted to the sunlight after the dark corridors of HQ and he took in the scene of the unit loading up the last of the equipment necessary for the defusal of the ordinance, the Second World War bomb discovered on Portland. Their next job; the Captain's last though Mike he wasn't to know that yet.

He made for the Captain who had his head in the cab of the Red Wing and rounded to the driver's side as he usually drove the Captain. Their heads met over the handbrake. The Captain had a quizzical look in his eye, 'Where's your family from, Sapper?' he asked immediately. None of the usual cheery affirmation.

'Err, Bretonside, Plymouth, sir.'

'Your family name is French then, is it?'

'From all over really. But yes, the name's French, sir. From a family of stonemasons that travelled Europe apparently. Why?'

'And what does it mean, boy?' All the avuncular humour gone, the same as the colour curiously drained from his face.

'Lapin? It means *rabbit* in French, sir.'

'It bloody well would, wouldn't it,' the Captain said under his breath to no-one, removing himself from the cab of the Red Wing and staring up at the sun questioningly, until he had to blink away those late afternoon sunspots.

'Alright, sir?'

'I've never liked surprises. They don't fit with this game,' replied the Captain with an air of distracted finality.

Perplexed, Sapper Mike watched him and decided to say nothing until whatever it was had cleared from the Captain's thoughts. However, for the moment nothing seemed to have cleared. The Captain had visibly paled at the mention of the word rabbit. As white as Portland stone, he was. To the Captain, it felt as if all the years of working to process, method and expediency to rid himself of his superstitions, his instinct and intuition, failed him in that instant so that he was filled with years-worth of fight or flight adrenalin.

He felt giddy, light-headed and leant heavily on the Red Wing to wait for the moment to pass. He had the briefest of concerns about his heart which was thumping out of his chest until he started taking in the here-and-now, what was outside, to Channel his senses away from what he felt inside.

Again, he looked up at the just visible, always reassuring dome of St Paul's Cathedral that even now dominated the London skyline. 'Imagine your first impression, arriving in London in the 1600's when all around were lilliputian wooden structures?' the Captain mused to himself.

The young Sapper followed his gaze and waited. He knew of old that the Captain was about to go into 'history mode' (as Sapper Mike had referred to it in his letters home) and impart something he felt worth sharing from the multitudes he held in that dome of his. Back to being the straight-backed Captain, he continued off topic. Strange: a butterfly mind was not something you'd have attributed to him.

'Have you had the chance to visit the cathedral yet?' the Captain asked. 'Got to get yourself up to that whispering gallery.' And before waiting for a reply, he chuntered on, 'Built of stone quarried in Portland and shipped on barges up the English Channel to the Thames. Just about all the public buildings of significance were hewn of Portland stone, including St Paul's Cathedral. He had a practice run on Portland—St George's—a sort of St Paul's in miniature.'

He paused, making sure he had the young man's attention. Activity in the courtyard compound had also paused to take in what was happening. While some of the less patient, younger men in the unit who didn't share a love of history shook their heads in dismissal, Sapper Lapin was all ears, so to speak.

'Something of a visionary was our Christopher Wren, Sapper. And not just in terms of his architectural savvy. He had this idea that the roads in the capital would need to be wide in the future. Wider than they were then by a long shot. I guess he had an idea that the future would bring more movement, that the traffic was going to get heavy as all sorts of produce and people were attracted to the capital. And being a public spirited sort, he petitioned the Burrough of London, the council, if you like.'

'I'm guessing the council didn't listen to him, sir?'

'Correct, Sapper. It was a visionary idea, but it was also common sense, practical. Hoping to save a lot of bother in the future. And like most self-important, starchy types when listening to a money saving, expedient idea, the council ignored it. Probably pooh-poohed it because they hadn't thought of it or couldn't imagine their way into it.' The two of them exchanged a wry smile before the Captain carried on; Sapper Mike at ease now that the Captain seemed to have returned to form.

'So, if you looked up the records who was in office then, you'd know who to blame when we hit the centre of London gridlock in a hurry! The other side of it is that down on Portland where you have next to no traffic, they have the most wonderfully wide roads to accommodate expansion and traffic. Arse backwards, I think you'd call it.'

After a few moments, the Captain returned to his usual self, fixed him with a purposeful eye and instructed him to double-check that the explosives in the back of the Red Wing were properly secured. No explanation of what had just occurred. Sapper Mike gently closed the driver's side door and did as requested, banishing the puzzlement.

Colonel Wildblood Has a Word

Colonel Wildblood's unmistakable brogue-click across the courtyard straightened postures and cleaned up the language. Captain Collins looked up from the cab of the Red Wing, put the antique field glasses in their leather case in the glove box, shut it sure and made off to engage the Colonel, his right hand extended ready to the greet of his superior and old friend. They had known each other for nigh on forty years, joining up within months of each other. Neither were National Service boys. Both had joined up because they wanted to. Both had fathers and grandfathers who had fought in the wars, although in that period it was pretty much the norm rather than the exception given the state of the world.

'Best of British.' There was a vague sense of a question in the statement.

'Just another job, Jonathon.' Out of earshot, they always reverted to first names.

'Is it, Bill? I had the feeling you might be making it your last.'

'As it happens, you're right, Jonathon. How did you know? It sort of came to me after the last job on Canary Wharf that I'd make the next one the last. I wasn't figuring it being on Portland...' he trailed.

'What difference does it make, Bill?'

'It's where I grew up. On Portland.'

'Oh! Portland? Really? You never made mention of that! I thought you were a Londoner with that accent? Didn't you once mention Yorkshire though, come to think of it?'

'Yes, I was evacuated to Harrogate. Just outside. From Portland though originally. Spent my first ten years there. Then London to live with my aunt after the war. Dalston in Hackney, or what was left of it. Couldn't face seeing Mum. Or going back to the island after what happened. Anyway, I had been *advised* not to return.'

'After what happened? Advised? What on earth are you talking about, Bill? You've lost me.'

'At best you could call it a ...' he searched for a word, '...*circularity*, a neatness returning to my home at the end of my career. Full circle.'

'Bill, Bill. You're not making sense or there's more here. But now's not the time. So, back to your place of birth as well. There's a neatness, don't you think? I would have thought you'd appreciate that?' he chuckled.

'It's a neatness I could well do without. Trying not to think about it Jonathon! Gives me the heebie-jeebies,' the Captain replied coolly.

'Are you going soft-headed on me, Captain?'

'No, Jonathon. It's just stirred up a few old ghosts and memories is all,' replied the Captain, forcing a return to his usual, characteristic confidence.

'Ah, well! Very good,' appraised the Colonel. 'No need to over think these things! Best keep the family box locked if it doesn't help is what I say! The past is gone. Forward we go!' And then changing the subject, he began a series of economical statements that he delivered like telegram messages. Stop.

'Sapper Lapin came to see me. A good chap, just as you said. Potential leadership material there. Not afraid to speak his mind either. Spot on you are with that one.'

From a faraway place, the Captain replied, 'Why'd he have to be called that?'

'What's that you say, Captain? Called what?' enquired the Colonel. The Colonel was having difficulty dealing with the doubt he was picking up on in his oldest comrade. The Captain didn't suffer from self-doubt. No doubt. It was what those who knew about him admired him for, amongst the plethora of other attributes. In the pause that ensued, the Colonel understood that the Captain wasn't about to answer the question or repeat what he'd said. Shaking away the moment, the Colonel continued, 'Of course, I told him not worry on your account. But I'm beginning to wonder if I gave him the right information?'

'Lapin, Colonel. It just doesn't feel right. My last job and all,' the Captain replied in a distant voice.

'Lapin? What doesn't feel right, Captain?' The Colonel shifted on his heels and his tone indicated that he wanted to get to the nub of the matter sooner rather than later, no shilly-shallying around.

'You speak French, Colonel, don't you?'

'Correct. I did it at school. Learned the language of diplomacy at University, even though it was an antiquated idea even then,' replied the Colonel, mildly reproaching himself before he started off philosophising, losing the thread of the matter before him.

'Well, you know what it means, then.'

'It means *rabbit*! What in God's name are you rambling about, man? This is getting tiresome, Captain Collins.'

'Portland is steeped in superstition. More so than tradition. Though that's there in buckets too. You can't say rabbit on Portland. It's like drawing bad luck to yourself. If ever something goes wrong on the island, it's usually put down to rabbits or the mention of.'

'Have you lost your mind, man? What, and you're thinking that because your Sapper is named Lapin, that's some sort of excuse for nerves? For God's sake!' replied the visibly exasperated Colonel.

The Captain sighed as he briefly considered the idea and then got a hold of himself for a swift response. 'No, I haven't lost my mind. His name and the fact it's in an old quarry. Well…it's just a couple of coincidences combined with the 'neatness' as you put it, I don't need.'

Bewildered by this previously unseen side of his colleague and choosing to take a gentler tact, 'Bill, what's this about? I can see that you're rattled. But what's behind all this? You can't seriously expect me to believe that an old war horse like yourself is going to get skittish about a rabbit. Or the mention of them?'

'No, Jon. I'll be alright. It's an old superstition I grew up with and old habits die hard. I must be getting soft in my old age.'

'Well, you can damn well get soft in your old age after this job. There's work to be done!' And softening again, 'But, tell me. Do you know where this idea has come from? Interesting. I had no idea.'

'Matter of fact, I do. Portland is famous for the lime stone that the City of London is mostly made from. The quarry men carved out huge slabs of the stuff which was shipped up to the Thames. It was back breaking, dusty dangerous work. Landslips, quarry falls were a regular occurrence. Hundreds of miners were crushed to death in them. My grandfather, for one. Survived the Somme and killed within a mile of home. An horrendous death.' And off he drifted into troubled reverie.

'And then with the man of the family gone, the family floundered and often perished. No insurance in those days. No hand-outs to hold them up.'

'Yairs, yairs. Get to the point, Bill! What's all this got to do with rabbits?'

'Oh, yes. Well, the miners noticed that whenever there was a quarry fall, there were always rabbits about. Rabbits and death: synonymous. And so, they came to be thought of as augurs and omens of bad luck. To this day, it's the same.'

With a crease of disquiet above the eyes, the Colonel replied, 'You're not seriously telling me that this old wives tale is affecting you, Bill?' His tone conveyed genuine discomfort at the thought he could have seriously have underestimated his colleague all these years. Their friendship had been forged sweating for years in fierce theatres of war poised over the promise of unexploded horror. Concern was there too. His perception of Captain Collins was a little diminished, tarnished by the revealing of an unexpected side of friend and colleague.

'No, I don't believe in rabbits as portends, bad luck or as a herald of impending disaster. Quite the reverse, truth be known. My grandfather worked it out. The islanders had it back to front.' He delivered this with a baffling gravitas.

The Colonel looked down, searching as he digested his friend's last remark. It made no rational sense and certainly wasn't the kind of talk that his unit needed to hear from him. Non-sensical whimsy had no place in the Royal Engineers, in bomb disposal. What was he thinking talking to a senior officer in this way, even if he was friend? The man was beginning to sound unhinged. That much was plain. Damage limitation. That was the only way forward. Contain the situation as best as possible. When push came to shove, professionally he trusted his old friend the Captain implicitly. Quickly he assessed that whatever it was would pass. *Bloody well had to!* And he wasn't about to take him off his last job. Just not the done thing. And how could *he* explain it?

The Colonel looked his old friend in the eye and planted the palms of his hands on his epaulettes for emphasis.

'I'm not quite sure what's going on here, Bill. More than that, I don't need to know. I get the feeling I don't need or want to dig too deep on this. Do yourself a favour, man and keep this all under your hat. Make no mention of it. I don't understand what this is about. But I do know that it'll pass. Even nerves of steel groan with the torque of the job from time to time and I'm sure that this is what it is. Put it to one side and focus on the job.'

And then, unwilling to be diverted onto an unknown path, 'Safest hands in the job, Bill. Better get there sharpish. Bit of a panic down on Portland. Talk of evacuating the entire island, the navy says. And would you believe it, but the CO there informs me that some of the older islanders have never left Portland in their lives!' By now, both men had resumed to straight back-backed, professional formality. Gone was the conspiratorial air of friendship. It was something of a relief to both.

'Oh, I would believe, Jonathon. Know it, in fact. To the point that I could probably put names to them if I thought about it long enough.'

'They have to be very, uh, what's the word. Insular? Strange types to do that, don't you think?'

'That's one way of looking at it. But as they'd see it: they've never trusted outsiders, people from the mainland. So, why leave home at the whim of someone unknown, someone you might not trust? Bomb or no bomb. They'll have job shifting them. It'll be like trying to pry limpets off the rocks.'

'If it be known that a prodigal son was returning home to Portland, they might take it from you though, Bill?' The crafty old stoat was keen-eyed.

'Oh, God! I'd not thought of that. But for purpose, it could work. I think I'd rather that aspect kept quiet, though. Prefer to just get on with it.' They exchanged a look and a change in the Colonel's demeanour told Captain Collins that the conversation was at a close. They'd given it more than enough air time already.

'Well Captain, whatever you think is best. Get these chaps organised and get going. Sooner you're gone, the sooner you're back.'

'Certainly, let's hope so, Jonathon,' the Captain quietly replied.

'What's that, Bill?' and caring not to hear what was said he continued, 'You better get going, old chap.'

46

'Less of the old, thank you, sir!' came the Captain's reply. It was plain to see that this was a forced return to his avuncular, playful self. The Colonel noted the old keenness in his subordinate's eye and decided that that was the moment to cut the communication. Job done.

'That's the spirit, Bill! Get that blue light on, man. Bit of adrenalin to sharpen the focus, what!'

What he couldn't know was that the Captain had absolutely no intention of blue-lighting it all the way to Portland. He wasn't going to rush into this one for all the tea in China. His gut told him that he needed as much time as possible to settle. *Slowly, slowly, catchy monkey*, he heard a distant voice tell him.

Colonel Wildblood had crossed the compound at pace, readying himself to return to the corridors of power. Having swiped his way into the building that sat in the lee of the Palace of Westminster, all bluster set to get back to it, he had turned to look through the reinforced spy window for a last look at his old friend. 'You'll be back, old boy. Never you worry,' he murmured to himself.

For a moment, he rested his forehead on the cool glass before deciding that it was a conversation best forgotten, buried. If it was never referred to again, then so be it. If reference be made, then a feigned memory lapse would do the trick. And with that decided, Colonel Julian Wildblood continued his day, remembering with irritation all the bloody interminable paperwork that was piling up on his desk. Lucky the pension was there. Couldn't come a moment too soon for him, and Bill to, it seemed. The job had changed too much for the Colonel. He hadn't signed to be a paper shifter, but he wouldn't want to have swapped places with his old friend, to be sure. Pressure had forged their friendship. He just hoped there were no flaws in this particular rough diamond.

The Captain watched as the Colonel, his oldest friend, crossed the yard. He'd only really had one other friend as close. But that was way back when he was a child on Portland. She'd often crept into his thoughts at the end of what usually had been a nerve-wracking day, though he'd never admit that. She was always there though, on the periphery. He didn't like to muse on why the memory of her would rise to the surface in that pattern. Watching the Colonel disappear through the security doors, the fleeting thought occurred to him that she might no longer be in the land of the living. But his instinct answered before he'd even finished the thought. Of course, she was. *She* was *there*. Captain Collins shook away the notion and about-faced with purpose. The courtyard grit scraped beneath his boots.

Chapter 5
Halcyon Days Out on the Salt

Billy Collins loved to fish. Nowhere was he happier than when he was on the rocks or out on the water in his red sailed skiff, jigging for whatever the sea would gift him. Gurnards, bass, dabs and other flatties. Mackerel and herring in the season by the stones worth, the weight of them almost drawing the water over the gunwales. He'd even caught tuna. Always caused a right sensation on the bluff quay. No-one else was catching them then and it was those fish that built his reputation. Something to be marvelled at those tuna: blue fins, yellow-green flanks, silver iridescent scales. Such powerful creatures, glinting sadly in the sunlight, drawing their last gasps on the dock with the crowds around. They'd been a common enough catch before he was born, coming up the Channel chasing the shoals of herring into the North Sea.

Billy's grandfather had heard tell of a beast of a tuna caught up near Scarborough in the 30s, which was the game fishing capital of the world for the upper crust, nearing seven hundred pounds, over eight feet long, worth over a quarter of a million in today's money. But that didn't happen anymore after the herring vanished into the First World War effort. No food for the tuna to chase from the Med, around Biscay to the North Sea via the Channel.

It didn't matter to Billy what he drew up from the depths though. It all brought the same thrill and fast twitch of anticipation and excitement. The fact that he kept his family in food and some money was a plus, but not what inspired him out in all weathers if he could get out quick before his mother noticed.

He enjoyed a reputation with the islands' fishermen, too. Billy had a knack for jigging with a hand line, sensitive to the subtlest of knocks and feline quick to jig to set the hook. No two ways about that. Born with it, as was the talk. Blessed in the eyes of the friends or born with the luck of the devil in the judgement of the foe. You couldn't teach what he could do. The summer before he'd rowed in with a silver monster of a fish that was nigh on as long as his boat after it had dragged Billy in the boat around for the best part of a couple of hours. Way too big for a lad of eleven to consider bringing over the side of the boat. Took him an age to row the half mile back to shore with the dying weight of the fish dragging behind him.

And there'd been a fidgety crowd waiting for him by the cranes on the south of the isle by the time he rowed in blistered and exhausted. Fidgety with anticipation they were. Word had got around on the shore that Billy had caught something so big it was towing him, oars shipped, he sat flummoxed as it drew him towards deeper water until it gave up the ghost, allowing him to head for shore. The beautiful silver fish had been identified as a tuna as all six foot of it hung by the tail from the crane over the quay-side bluff, its yellow dorsal fins glistening in the sunlight, the colours of the rainbow shifting over its silver flanks as the final twitches of life, the light in its eyes faded, dull.

Billy'd explained to the gathered old salts how he was in with a school of herring that was making the surface fizz and hiss all around the boat with activity as they were forced to the surface by a predator below. He knew it was big as the fish were schiz. How it was like watching shooting stars, a meteor storm in the water as the herring'd twist, exposing their silver bellies that caught the light and flashed in arcs. His description left some cold, the similes unnerved them. He should have known better and saved it for Maggie and his family. But he told how when the big fish had hit, nearly ripping the line out of his grasp and his fingers with it, he had fastened the line the portside row lock which had taken the force and turned the skiff in a spray of 180 degrees.

He'd known *something* was going to happen. He'd got that giddy, inward sense of premonition that started in his gut and made him hollow feeling with flight or flight. It had started with intermittent knocks on the hull of the skiff until it became a desperate pounding as if a crowd were thumping on a church door to be let in for sanctuary safe from pursuers. But when it passed, that stalling sense of premonition, his senses had sharpened. He was full of fire and he knew the fish was his. That was what set him apart and made some marvel and some suspicious of something other they couldn't know. He was clued up to know better than to share *that* information although he was always baffled why some just couldn't bring themselves to share in his good fortune.

It was tales of fortitude like these coupled with his patience out on the water or atop Pulpit Rock, to sit unmoving, stock still long after others' patience had given out and the elements had driven them home out of the wind and rain, that made his fame and his ignominy. Stoicism and patience, he had beyond his years when it came to fishing, his five senses acutely tuned to the weather and the water; his focus and attention undivided. He could read the shimmer and dazzle that left others blinking away their blindness and confusion.

But put him in a classroom with the school master, Mr Scriven, and he couldn't keep a thought in his head for a moment, notions slipped his grasp leaving him stammering incongruent nonsense. And keep still? Not a chance. His legs had minds of their own and that mind was obviously telling them to get up and get out of that classroom quick sharp. It didn't make their relationship a harmonious one. And that was before we even get to the family history.

But back to the fishing for a while longer before we get to the trouble with Mr Scriven. From spring to summer's end, when his face had darkened to a deep tan from hours watching the countless silver disks on the shimmer and dazzle, Billy was happiest. With the seas' breathing, its rise and fall shifting the hull about gently, with the familiar scents of wood and cork and salt, all was right in Billy's world. Like most brought up by the sea, he felt awkward, seasick, when he couldn't sense its presence.

First thing he'd do in the morning would be to rest his palms on the window sill and stare at the sea as if to assure himself it was still there. But he wouldn't know that until a few years later he was shipped inland against his will where the fields and moors stillness felt odd and silent eerie. He didn't know that he'd see out the three remaining years of the war away from home, the sea and his family and friends, hundreds of miles north alone on the moors.

Billy was perfectly happy in his skin, in his own company. The need to talk hadn't permanently passed him by, it just had never really been there. Though he could like the best of them when he was with his Maggie. She said he 'yapped like a gypo'. The Collins were all like it. Seemingly silent, watchful, with a less-is-more attitude to talk that set them apart from the rest of the islanders who were a close set bunch of gossipers. 'Like bloody starlings,' his grandfather would say.

Plain and simple, they were different and their dogged tenacity to not be drawn into idle chat, for good or bad, made them outsiders on an island. Maybe that was why he liked the freedom of the quiet out on the water. And why he couldn't abide the claustrophobia of the classroom. He'd always have his eye on the door—couldn't abide closed doors.

Billy had a map of the wrecks around Portland in his head. And there were a lot of them off the rocks off Portland. Plenty of places for the little fishes to hide. Plenty of room for the predators to circle. Little fish dark nooks. Bigger fishes shift in silence waiting for the opportunity. None of it was written down as it had been passed down word of mouth through the family. So, it wasn't so much unnatural luck as a close kept secret knowledge that had him bringing a good catch in when others would return to shore sullen with frustration that would turn to something else when they saw the bottom of his skiff busy with the flutter and slap of silver fish. As Billy noticed it, some wanted to share in his good fortune with a glint in the eye and smile when others looked on sullen, gaunt with displeasure.

So, out to the wrecks he'd row. Maggie and he would go together on the calm days, summertime of that year before they were made to leave. Maggie wasn't a fan of the motion of the sea, but she put up with it for friendship's sake. How he navigated out if sight of land was beyond her. But he knew what he was doing and she trusted him implicitly. To her it seemed he rowed till he got tired. He'd row with occasional heads up to keep note of the landmarks on the shore until they faded from view, plotting his course for whichever wreck beneath the waves he'd chosen that day. And there were plenty of those thanks to the islander's tradition of drawing the weary and unknowing with the promise of a safe passage by lantern light onto the rocks reef in order to run them aground and pillage the cargo and murder the crew. Couldn't have witnesses.

When Billy was happy with his position and after he'd gazed over the side with the glass bottom bucket his grandfather had made, he'd chuck the anchor over before baiting up the hand lines. They'd spend the day out on the water, Maggie lying in the bow of the boat with cut outs of her mother's photographic celluloid covering her tortoise shell glasses to soften the glare that Billy didn't seem to notice. She drifted in and out of sleep while Billy busied himself with the task at hand: fishing. Maggie was a tomboy and equally loved the fishing. She was happy to bait up, let it drop, snooze and think and wait, bring it up later, slow twitch.

Billy, on the other hand, preferred to keep his hands busy, fast twitch. And that concentration on the task at hand allowed him to follow and direct his thoughts. He wanted to be alongside them, his thoughts, whereas Maggie was quite happy to see where they took her. She got the same thrill out of hauling up a fish out of the depths but she liked as much to lie in the boat letting her thoughts drift. Starting off chatty, their words would dissipate as the sun rose and warmed the oak of the boat polished dark, smooth with a generation of use.

Out on the water, the sun could be relentless. With paler, freckled skin, an auburn red tinge to her complexion, Maggie would make her shade. Billy on the other hand, dark-haired, blue-eyed, olive-skinned, he didn't seem to burn. Never redden, just darken. His mum had an idea that their lot might have come from the Iberian peninsula back in the mists of time. The whole family was dark. Darker than the other Portlanders who were dark-haired and pale-skinned. There had to be some Mediterranean or North African blood in there somewhere that made them hardy to the sun. Maggie's family was the opposite. She'd have to cover up so as not to burn. Different skin altogether. Two more different looking kids you couldn't find on the island, nor closer either.

Their differences complemented each other, completing a puzzle that their mothers saw as written in the stars. Noting their closeness, Billy's mother thought that, had they been born a thousand miles apart rather than across a dirt lane on the smallest of islands, they'd still have found each other. 'Some things,' she'd say, 'are just meant to be.'

To all with a mind to see, theirs was a friendship that would stretch far out beyond adulthood. Not that their fresh, happy minds were bothered with anything but the here and now. And that here and now was the first taut line of the day biting into the calluses of Billy's fingers, lips pursed and the silver light of excitement flashing across his eyes, shoulders set.

Maggie had sat up, leaning in smiling at the cleverness of her friend who always seemed to know where the fish were.

'Get on, Bill! You're every bit the fish worrier!' Sometimes, he really didn't know what she was on about.

'There's at least 10lbs of fish on the end of that line. And he's not giving up just like that. Got to keep it taut before he makes for the wreck and we lose him.'

'How do you know it's a him?'

'What?'

'How do you know it's a male fish?' She smiled at his confusion. She'd get him yet.

'I don't! And I don't have time for this now! Get that gaff ready!'

She watched the animation crackle across his shoulders, every sinewy thought of her skinny friend was concentrated on the fish who, if she didn't know better, seemed to be listening to the line, to the water, head cocked sideways, attentive.

'What is it? Billy?'

'King of the Sea, Maggie! Put money on it!'

'How do you know?'

'I just know!' He gasped half with exasperation, half with good-natured complicity. 'Gotta get him up steady and quick or he'll be bending that hook! Sea bass alright. Gotta be. Look at the angle of the line to the water! Zigzags, then dives. He's not running!'

'He?' She questioned again. Billy shook his head, smile flat with confusion and a measure of amusement. Or it might just have been excitement about the catch.

But Maggie knew he was always right about fish. How he could tell what sort of fish, fathoms down on the end of his line, was one of the many enigmas about him that kept him interesting to her. Always, all ways. The whys and wherefores weren't worth pondering. They just were. Unconsciously, they knew the interest and kinship was mutual. But it would take years for it to dawn on him; her, not so long.

The summer before it happened, there were many days like this when they'd return from a day under the sun, out on the water with a motherload of bass, herring, mackerel, Spanish Horse mackerel and those weird, red wedge-shaped gurnards. Salt-caked, soporific and content, Billy would row them back to the bluffs and with the help of the old boys, too old to be out fishing, would man the winches to get the skiff up out of the water before it was battered on the rocks by the restless swell. Then came the job of gutting and cleaning the fish, sorting out the take homes and those to be sold. As has already been said, most were in awe of Billy's luck. "Do they just jump in yer boat, Billy boy?" the friendlies would ask. Others would look on, silent and surly; they'd go about their work unwilling to appraise his catch. They already knew.

Billy's luck came in a few different forms. When it came to fishing and cards, it remained constant and reliable as the turn of the seasons. In the evenings, he played cards. Canasta, a game his grandfather had picked up in Spain ten years previous in the 1930s. He'd gone there to fish, but had ended up running guns from North Africa to Spain and then he'd picked up a rifle himself to fight the fascists. But that was all Billy knew of that time. His grandfather didn't like to speak of those years away. However, with his father gone, Grandfather John had made it his purpose to pass on all that he knew to the lad save for that. He didn't want to put ideas in his head and join up to put him in harm's way: 'No need for you to be cannon fodder, my boy.'

One of the most valuable of Grandfather John's insights he passed on was how to catch bait to catch fish. He showed him how to collect dry summer grasses from the bluffs and how to pack it into the fissure cracks in the limestone at sea level. He showed him how to light the dry grasses with a tinder box and Billy was always delighted when the grass caught and the thick yellow brown smoke coiled away out of the rocks tasting the air. And then came the hurried creatures. Prehistoric-looking ear wig-cockroach like creatures that lived in the cracks scores of them. They'd flee the choking smoke and, quick and nimble, Billy would collect them up in glass jar, that first day under the contented, watchful eye of his grandfather who was sat a ways off in the sun, smoking his pipe.

When he'd collected a jar full and no more, as it was Grandfather John's maxim to take no more than was needed so there was enough for next time, he'd secure the lid as the buggers had a habit of clambering all over themselves to escape. Next was to use the roaches as bait to catch fish for the lobster pots. No need to get out in the boat if he didn't need to. Although he loved the sea, its promise of danger was always there. He'd had that knowledge passed on to him too. There was plenty of bait fish close in under the seaweed and kelp. Wrasse.

There were a couple of spots on the bluffs, close to home he liked to collect bait and catch bait fish. They were like his personal spots and to him as homely as Old Sea Dog Cottage. Just down off the first field, a hundred yards east of the new light hose (as I say new, it had been there since 1873), was a ledge he liked to fish for smaller Wrasse and it was close to the seams he mined for bugs. A creature of method and habit, Billy would unpack his ruck sack, the jar of bugs, two or three hand-lines wound around drift wood and whatever food he had for the day, he was ready. Billy'd pick out one of the bigger earwigs first between fore finger and thumb which was tricky enough as they curl into an armoured ball to the touch. Billy'd have to be very still until the earwig would think the danger had passed and it unfurled. In his other hand, he'd ready with his hook on a line and pierce the creature through its leggy belly so the barb passed out through the other side of its back securing it. He never did get used to crunch at that part and how they wriggled to free themselves, 'but needs must' as the old man would say. Besides, it was the wriggle that attracted the Wrasse. And now he was ready to go for them. He'd cast his line into the kelp where he knew from swimming that there was a concealed sandy patch where his hook wouldn't snag. Then, it was about patience, the waiting. That was the bit he wasn't so good at.

The Wrasse had an aggressive take. Even the little ones. They'd shake that line and dive for a hole for cover if he wasn't careful, leaving his fishing hand bound tight with line. His grandfather silently noted that he'd only had to have that happen once for the lad to learn that it wasn't to happen again. Better to let him learn himself, work out what to do and how to play it, that way he'd better understand the pride of working it out and remember it all the more. His grandfather believed that all the knowledge you could need was within you. It was just a matter of drawing it out.

So, Billy learned to react quickly to draw that line in hand over hand to counter the fishes' tactic. He wasn't going for the big ones for baiting up the lobster pots. Nothing too big as he needed to be able to put them in the pots. Two or three half pounders per pot would do the job. The rest could go back. Beautiful, but too bony for good eating unless it was a whopper good for fish cakes.

Wrasse were greedy for the bugs, it seemed to Billy. He wondered if they were like a sort of delicacy for them and they'd happily ignore strips of Pollock belly. It wouldn't be long before he had enough Wrasse needed for his half dozen pots, gasping, flopping then glass-eyed and still. He thought the Wrasse were beautiful. Camouflaged brown or green, some tending to yellow, there was nothing spectacular about how they'd evolved. It was the iridescent details, the turquoise, orange, azure and pink fin lines that his grandfather had pointed out to him that made each one as different as fingerprints and beautiful, if a bit thick-lipped and toothy.

He savoured the detail of each one. They were all different and it made the killing all the harder. But he'd learned that he couldn't linger on sentiment. He just had to get on with it. That was something Grandfather John said he'd learned in Spain though he didn't elaborate on what that meant. 'Get on with it, Bill!' he'd say to himself, mimicking the rough way his grandfather did as if to motivate himself.

Next came the hard bit. Billy had a length of copper wire about 18 inches long. Again he had to pierce a creature. He had to push the wire through the body of the Wrasse just behind the gills, through the resistant skin and again out the other side. He'd thread two or three fish on a wire and then he'd do the fiddly bit and secure the baited wire to the inside of a wicker lobster pot. The Wrasse would be the bait to entice the lobster into the pot. Once in, he couldn't manoeuvre himself out again. In the pot, he was ripe for the picking.

Billy timed the catching of the bugs and Wrasse for the baiting up of pots a couple of hours before low tide. That way, when he baited all six, he didn't have to lug them far. Each one was a two-hand job so it required the method and timing. At low water, Billy would weigh down each pot with enough pebbles to weigh and secure to each a length of rope with a rope basket containing a glass float. The glass floats were either green or blue glass orbs that were acted as markers so that he knew where the pots were at high tide when he returned six hours later in his skiff or twelve hours later rock-hopping on foot if it was an overnighter. He preferred a short retrieval in the skiff as, with a good catch, six water-logged, awkward pots heavy with snapping catch made for an arduous skitter across the kelpy rocks. Better to let the water do the work.

Chapter 4
The Long Way Home

The M25 hadn't done anything much to improve the Captain's mood or Sapper Mike's disquiet. The change in the old boy had affected him more than he bargained for. With the Captain not quite himself, the Sapper felt his age and lack of experience keenly. He snatched subtle, appraising glances at his mentor from time to time—as vigilant as a Jack Russel. The Captain had remained hunched over the wheel, gripping it was if he were intent on snapping it the whole way so far. Hearing the occasional low growl at the snarl of traffic, he'd decided by the time they'd hit the 303, he'd keep eyes front and just wait it out.

'What'll be'll be,' he counselled himself, using his mentor's words. Whatever was up, he couldn't change. He'd just have to leave it until the time was right. And besides, with the light fading, the glow of the dash board dials gave the Captain's face an eerie, ethereal glow which brightened the eyes and accentuated prominent chiselled features and darkened the hollows of age. It wasn't an approachable look. The passing flicker of hypnotic motorway dusk light took his attention and lulled him away from his thoughts.

After a quarter of an hour or so of open road, the tension eased out of the Captain's shoulders and he eased back into his seat. His left gear hand rested palm down on his knee, his right at twelve o'clock on the wheel. Somewhere around Portsmouth, Captain Collins looked over his apprentice who might have dropped off had he not roused him with the beginning of an apology. Unusually for his rank, Sapper Mike had noted that the Captain was not afraid to make an apology as and when. It was one of his quirks. He said he liked to keep his ship 'Bristol fashion, decks clear' and apologies, where due, kept things 'clear' and allowed him 'to sail on'. Sapper Mike hadn't quite fathomed what the old boy was on about. But doubtless there was some lore to be explored there. And so the Captain began, 'Wakey, wakey, lad!'

A shoulder roll followed by fingertips drawing the sleep that had begun to settle in the corners of his eyes. 'Yes sir? Can't be here yet surely?'

'No. Long way off yet. An hour and a half yet. Traffic willing,' replied the Captain, sounding reasonable.

'Oh, right you are, sir,' replied the Sapper, not understanding. He straightened himself in the seat and propped his 'rolled up no matter the weather/all business' sleeved elbow on the door sill. He'd noted the Captain's change in tone and demeanour but decided to still err on the side of caution and waited for the Captain to speak again. The old boy took it all in and smiled to himself, 'Right you are, lad. Appols for the flare of temper back there. Haven't been sleeping all that well. And I haven't been back to Portland since I was a lad. It's got me remembering all sorts of stuff that I thought I'd buried for all time. Or at least locked in a box in the attic. Not so, it seems!'

Sapper Mike took in his mentor's comic look of surprise, eyebrows raised up. 'How does that go, if you don't mind me asking, sir?'

'Hmm, maybe, lad. But not now. Got to get used to it myself first. I thought the past and its ghosts faded with time. Seems they're alive and well and as real as you and me sitting here.'

'I'm not getting this, sir. But as you say, as and when.'

The Captain seemed to be mulling something over and for a moment Sapper Mike wondered if he was going to let him know what the heck was going on. But when the Captain spoke again, it was on a completely different tack.

'I had a mentor when I first joined up. He was only 10 years older than me though he looked older. His experience did that. Excellent carpenter; master craftsman, you could have called him. Not that he'd have gone for a fancy title like that. He was too much of a salt for that. Anyway, the long and the short is that he lied about his age and joined up for the Second World War when he was 14. They didn't ask too many questions back then. They made port en route in Gibraltar where he said he got drunk for the first time on his fifteenth birthday and woke up in the morning with shame in his eyes, a sore head and a tattoo on his right wrist—two hands gripping each other by the wrist. Said he knew his mother would kill him. That was back when only crooks and spivs had tattoos.

'After a few more weeks at sea, around the Cape of Good Hope at the bottom of Africa and across the Indian Ocean to Singapore. Within days his unit was captured by the Japs and he spent the next six years on the River Kwai building the railway to link up Thailand and Burma to transport supplies. He had an appalling time of it and probably only survived because he'd grown up on a farm in Wales and so there was plenty of food about. Reckoned he only survived because he'd had a good start, physically. He hardly ever spoke of it.'

'He must have said something about it?' ventured Sapper Mike.

The Captain paused as he tried to recall detail. 'I remember he said that the hunger was worse than cruelty in some ways as it gnawed away constantly. He came back barely six stone. They'd sharpen shovel blades and stand in the paddy fields waiting for snakes to swim to them and then cut their heads off when they got within striking distance. And then they'd eat it still warm, raw. Reckoned you could squeeze the meat out of the skin like you see kids doing with ice pops at the beach. They needed the protein having only been fed rice. And then the irony of ironies, when the camps were liberated and the Americans were dropping crates of food. Many POWs were crushed to death by those crates of food as they were too weak to move out of the way...'

'Jeez,' exhaled the young Sapper with a shudder. Captain Collins looked across the cab, nodding silently.

'He never wanted to be drawn on it or make a fuss. There were a few more odd bits. But that was about it. Can't remember him saying much else about those six years as a prisoner of war except that that was where he learned to work with wood—building the bridge over the River Kwai. Best forgotten, he always said. Buried. Though that stuff never stays buried. That was the way then. Not blabbing *all* in counselling over and over.'

They continued in silence for a while as the Captain let his apprentice digest the information. 'Well, Alzheimer's got him in the end. Made him dream of the all the horrors of those six years in the POW camp. He'd wake up the other residents in the nursing home shouting in Japanese ...' The Captain trailed in the wake of the memory and then glanced back over at his apprentice who'd been concentrating hard. Realising he wasn't making perfect sense, the Captain continued in an effort to qualify himself, 'Point being, it seems that the past won't stay buried. Although you might stop the clock, real time ticks on with the past hot on its heels.'

'Right,' replied the young man unable to prevent it sounding like a question. Sapper Mike was following the story but was having a bit of a time of it trying to fit it in with what had gone before. Captain Collins wasn't slow on the uptake.

'Oh crap! Never mind all that. What I'm saying is, sorry about all that back there. I was out of line. I must be getting old and crotchety. No denying that anymore.'

'No problem, sir!' replied the Sapper, glad that the ramble had turned tangible at last.

'Good man, good man,' chuntered the Captain, winding down the window to let a bit of air in.

Sapper Mike thought better of making any further enquiries or offers of help. There was still a bit of an off-chord lingering in the air and the wonderment wasn't helpful. So, he got back to running through his duties and the protocols required when they got to Portland. The Captain had taught him that as a means of using ordering his thoughts this way in order to slow the mind down and focus on the tasks to come. After all, in the job, you had to be absolutely sure of what needed to be done and when push came to shove.

He checked the wing mirror for the seven and half tonner and the other two Red Wings. Equidistant, reassuring. The Captain had set the pace at a steady sixty. Certainly no rush apparent there. With a silent cab, the rain and tarmac hissed by for a score or so of miles. Wipers set the steady rhythm. Hypnotic until the Captain broke the silence, 'Where's your family again?'

Open questions were good even if he understood the Captain knew exactly where he hailed from. 'Plymouth, sir. Bretonside, down near Barbican, not far off the Citadel. All trawlers and gulls.'

'As good as it gets, I'm sure. Beautiful. Done a bit of work down there myself in the early days. Course, the Luftwaffe did it's best to flatten Plymouth and left me a livelihood. Jeopardy makes my opportunity, lad.' The Captain let that one sink in as was his habit, wanting the lad to profit by his experience. *No point reinventing the wheel!* He was a teacher alright in an avuncular sort of way. Not like school. There were rules, sure. But they were few and intuitive with the Captain. He had expectations of people who knew what was required of them without him having to say it. The pressure was positive which made the learning of the trade easy. Half the time, it was only after the event that he realised he'd picked up a load of new stuff, taught when he wasn't looking, so to speak.

The only thing teachery about the Captain was that he encouraged Mike to keep a notebook and write down in pencil (ink runs!) six new things learned. 'Make them bullet points! Don't need a bloody essay.' And so, as soon as Sapper Mike nodded an affirmation to himself, the old boy continued.

'I can remember the Barbican. And Plymouth Rock where the Pilgrim Father's set off from for the New World.'

'Port of bloody Janner pirates, Plymouth, as far as I can remember?'

'Still is, sir,' replied the Sapper grinning.

'Beautiful on a good day, grim with horizontal rain on a bad one! Reckon they invented the riot shield there. Just because of the rain!'

'Gawd, yes. That's one way of looking at it. Weather can be atrocious. My dad calls it wet rain! The famous, Plymouth wet rain! We get some right screamers there too. Blow up out of nowhere.'

'We don't need any of that!'

'What?'

'Things blowing up out of nowhere!'

'Ah, yes,' replied the Sapper, trying to suppress a bloom of self-consciousness when the Captain cut it short.

'You were saying?'

'Oh, yes. The wind. Bloody nightmare when you're out on the water in a hooly. Oh my days! Even the bigger trawlers get tossed about like balsa.' Sapper Mike quaked with the memory.

'Ha! Too right! Never been out on a trawler. But I put the hours in out in a skiff, way out past Portland Bill. It was a different world back then. No way you'd be letting a tacker out on their own in a boat nowadays. Gawd knows what the papers could make of that today.'

'I wasn't on my own.'

'I was mostly when my friend wasn't with me!' replied the Captain emphatically. 'Best days of my life.'

'You fished when you were younger. I didn't know that.'

'There's a lot about me you don't know, lad.'

'I'm beginning to see that, sir,' replied the Sapper, hoping for a level tone.

'Had a nine foot shallow skiff I used to take out jigging. Loved it. But enough about me. Carry on,' added the Captain, smiling to himself. Sapper Mike took him in a moment. That window into the Captain had shut as quickly as it had opened. There was a lot more there, Sapper noted intrigued, pausing before he continued.

'My uncle had a trawler. Because I liked fishing, Dad thought it might suit me and sorted it out with Uncle Brian.'

'Didn't suit then, I take it?'

'Nah. I stuck it out for a year after school. I couldn't find my sea legs. Plus, I was way out of my depth. Ten days out on the water and if the catch was good, my percentage? Well, the money doesn't get better. All that cash in my pocket and straight to the pub with all the older fellas to get rid of the *sea legs*...'

'Ah, that old euphemism. Doesn't work does it?'

'Dunno! But after days of rolling around on the salt, terra firma is horrible for a while. The balance is all out. Inner ear doesn't know if it's coming or going. But you're alright after a few pints. And then you have another four and you might as well be back out on the salt.'

'Sounds nice. No?'

'Yeah, sounds nice. Although, it only ever led to trouble. It was never just a couple of pints and I was a 17-year-old trying to keep up with the men. I was always more than half cut when they'd cart half of them off to sober up in Exeter.'

'What's that? I'm not following you. Why Exeter?'

'Half the crew were disappearing off to Exeter to sober up.'

'Still not following you, Sapper.'

'Exeter Prison, sir! Half the crew would get sozzled and get into some scrap or other and the judge would give them a couple of months to sober up. Most of them are 'regulars' up in Exeter. Serial in and outers so they end up getting months for minor misdemeanours. It's the way it works. Bane of Uncle Brian's life—getting crew that isn't half-soaked loony or inside half the time.'

'Never knew that. A long way from my experience of things.'

'Like most people, sir. Not mine though, sir. Half the family was 'away for a while' when I was growing up. It was just the way of things. Goes with the life. The other thing is that a lot of trawler men don't settle. No point in paying rent or mortgage when you're out at sea for months on end save for a few shore days here and there in the season. A lot'll just kip on the boat, do B&B's. But it just means that their out late, getting into bother with the Matlo's and anyone else stupid enough drunk to want to get into it.'

'Sounds like the wild west down in Plymouth, lad!'

'Dodge City, dad calls it.'

'So, fish worrying wasn't for you then?'

'No, sir. Nice as a hobby, crap as a job. That's why I got into carpentry. Kept me off the boats and out of the clink.'

'And a good job too. You're a lot better than that, lad.'

'Thank you, sir.'

'Done you proud the carpentry, Mike.' And they shared a look of complicity in the Red Wing cab, carpentry their bond. Both the Captain and his Sapper were clever with a hammer and nails, saws, chisels and hand drills. All the old school kit for carpenters and all the more remarkable to the Captain for an eighteen year old whose peer group had all flown with the times and gone electric. The Captain had a motivation encouraging the young man's idiosyncrasy: he was suspicious of over reliance on technology. What would happen if the power went? No electricity, no fuel. No fuel, no logistics to organise and transport food. No power, no TV, no news. What to do then?

It was what prompted him to fish, to grow food on his allotment, to do and make. He was fond of cryptically stating in a matter-of-fact tone, 'Come the apocalypse, only the useful people will be useful again!' smiling to himself all the while. It wasn't something he bandied about to all and sundry, just to a select few in his confidence.

Their first meeting in the woodwork shop, the Captain had been as close up as close up gets when he inspected the Sapper's handiwork. The lad had been making a lockable box for his personal effects in his free time. Notably, when all the other lads were off taking advantage of the Mess hall's cheap beer, Sapper Mike would be chiselling and sanding away in the workshop. When the Captain came to look over his apprentice's work, the joints on the box were squeaky tight. No glue required. Took some doing to be that precise. 'Beautiful work, son.'

It had made the Captain think. And it was then that he had turned and said, 'Come over here, lad. Something to show you that you might be interested in.' From a lower-level locker, the Captain removed a red velvet drawstring bag which he set on the workbench and asked the young man to open. Sensing that something important, delicate (was it a clockwork or mercury bomb timing mechanism?), Sapper Mike gingerly parted the leather pull cord clutched around neck of the velvet bag which revealed a pentangular wooden box some twelve inches by six across. He stood back level with the Captain to take it in. He looked from the beautiful object to the Captain and back again.

'What is it, sir?'

'It's a Chinese puzzle box, lad. Made it myself, too!'

'That's impressive, sir,' replied the Sapper, feeling a little humbled by his own box though he would learn that that was not the Captain's intention. Inspiration was the intended effect, always. The box was made of what looked like polished ebony with an inset of yellowy white wood. As the cat had got the Sapper's tongue, he invited him to open it. With exaggerated care, Sapper Mike picked up the box and turned it through 360 degrees inspecting what was undoubtedly a flawless bit of work. He traced the oriental design on the off-white inlay with the tip of his finger.

'It's not wood, sir?'

'Well spotted, lad. It's whale ivory. Carved from the tooth of a sperm whale. You wouldn't call it scrimshaw, but that's where the idea came from. Took me a whole year to make.'

'No?'

'Oh, yes. I wanted it to be perfect.'

'Well, you done that alright, sir!'

The Captain beamed his satisfaction. 'Open it then, lad.'

Sapper Mike carefully rotated the object, searching for a giveaway seam that might have indicated a lid. Not finding one, he began to gently twist the box with both hands in clockwise, anticlockwise directions for there were no hinges. For several perplexing minutes, this went on in vain until he ventured, 'It doesn't open, sir?'

'Oh, yes it does, lad!'

Sapper Lapin's brow creased as he scrutinised the box looking for joins. There certainly weren't any hinges.

'That's the puzzle. That's why it's called a Chinese puzzle box. Like the original safe for hiding precious objects or valuable or dangerous information. No key required, just a clever mind to outwit the maker. There are more puzzles inside. Sort of a three-dimensional puzzle.'

'Seems I've got a long way to go with mine then, sir,' replied the humbled Sapper.

'You've made a bloody good start, lad! Small steps, we'll take our time and I'll teach you. Now put it back in the bag and take it back to your quarters to work out.'

'Really, sir?' replied the slightly overwhelmed young man.

'Of course, lad. First task for you in order to be able to make one is to work out how to open one.' Sapper Mike carefully replaced the Chinese puzzle box in the red velvet sack and drew the cord firm and then, keeping hold of the string for added care, tucked it under his arm. Facing each other, that day, they exchanged a smile of complicity, Sapper Mike well aware and happy with the privilege. That was how it started. The Captain seemed to have a different manner and energy about him. He looked for the things to be gleaned and learned in a situation. Criticism was always constructive, framed in the positive, always solution focussed.

*

Back in the Red Wing, the Captain started up the conversation enthusiastically; keen to get the course on an even keel.

'But how come carpentry, then? Why not plastering or plumbing—or being sparky even? Good money in that.'

'Oh, I was always half good at it in school. Liked making things up with Dad. Plus, he didn't want me going into the family tradition.'

'And what was that?'

'Stonemasonry. Been the family trade for generations by all accounts. Dad said that our lot travelled all over Europe building bridges, churches and the like.'

'Good job though! Rewarding, too. How come the old man didn't want you going into that?'

'That's easy. Stone's heavier than wood. All there is to it. His back was ruined from all the lifting young. And his grandfather before him too.'

'Hmm, makes sense,' nodded the Captain ruminatively as they lapsed back into companionable silence, satisfied with where they'd got to in the conversation. It was an comfortable place after the *dis-ease* when they had left the compound. The Captain's wave of apprehension about returning to Portland seemed to have ebbed for the time being. The amicable chat had lulled them back to calm waters. But all was not to be right with the world for long. The associations were forming likes lines of swell on the horizon.

'Funny you should have stonemasons in your family. Same with ours. On Portland, you had two choices: it was either fishing or quarrying. Or both. Some became stonemasons, though, leaving the isle to follow the stone barges. Up to the London or wherever, looking for work, to ply a new trade. Some, but not many. Islanders mostly don't like to leave. Seems like it still the same today with those two refusing to leave even when they're practically sat on a bomb.'

'Sounds like a strange old place, sir, Portland?'

'Right you are, son. A beautiful place, battered by the elements. But eerie. A bit too full of history for my liking. Seeps out of the rocks. Maybe that's what makes the islanders a bit superstitious. Always poised for the unexpected. But maybe that's just the sea. You can never predict what she's going to do next. And the weather—a sunny day and then you look up to a darkening horizon. Something's always building there.'

Changing the subject, the Captain questioned, 'So, you mentioned a grandfather in Plymouth. How long has your family been down that way?'

'Not that long in terms of generations before him, sir.'

'Oh aye? And I suppose you're going to say that you've got a Portland connection, too?' replied the Captain, practically ninety degrees in his seat, right hand at the witching hour on the steering wheel, his left shifting down a gear making the engine whine over-revving complaint. Oblivious, the Captain scrutinised his apprentice with a hard, discomforting eye. But there was something else there too.

Sapper Mike had said something that had utterly wrong footed the Captain and vanished the good humour, *again*. Captain Collins, who took everything in his stride, with a career spanning nearly forty years making safe unexploded ordnance at home and in hostile environments was now decidedly looking undone by a mere snippet of information. That Mike also had relatives that lived on Portland should have such an effect on him on the Captain was peculiar to say the least. What could he say? Sodium motorway lights smudged past at clip behind over busy wipers; tyres hissed in the slick of the blacktop outside and he noticed the cab of the Red Wing had got a shade too stuffy for comfort. The Captain peered back at him and an involuntary swallow made the loose skin around his Adam's apple shift so that he more than ever looked his age. The intelligent keenness in his eye had been replaced by a wincing, worried look.

'Well?' primed the Captain flatly, clearly impatient for a response. Sapper Mike had a guilty, sick feeling that he hadn't felt since school. That wretched feeling you get when you're accused of something you haven't done *and* don't have an alibi to get you out of it.

'Sorry, sir!' he began weakly, already half-defeated before the Captain cut him short.

'Don't bloody apologise all the time. Just say what you've got to say.'

'Right, sir. I do, we do… have a family connection to Portland. When the family came across the Channel, they apparently landed at Portland and that's where they settled. Happy with the coincidence I suppose that they landed where stone was quarried. Must have just fitted perfect with their trade.'

'I'm not sure I believe in coincidences,' the Captain murmured. Another thought too uncharacteristic and open for the Captain who normally pretty much only dealt in absolutes, facts and what was right there in front of him. Determined not to be out off by this muddled side of the Captain, Sapper Mike continued hoping the momentum might carry them far enough off from these broiling waters.

'They had a good time of it by all accounts in spite of the language barrier. I reckon their stone cutting ability probably spoke enough to make the necessary introductions.' Having right himself in his seat to concentrate on the road again, the Captain replied, processing the information, 'Could be right there, Mike. Still, they did well to be accepted at all by Portlanders! But they obviously didn't stay though.'

'No, sir. Sounds incredible, but around that time some ship came in on the Norfolk coast with a monkey on board. The English, in their wisdom, thought it a French spy and promptly hanged it. With that sort of ignorance flying around, I guess they thought better of staying!'

'God Almighty! I remember reading about that. Norfolk, I think it was? Another odd breed of coastal people. Webbed feet with bones in their ears, no doubt.' They chuckled complicitly at the idea of a chimpanzee being thought to be a Frenchman and *therefore* capable of treasonable activity. Too bizarre to be true, by half. But it was. You just couldn't make stuff like that up. The Captain lapsed back to wherever he was in his head and Mike thought it best to leave him there.

Captain Collins had indeed been shocked to learn of the coincidence that his apprentice's family had a Portland connection. But something else was niggling him about it. He concentrated away from the problem, his tried and tested method of solving a puzzle when an answer didn't readily present itself. He'd ask himself a direct question and deliberately shunt it away, forget it, sleep on it. The answer would present itself when good and ready. Eyes fixed on the road, ears tuned to the thrum of the Red Wing, the mind filtering sequences of images and words just out of sight.

Sapper Mike slipped idly into the memory of the story his grandfather told of his ancestors leaving Portland, which he must have heard countless times.

In the story, his vantage point was about a half mile away from Portland Isle along Chesil Beach, looking back. He can see his grandfather, as he was then, in a white shirt, sleeves rolled up beneath a dark coloured waist coat. His grandfather is wearing some sort of hat that looks like a bowler. The wind is blowing and then some. It must be winter as the rain and sea spray sting his face and make him squint in the darkness as it is in the dead of night. There is fast moving cloud and the moon a sliver that is obscured for long moments that extinguish its' light and glow. The surf roars with the draw and drag release of thousands of tonnes of pebbles pulled and thrown back up the beach. From time to time, a bank of pebbles gives way nearby. There are what sound like detonations from the impact of the larger sets on the rocks as it approaches high tide.

The wind furies howl and scream in the rigging of a ship he can't see. A buoy bell tolls lonely a way off. Sapper Mike watches his grandfather in his black, felt hat check his pocket watch, expectant. Rain water or sea spray drips off the sodden, sagging rim. After a time, and there is no anxiety with it, the memory shows four lanterns, equally spaced, emerge from the top of the west cliffs of Portland where the silhouette of the rock meets the sky. They descend and traverse the cliff path. The lanterns make quick, but steady progress. And then a group of a dozen or so torches aflame appear at the top of the cliff moving much more quickly.

A flash of menace though the sodden man is unmoved. Satisfied with what he has seen, his grandfather turns his back on the scene, settled in the knowledge that all is as it should be and walks away along the uneven pebbles of Chesil Beach, away from Portland and fades.

That was how Sapper Mike remembered his grandfather's story.

Something in the atmosphere of the Red Wing shifted. Even in the dimness of the Red Wing cab, in the reflective glow of the dials of the dashboard, the young man could see that the Captain had paled again and he noticed the Captain did quite seem to fill his uniform. His scrupulously starched shirt hung loosely around his neck.

'Anything else you want to add to that story?' the Captain asked, wetting his lips.

'There was one other thing, now you come to mention it, sir.' And the Captain was already nodding. 'Well, I say there's another thing. I can't rightly remember. Something about our name. Don't know if it was because it was French or what exactly. It's been years since my grandfather told me the story.

Dad might know, I could ask him?' Mike was happy to have some sort of practical solution to proffer. He was out of his comfort zone with all these unexpected changes in the Captain's temperament.

The Captain replied with a reluctant resignation, 'It was about your name. Being French would have been enough to make you an outsider. That'd been enough for them to have to had to make a run for it sooner or later. Mainlanders are treated with suspicion and they're from within spitting distance. Being French would have made them the target of suspicion and unwanted attention. They must have got work and that spoke enough to make 'emselves of use until the islanders understood what their name meant.'

With a grim resolution, the Captain gripped the wheel. Sapper Mike felt tremors of irritation across his shoulders. Needles of heat and tension like ice crystals formed in his blood making him shudder and exhale noisily. This unexpected, unreliable side of his mentor was tiring. But more than that, it irritated him, triggering a hot pang of guilt that coloured him. He sat up in effort to banish the thought. He had no map of pre-experience to help him navigate this discomfort.

The two exchanged a look, checking in. Also annoyed with himself, the Captain sighed, 'Nothing wrong with your name to a rational mind, lad. But Portlanders aren't, weren't, known for rational responses. Just as likely to chuck rocks at you as good as look at you. That's why mainlanders called them Slingers.' The Captain indicated and overtook a crawler lorry before continuing, 'It's not you, it's me. When you're marked, you're marked, no escaping that. And it seems that I marked, still bear a mark. Like a tattoo, the story's indelibly etched on the skin.'

With an effort not to roll his eyes, Sapper Mike opted for candid, 'I'm not understanding all these riddles, sir! Shouldn't we be focussing on the job? Running through it, troubleshooting, Billy?' The familiar first name contraction hung there for a moment. He immediately regretted it.

'What did you call me?' The Captain's reply was disconcertingly mild.

'Billy, sir,' replied the Sapper, opting for brevity hoping to avoid further trouble.

'I've haven't been called that by anyone in years,' replied the Captain more to himself than for the benefit of the conversation. The name sounded curiously childlike when he said it out loud. Certainly it didn't fit for this leathery, wizened senior officer with a reputation for a having an anvil heart and nerves to go with it. His reputation in the Engineers was legendary with a courage came with a complete denial of risk that was just shy of absurd. And some might have described it as just so had it not been for his concentration and thoroughness had kept him alive long after it shouldn't have.

In some theatres of war, Sapper Mike well knew that the average life expectancy was ten weeks on the ground. Captain Collins had remained in one piece for over thirty years. His total score for the number of bombs defused was a thing to be marvelled at. He'd lost count way back. He didn't care to count the years either. He lived precisely in the moment to the exclusion of all else until now. His nerve should have given out a long time back and, by rights, he should have been warming his toes safe behind a smart desk like the Colonel, not still in the field dusting off unexploded ordnance with his paint brush.

But, in spite of all this, the Sapper was beginning to wonder about the Captain. He appeared to be fraying at the edges. And there was the knock-on effect that was making the young man squint at him. It was not in the manual for the Captain to show signs of weakness on any level.

Pulling rank would have been an option for a lesser man. Insubordination by way of over familiarity from a junior officer. Many colleagues would jump on the obvious challenge. But the Captain wasn't about that. And the dynamic between them didn't include it. Besides, since the call for this job, all bets were off. Division of rank seemed to be of no consequence to him. The call had had an equalising effect and the Captain couldn't escape the notion that they were just two people on the way to complete a piece of work together. The only aim was to get it done and stay alive.

Captain Collins was the young Sapper's mentor and a pettiness over rank would have undermined all that. Plus, he was not about to his personal maxim that 'the basic mark of an ass is that he always has to be right. And an ass always has to have the last word.'

'I better have a word with myself, don't you think, son?'

And, taking a risk, the Sapper replied, 'Might be an idea given the circs, sir!' Less than a heartbeat of silence broken only by a mutual chuckle that on any other day might have signalled resolute calm restored.

'But I've got to ask: what's the fuss about my name, sir?'

'Oh, it just seems like another in a long line of coincidences with this job. I haven't been called Billy by anyone since I was ten years. Although I'm not sure there's such a thing as a coincidence.'

'What does that mean—*no such thing as a coincidence?* All this …' he paused searching for a word that fit, '…*philosophy* is making my head hurt.' Sapper Mike shifted in his seat. It wasn't lost on the Captain either who was wincing inwardly at himself, but he had to say what he had to say.

'I've a feeling that there's a map, a blueprint of your life, and you can't escape what's meant to be. I've been drawn back to Portland, where I was born. Sort of completes the circle. And, I've got to be honest: it's half frightening me to death. It comes in waves. And when it does, I feel like I did when I was trapped under a fishing net when I was a kid. Seems like there's unfinished business. And although I've avoided going back to Portland all these years, the place just isn't going to leave me alone. No-one's called me Billy for a long, long time.'

'Not since you were last on Portland, let me guess?'

'That's right,' replied the Captain nodding. 'Everything's taking on a meaning.'

The young man just stared at his mentor. This confession was not something Sapper Mike wanted to hear. Captain Collins noted the disappointment. He'd said he'd have a word with himself and now he was babbling the inexplicable. For one, it was inconsistent. And two, it served no practical purpose. There was no accepting that. So, the Captain continued hoping that what he had to say next would make some sense and not have an ethereal taint that'd set him apart. He'd spent his entire life carving out a place for himself that was based on hands-on, can-do, dealing methodically with what was right there in front of him. The here and now was all that mattered. He'd made his reputation in the Engineers as a bomb disposal officer, as being as unshakeable as required, no more, no less. Focus on the here and now with certainly no room to allow hunches to slip through the fissures of concentration.

'As you've said, your name translated from the French means 'rabbit'. That's not a thing to say on Portland. Your whole family would have been seen as bad luck. A foreboding augur.'

'You've got to be kidding. Superstition is one thing. But that's just potty, surely? Do you really think that that was what it was about? That was the reason my family left Portland?'

'Yep. I don't know when the superstition started, that rabbits brought bad luck. And specifically rock falls. But I would put money on it. Pound to a penny that the Portlanders got wind of it and thought they had to be rid of your family.'

'You've got to understand the mind-set. It's like when you go overseas to the Middle East or wherever. You'll get briefed on the culture there so you don't go upsetting the natives unduly. Now, Portlanders could see the hand of the devil's work in just about everything. A bit of ash that floats out of the fire was known as a 'stranger' and a sign of bad luck to come. Says it all really …'

'What, do you think, they would have done if they'd caught up with my family, then when they fled?'

Looking across again to confirm his understanding of the question, the Captain replied, 'They'd have stoned them to death, in all likelihood. Simple as that.'

Sapper Mike's mouth made the 'o' of quiet disbelief, then, 'Living in the bloody dark ages, sir.'

'It's what they would have done. Portlanders were known for it. They were known as 'Slingers' for their habit of flinging rocks at strangers, mainlanders, that tried to come across the water onto the island. It's in one of Thomas Hardy's books. He documented it. A writer from Dorchester, he was.'

'That's just plain daft,' Mike added, ignoring the reference to some writer whose name rung a vague bell. 'Ironic too that a family of stonemasons from France come all that way just to be stoned to death because they were called 'rabbit'. Some crime!'

'Either that or hurled off the cliffs. Portlanders weren't above that sort of thing back along. Shaped by the elements—the wind, rain, sea and the rock itself. They were hard, insular, sometimes savage people.'

'Just gets better and better. I think I'll stick to carpentry.'

'Ha, you just do that, lad, you just do that!' It was all a bit too bizarre to contemplate. A non-starter, but enough to mull them back into companionable silence save for the burr it left in the Sapper's young mind. The weird history was one thing, but that these coincidences and all this superstitious mumbo jumbo weighed so heavily was more than a spanner in the works. And it left a tautness of thought behind his eyes.

Jeez! It was his common sense that had kept the old boy alive all these years as a bomb disposal officer, years after the law of averages should have had him blown to smithereens all over the shop. Just wasn't healthy. He didn't do negativity, for pity's sake. And then a thought occurred to Sapper Mike: *did the Captain think that this last job really would be his last?*

Chapter 6
The Road Is Long

The Captain drove on, keeping an eye on the rev counter, listening for any irregular thrum from the engine that might need thinking about and tinkering with. Either that or going through the inventory of the equipment needed for the job and the protocol for diffusing the bomb. He hoped to God that the timer was a simple clockwork job and not one of Jerry's boffins' more wily creations. He didn't feel up to a mercury timer. Not with these tremors in his hands that kept coming and going. He gripped the wheel, white knuckled. In short, he was trying to focus on anything tangible or practical that he could use to keep track of the direction his mind was travelling in. This was his ritual, his usual method to keep his mind ticking over with practical considerations and away from dwelling on the potential danger.

He'd really lost count over his career of how many bombs he'd rendered safe, innocuous save for a controlled explosion. He could have counted them all up if he wanted, but he didn't, for he wrote up each experience in a diary that was intended for others to find and learn from if he had that particular bad day at the office. He didn't fear death. He knew that if he was close enough to the device, he'd be gone before he could even finish thinking up an expletive.

And as *his* mentor had told him way back when he first started out in bomb disposal, 'Don't fear death, Collins. The lead up might be pretty awful but not the thing itself. Just hope you're close enough to one of Jerry's best when it goes up so you never have to know about! It's just lights out at the end of the day.' The coolness of the words had stung at the time, but as the years went on, they became something of a balm.

Captain Collins had decided that this Portland bomb, given the rough description the boys at the scene had given him, was either a Herman or Satan, in all likelihood dropped by one of the Luftwaffe's Dornier Do 17s. The Captain knew all there was to know about the Luftwaffe and drawing out his knowledge of the Do17, which was a *Schnell bomber,* a fast, light bomber that flew at low altitudes and was fast enough to outrun the RAF's Hurricanes and Spitfires kept him confident behind the controls in the cockpit of his mind. He nodded to himself as he recalled these reassuring facts, this knowledge that Jerry named it the *Fliegender Bleistift,* the flying pencil case, because of its shape. Remembering these hard facts kept the mind in check.

As the memory came into view, the here and now faded, the Land Rover's became the Do 17's throaty growl as it made a low pass over Portland. The past blindingly super imposed over the present and with it a fifty year blend of excitement and fear coursed through the Captain causing in him an impulse to put his foot down until he snapped out of it. Without looking at his apprentice, he knew it hadn't gone unnoticed. *I just hope this passes,* he mused to himself.

He couldn't be dealing with these fluxes of distracting memory. How to do his job? He'd put the rest of crew at risk. He didn't want to admit it, but the lack of control was turning from irritation to prickles of reminiscent of an old fear. And the responsibility he enjoyed for the lads was now beginning to feel like the proverbial albatross around the neck. *Oh, to be 10 years old out alone on the salt in his skiff now.* The Captain forced away the memory of his go-to calm and reset the rudder for hard facts…

Do17s were a work of genius: twin engine, BMW VI 7.3 engines (and you had to give Jerry his due there for his engineering ability—he was no slouch in that department), top speed of 410km/h, and the flight range given the size of the engine and the fuel tanks and a stack of other technical facts made it short range. That had meant that Jerry was getting close.

And then he hit another pocket of turbulence. An assault and updraft of cold air memory, a roaring wind and surge of panic. It wasn't quite a flat spin, but nigh on. His body was in the here and now, driving the Red Wing. A sixty-year-old fella with nearly forty years of bomb disposal experience, his apprentice beside him heading towards what should have been just another routine job. But this was shaping up to feel anything but routine.

'Shut the bloody window, lad, will you!' He drew a careless sleeve across his mouth to wipe away the white spittle.

'Just getting a bit of air, sir,' replied the young man startled-timid, incredulous by the Captain's outburst.

After a pause, 'Just shut it, please,' came the reply exhaled like a whistle of breath. The window went up and the boy folded his arms, his steady gaze fixed straight on the road ahead. Not that the Captain noticed for he was nauseous with the sodium light and fast disappearing down another rabbit hole of memory. Ten years old again and nearly sick with an acrid scent of memory, his eyes tearing with excitement and salt wind, nerves crackling across his shoulders but also terrified of the response he'd likely receive from Mr Scriven, his school master, with the news of what he had found at the beach.

Mr Scriven had returned to him in his dreams with a frightening regularity of late though a long, long time dead. These dream reminiscences of that choleric, cruel man dislodged whole slips of associated memory and detail day times for the Captain. Scalpel lines etched so deep and fine, there was no blanking them out.

*

Billy Collins burst through the school house door. It was a hot, mid-June morning, the year before Operation Tiger, and he was dusty and wheezy, out of breath. He was also very late for school having lost track of time while out at Old Harry checking some lobster pots he'd set. He'd clattered through the school house door with his boots causing it to bounce against the door jamb with displeasure. His shirt was slicked to his back and his lungs burned. His thoughts were no better. A school boy disarray of excitement and fear caused by what he had seen. He leant, palms on knees, prone in an effort to suck up the oxygen his body was crying out for.

Mr Scriven was predictably crackling-livid and the fact that Billy couldn't get a coherent sentence together by way of explanation just stoked the furnace of his rage all the more. Silent and imperiously, he glowered at the front of the class summoning every last ounce of fury he could muster. That was his way. He could start off cross and would let the momentum of his rage carry him into a fury. Maggie's mum thought it was his substitute for pleasure.

Billy was dumbstruck. What was making it all the more difficult for Billy was that the night before Billy had dreamt the scene of what he had just found over at Old Harry. It meant that he really didn't know where to start with it. What he had seen was so much like the vision of his dream, it had felt like... déjà vu? Was that what Maggie's mum called it? Or a premonition?

Well, he knew that that would be the wrong place to start with Mr Scriven who was nothing if he wasn't a lugubriously cold and rational. So, Billy just stood there, mute. He couldn't have played it worse if he tried. His face flushed with embarrassment as Mr Scriven stormed across the boards towards him, his academic black cloak billowing up a storm of dust about him, his right hand outstretched ready to grip Billy's hair for a nasty twist of mal-attention. Billy was well acquainted with Scriven's feeling for pain.

Across the classroom, having guarded a spot next to her for Billy, Maggie Golding winced inwardly, careful to try not to show her empathy. She knew full well that, for 'the Scriven', empathy meant complicity. And that meant a thick ear for her too if her mother wasn't around. There was nothing to be gained from Maggie getting herself involved. She'd be more use to him keeping quiet and being there for him afterwards. So, she studied her desk intently, all owl ears.

Billy'd been here before, so many times. His shoulders sagged and the rest of him wanted to go to ground too. He loathed this man with a passion that defeated him. But not this time. He knew what he'd seen and it was real. He was going to tell him and not let his anger render him speechless.

Maggie's mother, who helped out at the school house, had already noted with an affectionate resignation that, first thing, there was no Billy at roll call. Being the best friend of her daughter, she had a soft spot for him and knew well enough that whatever he was doing absorbed all his attention at that time and routine went by the by. She knew that his focus on whatever the task at hand was unswerving, complete and something to be applauded. She had a sneaky suspicion that the fact Mr Scriven, try as he might, couldn't attract this attention was a thread in the web of reasons that it irritated him well beyond the realms of rational behaviour.

Fact was that when Billy clattered the school house door open, she had heard, understood and quickly made up an excuse to enter the school room in the hope that her presence might distract Mr Scriven from his eruption of rage. She knew him for what he was: a lonely man with a depthless capacity for rage. So, on seeing her enter the school room, Billy side stepped Mr Scriven to avoid the menace of those outstretched skeletal fingers. Courage and the defiance that went with it made Billy glare back at the livid and incredulous teacher looming over him.

Mr Scriven raised his hand to administer another of his favourites, a flat palm clout to the ear that had left Billy's ear red sore and ringing more than many a time. Infuriated by what she saw, but quick to think, Sarah Golding announced her presence, 'I think Collins has something important to say, Mr Scriven?' She framed it like a question though there was another edge to her tone.

It had the desired effect and Mr Scriven quickly retracted his hand to smooth the back of his head. He paused and turned towards the voice and growled, 'Well, what is it this time, boy?' And so, Billy began his description of what he had found over at Old Harry.

Gulping to compose himself, Billy began, 'I was coming back from the Old Harry out past... when I came across the most incredible sight, sir! You've got to come quick. I've not never seen anything like it before. It's like a... a...giant...' he trailed off, too nervous to get his words out.

The pause made Mr Scriven twitch with irritation. He appraised the sorry creature before him and with a delivery that was unnervingly enunciated asked, 'Well, what is it that you think you've seen, boy?' The cool ferocity made the dozen or so other school children, who'd previously been interested to see the next Billy drama unfold, wince with fear and join Maggie in desk analysis.

Maggie tried to communicate wide-eyed with her mother who gave only an imperceptible, negative shake of the head. Billy understood that he couldn't rely on any more help, drew in his breath as he closed his eyes and clenched his fist for courage and, as calmly as his voice had let him, told what he'd discovered. He had a job steadying his voice and keeping the snot in his nose.

'Sir, there's what I think is an enormous whale skeleton over at Old Harry!'

Mr Scriven quickly considered this knowing that there'd been talk on Portland of whales spotted in the Channel by the navy. It was possible. But as a stickler for detail, he pounced on what he saw as a possible inconsistency, a way of humiliating the boy before him.

'A skeleton, you say?' And with that unnervingly demur tone, he continued, 'And how could a skeleton be washed up? Skeletons don't wash up. They sink, Collins.' Some of the less sympathetic wanted to laugh at this point but noted Miss Golding scanning the room with a look they instinctively understood.

Billy was not to be deflected. 'I know, sir. It shouldn't be there, but it is. It's about as long as ten skiffs and as high as three or more on its end! And it's on its back, sir. The ribs open to the sky.' He delivered the last bit with a finality that he hoped would be convincing. He didn't feel so confident about describing the even more unusual detail he'd discovered when he walked through the hall-like skeleton of what had to be one of the Great Whales, perhaps even a Blue Whale.

As he had passed through the skeleton at first along its spine, head inclined upwards, the sky had been an azure blue background for the dry white bones of the ribcage. How could they be dry? Absent-mindedly, his fingers had passed over the enormous trunks that formed the ribcage that were like the pillars of a cathedral. Maggie's mum had told them that the vaulted ceilings in cathedrals resembled an upside down boat or the skeleton of a great wale that Jonah had been trapped inside in the Bible. This felt a little like a church which must be like a cathedral, he reasoned. Only, he felt at ease among the bones, not self-conscious and uncomfortable as he did in church.

Something felt unusual to the touch and made him stop. Billy crouched and ran his fingertips vertically down one of the ribs. Billy squinted in the bright morning light to focus sharper on the whale bone to see what it was that gave it a strange texture. For it wasn't like old, white ossified sheep bones bleached white and dried out over time by the salt wind. This felt different altogether. It felt like it meant something, like braille to the blind.

He looked closer still and smoothed a thumb over the bone surface as to confirm the idea forming in his head. Momentarily, he became aware of the scent of the dried bladder wrack seaweed at his feet and then another, older unfamiliar scent. Billy was sure of what he saw before him. It didn't make sense, but he was sure of what his senses informed him.

Billy stood up and stared at the open cavern above him. He suddenly felt very small, but also very powerful with his knowledge, with his find. And then he hopped from rock to rock to avoid tripping on the great bones. Stopping every few yards to check what he already knew to be true. His intakes of breath rasped with the excitement boiling up in him. His eyes shone, keen.

After five long minutes, assured of his perceptions, Billy stood there on the creature's spine, hands on hips, looking upwards, full of wonderment, elated and breathing hard, squinting in the glare of the sun light reflected off the sea. The heat was rising in the day. He had to share this! And then he remembered Maggie, then school, and 'Oh Christmas, Mr Scriven!' School! He had totally forgotten it in his absorption. But the last person he wanted to share his extraordinary find with was his unforgiving sadist of a school teacher.

Initially disquieted, he resolved that Mr Scriven, and whatever he would predictably say or do, didn't matter. This had to be shared! And more than that, Maggie's mum would most likely know what to do with the knowledge. And it was a Tuesday—didn't she help out on a Tuesday? What luck! Yes, she did! And everyone looked forward to her being in charge. It made them look forward to the day rather than otherwise.

Tuesday was the day Mr Scriven was at the Admiralty all day doing important, secret things that he took very seriously. Billy knew Maggie's mum collected stones that had something called fossils in them, ancient creatures turned to stone. She took Maggie to a place called Lyme to look for them. And it seem like a some sort of a fossil? With the immensity of the thing, it couldn't have washed up though. And there was no matter, no flesh on it anywhere. Puzzling. His thoughts were too quick like spooked fish, silver flashes and bubbles, disappearing suggestions. He knew better than to try to catch them. He knew when he was beat.

Maggie's mum was the best bet. He always liked asking her questions. She would know what to do and maybe understand what all the carvings meant. He recognised some of the letters here and there but none of the words. In some places the carvings were like a series of curls and curves and dots. In others they were more like pictures drawn with a quill, full of exotic quick flourishes. Some places there were pictures of snakes, eyes in triangles, even lions. What it meant, he had no idea. The entire skeleton was completely covered in these cryptic etchings. What he did know as looked, before he set off was that he had dreamt of finding what he was sure was a whale skeleton the night before. And he had an impression of a crowd of people around all speaking at once in different sounding languages. He had to get to the school house as fast as possible for he had a vague sensation that there was no time to lose, that his find might disappear like a notion of smoke, just the scent of an impression left behind, if he wasn't quick about it.

'Mr Scriven!' gaped Billy with raw dread unmasked in his voice. And then, 'What are you doing here? It's Tuesday?' Billy had a rare talent for saying exactly the wrong thing at the wrong time to the wrong person. But slow on the uptake he wasn't. And so, pre-emptive staccato fashion, before Scriven's inevitable eruptive reaction, he rattled on:

'Sir, we've got to go now. Come and see it, please!' He was trying not to plead, but Mr Scriven heard the weakness, the falter in his voice and appeared to swoop down so that his face was not an inch from Billy's. Billy tried not to recoil from the school master's rancid breath and his body odour that smelled like something called ammonia. Billy's chin shrunk into his neck as he noticed that the livid scar tissue on the left side of Mr Scriven's face seemed to wriggle like a knot of rag worm as his anger flooded back and his self-control diminished proportionately.

Sarah Golding, unable to be a passive participant any longer, paced forward demonstratively across the floorboards which announced her presence before she uttered, 'I think Billy has something important to show us, Mr Scriven. What would it hurt for you to allow us to see this find and get out of the class room on a beautiful day?'

Mr Scriven wheeled and raised himself up like a predator disturbed from its gorging on a kill. For a long, silent moment, he appraised Miss Golding in that way that made her uncomfortable and then something else passed behind his eyes that she couldn't interpret. And then straightening himself, in a serpentine voice, disconcertingly pleasant, he acquiesced, 'Yes, Miss Golding. On a beautiful day, let's go and see what the boy thinks he has seen.'

Dust motes danced in the musty shafts of light as the school room shuffled self-consciously. Sarah Golding shook off her confusion and rested charge trying to find notes of enthusiasm and optimism. 'Right, children! Assemble in a line by the school gate. Alphabetically. Billy's going to show us what he's found.'

By the time they were lined up outside, gulping down the fresh air, emboldened by the heat of a morning sun in June, the school children were abuzz with excitement, giving each other playful shoves and pokes. They'd forgotten

Mr Scriven's mood and were just glad to be outside and not in the dark and musty, austere creaking classroom. They weren't there more than a few minutes before Mr Scriven gave the instruction for Billy to lead the way. And so, he set off at a walking jog. He wasn't going to hang about. They'd just have to keep up. It was going to take them a good twenty minutes to get over to the Old Harry on the South East corner of the isle across the cliff paths even at a brisk pace. They looked an odd troop that morning. Billy followed by Mr Scriven in the lead followed by a dozen children of various shapes and sizes with Miss Golding keeping an eye on the tail.

They were all drawing breath heavily by the time they arrived, scanning the beach for some sign of what Billy had described. There was no scent in the air save for the tangy spring scent of the mainland carried across the lagoon by a light north-westerly. Had it been blowing from the southeast, Billy might have got wind that something was not quite right, that what he had seen and what was there now were two quite entirely different things. But it was a north-westerly breeze and with a growing sense of triumph and excitement, he scrambled nimbly down the bluff followed by the billowing Mr Scriven's and the rising hubbub from his school friends who minded not a jot mirthfully losing their footing on the gravelly path. Only Miss Golding had a sense of a foreboding as she descended the bluff with exaggerated care.

Billy broke away from the group determined to be first to feast his eyes on the find. The ivory skeleton carved entirely with the strange symbols that he had seen not an hour before was already etched into his memory and imagination like a mariner's tattoo. He wondered if it must tell some sort of story as he deftly took the rock scramble. That was what he was thinking as he scaled the large spur of rock that separated him from his find, his sense of triumph overwhelming. But what he saw appalled him. More than that, the stench made him retch, bending him double.

He wasn't the only one as the children scrambled up onto the spur. First to assault the group's senses, the cloying carrion stench of the carcass that caught in their noses and throats. Then, the vision of the rotting carcass that the rooks and ravens and gulls, oblivious to the horror, ripping the blubber from the whale's bones with angry jabs were startled and scattered into the wind. In places, the whale's fatty white blubber gave way to holes of crimson gore where larger creatures over some time had gorged their fill.

And last of all to overwhelm the senses was the sound, the intense hum of thousands of flies settling and resettling on the carcass of the once great creature. The gulls bickered their shrill cries and quick-stepped. The ravens hopped meditatively, cawing, stony black-eyed, disappearing inside the maw.

With a wild look that spoke of more than confusion and disbelief, Billy Collins looked to Maggie's mum, Miss Golding, for some safe port. But there was none to be had. Maggie's hand brushed Billy's, but couldn't make more contact as he shifted fearfully towards Mr Scriven. No one spoke, all too horrified but with a unified expectation of Mr Scriven filling the void with a maelstrom of rage that would mirror the children's sense of revulsion. Billy was frightened now. Very frightened. But the storm didn't come. Instead, in a mild voice looking away to from the child to the sea, he said, 'It seems, Collins, that you have got it very wrong.'

Mr Scriven returned his stare to Billy for moment and then wordlessly descended the spur before announcing over his shoulder that school would finish early that day after the lunchtime bell. Looking to each other and none at Billy, the children followed Mr Scriven's lead and descended the rock outcrop and climbed up the bluff back to the school house, keen to distance themselves from the vision of the colossal, vile, rotting whale carcass.

And then there was only the three of them. Sarah Golding, her daughter and Billy. There was nothing to say and they just wanted to get away as well.

Back in the old school house, Portland's children sat in abject silence, afraid even to steal questioning glances at each other, under the brooding gaze of Mr Scriven who they had a feeling would be quick with an acerbic tongue for anyone not concentrating on the task at hand. As soon as they had arrived back, he set them silent reading: a Thomas Hardy novel none could quite get into.

All they wanted to talk about was the washed up whale; how awful it was and what Billy Collins could have meant by saying that its bones were stripped clean and carved with symbols and pictures and words. But Mr Scriven wouldn't have any discussion on the matter and flew into a rage when even the most innocuous of curious anatomical questions was asked. Chat about the subject he did not want, though it seemed to some that he must have been mulling it over. Those who dared look up at their school master noticed an uncharacteristic smile pass across his lips on occasion that dissolved into his down-turned, surly mask.

Mr Scriven stood up once when he heard the school gate hinge creak open. Chin up, eyes looking over the raised windowsill, he watched as Miss Golding asked Billy a question which was answered with a negative shake of the head. Carefully, Miss Golding closed the gate, felt the eyes on her through the school house window, the unrelenting glare of the school master. And then eyes down, she led Billy Collins and her daughter presumably towards home.

Some of the children guessed what was what, but daren't move in their seats. Mr Scriven's abrupt movements thereafter confirmed what some knew: that Billy Collins wouldn't be returning to school that day. Some wondered if at all. Although it provided a break in the learning day to see what had become Billy Collins' daily debacles with the school master, most were uncomfortable with it now.

Mrs Collins watched their approach along the lane to Old Sea Dog Cottage from the kitchen window. All three, heads down in line, uncharacteristically quiet together. She knotted her hands until the thought came to get the water on the boil for tea. Hastily she cut up some slices of bread and gathered herself before the front door opened and Miss Golding entered, the two children sat on the wall looking over to the lighthouse, far away looks in their eyes.

Quickly, before Maggie and Billy came in to sit down, for Sarah Golding knew it would not profit the children to discuss the mornings events with them again, she filled Billy's mother in with details. She was economical with her words so as to quickly convey the events without sentiment. She didn't want to worry Billy's mother any more than need be. She was anguished enough as it was since the news of the death of Billy's father on Flanders' fields. News that had turned her hair from raven black to silvery white overnight.

'Billy was sure of what he saw, Rebecca. You could see the dance in his eyes. He was late back from setting his pots and knew full well that Mr Scriven would give him a hiding for it. But he wasn't letting that put him off.'

'That boy! He'd be late for his own funeral…' she trailed off, unhappy with her analogy.

'Well, never mind that. I can't blame him for not wanting to be at school. Mr Scriven is a cruel man. Something's hardened his heart against the boy. He has never given Billy the benefit of the doubt. Can't! It's any excuse with him to give him a hard time. And I can't think for the life of me what's to be done about it. More'n that, I don't know how to come back from this.'

'And you say he was sure that he saw what he saw? That the whale skeleton was covered in carvings? Words and pictures? Symbols?' asked Billy's mother, shrill, imploring.

'That's what he said.' The two women again took a moment. They both knew that if Billy said he had seen the whale skeleton and that it had been covered in strange writings, he had. He simply wasn't capable of deceit or lies. It wasn't in his make-up any more than his inability to conceal his feelings. He was a perpetual open book. There was tacit agreement on that.

'What does it mean, Sarah?' Billy's mother asked. 'What was the scrimshaw?'

'I can't tell you that, Rebecca. But I think I know what the writings were.'

'You do?' Mrs Collins replied with stealth awe and dread in her voice.

'Yes, Rebecca. Some of it sounded like hieroglyphs. Egyptian symbols. Some like Japanese or Chinese characters. Some of it like Arabic script. Or how I've heard it described, as Billy described it to me on the way back. Elegant twists and curls and dots... he said there were printed words and words drawn with a quill and ink too. Some English. Some sounding like it looked like Latin. From what he said.' The last words hung in the air.

With widening eyes, the two women came to a tacit, silent understanding. They had been skirting the subject because they were at a loss as to how to say it. They were at a loss because normal chat hadn't yet shaped how to communicate such a thing. This was new and unfamiliar territory. For two women as close as sisters, they were cautious with each other for the first time.

'You saw it too, then Sarah?'

'No, Rebecca. I didn't see it. What we all saw on the beach was the rotting carcass of a whale. It might have been hit by one of those bloody war ships!'

'So, how are you sure that Billy saw what he says he saw then, Sarah?' Billy's mum questioned, deliberately enunciating each word of what otherwise what would have been a tongue twister. They both sensed that they were getting close to the admission of a shared experience.

Sarah Golding leant, both palms resting on the kitchen table, towards her friend before she spoke. She paused, trying to get her words straight.

'Because I dreamt of a great white whale skeleton on the beach here at the old quarry last night too. I walked inside it and trailed a hand over the carved surface. There were words and symbols and hieroglyphs etched all over it. You could trace it with a thumb. I remember thinking in my dream, "if only I could take a rubbing of some of it".'

They both fell silent and Billy's mother started to pour water into the teapot before she replaced it on the fire and sat down at the table. She composed herself before looking up at her friend. They had been friends since they could remember and had an implicit trust in each other.

Rebecca Collins then said to her friend, 'So, you saw it too? In a dream.'

'*We* saw, Rebecca. Billy said he saw it in his dream and then on the beach. And I'm pretty sure if we ask Maggie, she'll say the same too.'

'But what does it mean, Sarah?' she asked quietly drawing her shawl around her.

Sarah Golding clenched her jaw, thinking. 'I can't say, Becky. I think it's a gift. A troubling gift we've been given and Billy's the key to it. I have no idea what it means, but I have a feeling that there's change on the way. What I can say is that we don't share this outside us, outside of these four walls. This is to stay between us and the children like a shared family secret. It's not the type of idea that folk around here are going to take kindly to. It'd only make trouble for us. For Billy in particular. He's a sensitive enough fish as it is.'

'Yes, Sarah. We've got to bury it. We've have to make sure that the children know that too. But they're going to want to talk. Billy'll want to defend himself!'

'Well, he can't. Not on this. You know what folk are going to make of this if it becomes public knowledge. They'll run us off the island. Or worse,' she added quietly. 'Best not say a word and hope the other children just remember the carcass and not Billy's words about what he saw.'

'I just don't see how this can work out,' Billy's mother asked, imploring her friend for some comforting words.

'What I do know, Becky, is that Bill can't go back to school. You know how it's been between the two of them these last months. He has to be away from Mr Scriven and have the opportunity to save face. He's going to feel very strange and outside of it all after this experience. We both know that he's tough, but he's sensitive by the same measure. And what's more, I don't trust Mr Scriven to be near him.'

Soothed by the common sense, Rebecca Collins nodded and smiled a regretful smile at her friend before asking, 'What do you see for Billy, Sarah?'

Without hesitation that indicated that Sarah Golding had already given the question time already, Sarah Golding replied, 'I think that Billy'll probably have a life that leads him along paths that most would fear to tread.'

'As a quarryman, as a fisherman?' Billy's mum responded searchingly.

'I didn't mean for work, though I don't think he'll not do either of those things. I mean I think that he's marked out for something. I don't know. We've both said he's like he's been here before…'

Sarah Golding understood that her ethereal words weren't of much comfort to her friend and that she needed to speak plainly about the here and now, about practical things that they could do to try to mend the situation. They both understood that their feelings and observations about Billy were probably best kept between them. Salt crystals soaked and dried into the drift wood on the fire crackled and popped sending an ember arcing out onto the flag stone floor. A flake of ash caught on the heat in the air butterflied and disintegrated around them. The two women had both seen it and listened to the hiss of the fire until Sarah Golding resumed.

'You'll have to take him out of school. Tell the authorities that you have to set him to work as the man of the family. They won't argue with that.' They both knew this to be true as Billy was the only Collins male to left alive. Aged 11, he was in fact man of the house with all the responsibility to go with it, to provide. Thank goodness it was only the two of them.

'And I'll teach Billy in the evenings. I can do it with Maggie so he can catch up on what's been happening in school. That way, he won't feel so adrift.'

The two women exchanged a smile and a look of warmth. They grasped each other's hands as if to affirm the agreement and the emotions that went with it. This was what Maggie and Billy saw when they tentatively pushed open the kitchen door of Old Sea Dog Cottage. They looked worn and exhausted from the morning's experience.

And so that was how Billy was taken out of school and away from the influence of Mr Scriven. There were few references made to the events of that day, even between the two families. They all knew what they had seen and they had all shared the same dream. Only Billy thought he had seen it on the beach, daytime too. For all of them, the vision of the ivory skeleton with the unknown words and pictures and symbols and script, remained as clear in their memories as if they'd happened moments ago in their waking hours. Although the colours were pale, they were luminous too and defied the erosion of time. All four of them would wonder at the meaning of their shared dream as long as they lived.

*

Decades later, nearly a half century later, sat in the stuffy cab of a Red Wing Land Rover, Billy Collins could see the vision as clear as day, as if it was yesterday. What Captain Collins could also feel and know was that the story between him and Mr Scriven was already written by then and, try as they might to avoid each other, as clever and quick thinking as Maggie's mum had been to separate the two in the hope of preventing an escalation, the fates had conspired to make their experience a shared one and that the story between the two of them was far from over.

Chapter 7
Mike's School Days—A Near Miss

Back in the Red Wing, Captain Collins had fallen silent again with the sharp remembrance of these long buried memories. He was fairly astonished at how crisp and vivid they were after all these years. He wondered how jagged his recollections could and he couldn't escape the feeling of a dreadful momentum gathering the closer he got to Portland, his island, childhood home. The fly wheel of memory was set in motion like a spin blade.

His backside and legs cramping-sore, Sapper Mike shifted about still trying to get used to the unusual changes in his mentor's behaviour, now that they'd broken the ice and spoken a little more openly. However, his projection of potentials for things to come was far comfortable. Sapper Mike turned over their conversation in his mind in an effort to order and process it. But being barely eighteen, although old for his years as some said, he was fairly flummoxed as to what it all meant. So, he figuratively stamped it 'sensitive' and tried to file it away. Or, shove it to the back of his mind out of sight.

Despite being born into the fast changing, digital-media world where personal revelations, which perhaps should be kept shut tight in the family box, were the norm, Sapper Mike wasn't built like that. On a gut level, he knew that he wouldn't be sharing any of what had been said with the rest of the unit. Certainly not before a job, especially this job. That he didn't chat much and banter with the popular crowd—just didn't feel the need—meant that his peers often labelled him aloof, or no fun or arrogant. Truth be known, he was the converse of that. But people make their assumptions. Diffident maybe, arrogant no. It had been that way at school and was looking like it might be the way in the Engineers. None was true, but the result was that he was a bit of a loner with just a few close friends. The Captain being the mainstay.

Growing up, it had meant that many gave him a wide birth, mistrustful as they were of his difference, unnerved by his self-contained quiet. Or was it simply that they felt rejected? He didn't know and cared less. In a world where the noisy with little to say or those with the loudest shout in the playground held court, Michael Lapin was the odd one out. He came to be known as a dark horse to be watched particularly in school when he started getting taller and a more obvious target for the bullies. These musings sailed on the periphery of his thoughts that day as they travelled in silence. Then rather unexpectedly, it was Sapper Mike's turn to recall a series of events he'd rather not have had to remember in the Red Wing on the way to the Portland job, the Captain's last job.

*

'They always make you wait! It's all part of the game, Mike!' his father muttered gruffly as he rolled his restless shoulders. Had they not felt so uncomfortable waiting outside the headmaster's office, Mike and his father might have noticed the school secretary's momentary pause in the incessant, insect click of her typing as she clocked their discomfort and shrugged with mild irritation. To her, the scene was standard, seen it a thousand times and so the empathy had fatigued: they were nervous but didn't seem the types to make a fuss despite the father's grim countenance. That was fine with her. She had more important stuff to deal with unless there was trouble and she was fine to deal with that. The father would be a piece of cake, but the mother looked to be a shrewd cookie. No matter, she'd placate or eject them. She was the gatekeeper after all.

'Now now, Sam!' Mike's mother whispered, 'There's bound to be good reason for the delay.' She observed the secretary intently and quickly made her assessment: late forties, heals, pencil skirt and matching jacket, white blouse and pearls. Hair pinned up in a bun, functional. Tall, attractive, a tad too slim, with sharp features accentuated by fatigue, concealed with make-up. No rings on the left hand, but perhaps the vestiges of an indent where one had rested but had now been removed. This was not a woman to irritate. You didn't cross this one. She was the gate keeper and although there was a head teacher behind the tall double doors, this woman undoubtedly knew more about the goings-on in the school than he did.

Jenny reached across her son and put a hand on top her husband's white, calloused, shovel hands in an effort to placate him. She knew full well how uncomfortable her husband felt in formal, institutional settings. If they weren't called in soon, he was just as likely to get up and walk. And then they'd have no other option than to remove him from another school before this one took the initiative. They had talked about it the night before. Dad had framed it as 'taking control of the situation', but his mum had a different interpretation that went along the lines of 'walking the plank rather than joining the crew.'

She knew her role well enough. She'd mediate for a compromise and so long as Sam kept his hand in his pockets, she'd probably get her way. He was a man Sam took everything head on while she circled. As she remembered the measured, anxious tone of the conversation, hypnotised by the quietly raucous firelight, the head teacher's door opened and Mr McGuire greeted them with an air of enthusiastic decorum. Thank God.

'Mr and Mrs Lapin! Good of you to come. Please come in, please come in.' The headmaster held the door open with one hand while wafting them in with the other. He closed the door behind them with care then crossed carpet of the spacious office and took up his post behind his desk in an old-fashioned high-backed chair.

It was a bit off-putting. His ingratiating, cheery manner and tone was more like you'd expect from an old friend rather than a first time with the parents of a son who was likely about to be kicked out of school. Must have been a new breed in a changing world, she thought. The little family shambled into the head teacher's office. Mike's mother patted down her skirt and set her look straight ahead while his father crossed his arms over his chest, half sagged in the far-too-small chair, eyes down. Mike sat in the middle, unsure from whom to take his lead. He settled on sitting up straight and concentrated on a middle point on the headmaster's desk. He vaguely remembered something about others having to be present at the meeting, but they didn't seem to have arrived.

The headmaster shuffled and squared off some papers, put them in a tray, paused a moment to assess the three before him and then began, 'Good of you to come in today. I'll get straight to the point. I'm sorry to have kept you waiting. Now, as you well know, Michael, we cannot condone violence in any form at St Jude's. Bullying, physical or psychological is to be deplored. And deplore it, we do! Mark my words.' For all the friendliness to start, the man wasn't messing about, Sam noted as he martialled himself.

'Oh, Christmas! Here we go,' Mike thought to himself. He thought his ejection from school might have taken longer than this.

'Violence is not a viable solution to a long term problem. Though,' and the head teacher paused to carefully choose his words, 'in the short term, it may have its benefits. This is how the world works. Sharp intervention. We see it in the news every day. This is the example set by our government! How can we expect our children to behave differently?'

The family's collective head raised in unison as they tried to process the headmaster's statement. He grew quiet and pensive again, considering something he didn't seem about to share. Mike's mother raised an eyebrow to meet her husband's questioning look. They had talked well into the night about putting Mike's case forward. Essentially that he'd given in to a constant pressure from a bully and spoken to him in the only language he understood. They knew his position was indefensible in this day and age and that Mike shouldn't have 'shamed' the bully, as his mother put it, shouldn't have clouted him, as his father did. Mike's father, Sam Lapin, was beginning to bristle, fixed his eyes on the head teacher and looked as if he was about to say his piece. Mike closed his eyes with a wince. His father was as mild-mannered as it gets unless his sense of fair play was interfered with.

Nevertheless, the head teacher seemed to have anticipated something and placing both palms on the desk before him and with a tone less authoritarian by a measure or two, he continued, 'But the case in point is a delicate one and has required thorough examination. And I've have had to take counsel from many members of staff in order to come to a ...decision.' That last word lingered in the air of no-man's land between them.

'The calm before the storm?' Mike wondered.

'He's talking in riddles,' thought Sam. With the bile rising, he was having difficulty understanding where the conversation was going, tying up the threads.

And then the head teacher was off on a different track. 'And so, I understand that you are making excellent progress. English, History, Maths, Science, Design and Technology. And on the rugby field. According to Mr Philbrick, you had a 'clattering performance' against Bishop Gore School in North Prospect on Saturday.' He fixed Michael Lapin with a meaningful look that, if it was lost on Michael, it wasn't on his mother. 'I think this may be where you need to focus, how shall we put it? Your energies, Michael?' The head teacher seemed to be gaining a momentum that required the Lapins to hush and listen.

This was a good thing as they were truly foxed and weren't about to prevent him from taking what seemed like a promisingly optimistic course. The head teacher had let that last one hang in the air for a moment before clearing his throat to continue, 'And so, with these other considerations in mind, I have no option but to—' He was stopped mid-sentence as Sam Lapin's frustration took a turn for the defensive and he began to rise up from his chair. And he would have done had not Mike's mother flicked out her left hand whippet quick to grasp her husband's unclasping hands which arrived with a slapped report which sat him firmly back down in his chair.

The headmaster's chin and gaze had raised up and his mouth opened to take in more air. Mrs Lapin gave her confused husband a piercing look until she read his acquiescence and she turned to the head teacher to continue with a curt nod and flat smile. Mike scratched the side of his head for want of any better means to react.

'And so, with this in mind,' the head teacher continued from where he had paused as if reading from a script, 'we have no option other than to ask you to remain home for a week's suspension from school. Michael must remain at home for week. The Board of Governors took some convincing that permanent exclusion was not the only option. But furnished with a detailed description of this case and circumstances surrounding it, and Michael's academic and sporting progress, a week's suspension has been agreed upon. The only caveat is that his time is spent profitably, wisely. Mr Jones in CDT has said that he can enquire about a week's work experience with Armstrong and Sons, a reputable carpentry firm in the town. If that would be agreeable to you, all? That is your preferred interest, Michael?'

And without due pause for a reply, he continued, 'Well, I'm glad that's settled. I will ask Mr Jones in CDT to make the arrangements with the Armstrongs to commence Monday.'

The head teacher got up and so did the bemused Lapin family. The interview was over. He guided the family to the tall wooden doors. Sam Lapin turned the handle slowly with care, still thinking. He exited followed by his wife and turned to see the headmaster looking meaningfully at their son, one hand on his shoulder.

Mr and Mrs Lapin stared, it's fair to say, open mouthed at the head teacher. Perplexed and leaning forward as if awaiting something more from the head teacher who had turned and was now smiling broadly at them. Although Mike *was outwardly being punished, there appeared to something else at work that passed Mike and his father by. His mother was beginning to pick up on something else that she may or may not share later.*

With no audible reply from the Lapin family, Mr McGuire took up again. 'However, your presence on the rugby field on Saturday against Bishop Vaughan School will be required. You display an admirable hard work ethic and sense sportsmanship on the pitch that we want to see more of. Make sure you keep it that way and don't slip up again. I'm not sure I can speak up for you twice,' he added in a whisper. And with that he gently put a hand between Mike's shoulder blades to make sure of his exit and the door to the office closed decisively.

The three of them stood in a quiet triangle. The school secretary had stopped typing again, no doubt glad of a bit of drama to break up the day. Mike's father began to nod his head slowly, perhaps beginning to comprehend and definitely signalling the settling of the dust. With a definitive sigh, Sam Lapin smiled, 'I don't know quite what happened in there. But I'd certainly say that you were born under a lucky star, my lad!' This gained a conspiratorial smile from the school secretary who commenced her typing again. Cue to leave.

Sapper Mike Lapin remembered these decisive events as he sat in the Red Wing cab, the roadway hissing by, slicked with rain, on his way to diffuse a Second World War bomb on Portland, now as the youngest member of a unit of Royal Engineers Bomb Disposal Officers. And as proud as you like, too. There had been no more run-ins after that. He kept himself to himself.

Gusts of wind raked the Red Wing, smarts of rain lashed the windscreen like a cat o'nine tails, the wipers working overtime, a rhythmical wah-wah-reset, wah-wah-reset. It had been typical, filthy Plymouth weather that day when they'd driven back from his near expulsion. He remembered being sat in the back, taking in the relieved quiet of his parents up front, listening to the wipers then, head back on the headrest, eyes closed in relief.

Chapter 8
Biscuits and Field Glasses

Captain Collins had been glancing over from time to time at his apprentice when he roused from his thousand-yard stare. The lad also seemed stilled with memory. But now he was shifting in his seat, rolling his shoulders and he knew it wouldn't be long before the chat resumed.

'It comin' down in bloody stair rods, lad! You were away for a bit then. Thought you were going to doze off on me.'

'Order of the day, to be away with the fairies, sir!' He retorted, quick smart, eyes wide to emphasise the point.

'Cheeky bugger!' The Captain grinned back, letting the junior officer off the hook for his cheek. Things were back on track, relaxed. Might as well seal it with a biscuit.

'Hob nob, sir?' Mike enquired leaning forward, digging around in his rucksack for the biscuit tin.

'Now, you're talking, son. And get that flask of tea open, too. I could die of thirst over here if it was left up to you.' Jocular again. Camaraderie back on track.

'Yorkshire tea. White with one, reporting for duty, sir!' Intoned the Sapper with a mock seriousness pouring a mug, passing it over to the Captain who took it with his left and immediately had a noisy slurp of the scalding tea before placing in the holder to accept a biscuit. The Captain had a habit of staring at the remaining biscuit after he'd had a bite. They munched in contented silence for a while and after a bit of lip smacking, both drained their builder's brew.

They had a bit of a routine when it came to tea breaks. They discussed the merits of certain biscuits, agreeing that there could be no winner between the ginger nut and the hob nob and that you had to wash down the biscuit sweetness with strong tea to take the taste away. They had similar conversations every tea break, time and again. It was a ritual. Familiar, safe ground, affirming—that was what it was. And it often served the purpose of preparing the ground for a bit of learning or about a topic that might be bumpy and challenging. It was their tried and tested way of focussing away from the job, quelling nerves by sharing jokes, layering on the bravado before returning to the serious stuff.

Mike had found that there was a lot of this in the army. At first, it had been all a bit strange: that the same old jokes were repeated time and again and received the customary hearty laugh in reply as if never cracked before. But as time had passed, he'd got used to it and thought of it like swimming with the current—just let it carry you along. Never, though, did he drop his guard completely. That was what the army was like for Mike. It was like being in a perpetual state of relaxed vigilance.

Early on, soon after his arrival, when the Captain's tutelage had started, the old boy had warned him that there were a plethora of unspoken manners, jokes and traditions that Sapper Mike had to tune into, fit in with and be confident in, in order to be 'one of us' and remain safe and sane in bomb disposal. The Captain reckoned that if you thought about it too much, you'd go nuts or chuck in the towel. Always mindful of the job, following the process of diffusing each bomb, never letting your mind wonder into the territory of consequences or you'd be running for the hills before your noodle caught up with your legs.

No-one in their right mind would come within a country mile of unexploded ordnance if you stopped to think about it. The closest he reckoned he came to it was by thinking he was performing a public service, making the damn things safe so that they didn't blow civilians into kingdom come. But it was a long time ago that he'd stopped thinking about his own mortality until this, his last, job. With the curtains drawing on his career, the pages of the rule book appeared to be ruffling open, had become detached and were being carried off into the wind. So, he was glad that his apprentice asked him this next question even if it was a bit of a touchy subject.

'So, what was it with you and this Scriven fella then, sir?' Mike asked, keeping his eyes front. It was a trick he had noticed his parents using. Important questions were always put to him in the car when there wasn't eye contact to get in the way. It seemed to take the edge off whatever was being discussed. It was always this way when they wanted to sound him out about something. Whether he was aware of it, you couldn't say. But this was how he asked the Captain about Mr Scriven; something personal about his past. Personal was off limits usually. Too distracting.

The Captain surprisingly went straight into it. Any pause or reserve had packed up and gone as if he was glad of the opportunity to talk about something so long buried but no less poignant for all those years, it seemed.

'Oh, it was a number of things really. But it started out with the First World War. Both Mr Scriven and my grandfather joined up to do their duty for God and Country as they saw it. They didn't have to, mind you. Portland is the property of the crown. Goes back to Henry VIII or before, I think. I can't remember if it was because it was a deep water port or had something to do with the quarrying of the stone.

'But the long and the short of it was that the men of Portland had a pass. They weren't subject to conscription. So, when all the mainlander men were being enlisted into the First World War, Portlanders didn't have to. Thinking about it, it must have caused a right fuss when they volunteered for the war when they didn't have to. But that was what they did. They made the choice and went off to Portsmouth to join up. Walked all the way. Nearly one hundred miles as the crow flies. Wasn't unusual in those days to walk that far though. The choice to do it was though. More than unusual and must have made them close.

'They both made it through the duration of it. The lucky few. Through the Battles of the Somme and Ypres. The most fierce of the fighting. They came back quiet men, never speaking of those four years of the Great War. My grandfather never spoke of his time in the trenches, but quite often we'd hear him shouting in the night in German as he relived some memory that was still livid, fresh in his dreams. That was when he relived his experiences, I expect. And that was quite normal. Always at night, never in the day. Except the story of the field glasses.'

'The what, sir? The story of the field glasses?'

'Yes. They're in the glove box actually. Get them out. Have a look.'

Gingerly, perplexed, Sapper Mike lent forward and unclasped the glove box in front of him. He took out the leather binocular-shaped box with great care. He looked across at the Captain, 'Can I open them, sir?'

'Yes, Mike. They're for you. A parting gift, if you like.'

With a mixture of surprise and pride, Sapper Mike opened the grey leather case and took out a brass set of First World War field glasses. Binoculars to you and I. It was immediately obvious to Mike that the craftsmanship of them meant that they were worth a few quid, before he got to the fact that they were imbued with a certain significance; a significance that was about to be explained. 'You're giving these to me, sir?' The Captain simply nodded and returned his attention to the road ahead.

'I don't know what to say, sir.'

'Don't have to say anything, son. They're yours. I've collected so much over the years. Feel like I've got to get rid of a lot of it. Can't take it with you when you go. So, I thought you might as well have it.' Sapper Mike simply nodded his surprised thanks and waited for the Captain to continue, vaguely wondering, 'why the purge now?' He turned the field glasses over in his hands, massaged the leather, smoothing the polished brass with a thumb. They were a practical work of art, built to last—as they had. Clearly, the brass had been polished regular, the leather looked after too.

The Captain cleared his throat and began again, 'Yes. My grandfather never spoke of the war. Only the once about how he came by those field glasses when he gave them to me. We'd gone out to the Old Quarry on the South East of Portland, walking. Beautiful, clear, crisp day. You could see for miles. Thinking about it, he must have chosen that day to give them to me to show them off. Taken sandwiches with us, too. We stopped and sat to have them. When we had eaten, he presented me with the field glasses. I guess I felt a little like you do now.' It was a rhetorical question that he wasn't about to wait to be answered. Sapper Mike settled in, supping his tea.

'My grandfather was in the frontline trenches at the Battle of the Somme. The day it happened there was a ceasefire. You can pinpoint the day if you go through the history books. There weren't many ceasefires. He was on night sentry duty and said he could hear someone beyond the wire in no-man's land, obviously in pain. He said he'd listened to it for hours until he couldn't stick it no more. Some poor soul mangled up in the wire and mud that wasn't about to die quickly. So, what do you think the old man did, Sapper?'

'No idea, sir!' Sapper Mike replied, eager to hear the story unfold.

'He goes over the top is what he did to try and find the poor bugger moaning out there! But not until he'd argued with Mr Scriven, Captain Paul Scriven he was by then. Grandfather was a Corporal. Well, actually, it was more than an argument. They fought, by all accounts.' The Captain glanced across to check Sapper Mike had understood the import.

'Ah, problem there, sir! Arguing with a senior officer and disobeying a direct order?'

'Got it, lad! Bravery or stupidity, I don't know what you'd call. But bloody dangerous it was, without doubt. Even in a cease fire, to go over the top. He could have fallen off the duck boards; sloshed about and drowned in a water-filled shell crater; or he could have crawled over unexploded ordnance in the mud. And then there's the rogue snipers, shell shock-mad, stranded in no-man's land who would have shot at anyone, friend or foe for just being there.

'So, my grandfather and Paul Scriven had joined up together and made it through 4 years of the Great War together. That was something of a miracle to survive that long, so they were close. When you spend a lot of time in claustrophobic situations, fearful of being in the trench about to go over the top and torn apart by Gatling guns or fearful of Jerry tunnellers breaking through the mud with murderous intent, you get close. Same as with our unit. Pressure makes diamonds. You trust your colleagues with your life and you stick together. You have to. My grandfather broke the code, I suppose.' He was gathering momentum now.

'So, they argued about him going over the top to save the stranded soul out there. I can't remember if he told me about this or if I have created the memory. But, I can quite clearly see them arguing; Captain Scriven grabbing my grandfather's ankles as he climbed the ladder to go over the top to stop him, to probably save his life. Kicked him in the face in the process. I can see them, teeth bared in each other's faces, and then scrapping in the mud at the bottom of the trench.

'I don't know if it happened like that. Could be false memory syndrome. But I can feel the cold mud. See a dark clouded sky still heavy with scents or cordite and carrion and phosphorous flares and shit.' The Captain paused for a moment and finished the dregs of his tea before he continued.

'Well, G John, as I called him, got the better of Captain Scriven and got up that ladder and over the top. Must have clouted him good and proper too. Mr Scriven wasn't a small man. Said he crawled along the duckboards as far as he could. Then through the freezing mud, stopping to listen to try to locate the injured man. Said he kept low, even though there was a ceasefire. I imagine he thought he was doing the right thing, trying to save an injured Tommy at first. Of course, he couldn't know if the injured man was a Tommy or a Jerry.' The Captain let that sink in and watch the young Sapper's eyebrows arch. The Captain decided not to clarify further and get on with the story.

100

'I've got it in my head that G-John crawled around for a long time before he located the injured man. He said that he'd never seen eyes so white and wide against the mud when he found the man. But he'd found the man, frozen and tangled in barbed wire. Of course, with all the filth, he couldn't even guess the colour of the uniform in the dark. It was only when he started speaking that he twigged that he'd only gone and defied a senior officer and risked his life to save a Jerry!' Captain Collins looked across the cab at his apprentice.

Sapper Mike had placed the field glasses on his lap and had turned 45 degrees in his seat to watch the Captain as the story unfolded, left elbow on the rest. 'No, sir!' The 'o' was a long vowel. 'He hadn't gone and risked all that to save a German, sir? Surely not?'

Locking eyes, the Captain continued, 'And a bloody sniper to boot! It was one thing to fight in the Great War and rake the enemy lines indiscriminately with machine gun fire. Impersonal. To lock a soul in the crosshairs and pull the trigger is another thing altogether. And G-John knew that. God, would he have known that! And, if you think about it: he would have known what it took to be a sniper in a fox-hole with all hell breaking loose around you, too. Mortars and shells raining down an apocalypse on you and still be able to do your job. He would have known that.

'And he must have thought all of that when he saw the bright whites of the eyes in the dark when he fund that injured Jerry sniper. Perhaps the most hated and feared type of soldier on the frontline. That must have put a fly in the ointment for G-John. And then what to do? Save him or kill him? Quite a dilemma for some.'

Sapper Mike nodded quietly as he processed the import of the scene the Captain was describing. When he was satisfied, the Captain continued, but on another tack for a moment, 'His and Mr Scriven's friendship was strong. They wouldn't have fought otherwise. But there was still the disobeying of orders to get through if he'd come back alive. And then there's the idea of bringing an injured Jerry sniper back, saving him. I don't suppose that made him the most popular fella in their trench. But what was he supposed to do when he got there? He couldn't have known who was out there in all that mud and misery, dying. When he realised, what was he supposed to do? Just leave the man there freezing, half strangled in the wire, bleeding to death?' The Captain momentarily turned his attention from the road to his apprentice and asked, 'What would you have done in my grandfather's position, Sapper?'

They drove in silence for a while as the young man pondered the direct question. It crossed his mind as to whether it was some sort of trick question. But he quickly dismissed the notion. The Captain was straight up and didn't play games. Nevertheless, Sapper Mike replied slowly, tentatively, 'I would have snipped the wires and dragged the man back to our lines, sir!'

'You mulled that through, Sapper!'

'Not, sir! That's what I would have done! But that was my instinct,' he replied decisively.

'You really would have done that, come what may? Disobeying a direct order; fighting with a senior officer; bringing an injured Jerry sniper back to the home trench for treatment, saving him?'

'I would have, sir. That's my gut feeling.'

The Captain looked over at the young man quizzically before smiling and replying, 'I know you would, Sapper. And like my grandfather, you would have lain on your belly in the freezing mud, thinking it through until you decided to act. Feel first, think second. That'll change,' he added cryptically.

Ignoring the riddle, Sapper Mike questioned, 'And you, sir? Would you have done the same?'

The Captain looked thoughtful and paused before replying, 'Sat here with you now, it seems simple. As a younger man, the answer would have been simple for me. But time can change you. Preserving life, your life, not taking unnecessary risks and treading a straight path, staying out of bother comes to be more appealing. Like this last job, why do it? There's no need. I could delegate it.'

'It was supposed to be my first solo outing, sir?'

'No, flat no! Not this one. Gotta preserve you. Keep you safe!'

They fell silent again. What was the Captain driving at? There was a white elephant of a subtext here that Sapper Mike was damned if he could fathom. And then the Captain brought them back, 'Situations like my grandfather's, well, no matter what you think you might do. No matter how you run it through in your mind in preparation, I don't think you'll know how you'll react until you're in it. In that moment, in that situation, there's always an element of unpredictability. And you've just got to hope that you do the right thing and it comes good. Do whatever so that you're proud and stay alive. That's the goal.'

'More riddles,' thought the Sapper. The Captain didn't often go off on one and get all philosophical. So, when he did, Mike's brow furrowed eyes asquint as he tried to make links and slot the notions alongside similar ones. The Captain was being candid and this required careful attention. Like everyone else in the unit, he trusted the old boy with his life which meant that anything he said was to be digested for its nourishing content. Still, it didn't make a lot of sense until a long time after their chat when it was the right time to understand. He wasn't about beat himself up looking for meaning. It would happen when it happened. He knew better than to force it. That, he'd certainly learned from the old boy.

After a while, Sapper Mike massaged his temples, circles with his fingertips, before returning to the most tangible thread of the conversation, 'So, that was the defining moment then, sir? That was when your grandfather and Mr Scriven fell out?'

'Well, I don't know the ins-and-outs of it all. They never spoke after that. Not for the duration of the War or ever afterwards on Portland. Call it a silent family feud, if you will.'

'Do you think that that's why he had it in for you, sir?'

'Might well have been. Who knows what's in a man's mind and makes him do the things he does. It's certainly never just one thing. That's for sure.'

'What? A grown man with a grudge taking it out on the man's grandson?'

Captain Collins glanced at the young man noticing an emerging naivety that he hadn't previously spotted. He decided against commenting and continued, 'What I do know is that Captain Scriven must have kept quiet about their falling out, the fight and my grandfather's direct disobeying of orders.'

'How do you know that, sir? Did your grandfather tell you?' What with the heating blasting up the temperature in the cab, Sapper Mike was getting tired. Much as he wanted to learn, there were just too many hares running in the conversation.

'He didn't tell me. I must have worked it out somewhere along the line.'

'Worked what out, sir?' Sapper Mike had wound down the window and had his face turned to the cold air and rain in an effort to wake up. He couldn't hear that well either with the window open.

'That Captain Scriven kept schtum about it, of course, lad!' A crackle of frustration flashed across his eyes, his tone. Sapper Mike winced at his own incomprehension, but his jaw set tight with an angry tiredness. He was pretty much knackered out with all these uncertainties and changes in his mentor's character. Captain Collins looked across to see that the young man hadn't understood what he thought he would have and decided to let it go and explain.

'Captain Scriven must have kept quiet about his disagreement with my grandfather otherwise it's likely he would have been court-martialled and shot for disobeying direct orders.'

'Bloody hell, sir! It was that harsh then, back in the Great War?' The question was rhetorical and required nothing from the Captain, but a nod.

A few moments passed before the Captain continued, 'I don't know if Captain Scriven knew the German soldier was a sniper or not. I don't know that. But if he did, that would have meant two things covered up. Disobeying orders and the rank and function of the German soldier receiving our medical attention. I think that that's enough to sour a relationship for a few generations at least.'

Sapper Mike wound the window up, his eyes glassy with windburn but more awake for it. Wanting to drive the chat back to firmer ground, he asked 'What's the story with the binoculars then, sir? I'm guessing that they fit in here somehow?' The young man ran his thumbs appreciatively over the highly polished brass barrels of the binoculars. The leather handles and the case had also obviously had some sort of waxy polish rubbed into them too as they were no cracks and still supple to the touch.

'Quite right, lad,' replied the Captain. 'Fields glasses actually. First World War German field glasses. Polished once a week every week since my grandfather gave them to me when I was 10 years old.'

That the Old Boy had had the glasses for nearly a half century and had polished them every other week since he was a boy didn't come as a surprise to the Sapper. The Captain took painstaking care of all his possessions and tools alike. Everything was preserved to be in the best working order possible. The Captain believed in things that were built to last. But they only lasted if you looked after them. They had talked about this a fair bit as the Captain couldn't get to grips with the throwaway culture of Mike's generation.

He remembered this as he turned over the binoculars appreciatively and then carefully replaced them in their case. He snapped the catches shut and then Sapper Mike's eyes widened and he inhaled deeply as the origin of the field glasses dawned on him. The right side of his face creased as he asked, 'These are the sniper's field glasses, sir? The one your grandfather saved?'

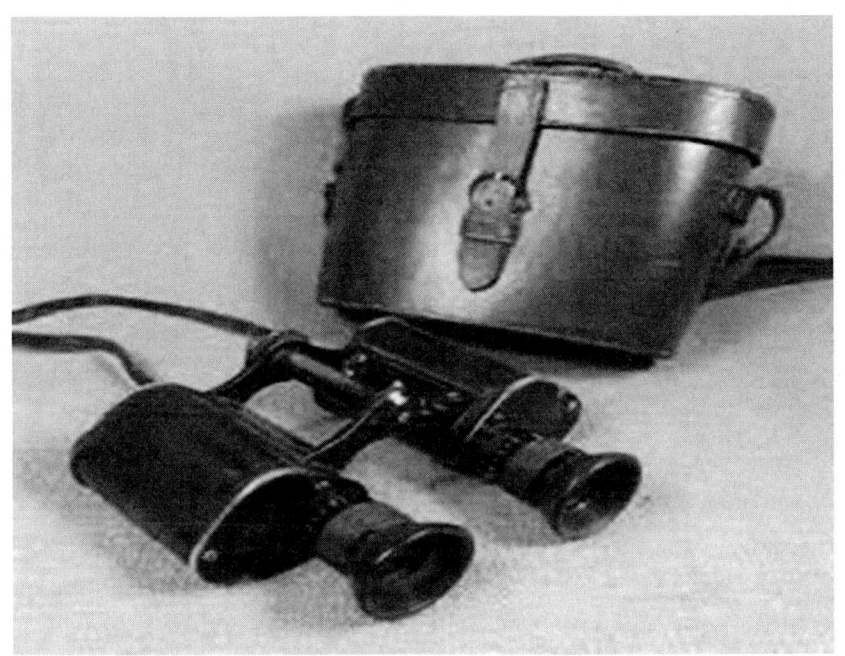

'Yes, lad. It seems that that Jerry sniper was as quick a thinker as he was with his trigger finger. He said he must have read the confusion in my grandfather's eyes and knew he was done for if he didn't act quick. Despite being tangled in the wire and with shrapnel wounds in his legs, he was at great pains for my grandfather to take the field glasses which would have been of quite some value. That made for a bond between them. Grandfather's German was reasonable and he understood the literal meaning of what was being said and he understood that the sniper wanted him to have them as a gift. The gift made the bond between them and ensured that my grandfather looked after him, got him back for medical treatment.'

As if to understand the information all the more, Sapper Mike once again removed the field glasses from their case. This time, he drew them up to his eyes to examine them more closely. And then he read aloud, the maker's mark, 'Zeiss Optics'.

'That's right, lad. There's another story there too: of how the British government bartered with a German company during the war for field glasses knowing there were of the most superior quality. But that's another story for you to look up. Nothing's black and white, lad.'

Sapper Mike whistled a long, single note of appreciation and again nodded at his mentor who paused before beginning again, 'There's more to it than you think though. And not just doing business with the Germans during the war for our war effort. On the home front, those glasses would have had a value for bartering for food, boots, all sorts.' The Captain paused to let the idea sink in before he relinquished the next part. 'And those glasses would have been of interest to British Intelligence for a couple of reasons. For one, the technology: a finer set of excellent binoculars with excellent lenses you couldn't find at that time. And they would have identified the German as a sniper. My grandfather would have realised this and been compelled to keep them hidden. Again, to potentially save his own skin. Clever Jerry, eh?'

'That's wily. And then some, sir! Do you think Captain Scriven ever knew of the field glasses?'

'I couldn't say he did or didn't during the war. But he knew I had a set of Jerry's field glasses. Oh yes, he knew that alright. And he was many things, but he wasn't a stupid man. He must have twigged that I'd got them from my grandfather. When the trouble between us really kicked off, he knew I had them!' Captain Collins hummed to himself and nodded and cryptically added, 'Maybe that I saw what I saw with those field glasses infuriated him and blinded him to the possibility I'd seen something he missed.'

There was obviously another dialogue playing in the Captain's mind, an overlay to their conversation. For an instant, he let himself wonder about it, but Sapper Mike dismissed the observation. There was already plenty enough to think on and he didn't need any more to distract him with questions. No, it would have to come from the Captain as and when, if at all. Sapper Mike felt relieved to have arrived at this conclusion and this gave him the confidence to focus and bring the conversation back around to tangibles again, 'So, your grandfather drags Jerry back through the mud and twisted wire of no-man's land to his home trench. Do you know any more about what happened after that?'

'I know that that they patched Jerry up and he must have spent the rest of the war safe as a POW. We had a good reputation for looking after our POWs. There's no reference to either Scriven or the Jerry after that in his journals. Didn't want to commit evidence to paper, I suspect. I know he was moved so that Captain Scriven was no longer his CO. Good thing too for him as if he'd stayed he might suffered the same fate as Captain Scriven who only just about survived the mustard gas.

'What happened to Captain Scriven then, sir?'

'The Germans gassed his trench a matter of weeks after my grandfather was redeployed. He was badly scarred across the left side of his face from exposure to the gas. Took his looks clean away. Poor sod. And when he got angry, the scar tissue went a livid red. Looked like it was alive. And he was angry just about all the time, mind you. Of course, you don't understand this when you're a kid, what he went through. To us he just looked and sounded terrifying. A very tall man like that in a billowing, academic gown and a glower that could make milk curdle.' Captain Collins shook his head as he considered this for moment and then lapsed into silence. Sapper Mike waited it out. It seemed like the thing to do. He kept his eyes on the road ahead and the wipers battling it out with the squalls of rain. There were a few questions he wanted to ask but wasn't sure if he wanted to hear the answers. It was all a far cry from the usual talk about the protocols of the job and the mental inventories they ran through. And then the Captain started up again, 'He must have covered the rest of his head with a pissy handkerchief as they weren't issuing gas masks as common place. Pretty much half burned his lungs out too. And when he got agitated, his throat'd dry out and his voice would seem to rasp and crackle. God only knows why the man smoked on top of his respiratory problems.

'All the stress of the classroom probably, sir!' They exchanged a look and chuckle. 'You're probably right!'

'So, he came back from the Great War and became the school master on Portland then, sir?'

'Yes, Mike for 20 odd years or so. Of course, when the Second World War broke out, he was one of the first to try to take the King's Shilling to give Jerry another bashing when Churchill announced that we were again at war with Germany. A real zealot of a man.'

'They wouldn't have taken him though, sir? Surely?'

'Nope, that's right. On account of those knackered lungs. Plus he was getting on a bit by then. How to make an angry man angrier, eh? So, he went for the Home Guard instead as an Air Raid Protection Warden which would have given him some clout on the island. He liked that. Always thought he was more of policeman than a teacher.'

Sapper Mike added, 'Oh, yeah they organised rescues, demolitions, supervising the air raid shelters, enforcing the night-time black out. I can see him now with the 'W' painted on his helmet.'

Captain Collins understood that he had probably learned this by rote—comprehensive as it was. The Captain could also see ARP Warden Scriven there in his tin hat. Unconsciously, he snorted with 50-year-old derision before continuing, 'That's right. In the 1930s, the fear was annihilation from the air. Every era has its specific fears. Like the 1960s was the threat of nuclear apocalypse. Nowadays, it's the terror threat from within. Sleeper cells. Of course, we had all of that during World War II—German Commandoes as sleeper cells as vicars, pillars of the community and the like who spoke better English than us as the story went. That was the fear anyhow. All part of the secret world. The world of espionage. Bletchley Park and the code breakers.' The Captain nodded slowly. 'Exciting stuff.'

'Really, sir? We didn't get taught any of this at school,' replied the intrigued Sapper.

'No, you wouldn't have. A lot of it has only become public domain of late. Before that it remained hidden by the Official Secrets Act. Only 50 or so years later do we have access to it. Oh, believe you me, there's aplenty that's not written in the history books. You've got a lot of reading ahead young man,' nodded the Captain meaningfully. 'Start with Zeiss Optics!'

'That I have, sir!' agreed the young man and he made a mental note to add that to the list. He didn't pause long on this as the Captain seemed relaxed, on a roll talking about the past. Better to let the old boy get it off his chest, he didn't wonder. Plus it was making the miles fly by and he was glad the heavy silences were gone. 'So, your Mr Scriven was the school master by day and ARP by night, sir?'

'Yairs, bloody responsible job with all that Ami Steel floating around Portland in readiness for the D Day landings. Half the American navy was there! And that clearly wasn't a secret,' the Captain added meaningfully. There was a lot of 'meaningfully' going on in the Red Wing that day.

'He would have had some responsibility for the barrage balloons, too. All the winching them up and down. He had intelligence gathering duties, as well. He was forever quizzing the old salts about anything they might happen to spot out in the Channel. Like a good intelligence officer, he listened to everyone. But not me, of course. That was his unravelling. His undoing.' *There was that 'meaningfully' again.* Sapper was getting used to it. It was followed by a pause and that thousand-yard stare. It needed derailing before it gathered speed and carried him away.

So, before the Captain had a chance to drift into reverie again, Sapper Mike gave him a nudge. 'This is where it gets interesting at a guess?'

'Right you are, smart lad. And it all goes back to those German field glasses you have in your mitts!'

'Intrigued, sir! But we're just heading past Bournemouth now. Only 40 or so miles to go, so you better get a move on with the story, sir!'

'You cheeky bugger!' guffawed the Captain when he twigged that Sapper Mike was taking the whatsit and he raised up his left hand off the wheel as if to cuff him on the back of the head. And then jabbed him in the ribs as to prove there was more than enough life left in the old dog yet. Sapper Mike yelped to go along with the mood.

'There's a lot more to this tale but I'll save it for another time, lad.' Sapper Mike nodded his agreement and turned his attention back to the binoculars glad to have something tangible to focus. And he was as pleased as punch at the Captain's gift. That was really something.

Contented silence once more settled over them and the remaining miles to Portland passed. The thrum of the diesel, the regular wiper wump punctuated by the occasional squall and pelt of rain marked their passage. When next he looked over at the Captain, Sapper Mike noted that his stare was a way out beyond the road steering wheel, the here and now superseded by the past. He was remembering again, reliving hours, days, weeks woven into a matter of super-accelerated moments of dense, clear experience and knowledge that need be revisited, scoured and searched for any remains, missed lessons could be learned from and hopefully laid to rest. Evidently, the Captain had to purge himself of an unnerving history and only then could it truly become a comfortable memory.

Chapter 9
Fear Confirmed

'Maggie! Wake up! Looked at this,' hissed Billy Collins. It was 4 am, 26 April 1944, two nights before it all happened and their shared experience of child hood would be cleaved cleanly and horribly apart. The two ten-year-old friends had snuck out of home at midnight to the bluffs on Portland to continue with their mission, as Billy saw it, their vigil as Maggie described it.

The wind was up, blowing furrows that raced through the grasses around them. But at least it was dry and comfortable enough for Maggie to have dozed off, wrapped up foetal, only her head showing from the quilt that she had brought with her, while Billy scoured and searched the horizon with the prized German field glasses that his grandfather had given him. In retrospect, you might be forgiven for thinking it an ironic twist of fate, the work of a mischievous trickster, that Billy Collins would see the threat through German field glasses, that only he saw what he saw, that everyone else had missed with the aid of precision German craftsmanship.

The moon was nigh on full, now small and faraway lowering silver disc in the West while Billy pressed the brass binoculars to eyes intensely, his mouth open in an effort to control his excited breathing. At 0400 hours, the moon's silvery path, six hours previous so clear Billy felt he could have walked on it, was fading fast now ephemeral and playing tricks with the light. And that was when his vision narrowed down as he registered faraway shifts in the light. He thought he'd glimpsed three dark shapes crossing the moon's silvery path when they'd first set up their watch.

But that had been hours ago and he was on the verge of self-doubt and giving up when his stubborn tenacity had been rewarded and he'd spotted them again, right out there on the curve of the horizon of the Channel, on the dark line that separated sea and sky like a dorsal line. Three then three. Then three again. If they were what he thought they were. And there were nine of them, the danger presenting was worse than he thought.

'Maggie! For goodness sake, wake up, will you!' He hissed again, clipping her foot with his to rouse her from her slumber.

'What time is it, Bill?' Maggie yawned. She was still wrapped up in the quilt and wriggled up next to him, both on their fronts leaning on their elbows now. And when he didn't reply, she asked again, 'What time is it now? How long have I been asleep for?'

'Dunno. Half four, coming up to five maybe?' he mumbled distractedly.

'I must have been out a couple of hours then?' And when he didn't reply, Maggie understood that something serious was happening and that her friend was too excited to get his words out. It was time to help coax it out of him.

Thoughts and observations ricocheted around in his mind, too quick and fleeting for him to really get a hold of them. What to do next? Who to tell? When to tell them? They'd broken the curfew—how could they get around that? The flood of thoughts made his limbs twitch restlessly in a fog apprehensive confusion. And that was why Maggie was with him, was good for him. She had a way of unknotting the tangles of his excitement, ordering them. She always had a keen sense of how and when to do things.

Billy lowered the field glasses realising only then that in his excitement that he had been painfully pressing them into his eyes. He rubbed the smart and wind tears away. 'There's something happening out there. Loads of activity in the last few hours. The landing craft have returned to port now and the big destroyer, HMS Scimitar I think, seems to be heading off back down the Channel towards Plymouth.' The profile silhouette of the destroyer that had dominated the bay west of Portland had turned through ninety degrees and was now a portrait of its bow trailing black smoke from its stack, the regular thrum of its engines diminishing.

'That's odd that the destroyer is leaving. But why the excitement, Bill? The exercises have been going on for days now.'

Billy took his attention away from the view west and turned to look at his friend. He handed the field glasses to Maggie and replied, 'It's not the exercises that are bothering me or the destroyer leaving. It's those dark, flickering shapes over there on the horizon!' And he pointed south east.

Maggie looked quizzical for a moment and then raised the field glasses to her eyes to look where Billy had indicated. Billy watched as she slowly scanned the horizon where the sun would rise and lighten the skies. Her slow scan stopped as she fixed on the target. After a pause, without lowering the binoculars, Maggie asked her friend, 'What am I looking at? They're too far away to be part of the exercises. Moving too quickly as well.'

'That's what I thought. And they're not ours. *Schnellenboot* is what they are, I think, Maggie. I've been watching them for the last twenty minutes. If only they'd come another mile closer, I'd be able to say for sure,' he replied breathlessly. 'Sounds stupid, but I thought they might have been whales to start with. I've seen humpback whales breach before now. Dark-backed, white-bellied, twisting out of the water.'

It was her turn to search her friend's face questioningly and guide him back although she did want to know why her friend who told her everything hadn't mentioned before that he'd seen a whale. She'd have to salt that one away for later.

'What's *Schnellenboot* when it's at home, Bill?' her tone quiet with the understanding that something important was happening.

'They are fast attack torpedo ships, Maggie. German fast attack vessels. E-boats. They must have come over from Cherbourg.'

'Why 'E' boats, Bill?'

Billy took back the binoculars, keen not to lose sight of them. Without lowering the field glasses, he replied, 'The E stands for enemy, Maggie!'

'What are they doing here?'

'Scouting for an attack I'd say!' Eyes widening as he lowered the binocs.

'Oh jeez, Bill! What does that mean? What do we have to do?'

'We should tell the Home Watch is what we *should* do!'

The moment stretched as they watched each other, beginning to understand the whole world of trouble they would be in if they told of what they had seen, which set itself against the unknown of what might happen if they didn't tell. If they *didn't* tell, then that'd make them responsible, wouldn't it? Neither option bode well for a happy prospect. Billy looked on expectantly at his friend who was usually so quick with answers or, failing that, possible solutions to problems.

He liked that she thought through problems out loud. She could always state clearly what Billy felt and could never quite get out straight himself. He didn't mind that she assumed control of situations either. Instinctively, Billy understood that her intentions were true and that her suggestions (as that was how she framed her ideas) were for the good of both of them. Between them, there didn't seem to exist any sort of competition. They were the best of friends and more than that, a team. So, when she wasn't forthcoming with the usual quick thinking and remained silent, baffled, Billy began to feel prickles of apprehension. He shifted uncomfortably.

'What do we do, Maggie?' he coaxed.

'As far as I can see, we've done the wrong thing to do the right thing. But now we've got here, I'm not sure that we can't get out of it without getting into a whole lot of trouble. And that's if they even believe us. We both know full well who we should tell,' she trailed off.

Billy nodded and unhappily added, 'Scriven!'

'And it's unlikely he's ever going to be in a frame of mind to believe you after the whale, Bill,' she nodded meaningfully, waiting for him to gather her import. He had two ideas to digest here. Billy's embarrassment about the whale was still acute and she was pretty sure he wouldn't have linked up that painful experience with these new, potentially dramatic events. Nor, she guessed, would he have factored in that his vision of the whale would have compounded the familial mistrust, though Billy was very much aware that breaking the night curfew was enough to have them 'slung in the brig' even if they were but children.

They both well knew Scard twins had spent a night in the brig after the finding of a lead-lined box of sticks of dynamite that they'd secreted under their families up-turned skiff to do God knows what with. But, knowing them, a plan for good use wouldn't have taken long in the formulating.

The south-easterly gusted and blew around them, flattening then releasing the longer grasses around them as it blew and lulled. The two friends sat by side staring out at the grey sea as white furls crackled restless across the shore break, their brows in consternation in their wordless communication echoing the scene. Occasionally, one would jut out a chin in an effort to see more clearly an option formulating only to shake it away as so much eddying flotsam in a tide pool. A mutual sigh and shrug called an end to the silent communication.

'Catch-22, Bill. Caught between a rock and hard place.'

'Yep. I'm going to have to bite the bullet and warn Mr Scriven.'

'Bloody won't, Bill!'

'What?' Billy replied in confusion.

'You'll be doing no such thing, Billy Collins. You're in enough trouble as it is. I'm going to tell Scriven about the E-boats. It's the only way to get the information across with the least bother for all of us.'

'But you'll get into all sorts of grief for breaking the curfew!'

'True. But what's the most important thing here, Bill?'

'Hey? I don't understand you, Maggie?'

'Well,' she murmured, paused and continued, 'the way I see it, the most important thing is to warn the navy that Jerry is close in the Channel. We can't rightly just swan into the dockyard and tell the Admiralty. So, we have to tell Scriven. Whatever happens, he's going to blow his top. That's a given as the man only has two moods: sullen and livid. If you tell him … Let's face it, he'll go apoplectic and he might not believe you. He's not going to want to believe you for a start. And more than that, if does believe you, he has to admit he hasn't been doing his job properly. He's a cornered rat.'

'And a cornered rat is always going to attack,' Billy added, nodding.

'If that happens, the message might get lost in his vanity.'

'You've lost me there, Maggie.'

'Well, that's not important right now. The point is we need the message to get to the navy and if you tell him, it might not. So, we owe it to all those servicemen and sailors to make sure the Admiralty knows and acts on the information. The best way for that to happen is if I tell him. I'll run it by mum. She'll know the best way of doing it. Maybe she'll come with me. I don't know.'

The two friends sat opposite each other, cross-legged, wordlessly for a moment before Billy patted Maggie's knee clumsily like he'd seen men do. The two staggered up, shaking out the numbness from their limbs. Billy broke the quiet again, 'I don't know why you think what you do, but I think you're probably right. What I do know though is that we better make tracks before we get into bother with the navy as well as Scriven if we're spotted. We've got a half hour to get home before he gets up and the Ami jeep patrol comes by.'

They exchanged a flat, pursed smile of grim accord and set off in crouched run. With a quick simian gait, the two friends were soon home outside Old Sea Dog Cottage. They'd kept low all the way not breaking their stride till they were safe from any Home Guard or Ami jeep patrol. Obscured from view, outside home, they allowed themselves to stand to get their breath back. Billy hands on knees, head down bent forward; Maggie leaning back hands on hips, stretching out a pain in the small of her back from all the sitting and then running back.

And then Billy did something he'd not often done before. Last minute, he decided to ditch his trust in Maggie and go with what he felt in his belly, what he knew intuitively. He hadn't thought about it on the run back, a new plan had flashed into his head and he characteristically just blurted it out. And knowing him was why Maggie accepted from him. In the same way, Billy relied on Maggie to meditate on a puzzle to find a solution, Maggie relied on flighty Billy's fly-by-the-seat-of-his-pants reactions which were usually, puzzlingly calm and correct when he'd stopped jigging about, nerves a-jangle. 'We're not going to do what you said, Maggie. It was a good idea though.'

Maggie was silent for a moment, digesting what Billy had said. And then, 'Ok Billy. What needs to happen?' She might not have let him get away with it so easily, but a wave of lethargy had crashed over her now that they were home, safe and her adrenalin was on the ebb.

'You're going to get a few hours kip before school so you're not too done in for tonight. You're going to have another long night ahead of you. The way I see it, we've got two chances at this, as you said. Me telling Scriven so he can tell the Admiralty. Or, so you or your mum can go to the Admiralty. There's a small chance that if I tell him that I've seen E-boats in the Channel, he'll claim it as his and he'll warn the Admiralty. If he gets lost in his rage as you said and doesn't, then he's going to be watching me like a hawk, making sure I don't get out and break curfew to go on watch again. He'll be distracted watching the house, so you can get out there with your mum and confirm it, without me, and let the navy know of the danger. Pound to a penny those E-boats'll be there. Third night in a row and that's proof enough for me. You might have to go straight to the Admiralty.'

As Maggie processed his rush of ideas, she watched Billy's eyes widen before he took to his heels, pushed past her and was off like a jackrabbit leaving the gate swinging behind him. And then her senses kicked in again and she heard the bolt of the front door of her cottage home being drawn back, the door opening. For a moment, Maggie was filled with an irrational dread that dropped in her stomach that Mr Scriven might be behind the door. But this was dispelled as her mum beckoned her in with a cupped-hand hiss so as to get the door shut on the last hours of curfew as quick as possible.

'You bugger, Billy Collins!' she thought with a smile of relief as her mother carefully closed the cottage door behind her. No Scriven. Maggie turned to see her mother framed in the closed doorway, arms folded across her chest, the scrutiny in her eyes asking, 'Well?'

Maggie sighed as she began to order her thoughts by way of beginning her explanation. Sarah Golding though had noticed the weariness in her daughter's loose limbs and saved her any further discomfort. The 'look' was clearly enough and she opened up her arms to gently usher Maggie into the warmth of the kitchen.

'In you go, darling. You can tell me about it over some tea and honey toast.' With that, the tension in Maggie's neck and shoulders dissipated and her head rolled back, safe in the knowledge that all was well in her world, home. She just hoped it would be in Billy's too. She didn't envy Billy in his task of telling Mr Scriven what he knew. Almost certainly it would be a horrid experience for him. And they both knew it. But Billy was task oriented and courageous to boot and bearing the brunt of Scriven's vents of anger was nothing new to Billy. He could take it. It was getting to the point where it was the norm. She'd noticed that when Scriven 'started', Billy would glaze over. He was taking himself to another place so that the here and now, or then and there of Mr Scriven was rendered mostly irrelevant.

'That Billy Collins has courage in spades,' she thought. A bloom of warmth enveloped her. Maggie sat down heavily at the kitchen table and noticed that a smile had crept into the corners of her mother's mouth as she watched her daughter. Maggie had the pleasantly strange feeling that her mother could hear her thoughts.

What Maggie couldn't have known was that Billy Collins had also turned a figurative corner and that she was party to some, but not all, of his thinking. The wind cooled the sweat on his temples making him shiver the way you do when someone walks over your grave. That galvanised Billy. Physicality always motivated him turning ephemeral, synaptic crackles and thoughts into motion and doing. As he'd later say to his apprentice, 'Character is all, Mike. And it's all in the doing. You learn by doing and thinking and you can't have one without the other. So, do and get on with it, lad!'

It might have been in that cooling moment that Billy came up with his raison d'être, his reason for being. Possibly, it came later from another source. Maybe it came from a point before but it was at that moment he understood that that no matter what sort of fall out and grief he got from Scriven, he had to do his duty and admit breaking the curfew and that he'd seen 3 or more *Schnellenboot* not 5

116

miles out from Portland on the horizon. He'd first heard tell on the Schnellenboot, or E-boats, from the old salts on the harbour. He knew that they were short range, fast attack diesels which meant that it was very likely that there were more of them close by.

With all the activity of the big American ships around Portland and Chesil of late, with all the servicemen involved in the manoeuvres, they were sitting ducks for these quick, slick torpedo boats. To Billy's mind, they could cause havoc and be gone before the navy even knew it, especially with this kamikaze frame of mind that he'd been hearing about since the bombing of Pearl Harbour that had brought the Amis into the Second World. No sense of self preservation, no rules of engagement, just hell-fire bent on destruction.

It made no sense to Billy. But nothing about wars made any sense to him. He just understood that that was the way it was and he had to do something about it and preserve life. That was the bottom line as he saw it and these thoughts chimed through him, clear as a bell. Billy had to tell Scriven. Pound to a penny Scriven would flip his lid, even give him a beating. But that would serve him well as all Scriven's attention would be on him, freeing up Maggie to move about more freely. And then when she confirmed it too, it would have come from two independent sources which would give it more veracity, more credibility. The navy would then surely have to act no matter what Mr Scriven's scruples and embarrassment might be. All that and a potential beating paled into insignificance given what those Schnellenboot could do to all those laden troop ships, each with hundreds of lives aboard.

He knew that his grandfather would have done the same. He felt as if he could feel his grandfather's encouragement in all of this. He'd described himself as a Utilitarian and he lived by the mantra, 'the greatest good for the greatest number.' And self-sacrifice was an integral part of that. Grandfather had probably got the idea from a priest. But it seemed sensible enough and so with this in mind, Billy Collins set off for Mr Scriven's house with an energetic mix of courage and trepidation in his heart. What Billy hadn't admitted to himself in all this was that one of his strongest emerging motivations was his want to prove Scriven wrong, to beat him, to humiliate him.

What it was, was that Billy was angry and he hadn't yet realised that no lasting good comes from anger, particularly avenging anger. What he didn't know was that he was tripping a timer switch. He was setting a mechanism of time in motion with consequences far beyond his understanding as a ten-year-old boy.

Mr Scriven's 5 am alarm went off and he rose automatically and swung his pyjamaed legs off the bed for his feet to find his slippers. He sat there for a moment to allow his senses to acclimatise to wakefulness. Blinking away the muddy, explosive, screaming dreams of Ypres with their acrid stench of mustard gas that arrived regular as clockwork nightly at 3 am, he reached across his nightstand for his matches and lit his Davey lamp, creating a warm glow in his otherwise lonely room. He leant forward and massaged his cheeks with the palms of his hands to shift the tiredness away. As the blood began to flow, he became more alert and the hornet angry fizz and burn of his gas scarring returned. That way he knew he was awake, painfully so.

Outside, Billy Collins had a tentative hand on the latch of the old school house gate. He looked up and saw a glow bloom in what must have been Mr Scriven's sleeping room. 'Now or never, mate. Damned if you do, damned if you don't. Nothing to lose,' he coached himself to repress a shudder of fear he could feel gathering in the wings of his mind. So, very deliberately but unsure why, Billy closed the garden gate behind him. He took a deep breath and marched with as much confidence he could muster to the front door of the school master's house. His knuckles hovered an inch off the surface of the windowless front door as he swallowed his fear away.

And then he rapped on the door evenly three times with enough force to be noticed, heard above the sound of the rising wind which was making the loose boards knock and the corrugated iron roof rattle on the dilapidated barn across the way. It must have housed livestock but they were long gone now by the looks. There was no movement around the school house save the angry clatter of the barn losing its roof, little by little.

After a few minutes, that for Billy could have been hours, he heard the latch drawn back and the door open as Mr Scriven, holding the Davey lamp before him, inched open the door. For a confusing instant, Mr Scriven appeared to look down kindly until his eyes adjusted to the light and he understood that it was the Collins boy who stood before him, kneading his fingers into the palm of one of hands, his lower lip beginning to tremble.

'Pathetic,' was the first contemptuous thought the school master thought as he gazed down at the child before him until the familiar wave of and anger and indignation crashed over his rocky sensibilities. No matter what the boy did, he elicited the same reaction from the school master and he roared, 'What the bloody hell do you think you're doing? Out breaking the curfew? There's a bloody war on in case you hadn't noticed, you bloody fool! Get inside now before the light attracts any more attention.'

Instinctively, Billy did as he was told and bolted into the house, though that was the last thing he wanted to do, Scriven's lair the last place he wanted to be. He had never been in before. And then he had two thoughts. The first being, 'But it was you who opened the door with a lamp in your hand? How is it my fault?' And the second was a resigned observation that it would always be the same in each and every interaction between them. They had been assigned their roles.

They were trapped. Both tormented in the play of the game.

Chapter 10
Maggie's Mum

Quiet people of a morning, Maggie and her mother, Sarah Golding, went about their breakfast routine. Padding feet, deliberate movements. The fire crackled, occasionally spitting, ash cakes falling. Maggie with her toast in hand; her mother with the heavy copper kettle for tea over the open kitchen fire. Maggie had slept solidly for two hours being out on the bluffs with Billy spying the *Schnellenboot*. Now they had pulled their chairs up to the fire to escape the damp and make the most of the warmth, moving only when the morning ritual required and then they moved around each other wordlessly, instinctively. Only when they were halfway down their first mug of tea and when a good quarter inch of salty butter had melted into their doorsteps of toast did Sarah Golding enquire of her daughter, with warmth in her eyes.

'So, what was it that happened out there last night? I'm imagining you were out with Billy judging by the flapping gate?' Her mum was always one step ahead of her and that was annoying even if she was always on her side. There was no point in concealing anything, particularly as they would need her mother's help.

'We went out onto the bluffs, out around Pulpit Rock. Billy said he's seen some strange shapes out on the water. Things that Scriven doesn't seem to have noticed!'

'Mr Scriven to you, young lady!'

'Oh, mum! He's been nothing but foul to Billy forever. But especially so since all this whale business. He's a dried up nasty old…!' Maggie surprised herself and her mother by the vehemence behind the statement.

Her mother paused, taking it in before carefully replying, 'True as that all might be, Maggie. You should always address him as Mr Scriven. You don't want to get out of the habit, let your guard down and have him as your enemy as well.'

Maggie couldn't quite get the sense of what her mother was saying, but she gained the import in her mother's definite words. She lowered her eyes and her mind quietened momentarily until she had to continue, 'But he really is horrible to him. He picks on Billy constantly. He just won't leave him alone. And Billy reckons he's not doing his job properly as head watch of the Home Guard. He should be out until 5 am, but Billy reckons he's back home by half two. And what with all the Amis here for Operation Tiger … Who knows what may happen?'

'What do you know of Operation Tiger, Maggie?' her mother asked with a concern in her tone that she couldn't place.

'Just that they are practicing for something big, something important, by the looks of all the manoeuvres.'

'Yes, but how do you know it's called Operation Tiger? Oh, of course. Billy!'

'Yes, Billy, mum. He hears all sorts of things from the old salts at the winches. He says the Amis are all talking about it as well.'

'Well, that's as maybe to know it. But you don't want others to hearing that you know it. What is Mr Scriven trying to instil in you all at school?'

And then with eyes rolled and a voice of parroting sarcasm, Maggie repeated the mantra that Mr Scriven had instilled in them daily for the last year that, '*Loose lips, sink ships!*'

'Exactly right, my girl! People are getting all fidgety and nervous with all the talk of German Commando *Abwehr* spies parachuting in disguised as farmers and priests and the such like, talking the King's English better than we do! The talk is of 5th columnists all over the South Coast!'

'Mum! What are you talking about? Abwehr 5th parachutists? You're not making sense!'

Sarah Golding scrutinised her daughter, as if from afar and then calmly replied having apparently gathered herself, 'You mustn't mention Operation Tiger outside these four walls, Maggie darling. If you must talk about it with Billy, make sure it is never outside this or Billy's house. And never around Mr Scriven, that's for sure.'

'But, why mum? I don't understand,' Maggie replied half-bewildered.

'It's because … what's the phrase?' Rhetorical question, eyes up to the left in an effort to remember, 'It's classified information. A military secret. Top secret, if you like. And anyone suspected of treachery, children included, could find themselves in a lot of hot water with British Intelligence Services.'

'A secret?' Maggie was incredulous. 'How can it be a secret if the whole world's talking about it? Anyone standing on Chesil Beach or 3 miles out in the Channel can see what's going on even if they don't know it's called Operation Tiger! Some of the American ships are as big as the Isle of White. How in heaven's name can that be a secret?'

Steadily eyeing her daughter over the rim of her tea mug, 'You'd have to call it an open secret. Like a secret that everyone knows. But one that you never openly admit to knowing because knowing it besmirches you, speaking of it incriminates you.'

'Riddles, Mum! Riddles!' Maggie responded struggling to keep up, 'How can it be a secret if everyone knows it?' Frustration thickened the edge of her voice.

'It's something that everyone knows and acknowledges very quietly and very much avoids saying out loud.'

Maggie stared at her mother and after some moments began to slowly nod. And then a smile crept over her face and she mischievously added, 'Like the open secret that women are cleverer than men!' They both covered their mouths repressing a giggle. Mother and daughter both winced a few tears which turned into belly laughs that salved the tension in the air. They had to put their mugs down. When their shoulders stopped twitching and they settled, 'Ooh, we can't be heard cackling like a pair of witches. People round here don't need any encouragement to go on a flight of fancy.'

Mother and daughter enjoyed the shared complicity and warmth.

Back to business though, Maggie coughed in all seriousness remembering Billy's predicament, 'The idea of an open secret is going to be lost on Billy. He wears his heart on his sleeve, mum. And if Billy has gone round there, Mr Scriven is surely going to be filled with rage.'

'I know, Maggie. I'm going to have to put my thinking cap on and get around there under some ruse to nip things in the bud and see what's what. If Operation Tiger really is an open secret, so wide open that danger is imminent, we really do have a duty to let the authorities know *and* try to get Billy out of this hitch.'

A brief silence followed while the two of them gathered their thoughts. Sarah Golding took up the gamut and broke the silence while pouring some more tea, 'Right, Maggie. Tell me exactly what Billy has seen, what you both saw and what you think it means.' Maggie proceeded to tell her mother about Billy's first surmise three nights back; about confirming that the dark shapes were in fact *Schnellenboot* how close they were seemingly unseen and the havoc they could wreak especially as the destroyer keeping watch over the naval manoeuvres appeared to have quit it's watch and was now heading west away from Portland. Maggie paused at the memory of the silhouette of the destroyer, trailing its fumes from its smoke stack, stark against the pewter light of dawn.

Sarah began to nod, her speech low and deliberate, 'Oh my. It seems that Operation Tiger is an open secret across the Channel too. The danger is here, now. And I have to do something, now.'

*

Billy stood shivering cold with nerves in Mr Scriven's kitchen, half transfixed by the mauve and burned orange chequered floor tiling that tilted musically under foot fall. He didn't notice Scriven carefully, quietly closing the kitchen door behind him. With a cruel, flat palmed shove between the shoulder blades, he'd been propelled into the dark hall way and instinctively made his way towards the kitchen. All the houses on the island were pretty much made from the same plan. The kitchen was perfectly still save for dust motes trapped in a ray of light that streamed through a crack in the black out blinds. Charcoal and ash collapsed in the grate of the kitchen fire.

Billy looked up quickly and then looked away so as not to focus on the livid scarring on the left side of Scriven's face. The school master was watching him intently. What he saw before him was a sallow-skinned boy, not tall, not short and as lean as a pickaxe handle. He was wearing one of those Breton fisherman's smocks from across the water. Too big for him by a long way and it certainly wouldn't keep out the drafts despite the density of the weave.

The kettle began to whistle and the creases of anger ebbed away momentarily from the tall man's face. He made to take the kettle off the heat and the familiarity of the action eased off some of his angular, usual tension. With his back now to Billy, he presented as a different sort of man in his house coat. A little stooped, older even. Billy noted that he had never seen Mr Scriven out of a uniform. Looking at him now, it seemed conceivable that this man and his grandfather had been the best of friends from childhood and had even joined the army to fight in the Great War together.

A confusing sense of affection crept over him. Mr Scriven was always either wearing his academic, black cloak or his Home Front serge uniform. But there was no denying his physicality. He was well over six feet, taller by a head than most men on the island. And then Billy took in the cruel, long-fingered hand grasping the kettle handle like a spider crab would its prey. He had felt the provocative jab of Scriven's index finger in his chest all too often.

'I suppose you're expecting some sort of admonition?' Mr Scriven asked calmly, his back still turned.

And then it came, *that* anger, as reliably as Billy knew it would almost as if in response to that momentary illusion of a shared experience. Mr Scriven flew at him.

'How in God's name are we supposed to win this war? How are we to retain discipline and order with children running around doing as they damn well please? Breaking curfew! I ask you? Obeying rules, doing as you're told is the only way we're going to win!'

Silence hung thick in the air like a cloying history. Billy opened his eyes, his body inert as his thoughts darted from corner to corner searching for words for a reply. With none forthcoming, Scriven took up the initiative and thundered on, true to form, 'Well, tell me, boy? Who do you think you are to defy me? To defy the Home Guard and the British Navy? A curfew is there for good reason. To keep us out of Jerry's sight. To save your, to save our, skins. You bloody fool! Well?'

Billy needed to pee badly and he couldn't summon a word or thought save for the impression that he wasn't entirely sure that Mr Scriven was asking questions that required an answer. That Y-shaped vein had started to pulse in the middle of Mr Scriven's forehead, the livid scarring seem to shift repulsively as if alive with ants. Billy banished the notion as unhelpful and placed his gaze just to the left of the school master's raging face and began, 'sir, there are German E-boats in the Channel, not three miles off Portland. Schnellenboot, I think they call them. Short range, fast attack boats. They know about Operation Tiger, sir. The Amis, the navy, we're all in danger, sir!'

Billy exhaled and his shoulders dropped with the end of his confession as that's what it felt like. The school master's eyes flashed and cast about wildly. He appeared momentarily to be too angry for words and then he recovered.

'What do you think you know about Operation Tiger, Collins?' Scriven's question sliced and seized on what he thought was a quantifiable fact.

Understanding that it was now or never, that this was the moment, Billy Collins cautiously emerged from a safe place in his mind to which the older man's anger had sent him scurrying. He replied matter-of-factly, 'Nothing, sir! Only what we've all seen off the island sir. The Amis are obviously practicing manoeuvres for a big push off Chesil Beach. And I think. No, I know sir that the Germans know it too. They know about the open secret. About Operation Tiger, sir!' There, he'd said it! No taking back the spoken. Not now, not never.

And as he quite expected, Mr Scriven was incredulous with rage. He couldn't conceal the fierce loathing he had for this boy and his self-contained confidence. What could he know about the German Navy, about the Schnellenboot? And then it dawned on him that the boy quite clearly thought him remiss in his duties as Home Front Warden, that perhaps he had seen him leaving his post hours early at 0200 hours rather than at five as agreed with the Admiralty when a coalition watch would take over. But how was anyone expected to exist on two hours sleep and then teach all those horrible children, for goodness sake?

And then another thought seared through his mind like a tracer shell. *Was the boy insinuating that somehow he had wilfully failed to inform the Admiralty of the Schnellenboot?* He'd heard whisper of these fast attack boats in the vicinity. But surely, even Jerry wasn't stupid enough to risk entering Portland waters with all that Ami firepower bobbing about? The quelling, momentary admission of guilt palled and vanished beneath a tidal surge of breaking anger. As the school master's fury of words again erupted, so did the spittle and that unwholesome foam that gathered at the corners of his mouth.

'German E-boats in the Channel? Who the hell do you think you are, Collins? Your arrogance appals me to my core. You really think a bloody schoolboy with some Jerry binoculars can do better that the Home Front Watch, better than the barrage balloons, the RAF and Her Majesty's British Naval reconnaissance?' The school master paused when no response came from the little boy. And then he verily screamed in a voice so cracked that he too was aware that his rage was about to cross a line. He paused to eye the furtive creature before him. And then, in a quiet voice, he continued, 'Do you really believe that?'

Speechless with fear, immobilised in thought and deed, Billy just stared back. It was too much for Mr Scriven to contain himself. 'Do you?' he bellowed.

Billy shrank back from the ferocity of the emotion displayed in the school master's contorted face and flashing eyes. Something more than usual was not right about Mr Scriven and Billy was frightened and weakly stammered his involuntary reply, 'No, sir. I'm not better than that!' And there he'd said it. Mr Scriven had forced the boy to retract what he knew to be true. Billy didn't know where those words had come from. But he'd heard himself say them. Bewildered by self-doubt, he asked himself why he'd taken back what he knew to be true.

Noting the boy's stammer, Mr Scriven seized the opportunity and launched again, 'Bloody pathetic you are, boy! You Collinses have always been a confused lot!' He had stepped forward and punctuated each word of what he had just said by jabbing Billy in the chest painfully with the index finger of his right hand. Each jab had forced Billy back a step until he was flat against the kitchen wall, the palms of his hands and his shoulders pinned against the damp, cold stone wall.

Towering above the child, clearly relishing his fear and submission, Mr Scriven exhaled a sharp breath of disgust and turned on his heal. He was ready to stride out of the kitchen, but stopped in his tracks. There framed in the doorway was Sarah Golding. She looked, well, she looked as she always did to him and he lowered his eyes in embarrassment. Sarah Golding shook her head as if to rid herself of his shame.

'I didn't hear you come in, Sarah,' the school master stammered in a gentle voice. How much had she heard?

'Well, you wouldn't have, would you?' she replied, her eyes flashing with a menace that unnerved as much as it interested him. Her eyes burned for a moment and then she averted her gaze to Billy and noticed that he had his eyes fixed on the heavy poker. Before Mr Scriven could also turn and notice, in a voice commanding, direct and gentle she told Billy, 'You'd better go now, Billy.'

The young boy snapped out of it and walked as if numbed in a slumber past his tormentor without a backward glance. He paused in front of Maggie's mother. With lost eyes, Billy looked up to her as she whispered something Mr Scriven couldn't make out, running a reassuring hand through his hair and then pulled him to her. Mr Scriven shuddered with jealousy. When Billy opened his eyes to look at Maggie's mum again, he knew tears were close. He needed to get out of there. And then he was gone, darting out of the school house cottage quick as a silver fish, up the lane as fast as he could, hoping to outrun the emotion, for the refuge of home.

Fifteen minutes beforehand, Sarah Golding had hugged her daughter Maggie. She had smoothed down the wind-whipped wisps of hair and said, 'Go on back to bed, Maggie. I don't think we'll be in school today. Get into mine.

There's still a bit of warmth in there. We don't want you looking all tired out today. We'll say you've got a fever. Save anyone asking questions.'

Maggie wasn't sure what was what and was too dog-tired to ponder it. No need either, really. She knew that whatever her mum had her sleeve would be right. Clumsily, she stumbled her boots off in the hall and wearily bent over to put them tidy against the wall. Training, now a habit. With lowered shoulders, she ascended the stairs and went in her mum's room. A small shaft of light had pushed the blackout curtains a shade apart and she was glad of that. She clambered into the creaky old wooden-framed bed. She hadn't noticed her mum following her up but was happily appreciative of her flapping the quilt and blankets over her, tucking them up under her chin. Safe.

'Sleep now, child.' As her eyes were closing, Maggie noticed her mother hadn't changed and was just wearing her housecoat over the clothes she slept in. She registered the familiar floorboard responses from her mother's gentle, careful gait. Down the wooden staircase, then a quiet shuffle along the hall tiles. Then the cottage door latch went. And before the shroud of sleep drew her in, a quiet voice in her mind noted, 'Funny to go out in her housecoat. She never leaves the house unless she's dressed for it.' And then she was asleep. Behind the blackout curtain, a bluff of wind made the glass in the kite window give a fraction.

Sarah Golding, all out of character outdoors in her night clothes, hair flailing in a sudden gust of wind, picked up the long hem of her housecoat and broke into a hurry towards old school house cottage. At the end of the lane, she started to run for all she was worth. She had one thought only in her mind and that was to shorten or prevent the exchange between her daughter's life-long best friend and the unpredictable Mr Scriven. She wasn't frightened of him or of any man. But she was rightly wary.

After what her daughter had told her of the events of the night, Sarah Golding had a hunch, had a feeling and then a certain knowledge that the school master and warden would react badly to what Billy would say to him. The family feud between Mr Scriven and the Collinses was one thing, but for Billy to suggest the warden had been remiss in his duties in keeping the island and Navies safe would be akin to cornering a rat. If he had been leaving his post early as the children had said (and why would they lie?), he was guilty as charged and cornered, dangerous. Nowhere to run he would have to fight and Sarah Golding knew that

Mr Scriven's unmasked loathing of the little boy would be unleashed and unchecked or tempered if they were left alone.

By the time she had reached the old school house cottage, Sarah Golding was breathless. She lent one hand on the gate post to catch her breath, the other over her heart. She straightened immediately as she heard the unmistakable sound of her colleague's raised voice in the wind—searing rage, the sound of which produced only two reactions. She banished one and set her shoulders to engage the other. Hoping Scriven hadn't locked the front door, Sarah Golding clanged open the garden gate with an unusually unmeasured sense of purpose. She didn't notice that she was narrowly missed by the rebounding gate and she was already up the steps and her hand compressing the cottage door latch. It had all happened in a fluid movement, uncontaminated by thought.

She strode the few steps through the gloom of the lightless hall towards the partially open kitchen door. There was light in there and she could see the back of her colleague Mr Scriven who was a head taller than the door frame and nearly as wide. To his right, she could see the diminutive figure of her daughter's friend Billy Collins, whose face was a contorted mask of fear and confusion as that grown man bawled at the boy, the bitterness in his voice erasing meaning, his arms rising and slapping at his hips in sharp, unnatural angular movements. She'd seen and heard the frightening spectacle of Mr Scriven venting his rage on a whole class for perceived transgressions, but never at a lone individual. It looked and felt very different.

It came as no surprise to her at all that the focus of the school master's unbridled rage would be Billy Collins, her daughter's best friend, her own friend's son. Instinctively, she knew it was wrong. Looked and felt wrong. His rage had an ugly momentum. And go on and potentially get further out of hand, it could not. She had to put a stop to it. Her pulse was also fairly racing now. But understanding the mind-set of an inadequate, she knew that she had to appear calm and show no sign of weakness. So, she pushed the door open hard enough to connect with the door frame behind, enough to alert the school master, but not too much so that he could not connect it with a nervous response.

'There you are, Billy!' she said as she opened the door. The words were innocuous sounding, not even directed at the school master, but were said with a mother's tone of finality that was unquestionable and that made him freeze momentarily. Shocked. Caught out. You might even wonder if he registered guilt at some level. Whatever it was, it was gone in a moment like a fish to the kelp sensing danger. He recovered, turning to her, a rictus smile forming. He spoke slowly, his composure regained, 'I didn't hear you come in, Miss Golding. Was the door open?'

Sarah Golding didn't immediately reply and he appraised her as she stood, framed in his kitchen doorway, surprisingly in her housecoat and hobnailed boots. He liked that and the embarrassment compelled him to shift his gaze from her to the flagstone tiles of the floor as he blanched. And then, as the colour in his neck rose and the scar tissue from the gas attack crackled painfully causing his hand to rise involuntarily to soothe the pain away, he caught that acrid, ammonia-like stink that he gave off when his feelings ran high, which had embarrassed him since he was old enough to notice. A fight or flight response, it nevertheless repulsed him as he knew it did others.

Sarah Golding registered his lidded intention as that acrid, ammoniac odour of his caught in her nose and throat. Usually an adept concealer of her thoughts and emotions as is characteristic of Portlanders, the tension and the repulsive scent caught her off guard and she visibly grimaced, emphasising her crow's feet. She shook her head in dismissal. There was no way back now, she knew that. And it caused her no discomfort.

'Leave that boy alone, Mr Scriven,' she repeated with that unmistakable tone of a woman whose mind is set. And then, as she turned her back on him and to complete his humiliation, because she knew that that was what he felt, she added, staring him down, 'Not now, not never.' She said the words gently and saw them home. When the school master's eyes dropped again, she knew that he understood and she left before his embarrassment caught like anger.

Sarah Golding did not turn to close doors behind her as felt the school master's eyes boring into her out past the front cottage door, down the garden path and even as she turned into the lane. She kept her pace measured and deliberate, resisting her rage and an instinct to run. To quell the turbulence she felt rising in her, she ran through a potential itinerary of her day, prioritising what needed to be done. The ordering of the day's events ahead calmed her mind.

Composure regained, Sarah's pace slowed as she reached her own garden gate. She looked up to her bedroom window where she knew Maggie should be sound asleep. 'You're going to need to be rested for tonight when you're out on the cliffs alone searching for those E-boats,' she thought. Billy Collins will be under a strict watch if not under lock and key. She too was more than ready for bed after those dramatic early-morning events.

Chapter 11
Police Meet Dead Men Walking

There was a pause in the conversation in the police car as the storm hurled hail as hard as gravel across the windows and the car moved visibly as the gust seemed to try to pry the car off the tarmac of the Causeway. Blue lights flashed intermittently and rain filled the beams of the head lights. The squad cars formed a 'V' shape facing away from the Portland preventing any access onto on the bridge road that connects Weymouth to the island of Portland. They hadn't bothered with cones as the island's population had been evacuated after the discovery of the bomb. Only two islanders remained. Two older traffic cops had joined the younger pair, sharing the ubiquitous flask of tea the younger two hadn't yet got into the habit of preparing.

The conversation, which was rather more like a series of statements than a conversation, had all but petered out as the four men in two cars had taken up night shift sentry duty on the Causeway. It'd be silent for a while until someone made an observation that usually didn't require a reply. The two older traffic policemen were quite content like this. They'd whiled away the last hour and a life time like this patiently, as happy in the silences as in the talk. The two younger ones in the front would have been happier passing the time chatting but had learned to acquiesce to their seniors' silence. Truth was, the younger pair was bored rigid, trying not to drum their fingers and annoy the two grumps in the back. Sitting in a squad car at 1 am on the deserted Causeway in the pitch black in a gale was a far cry from the excitement they'd hoped for. It was about as exciting and glamorous as paperwork.

'Only two left on the island now that won't leave,' murmured traffic cop burns from the back seat as he blew ruminatively across the top of his tea.

'Gotta be bloody potty!' came a reply from the front.

'Creepy old place. Have to be weird to want to stay.'

'One old bloke that won't leave without his pigeons and a certain *Ms* Golding (don't make the mistake of calling her Mrs, if I were you!) who refuses to leave and who won't disclose her reasons.'

'Young woman?' enquired the younger traffic cop in the driving seat.

'No,' came the reply with an extended vowel sound. 'About sixty if she's a day! Good-looking woman though. Well preserved. Hard as nails like all the old Portlanders. Don't make them like that anymore, even if they are a funny lot.' The two seniors in the back arched eyebrows at each other, nodding. The two in the front scrunched up their faces with half-hearted dismay. Neither was wearing rings unlike both in the back who were.

A few moments passed before a comment came from the back, 'We can't make them leave their homes. We can only advise them. If the thought of 2,000 kilos of explosive can't shift that lady, nothing will!'

'I think you underestimate the power of my charms, Clive!'

'Get on with you, you old goat!' The veterans in the back guffawed. The two in the front did their best to ignore them. After a few sighs, they lapsed into silence, watching for the arrival of the bomb disposal convoy. Predictably, it was the two in the front who started up again.

'They reckon the shockwaves might be enough to shake the old cottages to rubble if the bloody thing goes off.'

'Doesn't bear thinking about. I explained all that to *Ms* Golding. But she wasn't having any of it. Not rude, mind you. Just … what's the word?'

'Resolute?' offered the other older chap as if they were discussing crossword answers.

'That's it. Resolute. That's what she is. As unmoving as the rock she lives on. Apparently, she's never left the island save for three years as a child. 42-45. Says she didn't have any option as a child. But as an adult, she's not going anywhere. Bomb or no bomb. She won't be moved. Reckons she's lived through a lot worse.' All nodded, digesting.

'I think 'stubborn old boot' is what you're being too polite to say!' In the back, they shared a companionable chuckle. And then as the humour subsided each of the men drifted off into silence, into their thoughts, until the hail raked across the car, the angry squall of wind strong enough to shift the car on its suspension and then all four men were shocked into raised eyebrows and keen vigilance until the threat was assessed just as the wind.

The young blood in the front passenger seat broke the silence, 'I wonder what sort of person decides that what they most want to do in life is be a bomb disposal officer.'

'You've got to have a bloody screw loose, surely?' replied the driver, turning his head to make eye contact.

'I want to do my best, serve the public and all. But that's a bit far for me. These old bombs from the Second World War are so unstable, they're liable to go off at any time. They might have lain silent for 50 years but the minute you start messing about with them… There's no telling what might happen. I couldn't live like that …' he trailed off.

'Like what?'

'Like every day or each job might be your last.'

From the back came a sage observation, 'Suddenly lads, the dull bits of the job don't seem so bad after all when you think about what those bomb disposal fellas have to do, eh?' In the back, they smiled at each other. In the front, the two young officers scowled—youth never comfortable outwitted by experience.

The other old boy in the back decided to alleviate the chagrin in the front by asking his seasoned colleague, 'You were in the Royal Engineers though, weren't you, Clive?'

'Yairs, a long time ago now though. 12 years I did. But I was logistics, a driver. You won't nor would've caught me within a country mile of an unexploded bomb. No fear!'

'What are they like, the bomb disposal guys?' came the question from the front of the squad car.

'What're they like? Strangely quiet was my observation. The sort of person that you'd miss in the canteen unless you knew them,' replied Clive who was stroking his chin with the memory. And then all four men nodded as they gravely processed this observation, all intrigued. Clive took a good intake of breath before continuing, 'Tell you what though. I don't know what the survival rate is, but if you're known throughout the Armed Forces as 'Dead Men Walking', you'd think they go for a safer option. Never do, mind you. Totally committed. Another breed. No 'big-I-ams', muscled-up, covered in tattoos. Frightened the crap out of me if I'm honest. Sort of 'beware of the quiet ones'.' The four men digested this nugget.

'Here we are!' nodded Clive as he spotted the headlamps of the lead Red Wing in the convoy round the corner onto the Causeway, screwing the cup back onto his flask. But the two front doors were already slamming shut as the two young police officers bounded out of the car, oblivious to the howling gale around them, keen as mustard to get a rare look at a bomb disposal officer in the flesh.

*

It was just gone midnight when the convoy got off the A35 at Weymouth and began to snake its way through the Sunday night sleeping conurbation couched in sodium, orange street light through Weymouth to Portland Isle. The four Red Wings in front and the 7.5 tonner grunted and hissed through the unrelenting rain, their wipers earning their keep as they had all the way down. Keeping and marking time. A measured pace. No blue light, no need. The bomb had been there fifty years.

Another few hours wasn't going to make any difference to anyone, thought Captain Collins. He'd thought this thought for the best part of forty years on the job, before each job. It was a way of minimising the risk, a mantra repeated to normalise and assuage consternation, said or thought with a confident sigh of resignation. But tonight, the Captain inspected his words and found a hollowness that he'd not previously felt.

Instinctively, Sapper Mike glanced across at this boss. They exchanged the briefest of looks and then set eyes front again. Both noted the last of the night birds drawing curtains, lights out. Getting some sleep ready for the next working week. The Captain tried to shake away a gathering notion. But the question had formed, *Will I be here next week?*

Chapter 13
Public Services

Sapper Mike unwittingly derailed the Captain's thought process with his question. Decidedly, the Captain needed out from wherever he was. But a question put to a quiet man by a junior officer about a personal matter was probably not the order of the day. The Captain turned it over in his mind for a moment, considering if he wanted to reply.

The Sapper understood his faux-pas and then sighed his relief as Captain Collins began, 'Why did I never marry? That's a good question. Wrong time and wrong place, but I'll answer it now as it's in your best interests to know now and understand the job a little better. You might then beat a clearer path than me.' That was the mark of the man; why there was respect and trust; why he was his mentor. The young man's discomfort peaked and ebbed in an instant. The Captain winced and leant forward over the steering wheel to alleviate the pain in his lower back, settled back and continued, 'Good question. Requires an honest answer. Two reasons really. And funny we should be having this conversation on my way home, back to Portland.

'And then again, at my age, I've come to know that there are no coincidences. Nothing just happens by chance. There's a perfect architecture in life. A plan and map, the blue-prints of which you may glimpse a few times in a life time if you're lucky. You reach a fork in the road. Both routes look the same. But one of them is right and bright and positive for you. If your instinct is good, you may get a sneak at the blue print and you make the right choice. If you're disconnected, you just guess and pay the consequences.'

More bloody riddles for the young Sapper. He'd have to put up with it though. Par for the course on this job, the Sapper mused. But he had asked the question. Had to take the rough with the smooth.

The Captain ploughed on, 'Part of it is actually the job. The ladies, women I've met have been excited about the idea of a BDO. Conjures up all sorts of images and of course, you play to them. Courage in the face of danger, meticulous concentration, unshakeable conviction. All that stuff. And then there's the uniform! They love a uniform.

'I remember telling some about being first on the scene in a new war zone with the Paras, the most *efficient* of soldiers, toe-curling tales that I might have told you along the way. Of course, they loved them. They were impressed. And being a stupid, simple man, I was flattered and, not more than a few times, I thought *This is it! I've hit the jackpot*. In the retelling, you tend to skip to the moments of courage and triumph. But we're not stupid creatures entirely. And women get an instinct for what you're not telling them after a while.'

'How do you mean, sir? It's getting a bit vague again,' Sapper Mike added boldly.

The Captain blinked his eyes open before replying, duly noting the young man's query, 'They'll ask about your nerves and fears like jumping out of Red Wing and running for cover when you come under fire from a high-calibre rifle. You'll not want to be anywhere near Red Wing if a shot connects with 2,000 lbs worth of plastic explosive. That's 2,000 lbs worth of motivation for you to shift your arse clear of that going up. Gives me tremors now just remembering it.' He let that sink in for a moment, the retelling of a lived experience so close to death.

'You tend to leave all that out of the chat-up lines. But they work it out in the end. The banter and bravado fades. The cold light of day settles and romance is replaced by all the questions about the reality of the job.'

'And what do you mean by that, sir?'

'Oh, use your head, lad!' The young man stared ahead, expressionless trying to conceal his hurt. The Captain took it in and continued in a milder tone, 'What woman in their right mind is going to want to hang around with a man who is fairly likely to be blown to smithereens when he goes to work? That kind of bad day at the office is more than most women can bear. So, it goes either one of two ways. They'll either run for the hills or try to convince you to quit the job. Both are unenviable positions to be in, lad.' They continued in silence for a while, the Captain letting the young man digest this information.

A few minutes later, Sapper Mike picked up the thread, 'Must make for a lonely life, no?'

The Captain considered this before replying, 'Yes and no, lad. Nothing's black and white in life apart from the job. You have a profession and the army as family. All the banter, pension and perks. But, you might not have the wife and kids. My CO, when I started. And a right hard bastard, he was. He told me that if I wanted to have a *lovey-dovey* life on the sofa with the wife, then I had no place in the Royal Engineers as a BDO. Or words to that effect. Probably shot through with invective. He had a limited four-letter vocabulary and wasn't one to dress things up.' Sapper nodded his understanding and the tarmac passed by for another mile or so before the Captain resumed, 'The other part of it was that no-one ever measured up. That's the truth of it.'

'So, there was someone, sir?'

'Yes and no. There was someone I was close to. Someone I might have married had things been different. But that would have meant coming back to Portland. And I was in no hurry for that. Too many ghosts. The job was alibi enough, though. No, it was a lifetime ago when I was growing up here, the friend I'm talking about. Best friend I ever had, I'd say. And she'd always surface in my memory when I was getting close to someone. As soon as I remembered her, I'd lose interest in whoever I was with. And she was with me when I spotted the German E-boats.'

Back to riddles again, thought the Sapper. Although he had a hunch that they were getting closer to what it was that was troubling the old boy. Sapper Mike was tired now though, had had enough and didn't feel like pressing the Captain for more information. And besides, as he consulted the map in lap with a pen torch, they couldn't be more than twenty minutes away from their destination, the locus of the bomb.

'It's just another job. It's just another job,' murmured the Captain rounding the steering wheel through an s-bend. And then, 'My last job,' as a rasp.

'What was that, sir?' But the Captain hadn't heard him, so far deep in thought he was. Sapper Mike had taken the familiar silence for the Captain concentrating on the task at hand, the driving as the kind of practical task he liked while thinking through and trouble-shooting the real task: the diffusing of a 2,000 kilo Second World War bomb. But that didn't seem to be the case. Nerves were evidently getting the better of his mentor. He was having a tough time of this one and the young man didn't how to go about broaching it as a subject, so out of character as the behaviour seemed.

Back on the straight, the Captain clocked Sapper Mike's gaze, a question in his eyes. The Captain took a moment and then enquired, 'Did I say that out loud?'

'Yes, sir!' came the matter of fact reply. *In for a penny, in for a pound*, he thought. 'You're not alright with this at all actually, are you, sir?'

'No, it would seem not,' he replied, licking his lips, dry-mouthed. 'It seems this job has got me spooked. Being my last one and all. Returning back to Portland, the island I grew up on and haven't returned to in nearly fifty years. It all just seems like all too much of a coincidence, lad, for my liking.'

There was a brief pause before Sapper Mike chuckled, 'Bloody hell, sir! For a moment, I thought you were sounding superstitious there! No room for that sort of hogwash in the job though, eh sir!' Sapper Mike was smiling broadly as he said it as it sounded so preposterous. That his mentor, who had never been anything but straight ahead, down the line and hands-on practical could for a moment, entertain a superstitious thought, was nothing short of unthinkable.

It was also a ball of banter they had kicked around plenty of times, pouring scorn on doo-lallies, unicorn spotters, horoscopers, stargazers and other hopeless types. Their exchanges had always ended the same way, with the Captain concluding authoritatively that, '…the here and now is all there was to this world. What is right in front of you is what matters in this world, no room for nothing else. Not now, not never!' Sapper Mike smiled to himself, confident in the memories.

Another pause and then the Captain spat out a short sentence the young man would never forget, 'For God's sake, lad, the whole world is superstitious!'

'But I thought you'd always said there was no room for that in the job?' Fissures forming in the confidence, trust. Involuntarily, Sapper Mike had the idea of ice floes splitting and collapsing into the sea. Immediately, he banished the idea to focus on the Captain.

'There is no room for it in the job. But that doesn't mean to say we don't have our idiosyncrasies and odd beliefs.'

Sapper Mike had known the Captain now for nigh on two years. More or less as soon as he arrived, the old boy had tucked him under his wing to look out for him—his first time away from home at 17. He had a sense that the boy could go far. The Captain also knew first-hand how disconnected and dislocated it could feel to be away from your home and family at a young age. Sapper Mike had hung off the Captain's every word—smart enough to recognise a good man and friend when he saw one and eager to learn from the Captain's age and experience.

He'd learned from his father of the folly of reinventing the wheel and was no longer burdened by the sense that he was the first to experience whatever it was he was going through. Pound to penny, someone had already got the t-shirt, so you might as well listen to what they have to say and then beat your own path.

No, Mike's father had taught him that although the world may have moved on technologically, people were still as bovine stupid as they ever had been. 'We're still subject to the same fears, desires, wants, considerations as we were when the Bible was written, probably since we were sharpening flints. We just have different names for stuff now. Atavistic motivations,' his father had said, though he had no idea what atavistic meant to this day.

So, if there was the opportunity to listen to wisdom of experience, he reckoned he might as well save himself the bother of having to start from scratch on any endeavour, personal or professional. Sapper Mike found that the idea freed him up and he liked being a part of the wheel of experience gathering speed. Consequently, he'd lapped up the Captain's observations and tips about the job and anything else he had an opinion on. That was the level of trust. Even if it all got a bit dull, long-winded or tangential, it was said from the heart and there were seeds to be gleaned.

He'd learned that it was always worth following the Captain's rambles even if the other young lads had got bored, 'timed out' and double backed to thinking the old boy had lost his marbles. But there really was always something to learn from the old boy's anecdotes. Maybe the way his mind worked was from another era, but his mind was sharp, the edge fine honed. And because the Captain always came from a positive place, never to demean or castigate, Sapper Mike trusted the old boy. That was the SP, the bottom line.

Clouds of disquiet, however, seemed to be accumulating on the horizon of their shared experience. He'd never once thought that the Captain held back and didn't tell it exactly as it is or was.

'Lad, I can't tell you everything…' the Captain trailed off in what sounded confusingly like defeat. The Captain simply didn't have chinks in the armour. Or had he misjudged his mentor? Crow's feet formed at the corner of the young Sapper's eyes as he pondered, his thoughts stuck between gears. Sapper Mike said nothing when usually he would have. Instinctively, the Captain filled the void.

'Listen, Mike. Everyone has their quirks and foibles, fears and doubts. Many of us, most of us have a superstitious side. Whether that means a belief in God, the Fates or even rabbits being omens and augurs of bad luck. It's part of being human. It's a hook to put your hat on when there's nowhere else for it. For me, it all amounts to the same thing. That there's more to this world than meets the eye, without a shadow of doubt. On Portland, it's rabbits. Other places, you never put a hat on a bed. Fears and superstitions. People on Portland will get snotty and angry with you for even saying the word out loud. They've got it all back to front, as it happens.'

Sapper Mike paused before replying. He was put out by this turnaround, confused. So, he latched on to what at least seemed partially tangible, graspable, 'What's that, sir? Back-to-front? *Rabbits* aren't omens of bad luck?'

'Of course, they're not. They're rabbits, for goodness sake! They have got it the wrong way around though. They are the opposite. You spot a rabbit on Portland and you pay attention. They'll help you live.'

'Oh, bloody hell, sir. You've really lost me now!'

'Well, that's as may be but you've got to respect the local traditions and keep quiet about rabbits around the islanders. It's just not worth the bother.'

'Right you are, sir. I just didn't think you believed in all that mumbo jumbo. I thought you were all about the here and now, what you see is what you get,' replied Sapper Mike unenthusiastically, perplexed.

'Well, that's true still. I'm no different to anyone else despite what you might have thought. I grew up on Portland. As did my father, grandfather and grandfather's father as far as I know. And all those traditions and myths and superstitions do stick. Funny ideas, I know. But it is what it is. I had a great experience growing up fishing and mucking about on the isle as a lad. Happy times. Even through the war, right up until the last few months before I was *made* to leave it all behind.' Sapper Mike noted the emphasis, but thought better of delving into whatever that can of worms. He had plenty to chew on, so he kept quiet.

'Then it all took a turn for the strange that I can't explain even to this day. I haven't been back in 50 years and it all feels a bit odd coming back here for me last job. I'm remembering things that have been locked in the puzzle box at the back of my mind, forgotten for all my adult life and now the box is open, unfolding. All those long forgotten ghosts are out and making me remember all sorts of strangeness. Much as I'd like to pretend that inexplicable things don't happen, the truth is they do. That's my experience. And remembering that is, quite frankly, making me nervous.'

Sapper Mike was pretty much astounded by his mentor's revelation. But as he was trying to explain (even if it was vague and nebulous), he had decided just to go with it. To him, their friendship was a lot more than a hiccup of trust. Friendship overrode disappointment.

'As I say, my last month on the isle was uncomfortable to say the least for a number of reasons that I'll explain to you when we get through this. And we will. I'm sorry if I've misled you. But, for what it's worth, there is no room for superstition in the job. You have to have all your wits about you, focussed on what's in front of you, the here and now. Understanding that and concentrating on the detail is what'll keep you alive, *save you from having a bad day at the office*, if you like. But, and it's an unwieldy but. Leave a little room for your instinct, your spooky hunches. There's got to be room for that too as that's what's helped us evolve over the millennia.

'Hunters and gatherers couldn't see or hear the wolves in the forests in the dark, but their instinct could feel them, so the clever ones didn't go into the woods. Those that ignored their instincts went in and had a horrible end, got eaten alive. Those that paid attention to their instinct made for the high ground and it's them that we're descended from—those that listen to their instincts. If you ask me, that's why we're here and Neanderthal isn't. He didn't have the same basic instinct: intuition…'

'Eh? Too many hares running again, sir. And that's two confusing messages, pulling in opposite directions, surely though, sir?'

'Yes, lad. Exactly! And managing to keep them together and not let either run away from the other is what'll makes you clever. All life's a precarious balance. Bomb disposal especially so. Bear that in mind! Now I've just got to heed my own advice and I'll get through the next twenty four hours.'

'You don't have to be the one doing the hands-on, though? You can delegate. You're the Captain and it's your last job!'

'Precisely, lad. It's my last job and I decided years ago that whatever or wherever the last job was, I'd take care of it myself. I just never imagined that it'd be here, where I grew up! Too many bloody ghosts!' The Captain checked himself, hoping that the mention of ghosts hadn't undone all the shoring up he'd just done.

'Well, if that's the way you planned it, sir? But you don't have to.'

'It's not the way I've planned anything, lad you see? That's the point. It was written in the stars long before me and my making decisions. These are the cards I've been dealt and I have to play them, no matter the consequence.'

Sapper Mike appraised this new side of his character the Captain had presented. At first he had resented him for it, only a few hours ago. But actually, what was different really? Nothing *had* changed: he was still the same good-natured, clever old fella. He just had a bit more going on upstairs than met the eye. And he couldn't rightly knock the man for his beliefs. After all, he'd grown up with it! He knew very well that his Aunty Eileen read tea leaves and playing cards for people, reading their fortunes or failures. His own father was said to have 'the gift', though he never spoke of it. *None of it was anything new*, so why let himself get upset about it? He reasoned. There was just more to the Captain than met the eye and surely that's what made him interesting to be around? *Best just help out the Captain as best he could.*

The Captain had been keeping one eye on the road and the other on his apprentice as he noodled it through. When he saw the light dawning in his favour, Captain Collins smiled the first genuinely happy smile of the day. He had put a lot of store in the lad.

It was Sapper Mike who fired up the conversation again, 'So, they really found the unexploded bomb on the football pitch of Portland United, sir?'

'Correct, lad. But not just on the pitch either. No less than a metre from the centre kick-off spot, it was. Reckon they've played hundreds of games on that pitch. Hundreds!' The Captain added for emphasis.

'All of which could have gone off with a bang, sir!'

'Streuth, lad. Doesn't bear thinking about. How many lives? And a bomb like that would have taken out all the supporters, not to mention all those at home on Grove Road that runs along the side line.' Mike tilted his head back and noisily exhaled at the thought of the happy blare of a football match, all that enthusiastic emotion shattered in a split second and the horror of realisation after in a smoky split second, the mayhem that could have been—the ref and all the players and supporters: mothers, brothers, fathers, sisters, sons, aunties, uncles, cousins blown to smithereens decades after the end of a war most could scarcely remember if at all.

And how people and the media would have reacted to such an event? People would doubtless look to Germany. But the Germany they were looking at was not the Germany that dropped the bomb and could also barely remember events pre-1945 and if they could, they'd have wanted to forget more than anyone. Just as well the damn thing didn't go off. The ramifications were like a hall of mirrors echoing, ricocheting off in to the distance.

You still heard about the odd unfortunate farmer in Normandy who happened to feel too much give as he ploughed his fields and snagged some unexploded ordnance from the First World War, his last thought a momentary 'Merde!' before all that remained of him were smears of his former self splashed on the twisted metal of his tractor in the stillness that follows. But that happened less and less these days with the diminishing odds.

That was just one solitary man on his own though, not two entire football teams and their supporters, potentially half an island's population, certainly the male population. Didn't bare thinking about, if you didn't have to. But the old man and his apprentice *did* have to think through the grim consequences and it was these thoughts that gave meaning to their job, *the job*—to make the world safer and stave off catastrophe and the aftermath of misery that could echo down through the generations, the potential bereavements bruising and scarring the lives of the yet unborn. Both the Captain and the lad were nodding in unison having reached similar conclusions having thought it all through, start to finish, hearing the detonation, the silence that follows and the rush and roar of terror and confusion that fills the void when the smoke clears and the vision of hell itself.

Sapper Mike and the Captain simultaneously snapped out of their grim reverie and returned to their professional selves as BDO's Bomb Disposal Officers. Apprehension and fear were consigned to a lead-lined locked box in the back of their minds as the convoy slowed at the head of the Causeway to greet the local police, two squad cars convened in 'V' to prevent civilians from returning to the island before the bomb was made safe. The sight of the police cars galvanised a sense of purpose in the old boy and his apprentice. Back to business.

The Captain had rolled his window down, elbow out as he exchanged formalities with the bobby in his mid-to-late 20s who had braved the elements. The other older three policemen had stayed put in the warmth of their cars, out of the driving wind and rain. Sapper Mike wondered if the policeman's youth meant that he'd drawn the short straw. Probably.

Clear-skinned and square-jawed, visibly freshly shaven even at 1 am, the young policeman lowered and inclined his head to speak to the Captain who confirmed the purpose of their presence as if it could ever have been in doubt. Sapper Mike noted the deference in the bobby's demeanour. He wondered if the conversation in the squad cars might have rounded on the topic of what sort of person decides to be BDO, much the same as he had. And they would have come upon the same list of characteristics that Sapper Mike had: risk takers who like to live on their nerves, but with an iron sense of self control to counter balance.

Either way, the deference was there, plain and simple. He wasn't quite falling over himself to be helpful, but he wasn't far off it. The young policeman was about to give the Captain directions to the dockyard naval base when the Captain politely cut him short, thanked him, told him he knew where he was going and pulled off, causing the young policeman to step away. The policeman stood in the driving rain and watched as the convoy passed him before returning his cap to his head and then, having evidently gathered himself, turned on his heel and returned to the squad car.

Careful, cautious, the convoy of bomb disposal vehicles made its progress along the Causeway—a low viaduct that connects the mainland, Dorset, to the island of Portland. On the landward side, Fleet Lagoon sheltered by the barrier beach of Chesil and the island that was once dominated by the hulks of the British and American navy during the Second World War. On the seaward side, the pebble barrier that characterises Chesil Beach.

Sapper Mike couldn't get a sense of it in the dark, but was very much aware that they were soon to be upon an island that at one time would have been quite cut off from the mainland were it not for the building of the half mile long bridge. He remembered the Captain telling him the stories of the islanders that were known as 'Slingers' for their habit of hurling stones at unwanted visitors from the mainland who, in turn had at times, prevented the islanders from landing on the mainland for provisions, effectively reversing a siege by keeping the islanders on the point of starvation. Such was the habit of their happy cohabitation!

'Listen to that, lad! That's some storm. It would be impressive to see those waves now. Reminds me that I read a few years back that a monster of a wave broke through the third-story window of the pub, The Cove House Inn, at the end of the beach there!'

Sapper Mike looked sceptical. 'What a wave to break high enough to get in through a third-floor window?'

'Yep! The sea can really get up around Portland when there's a blow on, lad. Can't you hear the rumble?'

Sapper Mike listened more carefully and then distinguished another sound above the sound of the diesel. 'What's that?'

'That rumble is the sound of the waves, the suck and draw up of thousands of tonnes of pebbles on the ebb and spat out on the shoreline. That's the sound of the power of the sea.'

And that's what it was, the sound of the sea thrashing the pebble coast as if to assert its boundary with regular detonations. It made Sapper Mike thoughtful.

'Enough of that for now though,' stated the Captain winding up his window as the rain began to lash the Land Rover with a scattering sound of viciousness. 'I just wanted to hear it again for a moment. It's been fifty years since I've heard that sound and it still has the power to make me go quiet. And I can see that it's the same for you!' But the young man's attention had been diverted away from the titanic sound of the power of the sea as the mass of rock that is Portland Isle loomed before them.

At 2 am, with the police roadblock in place, the convoy of four Red Wings and the seven and half-tonner was the only single movement progressing along the Causeway, glow worm like those in the grasses on the rock that Billy Collins remembered from a lifetime ago. The shadow of the island in the stormy darkness quietened both men. After the angular order of built-up suburbia and a seaside town on the way there, it was the rugged wildness of the place that impressed and in some way intimidated the young man though he couldn't rationally explain *that*.

The Captain shook away the looming bank of memories gathering before him silently. Having very deliberately tried to forget his childhood on Portland for nearly a half century, the tidal pull it had on him, the listless tide of memories still were beginning to surge and draw, forgotten seas of emotion still angry in him all these years later and he knew he was here for the reckoning. But right now, on arrival, was not the time to be reflecting on his own story, though with the sight and sound of the island he knew that it was just a matter of time before the choice would no longer be his to make.

In that moment, the Captain understood that he was not reconciled to his past, to his experiences—that all the adrenalin and method involved in his career in theatres of war all over the world had not quietened his mind a jot. He could feel the emotions he felt as child fifty years previous like a rogue swell in him as fresh today as the sea spray and squalling rain that was over-working the wipers.

Sapper Mike was tired out, quiet now from the journey down which seemed to have taken an age. Sure, it was late now and up since dawn, 14 hours had made for a long day with a job ahead. Usually, he was fine with the long days. And he was fine with the thought of a job. Fear gave the edge to caution, as they say. Made you careful. And he'd got used to that too.

But there was another new variable in the equation. A variable that had tired him out, and that was the Captain's change in manner. To the young man, the Captain was a rock, a diamond—clear cut, transparent and as hard as. Come to that he'd seemed ageless, but much more like a young man than one of nearly sixty, such was his vitality and dauntless good humour just 24 hours previous. The man sat next to him now, however, was hard to read, exuding a mood that was distracting. And God, he appeared to have aged, even acquired a stoop, hunched forward as he was over the wheel. But more than that, to Sapper Mike, the Captain seemed human, fallible and subject to winds of change and ravages of time that he'd seemed impervious to.

It dawned on the young man that in the two and bit hours since London: gone was the hero, always ahead of the game, unquestionably self-assured and forever ready with a quip to steady the nerves. Now, beside him was an old fella, like anyone you might find yourself sat next to on the bus, frayed and made frail by the ravages of time, resting on a stick wondering, mind wandering, no longer sure. Mike was uneasy now in his presence. More uncomfortable still was the sense of disappointment he felt. And that forged a guilt in him. It felt like a betrayal on his part—a jagged and distracting feeling that made his mind drift.

An odd conversation he'd had with the Captain in his workshop a few weeks back came back to Sapper Mike.

He'd been sanding down the top of his first attempt at making a Chinese puzzle box. It was rosewood. He'd clamped it in the workbench vice between protective strips of rubber to sand it carefully. He was resting the palms of his hands on his kneecaps, bent down, one eye closed, checking that the top surface was as level as could be. He opened both eyes, nodding to himself, and raised himself up in a fluid motion. The Captain had his back to his apprentice and the young man noted he'd put his silver-rimmed spectacles back on. And then he began.

'I've been thinking. I have to say that you are one of the most 'capable' Sappers I've met. And that's saying something given the span of my career and the services and theatres I've fought in.

'What do you mean capable? Of doing the job?'

'It means that I have no doubt that come the time (and I hope that it doesn't come to you) when you have to be prepared to do anything. And I mean anything to stay alive, you wouldn't hesitate.'

After a pause, the young man replied not without a hint of irritation, 'Not following you, sir.' But the Captain was off again wistfully. Evidently hadn't heard the young man.

'Capable comes in surprising packages. Like your good self. Never really associating with those your own age, sky-larking. Preferring to get your head in a book or write a letter home. And too vigilant by half. Maybe that's what it is about you ... Your diffidence conceals your nature and critical ability.'

'Uh, come again, sir! I haven't the foggiest what you're talking about,' came the young Sapper's reply as he turned to face the Captain. But again the Captain continued with his monologue, oblivious.

'Don't fear death, lad. I've been near it plenty of times in the job and when you think the time is near, your brain floods with chemicals and the fear's cast away, the darkness recedes with the coming of the light. Completely gone. A warmth like no other envelopes you. Like a bath of olive oil or morphine ... Having said that, the build-up to it might be truly bloody awful. And that may be something to fear. Just not fear itself. Don't fear the unknown.'

'Lost me completely, sir!' Sapper Mike replied, frustrated as much as disconcerted.

The old boy snapped out of whatever it was and leant over the steering wheel, cradling it as he looked up. 'So much has changed, lad, save for the feel of the place,' and he turned and winked reassuringly at his apprentice who replied with a thinning, flat smile.

'Five minutes and we're at the Admiralty. Or where it was a half century ago. Called something completely different now, no doubt.' Sapper Mike understood that the old boy was remembering, connecting the here and now with the there and then. But no more than that was forthcoming and he was in no mood to ask questions. Frankly, this journey had been long enough and he just wanted to get the briefing over with and get his head down for a while to reset the brain.

Instinctively, that was what the young man knew, as well as that the idea of pursuing truths tired at that time of night was only going to confuse the issue potentially with a whole lot of other unknowns and variables. Best let the old chap get on with it and he'd deal with the here and now and get what needed unloading out of the Red Wing.

First though, Sapper Mike set about straightening his collars and smoothing imaginary creases out of his service sweater and fatigues. Truth was, even after nigh on three hours of travel, his uniform was immaculate, as was the Captain's. Only the space around the eyes related another story.

By now, they had traversed the Causeway. The Captain rolled his shoulders, cleared his throat and with it any vestiges of fatigue or whatever it was that was going on with him.

'Oh my days, it's changed! Most of this wasn't here back along. As you'd expect though, lad. March of progress and all that!' Sapper Mike expected his mentor to go into a monologue reverie as they began their ascent of the rock. One hundred and fifty metres up of long curves and s-bends. But the Captain just swore a colourful four-letter exchange to himself.

'Whassup, sir?'

'Wrong turn, lad. We shouldn't be climbing the rock. It's changed so much. I've taken us onto the rock rather than the Admiralty. No turning around on these bends though. Just have to turn around at the top and come back down. On automatic, I suppose. Heading back to Old Sea Dog Cottage. Old habits really do die hard, even after fifty years.' He paused a moment before continuing and concentrated on steering the s-bend at hand, 'My old homing beacon started emitting a signal again. Let's just say it never happened, eh?'

Sapper Mike quickly decided that whatever it was that was bothering the old boy would have to settle soon enough and he was of no mind to make anything of it and replied curtly, 'Best course of action, sir!' Eyes front, he didn't spot the Captain's quizzical grimace turn to acceptance.

'I'm going to need your help on this one, lad. A lot of help,' he added, nodding.

'Of course, sir! Whatever needs to be done. All hands on deck!' Sapper Mike said emphasised with a finality as if to confirm he wasn't about to speak again anytime soon, for the rest of the journey to the naval base, he kept his eyes fixed on the progress of the convoy in the wing mirror.

A few minutes earlier, tracking their progress from the police car, the square-jawed young policeman paused before taking a sip from the flask of tea proffered. 'I bloody hope those BDOs know more about what they're doing than where they're going!'

The two more senior policemen in the back leant forward to see what he was talking about, as did the other young man in the front passenger seat.

'They're going straight up on to Portland, by the looks.'

'Bloody right they are!'

'Thought the briefing was at the naval base?'

'It is! I was just about to tell them and give 'em directions when the miserable old duffer driving, pulled off. Told me he knew where he was going. Could've taken my head off. Bloody old fool!'

'Oi!' came a searing rasp from the back seat and then one of the old boys took up the gauntlet with a fierce, throaty growl. 'Less of the old, young man! What you were looking at there was experience and time served. Stands to reason that a bomb disposal officer that senior has put his life on the line and diffused more bombs in war zones than you've had hot dinners, mi'laddo! Have a bit of respect. Those lads were right up front with the Paras in the Falklands making areas safe for the initial landings. More nerve in their little fingers than you've got in your whole body! So, pack it in, you whippersnapper.' And to drive his point home, he thumped the headrest of the driver's seat with the flat of his hand. The young officer's head jolted forward.

Though the young officer couldn't see it, the speaker was fairly puce with rage, spittle at the corners of his mouth and a tremor in his voice that belied experience that the two young officers in the front couldn't have guessed at. A thick, livid silence settled in the police car—the back in their brinkmanship, the front cowed acquiescent. The young officer thought several quick replies at once, but remembered himself, exhaled and reluctantly replied, 'Yes, sir.'

'Glad we've got that sorted. You might want to think before you speak and engage that tiny mind of yours.' He let that settle and his shoulders loosened as there was no reply forthcoming.

Satisfied that the young buck was back in his box, the two in the back settled into their seats. The young man, though, was hunched over the wheel and watched the progress of the convoy as it snaked its way up the rock and looped back around to make its descent of the hairpins again. He too settled back into his seat then, shaking his head as imperceptibly as possible with irritation and disbelief. The two in the front shared a meaningful glance that suggested, 'What the heck was that all about?' shocked by the ferocity of the reprimand. A mutual shrug: constructively, nothing more to say.

In a lull in the storm, they watched the convoy, like a procession of glow worms, meander back down the rock. And then a squall of rain lashed the patrol car. A gust with a force that would have set Richter to recalibrating had the car shift on its suspension even with four, well-fed policemen in it—the elements reminding them really who's boss.

A few minutes later, the convoy pulled up at the Admiralty checkpoint barrier. The Captain flicked the gearstick into neutral, leaving the Land Rover's diesel pulsing as it idled. Both in the cab noted the irregularity; something to be investigated later. They waited for the armed guard in the beret, stocky fella in his forties and an older chap, to come out of the hut. Beyond, the red and white striped barrier floodlights illuminated a still fairly busy scene despite the hour—uniforms loading and unloading this and that.

Even though it was blatantly obvious why they were there, the armed guard eyed them with something akin to suspicion before lowering his capped head to the Red Wing window to ask for the Captain's ID and purpose. He gave the appearance of scrutinising the Captain's papers, even checking the photo before returning them with a curt nod. And then his expression softened and he added in a friendlier tone, 'Good to see you, sir. And welcome.'

With that, he turned to the hut and gave another decisive nod and the red and white barrier raised in three halting motions. Captain Collins leant forward over the steering wheel as he engaged the clutch and put the Red Wing in gear. He turned his head and spoke loudly enough so the armed guard could hear him, 'Need to have a look at that, young man!' stated the Captain with a genuine look of irritation and he pulled off, leaving the guard in a wake of diesel fumes. It took the guard a moment to work out that the old boy was talking about the barrier.

'Bloody Royal Engineers,' mouthed the guard while shaking his head dismissively.

True enough, Sapper Mike had thought that if it was his barrier, he'd want the mechanism functioning perfectly. But he wasn't about to tell the man there and then and he certainly wasn't expecting the Captain to point it out either. A lot of other colleagues would have engaged in that sort of inter-service personnel banter. But it wasn't either his or the Captain's personal style to be abrupt in that way. Not unless pushed, that is.

The Captain was old school, impeccably mannered and although he had worked his way up through the ranks, he'd never been one to pull rank and never really seen himself as officer class though the braiding on his shoulders told a different story. Rank and file had to be observed but both men had a sort of egalitarianism in common that meant they would treat the most highly and lowly placed with an equal respect. An ideal popular with the lowly, but not so with the highly placed in life. Potentially disruptive, it rubbed some completely up the wrong way.

'Everyone deserves respect in the first instance,' Sapper Mike remembered the Captain once saying, 'and then it's up to them to maintain or not as the case may be,' he'd finished. The Captain often came out with these observations and sayings for Mike to digest and he'd said things alike and enough times for it to sink in so that Mike digested and made it his own. That was why it was an uncharacteristic burr of behaviour for the Captain to pick someone up on something that really he had nothing to do with. Smacked a bit of 'jobs-worth'. And that, the Captain was definitely not.

After the journey they'd had, he wasn't about to mention or even ruminate on it. 'Eyes front, move forward. What's done is done. That's why the windscreen is bigger than the rear-view mirror. Don't delay on what's behind you,' murmured the young man. Another of the Captain's sayings! Not that the Captain noticed as he was staring intently at the old fella of similar age to himself in the hi-vis in the guard hut. And then he pushed the shift into second and faced forward. He was quiet a few moments as he concentrated on where the uniforms were directing them to park up in the service yard before he exclaimed, 'Jee-free-Moses!'

This time Sapper Mike enquired, 'What is it, sir?' as they parked up, hand brake on, knocked out of gear, ignition off, twist.

'If I'm not very much mistaken, the fella sat in the guard hut operating the barrier was an old school friend of mine, Paul Scard. One of the Scard twins. Right pair of mischievous buggers they were. Christ, he's changed a bit. Passage of time isn't too kind to any of us and fifty years is certainly going to do that. Funny how your memory stops in time and don't catch up till you see 'em next.

'One moment they are ten years old scaling Pulpit Rock in the summer sun, next moment 60 years old, no hair, sat in a hut manning a barrier. Oh yes, and that reminds me,' he added leaning forward to the glove box to retrieve a green, two-inch long Velcro strip that he held up between thumb and forefinger for

Sapper Mike to register. 'You'll be needing this! Standard army issue.' Deftly, in a single movement, he applied the Velcro strip to the young man's field green jumper concealing his rank as Sapper and surname 'Lapin'.

The young man had lowered his chin to breast bone to watch the application of the Velcro tab and then looked up at the Captain with a question in his eyes. 'You can't be serious. Really?'

'Really, yes. We don't want the locals making those connections,' and then he paused before adding, 'and making associations with underground mutton bunnies.'

'Got to be kidding.' Mike shook his head. He still couldn't quite get his head around how crackers the idea was that Portlanders saw rabbits as omens of bad luck and worse. More than that, that he had to cover his own name was ludicrous. Just didn't make sense. But then the Captain, who had always made sense, had been nothing short of peculiar since the phone call for this job came in.

'Nope. Deadly serious, lad! Keep calm and carry on!' The Captain stared straight ahead a moment, checked himself, flicked off the cab lights and hopped out in one fluid, youthful motion. He marched off towards what Sapper Mike took as the waiting dignitaries. The young man took his time getting out of the Red Wing and stood to take in the quiet a moment after the last few incessant hours of noise of the wipers battling the lashing rain, the throaty rumble of the diesel chucking out fumes all down the motorway.

The air was clean now and the wind seemed to have eased off. He stretched a moment, picking up the scent of the sea and the sound of the surf some way off. Slamming the Red Wing door behind him, Sapper Mike donned then straightened his beret and moved off double time to catch up with the Captain who looked to being 'all back to business'.

Chapter 14
The Briefing

After the convoy had parked up, careful and precise as to the millimetre, the unit proceeded to the Admiralty Officers' Mess for the usual formal introductions and briefing. They'd had their brief in London and now was the chance to hear the information gathered on the ground to date: the exact location of the bomb in relation to local infrastructure potentially within the blast zone and the identification of the explosive ordinance confirmed as a 2,000 lb Second World bomb, the largest of Luftwaffe's arsenal and colloquially known as a 'Satan'.

The briefing began under dimmed lights in the Mess with the aid of a dinosaurian overhead projector on the raised dais. It conveyed the image of a map of the island, the immediate blast zone and its furthest reaches were indicated by a circular, red, transparency which extended more than inch into the sea, therefore covering the whole island. That meant that the whole of Portland was under threat of the bomb blast and subsequent shockwave.

As most of the cottages on the island were one hundred years old and plus, they were deemed to be likely to crumble if the UXB (unexploded bomb) detonated. In short, it needed to be made safe. No explosions expected or otherwise. As ever, there was only one expected outcome. Any other was unthinkable, at least Captain Collins' unit, anyway.

The briefing was conducted CO Colonel David Somerfield who was at least a head taller than the other five in his entourage of locals and evidently from generations of well-fed stock. He had a shock of thick white hair and hairline that should have belonged to someone 25 years his junior. He only had to clear his throat and the hubbub in the room died instantly like a lightning strike evaporating mist on a calm sea as Mike had once seen on exercise off Cyprus.

'Ok, gents! Let's get to the facts of the matter at hand! Preliminary intel suggests we have 2,000 lb WWII bomb.' Someone whistled as if to accentuate the destructive power of the bomb that had rested easy for fifty years (the War on Pause as the Captain put it) while Portland United played their beautiful game only inches above.

'Colloquially known as a 'Satan' if I am correct, Captain Collins?' With his hands clasped behind his back, legs at ease, Colonel Somerfield flexed his shoulders and rolled on his toes as if for emphasis.

'Correct!' confirmed Captain Collins from the floor with a true-to-form unquestionable authority with a curt nod. All those in the room gave a short, affirmative murmur of mirth that was both polite and conveyed 'confidence in the face of death.'

Colonel Somerfield continued matter-of-factly as if reading bullet points, 'She's been there since 1942 as far as we can tell. As a precaution we've cleared the island of all inhabitants. All bar two. A pigeon fancier who, to quote, 'is damned if he's going to leave his birds to be blown to smithereens'. And an older lady who I'm told is the personification of stubborn. She, unlike the pigeon fancier, appears to be in complete possession her faculties. Her reason is that, Jerry never made her leave the island *of her own accord* and she is of no mind to have one of his ghosts make her do so *now*!' This was met with a murmur of approval.

As this line was delivered, Sapper Mike's gaze rested on the Captain who appeared to evaluate this nugget of information by pursing his lips and questioning with his eyebrows. It had evidently set off a train of thought. And, as soon as the idea had formed, the Captain squinted and dispelled the thought. Sapper Mike wondered idly for a moment as to the cause and then concentrated his attentions back on the CO.

'Lovely lady, as I say. The rest of 'Joe Public' have been evacuated to a holiday camp in Weymouth. Safe and sound and out of harm's way. All having a jolly old time, by all accounts. All bunting and Vera Lynn parties. Local primary school has gone to town with it. Turned it into a learning experience. Gas masks, rations, building Anderson shelters. Keep calm and carry on. All very British. Spirit of resilience our nation's known the world over for.' All those present again murmured their affirmation—*meh!* Sapper Mike, who wasn't used to this degree of nationalism, wondered if proceedings might conclude with a rendition of the national anthem.

When the murmur had subsided, the Colonel continued, 'As to the position of the device, it is practically beneath the centre spot of the Portland United football pitch.' He paused for effect and then uncannily used the same words Sapper Mike had heard the Captain use, 'So, there's many a match played by Portland United that might have gone off with a bang!' Colonel David Somerfield paused as those assembled chuckled politely. He was clearly enjoying himself though Sapper Mike could have done with a little less forced mirth at that time of night.

With patience thinning, he was beginning to resent the obligation to laugh. Nonetheless, Sapper Mike was beginning to understand that these briefings, with the 'dad joke humour' and the expected responses helped bond personnel as a family in the same way you might humour doddering relatives who had long ago ceased to make sense. Back at the beginning, when he'd first joined the Engineers, he'd had to ask the Captain about it. Other recruits probably just accepted and got on with it. Wouldn't dream of asking a senior officer about it, but Sapper Mike did. Such as he was and such was the trust. He could ask the Captain just about anything providing no-one else was within earshot.

'What's with dreadful jokes in the briefings, sir?' He'd asked while they were in the workshop.

The Captain had paused, lifted his head and attention away from the task at hand and replied, 'It is what it is. It might rankle. But that's all. Just move on. No point in digging too deep on some things. It'll make sense in time.' It was a fairly cryptic reply from the old man and he'd come out with all manner of similar such epithets along the way that Sapper Mike filed in his mind under the title of 'how to get along in a new environment.' He must have got that from the Captain too, though he couldn't remember where or when.

'Not always helpful to be too bright and enquiring, lad,' was another, 'Particularly if those around you aren't! You don't want to stand out in crowd. Sometimes it's best not to speak up, even if you know you're right and certainly don't question if it's not your place. Keep a low profile, that's what I say. And be grateful if things go your way.' The young man let these thoughts dissipate. It was no time of night letting the mind wander and so he marshalled his concentration back to the briefing.

Sapper Mike understood the danger to the pigeon fancier who wouldn't leave his beloved birds and the 'stubborn old lady' who apparently had *never left of her own accord on Jerry's account and wasn't about to start now.* The line had been delivered by the moustachioed CO who had clearly anticipated the moment of levity it would bring—the reciprocal bray of laughter from twenty or so assembled. With the mood momentarily lightened, pressure released, he got back to business with a serious tone and an economy of words mostly what they already knew: explaining that local infrastructure including schools, a medical centre, and a central council office not to mention the Admiralty buildings *could* be affected by a bomb blast. As would all the housing on the isle as the majority of it was built 50-100 years ago and could be subject to subsidence after the shock wave.

He announced the time of reveille and breakfast at first light at 0600 hours by which time a decision would have been made by the Prison Service as to whether the six hundred prisoners within the blast zone would be evacuated from the island (a logistical nightmare) and who would visit the last two remaining islanders in a last-ditch attempt to persuade them to evacuate in leaving the BDOs to get on with it, safe in the knowledge that there was no imminent threat to civilian life—the essence of public service.

'AOB?' barked Colonel Somerfield. His neck snapped back and forth, eyes scanning the hall for a question Sapper Mike felt wouldn't be asked and then closed the meeting. The hall emptied in a matter of minutes, all keen to get some kip and prep for the day ahead which was already looming. Sapper Mike had taken his lead from the Captain who still had not moved despite the meeting disbanding. Hands clasped behind his back, he was deep in thought again, ostensibly contemplating the regimental coat of arms above the stage. Sapper Mike had the impression that this wasn't the Captain's focus. He decided to chime in, 'Ready then, sir?'

Slowly, the Captain turned to his Sapper. 'What was that, lad?'

'Time to get some shuteye, sir!'

'Right, you are. Let's go.' With that, they left the Mess hall. At the last moment, the Captain turned on his heels and returned to the door, took a last look around and clicked the lights off. They made their way to their sleeping quarters in silence, too tired for chat. As they unlocked the doors to their allocated rooms above the Officer's Mess, Sapper Mike turned to the Captain, 'Give you a knock first thing, sir?'

'Not if I'm up before you, lad!'

They exchanged a smile and looked at their boots, before Mike added, 'Whatever became of your friend Maggie, sir?' The question had passed his lips before he knew it. Tired.

'Had a feeling you were going to ask me that. Sharp lad.' He paused before adding, 'Truth is, I don't know. After we were evacuated, I never came back to Portland until now. Haven't set eyes on her for fifty years. Not that I haven't thought of her though. If I'm honest, I can't say that many days have passed when I haven't asked myself that very same question.'

This reply was perplexing for the young man. It simply didn't add up to what he knew of the Captain. Another incongruency and again he replied without filtering the words and they were out before he could grasp them by the tale and haul them back in. As soon as he said them, he knew it was too direct, too personal a question for that fatigued time of night.

'What? You thought about her daily but made no effort to get in touch? That's not like you, sir. Bit odd, sir?'

The Captain was some moments in replying, 'Quite right, lad. It's not like me. I don't know if I was afraid she hadn't made it through the war or what really. Countless times I thought about coming back here, looking for her. She was like family, only more so. But I didn't. I can't really explain it.'

'Seems that way,' replied the young man and both were conscious that some sort of role reversal had just taken place. Consequently, in an effort to right things, Sapper Mike waited for the Captain to reply and wrest back control of the usual order.

'No, it doesn't make sense. Those thoughts bring me to a standstill. All sorts of unanswered questions. But what became of her? I have a sense that I will find out soon enough. Goodnight, lad.' And before Mike could answer, the Captain had disappeared behind his closed door. Sapper Mike shook his head and did much the same thing, yearning for sleep and the hope of a clearer head in the morning.

Chapter 15
Three Dreams in a Sleepless Night

Captain Collins turned the key in the door and sat down heavily on the iron frame bed. He removed his glasses and stretched out to place them carefully on the bedside table. He unlaced his boots and placed them beneath the chair beside the bedside table, the same routine he'd observed in scores of military quarters the world over. Standard 12 by 8 rooms, all kitted out the same—basic, functional. At the end of the bed: an open wardrobe-locker the height of a man and as wide as the single bed—fit for a uniform and suit. Opposite: writing desk and chair, mirror above the sink and bedside short boy and lamp. No frills. Job done.

With no-one to observe him, the Captain moved with the deliberation of a tired man, his age. Gone was the straight-backed, brisk and vital serviceman, replaced by someone altogether more measured in thought and deed. Time was, he could have driven a thousand miles, got out, put a sixty pound pack on his back and then run another fifteen. Different story now though—try just under two hundred and that was him *done*.

To you and I, he appeared to have aged 30 years in the turning of a key. He removed 'woolly pulley' as they were known and placed them individually on two of the hangars in the suit locker. Then, still in his cargo-fatigues and vest, he stretched out on the cot, hands behind his head, not for a minute expecting sleep to come. But it did. Had he been counting, he wouldn't have got past seven. Closed the eyes to concentrate on the breathing: in through the nose, short; out through the mouth, long. Gone …

The Flying Scotsman was blistering along. Billy Collins had his head out of the carriage window, eyes watering with glee as he stared at the funnel billowing out pressurised steam, smoke, sparks and excitement. For a few exhilarated moments, he quite forgot the events of the previous few days on Portland and that he was being 'evacuated' from his home and family on Portland, headed for Harrogate, hundreds of miles north in Yorkshire to live with strangers for an unspecified length of time. For, who knew how long the war would last? No-one could know. It had been 3 years already. And the history books suggested that it could go on for decades. Uncertain times.

For the ten-year-old Billy, time shifted differently—a summer holiday could feel like a lifetime unlike for a sixty-year-old Captain for whom the reels of time spun forever faster. For a boy who had never left Portland or ever seen a steam engine, the experience was enervating and daunting in equal measure. With gathering speed as rural England passed him by, Billy Collins' experience was tinged with apprehension as the distance between himself and his family and all he had known grew.

Outwardly, it might have been spring in England's green and pleasant land. Inwardly, it felt still in the winter dark. It hit him in the pit of his stomach, a searing glee that made him wonder if the tears in his eyes were wind-blown or anguish fed. In the end, he reasoned it didn't matter as he felt both. After the initial excitement, Billy barely moved, sat alone in the train carriage with his wooden gas mask box on his lap. He had no interest in it. Plenty of people got on and off at Southampton and Oxford. There was a whole rabble of other kids, presumably being evacuated too, down the carriage.

Billy stayed put, though. Idly he watched the countryside go by as the catastrophic events of his last few days on Portland played and replayed in his mind, searing deeper with each remembrance.

The Flying Scotsman eventually wheezed in at York after fourteen syncopated hours of rail track. The other couple of dozen or so kids, also being evacuated from cities that the Luftwaffe had been taking more than a small interest, clamoured for release. All of them were supposed to be met by host families who would look after them. They'd see the rest of the war out with these families, safe in the countryside away from the bombs raining down on their city homes. Their excitement was as a palpable and the train's tired exhalations after the journey. He guessed that many of the city kids had never seen the countryside before. He wondered what those, who hadn't seen it, would make of the sea?

Despite the bright sun of the spring morning, Billy Collins didn't feel warmed or a part of the scene unfolding though and waited until the crush was over before making his way to the carriage door. That 'outsider' feeling was keeping him away from the throng and quiet with it, too. He watched the arriving families hoping for a smiling face and the promise of a happy family and times ahead. But in the pit of his stomach he felt an intuition that this wasn't going to be the case.

And at that moment as if to confirm it, he spotted two hard, grim-faced soldiers asking the kindly lady-chaperone who had accompanied them up from Southampton, what seemed to be a set of urgent questions that might have been commands. An anxiousness lined her brow as the chaperone scanned the gathered, chatting children for a particular face. The soldiers with the initials 'MP' on their helmets followed her gaze and Billy knew that they were there for him. He was stood framed in the carriage door in plain sight when her gaze alighted on him and he watched her mouth, 'There, in the carriage doorway!' as her arm raised to point him out.

The soldiers, military policemen, Americans, judging by the uniform, didn't wait for confirmation and made directly and roughly towards him through the platform crowd.

'Billy Collins?' one asked.

'Yes, sir,' Billy meekly replied, trying desperately to manage the quaver of fear in his voice.

'You're with us.' And that was all they said. They weren't like the other American service personnel he had met at home at Portland. No easy smiles or chocolate for the children; no cigarettes or jokes for the ladies. These were a different kind of soldier. Mirthless, ruthless types of men focussed solely on the job which appeared to be to whisk Billy Collins away without more ado. With one in front and one behind the soldiers marched Billy off the platform, the crowd parting before them, the excited hubbub quelled as they watched him go to the jeep waiting for them, the engine running already. Billy hadn't managed to take his bag and gas mask box off in the back of the jeep before they lurched off confirming whatever the urgency was. Disconcerting.

Billy didn't have a watch but thought that they had driven through lanes up onto the moorland for more an hour before they pulled over a stone, hump back bridge to Muker, a village at the foot of the Yorkshire dales which rose up behind it, the river before it. They were patches of snow melting on the hills and Billy noticed that spring was about a month behind Portland. The landscape was barren, the trees leafless and the sky had greyed merging into a stony outcrop of horizon, the initial bright rays of morning sun obscured. He thought the village might have been the destination. The river looked promising for trapping fish, even. But, no. They passed through Muker.

For half as much time again, travelling not much faster than a walk, after negotiating a stone track that a pony might have issue with, the jeep bumped up a puddled lane that had stone walls either side making two enclosures before a solitary, small windowed, stone house with several farm out buildings either side. It might have been a working farm at some point, but not for quite some time. As they neared further still, Billy could see the front door open and a very tall man in a suit stoop to emerge from the house and stand on the bottom door step. He appeared to be puffing on a pipe and Billy felt his throat tighten as he thought of Mr Scriven and the stench of his pipe. He certainly couldn't have been all the way up here, surely?

As the jeep circled into the muddy yard, Billy closed his eyes in relief as he got a look at the tall man and confirmed that it was not in fact Mr Scriven, just someone that looked like him though maybe taller. Billy watched the tall, sallow looking man, somewhere in his late forties, appraising them. He nodded curtly at the two MPs in the front on the jeep as they came to a stop. The MP in the back with Billy picked him up like a sack of spuds and dump him on the yard floor.

Picking up his bag and gas mask, one in each hand, he placed them in Billy's before hopping back into the jeep. The tall man nodded again, puffing on his pipe. Without even having turned the jeep ignition off, the driver put it into reverse, swung back out onto the track and was away. Not a word had been spoken since York. Billy watched it the half mile to the end of the lane and then it was gone from view. He turned to see the tall man puffing, scrutinising him. He suddenly felt very alone, hundreds of miles from everyone and all he knew. He didn't know where York was and he knew he was now miles from Muker. There was no way he could find his way back, even with all his determination. It was simply too far.

Drizzle settled on his face. He looked at the tall man who seemed to have a gentleness in his eye despite the severe, angular shape of his face, 'Best get in before the weather really turns, Collins,' the tall man said as he turned back into the house. With a bag and mask in each hand, Billy stood for a moment as he wondered how the man knew his name. No-one had mentioned it. He understood then that much more was at work and had been put in place to bring him to the middle of nowhere away from all the other children. His shoulders drooping, Billy climbed the house steps and closed the door on the light behind him.

And then he heard the sallow man say over his shoulder, 'You won't be needing that gas mask here either, lad. Jerry has no interest, even in this God-forgotten corner of the world. Don't suppose he even knows it's here. Come into the kitchen, lad, and close the door behind you.' Billy noted the acerbic edge to his words. He wasn't thrilled to be here either, by the sound of it.

Billy closed the door behind him and took in the kitchen in front of him—rough oak table and four chairs and a more comfortable looking arm chair by the wood burner. Billy took a step forwards only to hear a menacing, low growl. It was only then that Billy noticed the Border collie under the kitchen table baring its teeth at him. One blue eye, one brown. The tall man clicked his finger and the growling ceased.

'Don't think of trying to leave this place, William Collins. Bob and I are here to make sure that you don't. That dog will keep a good eye on you. And please don't try and test us. It's in nobody's best interests that you leave here. And in time you will forget all that happened on Portland. You will sit out the rest of the war here with me. However long that may be. So, get used to the idea quickly and we shall get along fine.'

He let that sink in and then offered, 'Tea? Bread and jam? The one good thing about being up here is that the MOD will look after us. We even have honey, eggs and sugar, bacon and chickens. Dealing with them can be your job. Got to keep a routine. Keep busy and concentrate on the here and now and time will pass more quickly. And forget your past. That's all gone now.' The tall man then busied himself making the tea and slicing the bread. Billy had to admit that he hadn't seen such thick slices in years and the jam looked like, well, jam!

'As it is or toasted?' the sallow man intoned, nodding his head towards the thick sliced bread.

'Toasted, please sir.'

The tall man deftly speared the thick sliced bread and set it above the fire to toast. Billy watched as it quickly browned and his new guardian turned it over. Just as quickly, the other side was done and the man was buttering it up with enough butter to last a week at home. As he did this, he seemed to be considering something. Was that look friendliness or intrigue in his eyes?

Billy had noted the man's economy of words—never more than necessary with a very deliberate, clear delivery which ran at odds with his physical movement which was quick, purposeful and belied a latent energy and tension. Somehow it made Billy nervous and want to make a break for it, there and then. He even anticipated the sound of the cup and saucer up ending before him, the scrape and clatter of the wooden chair legs across the flag stone floor, that is until the Bob's tail whipped across his shin—a reminder.

The thought of his mum and Maggie at home on Portland made him feel very much remote and alone in the world. His mother had, what Sarah Golding described as, a warm soul. Billy had the feeling she'd describe this man's soul in much cooler terms and the sense occurred to him that this level of friendliness was as good as it would get. The man was here to do a job, with a modicum of reluctance it seemed and warmth or friendless was clearly absent from his brief. Billy walked out of the kitchen back to the front door. He drew back the latch and opened it. The drizzle had thickened into cold rain pitting the puddles in the yard.

The scene before him was devoid of colour. Grey stone and sky. Course grass and bracken browned, dull. A scent of stagnant water crossed him. And there was no movement. He was used to bright, sea reflected light, endlessly shifting and changing. It kept him alert and energised. Here, he already felt inert. No even listless. With no options, it felt like the perfect prison.

With that thought, Billy's sense of isolation was complete and would remain so for the remaining three years of the war. Billy did not leave the farm in that time and neither did he learn his guard's name. The sallow man would leave in the morning once a month only to return as darkness fell. Any hopes of escape dissipated quickly as he couldn't get past the yard gate without hearing that low growl, the black and white dog patiently stalking him. He didn't have to test that sort of dog to know its intent. He was quite clearly under house arrest. The thought closed in on him, made him nauseous. What sounded like loose corrugated iron edged and scarped back and forth nearby. And then he felt the eyes of the dog on him.

*

Captain Collins woke with a start and swung his legs out over the bed edge in fight or flight readiness. Planting his feet, he took in his surroundings. Nothing unusual. He made for the door, but stalled himself before opening it. *Calm! Pull yourself together, Collins.* Must have just been the dream, but it made him set himself heavily down on the bed. He rubbed his palms over his face to try to wake up, orient and rid himself of that limbo feeling.

An oily memory of dream settled behind his eyes. Then it turned uncomfortably sharp, astringent clarity that left him scratching the back of his neck vigorously. And then he realised that it wasn't a dream, so much as a memory from fifty years previous that felt closer to the here and now than the briefing just an hour ago. He exhaled wearily.

Captain Collins anticipated a long night of wakefulness ahead. The nerves across his shoulders, still tingling with fight or flight energies were at odds with a leaden feeling of torpor that had settled in the rest of him. He'd have to do something to regulate his fly-wheel-mind before it gathered speed. He could well have done without a trip down memory lane at that time of night. He had to be up in a few hours, fit for the job, for Christ's sake.

He needed a distraction. A newspaper or something, but he hadn't packed anything suitable such was his distraction before leaving London. For want of a decisive action, he snapped off the main light hoping that maybe a lower light would make for an easier passage to the land of nod. Nothing to do but concentrate on his breathing in an effort to relax. He didn't get to count a dozen repetitions though before his eyes, flickered and closed. Soon he was falling down the rabbit hole of dreams *again*.

*

Once the feeling of falling had stopped, Billy Collins woke on his bed at Black Gate Farm. The mind of veteran bomb disposal officer taking in his skinny limbs of a half century before, not with a little irritation. His eyes alighted on the window. Bright light incongruous to the moors poured in. It was like sea light. Despite his disquiet, he could not ignore the compulsion to investigate. Gingerly, he made his way across the creaking floor boards to the window. The view was not of the dull browns and greys of the moors, the usual drizzle.

He was looking at Red Pool on Portland, the English Channel, morning sun-lit. Resting across the rocks was the colossal, unmistakable skeleton of the whale, perhaps two hundred feet long and some seventy feet high, as if carved of sandstone. As he looked, he saw himself inside the skeleton. And then that was where he was, the palm of one hand flattened on one of the leviathan ribs that towered above him. The girth of each rib was such that even with both arms, he could nowhere near put his arms around.

There was no doubt about it. It was the same whale skeleton that he had dreamt of as a child. Only now in his dream, he could examine with an adult scrutiny, even if he had the body of his ten year old self. Some things don't change. The entirety of the leviathan structure was covered with intricate, ornate scrimshaw that was turning to filigree before his eyes. It was a work in progress, working. His fingers traced the patterns carved into the bones. Some looked like hieroglyphs, all differing types of curling calligraphic script, some that looked like Arabic, some Indian, some Egyptian.

The entire skeleton was completely covered with the carvings of which he had no idea of the meaning. But that didn't mean he didn't feel its potency. Each moment of looking felt like a thousand years, as if he was looking at the history of the world carved into the bones of a long-dead colossus. And then he noticed the sound. Though he could see the sea, not more than a few feet away, the sound was like the great echoing emptiness of a stone cathedral full of whispers, muffled footsteps and cloaks retreating into the shadows. Not the familiar, reassuring soundscape of the sea.

And then there was also that musty odour. A deep, intense scent akin to incense, candles and wine, cloying and neither pleasant or otherwise but that magnified the feeling that Billy had that he was in the presence of something powerful, awe inspiring, unknowably greater than himself. He felt many things at once: enervated, inspired, fear tempered with caution, his senses honed, blade-sharp. Ambergris? Was that what it was called?

Being inside the whale, the vaulted skeleton ceiling above, was an assault on all six senses. On an instinctive, animal level the monolith created in him a searing feeling in his gut that made him white across the knuckles and burn across the shoulders. But just as he registered this, he noticed the vast ivory tusks seemed moist, that they were exuding an oil of some sort that made the carvings glisten the sun light. Billy Collins looked up through vast, leviathan skeleton and tried to imagine it alive. Paradoxically, his sense was that it was alive. What he saw before him may have been the ancient bones of a long since living, swimming creature.

But his intuition told him otherwise. It was cognisant, very much aware of his presence. It was watching him. His eyes focussed on the sun above which blinded him and he lost the image in a swirl of hieroglyphs. A white, visible wind howled and filled the monolith. Tectonic vibration shuddered the structure. Terror enveloped him.

Captain William Collins gasped awake for the second time that night in the Officer's Mess accommodation at the Admiralty at Portland, panting like a sight hound after the chase. He swung his legs off the bed wearily, angrily so as to be ready if need be. Mind racing, body on automatic. He scanned the room, focussed on the door, then the rest of the room and was reassured by its Spartan normalcy, no room for misinterpretation—all as banal and functional as needs be. He just had to calm his breathing.

After a few moments sat on the edge of his cot bed, his breathing returned to normal. He walked to the sink and drew himself a cup of water, careful not to meet eyes with his reflection in the mirror. As a man, as BDO with over forty years' worth of experience, Captain Collins had absolutely no wish to see what he knew would be fear in his own eyes. And it was a fear akin to no other, something that he hadn't felt since he was last on Portland, a half century ago.

Captain Collins lay down heavily on the bed again lacing his fingers behind his head, exhausted. He glanced at the red digital display on the radio clock by his bed. 3.06am. He exhaled a long sigh, sure in the knowledge that this was to be a very long three hours. He knew that his dreams would not leave him be that night and that, without doubt, a tsunami of memory was merely gathering momentum, crossing the oceans and depths of his memory, ripping and churning all in its path.

Chapter 16
The Last Dream of Three

Sleep didn't take him so quick this time. He nodded out into that limbo between the physical world and the luminous, preternatural world of dreams half a dozen times before eventually leaden, he sank beneath the surface. Quick breathing, panicky, Captain Collins woke in a dream fumbling wires of a detonator. His fingers wouldn't behave. They seemed numb, oversized and beset by unpredictable tremors, hearing the click of the firing pin, wide-eyed with the knowledge that that was his final moment.

In another fragment of dream, the Captain crouched by the Satan drilling out the mechanism while giant rabbits, the size of donkeys, thumped around him so heavily pawed that he knew it was only a matter of time that if he did not disconnect the timer, the vibrations would inadvertently set off the timer. And then, having unscrewed the mechanism, he was horrified to see that all the wires were the same colour—how in God's name to tell which was which; which one to snip to ensure that the bomb was made safe, so that he wasn't decommissioned, vaporised into a spray of chum. That endless moment, Though I do not fear to walk in the Valley of death ...

Sweating, tense, poised, heart pounding with adrenalin wakefulness, his mouth filled with coppery saliva Captain Collins dreamt over and over of making a fatal mistake, ending his days on Portland where he began. A dark master marionettist had Captain Collins dancing like a puppet on a string until he was drawn under the meniscus of sleep. Sound, feeling and light faded. And then he was back down the rabbit hole, ten years old again.

A heavy oak door closed with certainty behind him. The hall was large, oak panelled, the floor a chess board of foot square black and white tiles. Billy Collins, with trepidation in his step, proceeded along the hall drawn towards the staircase. At the foot of the staircase, he timidly gripped the banister understanding that the reason he was there was upstairs in this house he had never previously visited but that was also instinctively familiar. He paused before ascending the staircase, suddenly alerted to the swinging pendulum of the sentinel grandfather clock at the foot of the stair case.

With a shudder, he realised that it was large enough so that he could fit inside the body of the clock. And then he understood that it was in fact a clock made out of a coffin. He heard his grandfather's voice, 'Tick tock, time waits for no man, William Collins.' Quickening his step, now grasping the banister tightly he pulled himself up the stairs eager to be away from the clock, its voice and what it represented. He bounded up the last steps and the hall fell away into cloud in that way that happens when you climb the stairs in the dark and anticipate a last step that isn't there. And then Billy was falling.

The Captain woke on the creaking, single cot bed, his hands resting his sides. With his finger and thumb of his right, he squeezed the bridge of his nose to try to ease his tension away. He understood that a dreamless, restorative sleep was not in the offing on this of all nights. If he'd have been a betting man, which he wasn't as he'd left nothing to chance since he was a lad (the job having taught him that), he'd have put a tenner on where his dreams were taking him.

Since the call in London for this, his last job, on his home isle of Portland, the screws of the locked box of his childhood memories in the attic of his mind had been slowly unscrewing until now, back on Portland, the lid was loose, free and those thousands of thoughts, feelings, memories and other associations had pushed the lid off and out they escaped as if luminous genies escaping the confines of a lamp.

Again, another unfamiliar front door closed behind him, a key turning definitively in the lock, the latches and bolts, top and bottom, rattling shut too. The Billy Collins in his course haired knee length trousers and navy fisherman's tunic turned away from the door and took in the hall of the house before him. It was light and airy, again black and white chequered tiles leading to staircase with white banisters, a dark wood mahogany rail. Halfway up was a frosted glass window with stained glass, yellows, reds, greens and blues. At its centre was a blue disk, the picture of a three-masted, clipper type ship battling a tempestuous sea, a whale twisting and thrashing below it.

To Billy, as he climbed the stairs assessing the image, it seemed that both ship and whale were locked in an earnest struggle. He noted that outside, beyond the light was bright as if reflected off the sea. As the door had closed, he caught the scent of ozone, brine and kelp. He must have been near the sea. He shook away the thought and turned the corner of the stairs pulling himself up with a renewed energy, feeling the compulsion to find what he intuited he was supposed to.

At the top of the stairs, another well-maintained white-painted corridor. He'd never been somewhere so light and clean feeling. The stained glass window behind him caught the light which sent shimmering, coloured patterns on the paint work. There were three doors on either side of the corridor, all closed, but it was the one at the end directly in front him that called him, drew him. Tentatively, the polished floorboards creaking beneath him, he proceeded to the door.

He paused, summoning up courage and with an intake of breath, Billy turned the round, brass door knob and pushed the door open, his presence announced to anyone inside with an incongruous creak. This room was even lighter still. The room was round, as if in a tower with four tall windows uncurtained. The floor was wooden and again well-polished. Against one wall, with a table with a jug of water and cup on one side, a chair on the other, was a large metal framed bed. Billy squinted to be sure of himself. There was someone in the bed.

Billy crept forward, curiosity the better of him, fearful but determined to know who lay beneath the covers, all the while feeling as if he had ghostly palms on his shoulder blades pushing him forward. Arriving at the beds edge, arms dangling, tingling at his sides, Billy with a sense of dread pondered who it might be: faces flashed before his mind's eye, his mother, a dim memory of a man who may have been his father or grandfather, a fisherman from the dock? Mr Scriven? Were they alive? That incense-like, ambergris scent filled the room. Carefully, fearfully, Billy drew back the blanket. As he did so, the person beneath shuffled, roused to wakefulness. The person sat up, rubbing her eyes, blinking to focus. He took a step back, shocked.

'Billy, you came! I knew you would. I've thought about you every day. But I feel as if I've been sleeping for an eternity. But it's you, Billy! You! Oh, how I've missed you!' said a voice that Captain Collins had not heard for fifty years, but that Billy knew as perhaps the most comforting he had ever known.

Despite the shock, with the eyes of the Captain racing back through the decades, the moments previously sleeping person before was unmistakably Maggie Golding, his childhood and best friend he had ever had. With that,

Maggie flung her arms around him, squeezing and smothering his astonished body with a hug. She released him and looked him up and down.

'Why, you haven't changed a bit. Well, a few years older since I last saw you, you rascal!' Billy remained speechless, dumbfounded. 'Haven't you anything to say after all this time?' Maggie prompted.

Billy blinked and eventually stuttered, 'I didn't think I'd see you again. I'd, I'd, I'd given up hope, I suppose.'

With mock dismay, Maggie shook her head. 'Yea of little faith, as mother used to say! We're bound together. Always have been. And here we are again!'

'Where have you been, Maggie? Where are we?' struggled Billy.

Maggie looked pensive and then began, 'After what happened, after they shipped you off to Yorkshire. They sent me to Cornwall, near Zennor. They thought they had to separate us, to make sure the story never got out. Save the Admiralty the embarrassment, something to do with losing moral if the public knew what had really happened. That's why they sent you up there and me here. Three years I've been here. Nice enough, but I've missed mum, you, home, Portland. They've been good to me here and have given me a free rein. Out here, so far away from everything, there's nowhere to go. Next stop, the Scilly Isles! I guess that's why they sent you to Yorkshire too. Far away enough that the story couldn't get out.'

'I don't understand, Maggie.'

'Well, you don't change, do you, Billy? For someone so sharp, you can be really slow! There'll be time enough for all that. Not now though. Come on now, there's things we've got to do; things I've got to show you.' And with that, Maggie jumped out of bed as only children can just wakened from deep sleep. She took Billy's hand. She pulled him towards the largest of the windows.

Billy's body was resisting. She gave his arms a gentle but purposeful tug, 'Come on, Billy! Clock's ticking you know what time's like in sleep, years in the blink of an eye and we don't want anyone waking you up before we've done what needs to be done!' The look Maggie gave him left him with the clear understanding was that there was no choice and procrastination wasn't an option either.

Apprehensively, Billy asked, 'What are you showing me, Maggie?'

'What you need to see, Bill, of course! What you need to make sense of things before it's too late.' There was something knowing in her tone that seemed strange to him, unlike the Maggie he remembered. He felt the tinge of discomfort *when mocked. They'd always shared secrets and there had never been any between them. Complete trust had always been the mark of their friendship. That she seemed one step ahead of him somehow was disconcerting.*

After his experience of being 'evacuated' to Yorkshire, Billy'd developed something of a sensitivity of the unknown, a fear flinted-sharp with caution. But Maggie had always been a force to be reckoned with and he knew that he'd not be able to dissuade her once her mind was made up. That much he had always known and she of him too. Her frown wasn't working so she smiled a familiar smile and inclined her head to the window, 'Come dafty! Nothing to be frightened of. And we've got to get this job jobbed!' Billy smiled, remembering this was her mother's phrase she'd picked up. He allowed himself to be drawn to the window, to the light.

From here on in, events moved rapidly. Successions of images piled on images, some still, some moving and some that made fear surge through his chest and his heart beat like never before, tinged and tempered intermittently with elation, fear and everything else in between. They peered through the window. To begin, all was calm. They were on a cliff top, a short stretch to tufty grass leading to the cliff edge, a rocky enclosed horse bay below, sand at the water's edge and sea in all directions as far as the eye could see.

At the window, Maggie nodded encouragingly, 'Look, Billy, look!' she implored. Furrowing his brow, squinting in the bright reflected light, Billy scanned the horizon in the same way he'd done as a boy fishing in his skiff, mindful of squalls and quick shifts of weather. The sea was calm, iridescent fading away to the horizon and sky.

For the life of him, he couldn't see what he was supposed to see and it set off a frustration in him—that feeling of being mocked again. But he banished the perishing thought, knowing and trusting Maggie better than that, even if they were in what on some level he knew to be dream. And then his gaze slowed as he focussed on a small black triangular shape that had pierced the surface, miles off. His heart skipped a beat as the dark triangle grew. He couldn't put a size on it as it was about three miles off, he guessed knowing that the eye could only pitch the horizon as five miles off. What he did know, was that at that distance, it was large. Very large.

Excitedly, Billy pointed, 'A sail, sail!' He looked to Maggie for affirmation, but found none, just a shake of the head. They shifted stance and looked again.

'It's too big to be a Jerry E-Boat, Maggie. Wrong shape too,' he uttered, neither now taking their eyes off the dark shape.

'Not an E-boat, Bill, that's later,' she announced with that confidence again. The black sail appeared to be traversing back and forth between two points. How long for they watched was anyone's guess. This was dream time, but it held both their awe and fear. And then it happened. Slowly, whatever it was breached the surface in its entirety revealing what had lain beneath the surface. Billy had heard of them, he may even have paused on a page with a picture of one, but never had he seen one before.

Almost silently, Billy mouthed, 'It's a whale, Maggie. It's a whale! But it's enormous. Bigger than any ship I've ever seen!'

'It's not just a whale, Billy. It's the whale. It's the one we all saw in our dreams. You, me, your mother, my mother. We all dreamt of this whale. Same time same night. You must have dreamt of it since. You must have known it wasn't going to leave us alone?'

'I have dreamt of it. All my adult life, every few months it has come back to me.'

'You and me both. Our mothers too before they passed,' she added without emotion.

'But that whale was just a massive skeleton?'

'Yes, the one on the shoreline at Red Pool at Portland.'

'It was covered in strange symbols, hieroglyphs and scripts. In languages I'd never seen before. All of it was covered, as if carved. Over thousands of years, if it had been carved...? He trailed.

'Yes, Billy. But that's no concern of ours now.'

'But what was the writing? What did it say? What did it mean?'

Matter-of-factly, Maggie replied, 'They are religious texts. All the texts, all the beliefs and myths and legends of all the peoples of the world all recorded on the skeleton of the whale, of course. It's all our histories. Just watch now, Billy. It's about to happen. Quiet yourself.'

It made no sense. Billy stood transfixed, too incredulous to process what his friend had said. All his attention was on the terrifying majesty and size of the creature out to sea. To our eyes it looked somewhere between an orca and a baleen whale. But that was not apparent to the two friends for the moment. The creature continued to traverse unhurriedly between the two invisible points on the featureless sea as if restless, as if prowling, as if waiting for a moment.

After a time, it visibly began to move with more speed. Instinctively, Billy felt something monumental was about to happen. And then with a visible bow wave the creature turned and began to thrash its colossal tail to gain speed. White water sprayed with this new frenzied movement. Billy had a memory, as a boy, of the thrashing death throes and shudders of large fish he'd landed in the bottom of his skiff. The image infused with awe and regret as the silver fish turned through the spectrum of colours vanished. His attention fastened on the whale which was heading towards the beach below with gathering speed, its tale now thrashing ferociously, bow waves growing with each stroke.

A thought began to form in Billy's mind, 'What would happen when the whale beached?'

'Just watch, Bill,' Maggie mildly admonished, seemingly aware of his thought. The closer the whale got to the beach, now only half a mile away, the more the pounding and blood rushed in Billy's ears. His breathing quickened, his palms were damp. Closer, closer. Involuntarily, he moved into his friend. Without looking at him, Maggie threaded her arm around his waist. And then they were holding their breath. Billy started counting down in fathoms.

The whale was not slowing down, if anything it was gaining speed. Its huge, unreadable eyes gleamed. Twenty fathoms, ten, five and then with a final and massive flick of its tale, the whale launched itself on to the beach. Shock made both take a sharp, rasp intake of breath. A simultaneous, soundless white flash marked the beaching. Sunspots, green and blue danced in front of the children's eyes followed by a blankness until their vision reasserted itself.

'Look,' said Maggie, inclining her head to the beach. Billy did and there was the leviathan whale skeleton inscribed with the strange symbols and writings that had become familiar and as equally unfathomable to him. Billy looked at Maggie. He searched her eyes trying to derive some sort of meaning or understanding. As he looked into her green eyes whose irises were spotted with red and orange flecks, he noticed a yellow ring of sunburst around her pupils.

Billy's vision disappeared into the darkness of her pupils and he saw himself as his rightful age, sixty plus, as Captain Collins in his Royal Engineers uniform unscrewing the mechanism of the bomb, of the Satan that had been buried on Portland for 50 years as if waiting for him. He could see he was his patient, unhurried methodical self as he unscrewed the bomb's detonator and then he heard the click like a latch being drawn as the timing mechanism moved horribly into effect. Three seconds of life if that. This was it, the Captain's final moment.

Shards of fear erupted coursing through his chest, 'Oh my…!' he began and then came the inevitable, final, soundless white flash. And then, nothing.

Chapter 17
Some Things Don't Change:
The Scard Twins

'What? What!' he shouted. The light was blinding. Broken fragments of memory and dream fused together as he realised he was alive and looking at the bare light bulb above his bed. There was a hammering at the door. Someone was calling his name. He swung his legs out of the bed, noting he was still in his clothes. What time was it? Didn't matter. 'Yes, yes!' he growled, trying to shake sleep from his limbs and his mind. He staggered to the door. The knocking was incessant and, just roused from sleep, irritating.

'Just give me a minute, Lapin, will you,' groused the Captain, turning the key in the lock, yanking the door open. The face that greeted him didn't make sense. It was Sapper Mike. It was an old face staring back at him. Similar age to himself, weathered, mottled with liver spots, the remaining hair on the side of his skull cropped short and neat. There was an expectant recognition in his eyes. The man was clearly waiting for the penny to drop. When it didn't, he looked the Captain up and down stood there unshaven, bewildered in his fatigues and white vest. It didn't help that Sapper Mike, appearing as spritely and bright as a polished button, had loomed into view looking quizzical about the racket.

'Christ, Billy! Don't you recognise me?' nodded the man encouragingly.

Glancing from the young to the old, Captain Collins paused, giving himself time to gather his wits and stepped forward with an outstretched hand to engage his old friend and reassure him that he was still in command of his faculties and uttered, 'Paul Scard! Well, I never!' They clenched hands, white knuckle and sinew, and shared a keen look in the eye. Captain Collins clapped his old friend on the arm for good measure, released him and stood back in silent appraisal. He was shorter that the Captain by a head, but wider across the shoulders and both shared a barrel-chestedness that illustrated a life of fitness and showed a commitment to their want to never wither despite their heading to their sixth decade apiece. Sapper Mike thought it was the second guard on the gate, in the hut, that the Captain had uncharacteristically given short shrift.

'Billy Collins, my goodness me! I knew it was you from the first instant! I was at the door in the meeting when I spotted you. Couldn't believe my eyes after all these years. I doubted myself for a moment. But that faraway look you had in your eyes is unmistakable. Away in dream, no doubt!' cajoled the Captain's old friend.

It took the young Sapper a little by surprise to hear someone being so familiar with the Captain that he felt comfortable taking the whatsit. They must have been close and it seemed the intervening fifty years had just fallen away before them. As the Captain wasn't quick with a rejoinder, the stocky man continued, 'Gave Pete something of a lash of the tongue on the gate, so I hear? It was him that mentioned it. When we sat down for a brew, he says, 'Some rude bastard from the bomb squad just gave me a bit of verbal. But the funny thing is, I could have sworn it was Billy Collins!'

'Of course, we've not seen or heard hide nor hair from you in the last fifty years. Word travelled back on the jungle drums that you survived the war somewhere up north and joined the Royal Engineers. As we'd heard nothing since, we feared that you might be scattered in little pieces somewhere. But no! Here you are larger than life!' And turning to Mike, 'And so who's this whippersnapper you've got in tow, then?'

The Captain rubbed his cheek with the palm of his hand and introduced Sapper Mike who simply nodded a silent greeting as the two shook hands. Captain Collins scratched his head and put his hands on his hips and answered the young man's silent question, 'This is Paul Scard and his twin brother Pete was the guard on the gate I gave short shrift to. We grew up together on the isle. And never a more perilous pair of buggers could you have ever cared to meet. If ever there was a scrape to be scraped, Peter and Paul always in the middle of it!'

'Only if you hadn't got there first, Billy,' added the Scard Twin. 'Bet he didn't tell you that, lad, did he? Christ, if there was mischief to be had!' He shook his head in happy reminisce, before continuing, 'So, you've worked out the difference between Pete and I after all these years? Perhaps you have learned with age!' An ever present glint of banter in his eye.

Sapper Mike had the impression that the Captain's old friend probably never spoke without sparring. Life was probably like one long verbal joust for him.

He'd met others like that in the Engineers. Chatty buggers, every one of them. He wondered if it had something to do with having siblings? And a twin to boot. God, they'd have had to fight to get the attention. Maybe that was where it came from.

'Nearly fifty years, Paul,' trailed the Captain.

'That it is, Bill. And you look don't a day over …' it was the Scard Twin's turn to trail off. Reciprocal eyes twinkled as they enjoyed the banter. They continued their silent appraisal. Countless genies escaped and rekindled after life times in the lamps of memory.

And then to anchor them back in the here and now, Captain Collins continued, 'So, you opted a public service too, Paul.'

'Yes, Bill. Well, I never could stand the smell of fish, so that was out. Quarrying wasn't my cup of tea. So, it was either work in the prisons or see the world with the Royal Marines. And that I have. No-brainer, really. Paul did too. As luck would have it, we've hardly been apart. All over the world wherever the curtain went up for a theatre of war. The Scards were there delivering the good news.'

Sapper Mike noted that he emphasised the euphemism with a piratical guffaw and how the Captain simply nodded, ingesting, understanding the gravity of such a simple statement—the enormous intensity of experience that went with such an understatement. Sapper Mike salted it away and added it to his list of other blithely-used-played down, every day public service sayings such as, 'having a bad day at the office' meaning being unexpectedly atomised by a wrong move diffusing a bomb. That one still made him shudder.

'Bet you've seen your fair share of that too, Bill? A little hairy on occasion too what with all the IEDs (improvised explosive devices) that are doing the rounds these days, eh? Nothing like the dependable Jerry technology you've got to deal with up on Portland now,' he joked.

Sapper Mike could have sworn the Captain paled for an instant before he returned with a sharp edge, 'There's never been anything straightforward about Jerry technology. Lethal then, lethal now,' all friendliness removed from his tone, his expression grave.

The Scard Twin took half a step back in confusion, his already rugged face creased with perplexity before he continued, unwilling to be put off stride by a rebuff, 'Not long now though, Bill. Paul and I retire at the end of the month.'

'You, too, eh Paul? This is my last job before I hang up my boots and pliers.'

'I thought you weren't supposed to announce what was to be your last job as BDO? Not wanting to tempt providence and jinx yourself?'

'You think I believe all that superstitious hogwash, Paul? Haven't got time for it. WYSIWYG. What you see is what you get. And if you don't see it. You deserve what follows!'

'Well, maybe you don't now. But we all did back in the old days. You well know that you couldn't meet a more superstitious bunch of buggers as Portlanders!'

'I guess the job drummed all that out of me,' added the Captain but it was clear that neither the Scard Twin nor Sapper Mike were buying, particularly Mike after the less than reassuring journey down to Portland. An awkward silence followed as the Captain about-faced and walked back into his room and began putting on his shirt and woolly pulley. Sapper Mike and the Scard Twin exchanged a look and shrug as they watched the Captain lace and buff his boots and wet and rake a comb through his hair, side parting as per. Shipshape and amazingly without a crease out of place, the Captain turned on his heel, backed out of the door without so much as an excuse me, locked it, pocketed the key and marched off, all purpose.

'Better get to breakfast, ladies. Early bird and all. Can't think on an empty stomach!'

Sapper Mike raised his eyebrows to himself and followed the Scard Twin who was muttering something along the lines of, 'Still not the full shilling, then!' On the way to the Mess hall, Sapper Mike digested the comment. Over the last 12 hours, with all these other sides to the Captain presenting themselves, he was having a serious concern about the old boy. It was all a bit queasy. Christ, was he fit to command the unit? Let alone doing the damned job himself?

Doubt spread like ink through water. No matter how diluted it might become, he'd now always know it was there. The burden of a realisation poured down through him like mercury through a timer, Should he express his concern to a senior officer? That would feel like a betrayal of a friend though. But what if he was putting his and other's lives at risk? Would he be laughed at? Would they take the word of the most junior officer in the unit over the reputation of the most senior? And not only that, possibly one of the most respected senior officers in the Royal Engineers of that era. Oh, hell! This was going to be hard.

The clack of boots on the Mess hall parquet floor snapped him out of it. Crockery clink and the fug of full Englishes brought him back in the room. With all the questions flapping around his head, he just pointed at the scrambled eggs, bacon and whatnot he wanted and walked over to join the Captain who was grinning with a mouthful of food as he'd now been joined by the other identical twin, Peter.

The Scard twins were, in fact, eerily identical. Age hadn't changed the mould as is often the case. Though Sapper Mike wasn't in the mood for marvelling at the wonders of biology and genetics. Putting his tray down, he knew he'd come to his decision. He wasn't comfortable in it. And it smacked of procrastination, but he'd decided that for the time being, he would just keep an eye on the Captain. Fortunately, with the promise of food came a return to good humour.

Sapper Mike tuned in and out of the conversation, quiet content to mull things over and get stuck into breakfast. The other three were pretty much oblivious to his presence as they shared reminisces. All three were animated and on form despite the early hour. They guzzled and slurped and laughed, despatching breakfast with gusto. They hardly paused for breath. As one finished recounting one tale another took up the baton. He couldn't have got a word in edge ways, even if he'd wanted to. But it was nice to see. The Captain seemed like his old self, relaxed, in command of himself, perhaps even more in the company of his boyhood friends.

Sapper Mike marvelled at how they'd simply clicked back into a communication that meant that the intervening half century might only have been a few seconds. The thought occurred to him that he hoped he'd have this sort of rapport and stock of memories to share when he was their age, if he got to their age. Another sobering thought paused his fork before his mouth as a very rational part of his mind asked the question, 'What are the stats of survival for a BDO? And what were they compared to other professions in the army?' Suddenly, the sausage wasn't as tasty as it had been.

'You alright, lad?' asked the Scard twins in stereo unison. All three were staring at him.

'You look a little pale there, Mike? You fit, lad?' asked the Captain who rested an elbow on the table and took an emphatic slurp from his mug of tea.

Before he had a chance to reply, Paul Scard, who had noticed the Velcro tab across Mike's surname on his pullover, was leaning forward with the obvious intention of pulling it off when the Captain leant forward and rapped an eggy fork on Paul's knuckles.

'Ouch, you bugger. That hurt!' Irritation and injury scoring his forehead.

'Sorry, Paul! Just there's been a lot of that in the Mess back home. Spelling's wrong on the stitching of his name. Mike's surname is, er … Ratt. Which is bad enough as it is. Except the stitching says 'Pratt', to add insult to injury! Some wag in production having his fun no doubt.'

The lie was unconvincing, but the twins seemed satisfied with that and whistled what appeared to be a choreographed intake of breath, nodded and got back to their polishing off their breakfast. Mike blinked a few times at the Captain in an attempt to conceal his disbelief and averted his eyes back to breakfast, thinking, 'And there it is again: surely these people aren't doolally enough to think that my name, Lapin, is enough to jinx a job?'

Clearly, the Captain still seemed to think so. Mike had thought it must have been some sort joke, a ruse. But given the Captain's swift reaction and lies, he had to cast that firmly into doubt. And then he felt a spike of anger towards the Captain—which might have been a first. 'Christ, it's not my name which might jeopardise the disarming of the bomb; it's that old duffer's peculiar behaviour, for goodness sake!' Best keep that to himself. He redoubled his concentration on the task at hand. Eggs.

Chapter 18
26 April 1944: Two Days before Operation Tiger

Maggie drained off the last of her tea and set the enamel cup deliberately on the kitchen table. The Davey lamp on the table cast the only light save for the orange embers aglow in the fireplace. Occasionally, the burned out grey coals would collapse into dust, ashen-spent. Earlier on in the evening when the fire was first lit, the salt in the driftwood crackled and spat, sending burning embers arcing out into the room or a 'stranger', a wisp of black butterfly ash, out into the kitchen to rest on the flagstone floor, extinguished. These were said to be 'strangers' sent from the spirit world to augur a change or calamity. Two floated out of the fireplace and danced whimsically around Maggie's bowed head. Mother and daughter affected not to notice, but their eyes met fleetingly, knowing. Maggie then watched as Sarah Golding turned towards the window and parted the curtain a fraction.

'More or less a cloudless night, Maggie. Plenty of stars and the moon looks to be three-quarters full. You'll have to fade into the shadows to keep from being seen. The wind's getting up too, so wrap up. Don't want you getting a chill out there. Find hollows in the grass to lie in on the bluffs out of sight, out of the wind on the way to the rock. Then you know the dip at the top of the rock.' She was speaking into a half inch parting in the blackout curtains at the window.

Then she turned to look at her daughter sat at the table. Adrenalin, keening all her senses, made her tingle, sharpening her acute in readiness, crackly alert in anticipation. But to look at Maggie, you wouldn't know it. So naturally self-contained was she. Maggie had perfected dumb innocuousness at school, something Billy, who was all impulse and energy, had not. Scriven had had his uses.

'Now, on your way out to Pulpit Rock, keep low and close to the walls out of sight, hood up. And if you come across Mr Scriven, a Home Guard or an Ami patrol, go to ground, eyes down so the whites of your eyes don't reflect the light. Don't move till they're well out of earshot. In fact, count to a hundred in your head till they're gone to make sure there's a good space between you and them before you make a move. The shadows are your friends, maid.' Maggie nodded once, her silent assent.

'Now remember, Maggie, you've got to be absolutely sure that what Billy says are out there, really are there. The clock is ticking. If there are German E-boats in the Channel, they could wreak havoc with all the manoeuvres going on. Something big is in the offing. Jerry's onto it and getting bold.'

'Billy thinks they may be painted funny to make them more difficult to see, mum.'

'Really? Well, I wouldn't put anything past anybody in this war. Never underestimate an adversary, Maggie. That way, you'll never be surprised. And judging by the whispers coming from the Continent, anything is possible. The Germans are ruthless and clever.

'Now, if Mr Scriven and the Home Guard watch have missed what Billy has seen, there could be all manner of trouble. We'll have to go and present it to the Amis and Naval Command. No two ways about that, it's our duty for the War effort. There will be trouble for us. You mark my words. But there is no alternative given all the lives at stake.'

For a moment, noting the acceleration in her mother's speech, Maggie wondered if her mother was nervous. A show of nerves? Now, that would have been way out of character. Maggie shooed away the idea and replied, 'I know where to go and what needs to be done. I'll be fine, mum!' imagining and echoing how Billy might have put if he was there. Sure of his ground, away from school, his courage made him positive, definite—*always, all ways,* as he put it.

Sarah noted her daughter's steel. Her eyes brightened and, with a smile, she complimented her, 'That's my girl! I'll stop rattling on, now. You go on now and do what you've got to do.' For Maggie, the echo of her own words was reassuring.

'Yes, mum!' her daughter replied with a self-conscious-sort-of-salute, tucking her chair soundlessly under the kitchen table. Maggie took her duffle coat off the hook on the back of the kitchen door and buttoned herself up, collars up, hair flicked up and over in one motion. She'd watched her mother carefully and mimicked her habits in many other ways too.

'Hood up now! Go and be lucky, Maggie. As soon as you're sure, get home quick. If we're as sure as Billy is confident, there may be more Home Front and MPs about and they won't take kindly to us girls being out and about doing a *man's work*!' Sarah Golding emphasised her last words and rolled her eyes in mild irritation, but not without a reciprocated flat smile of humour, their shared amusement.

And with that, Maggie quietly and carefully, with a feline stealth, slipped the latch and was out into the night, into the buffeting winds that were constant and as reassuring as sunrise on Portland. The wind pressed heavy on the oak door desperate to fill the kitchen. As Maggie left, the shadows danced from the Davey lamp and stilled. Sarah Golding took the door in both hands to steady it before it slammed in the draught and shut it carefully after watching her brave little girl take off low, down the lane.

Sarah placed her forehead on the door. Such a brief prayer that her daughter would not be discovered and allowed herself a brief moment of concern. Climbing Pulpit Rock took audacious soul daytimes in the calm, let alone with half-gale gusts in the dark. Sarah Golding extinguished the lamp and the thought. *No good worriting. What'll be will be,* she mused, making her progress upstairs, through the dark, by touch alone.

The three-quarter moon was rising in the southeast, turning the uneasy sea to pewter before delivering its alluring path and promise of silver. A south-westerly with occasional menace buffeted the grasses flat. Loose rigging on the masted skiffs down at the water whistled and clacked and stilled ominously. The events of the next forty-eight hours would pull the weave of the lives of the Collinses and Goldings apart.

Concentrating on her task, her role in the play of events, Maggie Golding kept low to the shadow of the small holding walls and quarry pits where the islanders grew, grazed or carved a living. In her mind, Maggie saluted Billy as she scuttled passed Old Sea Dog Cottage, wishing her friend was with her for company and courage. Billy's reaction to unforeseen events and challenges was spot on, instinctive. They were a good team of two—she was reason, he was response. She reined him in when Billy's natural risk taking needed tempering. He inspired her out of over caution.

Billy's sometime impulsiveness and apparent lack of a sense of preservation had put them in a few awkward spots, particularly out on the water. True enough, he sailed closer to the wind than most in all things, but he'd never put her in harm's way. No question of that. And that was what made her confident in him and what made him need watching over too. If only he was here now! She knew he'd be fidgeting like a ferret on a scent worrying about her. Low and bold, Maggie made her way to Pulpit Rock. This was her chance to prove herself to him. That night, she was taking the helm.

Billy had told her to make for the Rock, risky as it was, being pretty much beneath the lighthouse. That it hadn't shone its reassuring beam since the blackout began made it no less of problem. At one hundred and thirty five feet high and striped red and white, people were drawn to it like a totem. The Amis parked up there in the shadow of it nightly on their patrols ready to catch Wrasse fishermen making for the Rock.

Pulpit Rock was the highest point on that part of Portland headland. It had a view due south to Cherbourg, France and South West down the Channel. If those German E-boats were out there, their menace of destructive potential would come from that direction, Billy reckoned. Maggie had to remind herself to stop thinking about what Billy would do and concentrate of what she was doing in the here and now. She'd nearly made it to the lighthouse.

Though Maggie had caught the scent of tobacco smoke moments before, she was so intent on keeping low that she nearly ran headlong into Mr Scriven who was leaning into the cab of an Amis MP jeep with its distinctive white stars on the bonnet and doors. The more he leant in, the more the driver leant back. She'd been thinking, not concentrating. She had to empty her mind of her thoughts. She was glad of the discomfort of the wall against her shoulder blades, pinned as she was to it now, breathing into her lapel to dampen the sound of her excited breathing. She stole a glance. They were there in the shadow of the lighthouse. Beyond them, the moon's silvery path led out across Chesil Bay to the dark horizon.

Fortune smiled on Maggie that night. The winds had swung around and being downwind of them her gravelly scrunch had been carried away rather than towards the MPs who also just fired up the noisy diesel engine, evidently about to leave. She hated that nauseous stink. That and the cloying fug of the smokes the three of them had lit up another. And on a third light too, she noted. Dead as doornails they'd have been, Billy would've said, had he been there. She didn't know why he said that, but she knew it was something to do with his grandfather who had been emphatic about it after he came back from the First World War.

Maggie made a mental note to ask Billy to explain it to her, by way of calming herself as she sat with her back against a wall with her heart pounding out of her chest. Thank God she'd kept to the field side of the wall as Billy had advised rather than on the track. The other side, she'd have been caught for sure.

As her adrenalin spiked with fright, her senses tuned back in, Maggie heard that hollow-confident laugh of Scriven's as he tried to ingratiate himself with the ever cheerful Amis in the jeep. My God! He was telling them where Billy lived and his *laughable* account of there being German E-boats in the bay. So, it was common knowledge now, Maggie mused.

'No such thing as too careful though, sir!' twanged one of the American servicemen amicably.

'As if!' replied Mr Scriven, attempting to conceal his contempt and querulousness. The Amis exchanged a querying look. But, not to be deterred, Mr Scriven continued with what he hoped for was a complimentary tone, 'With all that American steel in the bay!' And then preening, 'Besides, I'd have spotted them long ago if there were. Stupid brat doesn't know his *Kreigsmarine* from his Kartofel salat!'

'Right, sir!' They twanged in bemused unison and then, 'We'll swing by Old Sea Dog cottage, then. Make sure all's quiet and he's indoors safe. Goodnight, sir!'

Mr Scriven watched them pull off in a fug of diesel fumes, heading up to Fortuneswell to Old Sea Dog Cottage to check Billy was not breaking the curfew. He wouldn't have heard they refer to him as a 'dumb Limey'. Oblivious, Mr Scriven raised his right arm in a self-conscious salute-wave, irritated that the Americans should be more concerned for the boy's apparent stupidity.

Maggie turned her cheek, terrified he'd sense her and fix her with that prehistoric gaze of his. A salty gust scorched her face and a teary glaze formed over her eyes, so she straightened her back against the wall and drew her knees up to her chest protectively.

From only six feet away, the other side of the wall of the cross roads, Maggie heard Mr Scriven begin a hacking, coughing fit that went on for far longer than should have been healthy. Finally, he concluded his repulsive respiratory issue with a retching hawk and spat over into the field where Maggie hid. She closed her eyes as she grimaced. *Disgusting.*

Then quite clearly, in a lull in the wind, Maggie heard her teacher, Mr Scriven complain, 'Bloody Yanks, cocksure with all their flipping kit, manners, chocolate and tights. How bloody degrading to have to rely on the likes of them.' The charm of moments before was flat gone. There was a breath-taking, acid-coldness in his tone.

A tremor of confusion passed through Maggie Golding. She couldn't marry up this vitriolic statement with the friendly exchange she'd only heard moments before.

'Not the time to be fathoming contradictions,' she reminded herself, remembering her mother's counsel. 'Focus on precisely what you need to and banish all other thoughts.' *Focus*, she chided quietly in her mind.

At that moment, the withering ember of Scriven's flicked fag-end arced into the night air and distracted her from herself and then the choking fear as her heart nearly flew out of her mouth as Mr Scriven strode, scrunching past in his hobnailed boots, head up, not feet away from the brave little girl pulled up tight to herself on the other side of the wall. 'He has all the awareness of a stone,' she could hear her mother comment.

Eyes as wide as can be, whites fiery aglow, breath held as she watched him for a full minute of eternity, disbelieving her luck and grateful for his conceited self-belief.

She was fairly incensed by Mr Scriven's irresponsibility too, flipping his fag into grass that was blown bone-dry and brittle by the island winds. 'It could go up in a second!' she thought with a flash of anger. 'Then Jerry would have the perfect point of light to navigate by. Bloody fool!' Maggie slapped a palm to her mouth in embarrassment at her language. Then she smiled to herself, noticing the North Star.

'Time to do what needs to be done!' she encouraged herself.

Maggie waited until Scriven was a good hundred yards back up the track towards Fortuneswell, then she hopped over the dry-stone wall, careful not to dislodge the loose rocks at the top. She kept low, crouched in a run and continued to Pulpit Rock. She dragged a hand over the rough stone wall as she made her way, comforted by the sharp texture of the familiar touch. Maggie kept her focus and was not distracted by the luminous fireflies she spotted in the bracken and nooks in the wall. Usually she would have peered, mesmerised by their radiant, tiny glow, resisting the urge to cup the brittle, fragile creatures in her hands. Not now though, fixed as she was on getting to Pulpit Rock.

At the end of the track, past the lighthouse, Maggie Golding scanned the area for movement, a shadow of authority. She had to be careful of Amis MP foot patrols also. Billy said they could be a cunning lot waiting in the shadows until you were almost upon them before they made their move and rumbled you. They were good at their job. You had to give it to them.

Maggie waited a good few minutes until she was satisfied there was no-one about. She reasoned any foot patrol would have caught a lift back in the jeep back down off Portland. Nothing had stirred, so after a few deep breaths, Maggie broke her cover to quickly cross the open ground around to the seaward side of the light house. She had to move rapidly in a simian stooped-gait, right hand pumping to keep the stitch at bay, the left keeping Billy's binoculars from knocking against her chest. She had to get to the bluffs at the water's edge, the part mined eight foot step that marked a no-man's land between Bill Quarry and the lashing waves below.

Nearly there, Maggie hopped in a zigzag fashion as Billy had taught her over the last rocks before the step, half expecting to be paralysed by a beam of torchlight or an angry shout. But all she heard was the endless roar of the surf battering the cliffs around Pulpit Rock and the relentless draw, drag, and crash of the waves endlessly shifting tonnes of pebbles at a time on Chesil Beach. The awe-inspiring sound was both a comfort and something fearful. Familiar but frightening also: if the sea could shift thousands of tonnes of rock, it would have no qualms dashing her about like balsa and drowning her in the kelpy, black water at the foot of the rock.

And with these thoughts roaring like a cloud of butterflies in the back of her mind, she'd made it to the bluff. Maggie turned herself around to lower herself down the eight foot step. She extended herself to her full length to minimise the distance she had to fall, paused to steady herself as she'd seen Billy do a thousand times and then let go. As she landed, she lost her footing on the uneven surface and fell backwards painfully on her backside. The pain that shot through her hip flashed white in her mind, her eyes filled with painful tears and an acidic taste of fear filled her mouth. She swallowed it away, thinking of Billy and his indefatigable courage.

Lifting herself gingerly on her knees, she checked to see that nothing was broken, then she plotted a path across the bluff, close in to the shadow of the bluff out to Pulpit Rock. She had one more 'challenge' to face and that was the narrow Causeway over the broiling sea some sixty foot below which was nerve-racking in the daylight, let alone in the dark in the rising winds.

The pain in her hip had sharpened her caution. She was all careful adrenalin now. With it came a confidence as she bounced across the Causeway and the swirling whorls of sea below that would have smashed her against the rocks before drowning her quietly, alone with no-one to hear her fear. However, before she could begin to process her thoughts, she was at the base of Pulpit Rock, exhilarated, breathless.

Now the *only* thing left was climbing thirty metres to the top of the Rock and her lookout spot. Maggie prayed that she would not freeze mid-rock as she'd done the first time she'd made the climb. Unable to feel the next handhold, she had found herself limpet-clinging to the rock face, paralysed with fear. Not wanting a repeat, Maggie had shared her worry with Billy who, after the usual pause while he thought things through, brow furrowed in a way that, to those who didn't know him, made him look a little hostile, gave his best suggestion.

'Take a mo, Maggie, to map a path in the footholds cut into the Rock, so you know where you are going to plant your hands and feet. The moon is three quarters full and there should be enough light from the east to cast shadows in the foot holds so you can see them. When you're happy you know where you're going, just do it. Don't think about, don't hurry but be as quick and sure-footed as possible. No big stretches and don't stop for doubt!'

As she looked up at the chiselled foot holes in the rock, Maggie played back through Billy's counsel and when she was satisfied with her route, she climbed the rock face in a series of fluid moves—a single purpose of mind pausing momentarily only to catch her breath an feel for her next handhold. Like a gecko, tick-tack, tick tack and up. She was there. Half-amazed at herself, Maggie scrambled over the top of the rock, keeping low and mindful that she was over 60 feet above the broiling rush of water and rocks.

It was the optimum lookout point which meant it was about as windy as it got on Portland. And then did it gust, hellishly. Her hair whipped at her eyes and face, folded into her mouth and wrapped around her and like a giant's arm her waist tugged at her distinctly three times, each followed by a pause. It was only a matter of seconds that stretched into physical ordeal. At least it was reassuring that the gusts hadn't hit minutes before as she might well have lost her hold on her ascent and plunged to the base of the cliff. *There for the grace of God go I,* she panted.

187

Instinctively, Maggie flattened herself face down, pinned flat so that the wind had less purchase but not before she got a sickening, vertiginous, snatch of glance at the whorls of roiling sea, foam and black kelp lashing beneath her. Flat on her belly she inched her way to a depression scalloped out of the rock and squeezed herself down and in, glad to be a little out of the wind and waited for her breathing, pulse and thoughts to calm.

What can you see, Maggie? Came Billy's voice. Chesil Bay stretched out before her for eighteen miles she knew. In the daylight, the horizon was five miles away, much less that in the dark. She wondered how far the naked eye could see in miles in the moonlight? Had to be less, she told herself. That meant that if she could see them, the *enemy boats were within five miles of Allied Operation Tiger*. That was what the Admiralty had to know.

If she was going to prove those German E-boats were out there, this was the spot from which she could do it. Maggie reminded herself of her mantra of purpose as she pulled her overcoat tight to her, collar up to keep out the draughts. She methodically identified the ships at anchor in the bay as best she could and took sips of water waiting for routine to regulate her being. 'Enough for thirst, not enough to pee!' her mum had warned.

With Billy's binoculars, Maggie scanned and waited and scanned and waited. Every ten minutes, she noted the time by her mum's pocket watch and wrote the time with a stub of pencil in her little notebook that was usually kept for drawings, thoughts and descriptions of her dreams. Her mum had suggested it as a way of making a routine to stay awake. Also, if she did see the E-boats, they would have a time and direction log which could help guestimate the distance they had to travel to attack and therefore for 'our boys', as Billy called them, to prepare for attack.

It was now going on for two in the morning and would have been nigh on pitch black, were it not for the moon which was about overhead now. Maggie Golding half lay, knees up in nook at the top of Pulpit Rock, careful to keep those knees in the moon shadow, out of sight of the Amis MP's and the Home Watch. As Billy had put it, 'the only thing wrong with the best of lookout points is that, if you're not careful, everyone can see you too!'

Being at the highest point of lower Portland on the rock, Maggie would be at the optimum vantage point for looking out for those Jerry E-boats, as Billy called them. 'Always the other side of the coin to consider, always another way of looking at things,' she thought as she scanned the pewter, moon-blown waters beneath her. Maggie noted the couple of constellations that her mum had pointed out and put names to. The Bear and Orion's belt were the easiest to spot. Orion's belt was that the one that got her. Three stars in an almost straight line. The middle star a half an inch out to the naked eye, but millions of light years according to the 'physicists' whatever they were, mum said.

For a good hour, Maggie kept an intense vigil, fairly prickling with the twitches of adrenalin scanning and re-scanning the horizon, the binoculars clamped to her skull giving her an odd, other worldly shadow in the silvery light. Unlike every night for the last week, Chisel Bay was quiet. Operation Tiger seemed to be taking a rest, she thought with a half chuckle. Sleeping Tiger, beautiful, to be respected and awed, rather like the half dozen silhouettes of frigates and the destroyer anchored a three quarter mile out of Chisel Bay, listless at anchor, ominous angular man-made shapes set against the curves of nature. On the shoreline were dozens and dozens of landing craft as far as the eye could see.

Charcoal drawing of the silhouettes of the landing craft, frigates and the destroyer

Seeing nothing, and not with a mild sense of frustration, Maggie let the binoculars rest on her chest, quite exhausted by the evening's intense activities and unrequited excitement. In spite of the buffeting sea winds there atop Pulpit Rock, she felt the warmth of drowsiness flicker her eyelids. Annoyed with herself, Maggie adjusted her position to set the circulation going again in her legs, raising herself up a little, but not so much as to be out of the shadows.

Nothing shifted or stirred for the first couple of hours. As her adrenalin ebbed, the cold from the wind and the rock pressed into her bones, through her hips and ran across her shoulders causing involuntary shivers and occasional teeth chatter. It was a north-easterly wind, perhaps down off the Russian Steppes, and had a bite to it that got into her knees. Maggie got herself into the routine of shifting her position every few minutes, nibbling on the crusts of bread her mother had filled her pockets with and scanning the horizon with Billy's binoculars.

But by the close of her third hour of vigil, when she had observed no discernible activity, Maggie wondered if she was on a fool's errand. Her mind drifted and her confidence tugged on its mooring. Outrightly, she dismissed Mr

Scriven's denigrating assessment of Billy 'that he had a fanciful, overactive imagination and would never be useful to man or beast. And certainly not credible.' That was how he described him to the Amis in the jeep. Out of the classroom, you couldn't hope to meet a more practical, smart young man as Billy—forever swift and sure-footed.

That incident with the rotting whale, just days ago, had put a shadow of doubt in her mind, she had to admit. Had their eyes deceived them about these E-boats? Had Billy got it wrong? And then, while examining the binoculars almost as if to check for a fault in the lenses, Maggie slapped herself on the thigh to dispel the doubt gathering on the periphery of her mind. *Billy was her best friend.* She had seen the E-boats with her own eyes. But still the shadows of doubt had grown long. Mr Scriven was the School Master and Head of the Home Watch. His father had been the Sherriff of Portland, surely he was an authority figure to be trusted?

'For goodness sake!' she chided herself, 'I saw those dark shapes with my own eyes, with *these* field glasses. Billy's grandfather's field glasses.' She exhaled, feeling more than a little guilty for doubting Billy.

But with that, Maggie heard the unmistakable rumble of one of the larger ship's engine firing up. *What was going on?* Without the aid of Billy's field glasses, Maggie saw the plumes of smoke flare and spark from the main stack of the destroyer, guarding the Amis flotilla, Operation Tiger. There were a couple dozen or so landing craft anchored, low and sleepy in the water, close and large enough to see without the field glasses.

Maggie hurriedly counted and recounted the landing craft as the dawning shadow light played tricks with her vision. Maggie settled on a figure of fifty or so landing craft. And there must have been nigh on triple that safe in the lagoon in Portland Harbour if the gossip be believed. It was now getting on for gone four AM, or 0400 hours as Billy put it in his newly adopted 'marshal-mission manner'. She'd giggled when he'd said the time in this way when he'd described her 'mission', which route to take to Pulpit Rock; how to avoid the Amis and the Home Front by waiting until 0100 hours; and the times, usually around 0500, an hour before dawn, in the light just before the shadows of night faded and played tricks on you.

It had been around that time when two nights previously he'd seen what he was convinced were the fast attack, German E-boats. The 'E' stood for *enemy.* Maggie had been nodding seriously, but she found something amusing in the phrases of 'O' few hundred hours. It just sounded funny, Billy saying it. Too grown up or something. She supposed it might have been nerves at the thought of breaking the curfew; being caught and confronted by Scriven and the trouble she'd get into if she got caught by the Amis MPs or, God forbid, if she fell alone in the dark off Pulpit Rock. And she still had to get down off the darn thing— down and backwards was a whole lot worse than going down.

So Maggie had laughed, involuntarily, and then abruptly stopped at a wash of hurt. It was a flicker, there only for an instant blinked away as he reprimanded her, 'Stay sharp, Maggie. This isn't a game. There are lives at stake. We're doing this for king and country!'

She had quickly replied, 'Of course, Billy! Don't pay any attention to me. It's just nerves.' Clearly, why anyone would laugh when they were nervous was an enigma to Billy. Maggie had beamed encouragement back and the squall cleared. Her mind was drifting. She was finding it hard to keep on track, tired as she was.

When she looked up again, the destroyer was no longer on watch presenting its bow in silhouette. It had turned its stern to Pulpit Rock and was about a mile off heading southwest down to Plymouth, she supposed. Coke smoke from the stacks trailed behind it. It was quite a breath-taking, inspiring sight. And then it dawned on her—if the destroyer, *HMS Scimitar,* guarding Operation Tiger was leaving, those E-boats had an ideal opportunity to attack. Operation Tiger was as vulnerable as a kitten.

Oh, Lordy…! As her mouth opened, she caught a movement, a quick dark shape in the corner of her eye, causing her to raise the field glasses to her eyes with one hand, the other hand to her mouth as she spotted movement on the horizon due south. It was odd. They were there and then vanished. She peered through the field glasses then drew them away to look with her own eyes. She did this half a dozen times with growing disbelief. She couldn't help remembering leafing through one of her mother's books about Africa. And then she made the connection.

There were craft out there moving rapidly. They just didn't *look* like boats. She kept thinking zebra. Completely incongruous, but there it was. In the pre-dawn light, the white stripes caught the light. It was astonishing. She watched for a few minutes to be sure it wasn't a trick of the half-light. Astounding as it was, the enemy boats were there. Just as Billy had said, but what she was sure of was that they had been painted with black and white stripes. That had made them difficult to spot and even harder to ascertain how many there were. Maybe that was why Billy had doubted himself. But they were there.

There was no doubt about that now. Billy was right. So much for him being fanciful and useless! It seemed that Scriven was in fact all the things that he had said Billy was. *It was funny how people did that: accused other people of having of the faults they possessed.* Maggie didn't have time to consider that then though. But, Mr Scriven *had* missed this very definite threat. Maggie had to warn someone of the terrible danger. She scribbled the time, the direction, SSE of the E-boats, approximate distance 4 miles, number. Then she pocketed the notebook and morsels of food left over. She didn't want to leave evidence that she had been there.

Maggie Golding slipped, skidded down the rock blurred in a rush of excitement and fear, mindful that it was nearly dawn and the shadows were slipping back into the land. At that moment, the grey dawn light was not her friend. There were no shadows to keep to. If there was anyone on watch, now was the time she would be spotted. Down off Pulpit Rock, she then ran along the step until she was level with the lighthouse, then with no sign of man or jeep back up the track to Fortuneswell. The sky was brightening in the east. The sun had not yet come up, but as soon as it hit the horizon, she would be all too visible.

Gingerly, like a fox she traversed the island; Maggie kept to the seaward side the walls, between the huts, scanning for movement, careful to have cover between her and the north of island from where her trouble might come. She wasn't worried about the islanders; they wouldn't break with tradition and would keep shtum. It was the Amis and the school master she had to watch out for.

Passing Mr Scriven's cottage at the back of the school house gave her cause for concern but she'd planned a route home while on the rock to avoid it. Mr Scriven's cruel ways had made her wily.

Before she knew it, Maggie burst through her front door with an unexpected urgency that had her mother nearly knocking over her chair as she stood up from the kitchen table. Sarah Golding had been keeping her own anxious vigil. And with it still before six and the blackout blinds still closed, Sarah Golding had had no warning of Maggie's arrival, but she was soon in action, closing the door firmly shut. Open doors were evidence of activity and with sunrise still twenty-or-so minutes off, the curfew still very much in place.

Maggie gathered herself as she calmly removed her toggled-up duffle coat and placed it on the back of a kitchen chair. Sarah observed her daughter's calm and set about deliberately pouring their tea and buttering up the toast with jam, giving them both time to settle and be calm and speak without distractions. They both sat and took bites of the bread and jam followed by mouthfuls of tea to dilute the sugary taste, all the while keeping a watch on each other in anticipation. It fairly killed them to contain their nervous excitement, eyes a-shine. But with the toast finished, ready to talk freely, Sarah Golding began, 'I'm guessing by the look of things that Billy was right? You've been out so long! You didn't fall asleep, did you?'

'No mum! Have you ever tried to sleep on top of Pulpit Rock in a half gale?' she replied excitedly, unable to contain the news and her nervous tension. 'And yes, Billy *was* right!'

'You must be exhausted, Maggie! Well, you will be when the excitement ebbs.'

Maggie skipped, replying about herself and went straight to the story, 'Nothing happened for hours. No Operation Tiger activity. Must be a rest day or rest night. There's a half dozen or so boats moored up a three quarter mile out, with that ship with the massive guns being the biggest of them. But it was all quiet. And with that north-easterly, it was freezing too, not to mention uncomfortable up on Pulpit. My behind and legs kept going to sleep, had to keep shifting about to keep the blood flowing.'

'You must have been freezing! No rain, though, thank goodness. So, what happened?'

'Well, it must have been an hour ago. I was nearly dozing off when they fired up the engines on that destructor. The one that Billy said was named after … what was it? A sword?'

'It's a destroyer, darling! The big ship that is guarding the landing craft is called a destroyer! We've got to get this right if we're to be taken seriously.' And then, after a moment searching her memory, she exclaimed, 'HMS Scimitar! That's what it's called. I heard them talking about it on the quay. Sounded like it had had a collision yesterday with one of the American vessels and might need repairs…' she trailed as she recalled.

With a little exasperation, Maggie continued, 'Oh, mum! So, the engine noise of the destroyer caught my attention. I watched the smoke coming from the stacks. Just a little at first then great whorls of it echoing across the water. It felt like I was being hypnotised and when I looked again the destroyer had turned and was, *is* sailing away!' She trailed now, waiting for the significance to hit her mother. Her mother was staring with pensive intensity down at the kitchen table, her mind evidently at work.

It must have been important as her mother had risen up from her chair and planted her hands, palms flat down on the table. When she next spoke, she didn't raise her eyes. 'What happened next, Maggie?'

Maggie involuntarily gulped before she replied, 'Something caught in the corner of my eye. When I scanned the horizon with the field glasses, I spotted movement. At first, I wasn't sure what I was seeing. Whatever it was, it was striped like a zebra!' She paused to let this sink in.

'What?' Sarah Golding replied, suddenly unsure where the story was heading.

'They've painted the E-boats with black and white stripes, mum. Makes them really hard to see! Maybe a half dozen of them, just as Billy said. They seem to disappear and reappear.'

'So, the Germans have learned to camouflage boats at sea,' observed Sarah Golding.

'I didn't know you could camouflage ships at sea?'

'Neither did I, but if you can camouflage on land, I suppose you can at sea. Just takes a bigger imaginative leap.'

They both thought about this for moment before Maggie continued, 'It was kind of eerie the way E-boats appeared just as the destroyer had set sail. Almost as if they were lying in wait.'

'Oh God, Maggie, they might have been lying in wait like jackals. We've got to do something now!' This was the first time Maggie had even heard her mother use language like that. It must be serious! Maggie's mum's eyes had a startled watery look to them and she'd raised her hand to cover her mouth …

'They were what, mum?'

'The E-boats could have waiting been waiting for the destroyer to leave if they'd been eavesdropping on radio communications. Or they could have been on a reconnaissance mission. Either way, they know what you know now. The important thing is that they've seen what you have seen. The Kreigsmarine know that Operation Tiger has no guardian. With HMS Scimitar out of the picture, Operation Tiger is wide open to attack. There are no big guns to ward them off. With that sort of confusion, the entire navy is at risk too. They could sail right into the harbour and destroy the fleet like sir Francis Drake did the Armada at Cadiz. The Singeing of the King of Spain's Beard.'

In response, Maggie's mouth made a silent 'O', understanding the import if not the reference. All business now, straightening herself, Sarah Golding informed her daughter, 'I've got to go to the Admiralty, to the Amis, and tell them what you've seen!'

'But mum! You'll get a quarry load of trouble for this, it's still curfew for another hour yet. Can't they put us in the brig for this? And if Mr Scriven has anything to do with it, they surely will, mum!'

'I know, Maggie. This is going to be a bumpy old road of trouble for us. But better to beat a straight path with a crooked stick than…'

'Uh, what are you saying, mum? I don't understand.'

'We've got to be utilitarian about this. The greatest good for the greatest number.'

'What does that mean, mum?'

'It means that we are a few who know of the danger. People get it wrong. They make mistakes. Whole islands, towns, governments, armies, countries do. If the navy isn't aware of the E-boats, then they need to be, no matter how uncomfortable that may be for us. Hundreds of lives may be at stake. They are sitting ducks. And if half of the navy is destroyed, it could be the turning point in the … It's not just Portland that is in danger. It might bear the brunt, but this could have repercussion for the whole…'

'Sitting ducks, mum?' Maggie interrupted, foxed.

'Yes, sitting ducks … There's no time to explain now. We've got to be practical about this. It's not about us and *there will* be trouble. But that's just as may be. That's a small compromise considering what's at stake.'

Things seemed to have gone up a gear or five. To Maggie, it didn't just seem as if the Amis and Operation Tiger were in danger. Her mum seemed to be implying something far more serious.

'Oh God, Maggie! This could be Pearl Harbour all over again. If they have missed what Billy has seen, the repercussions could change the whole outcome of the war. They aren't going to like this one bit.'

Maggie tried to let the words and ideas settle in her mind. Her mother's countenance had changed from excitement, determination and focus to something that altogether had quelled her. Sarah Golding was ashen-faced, disconcerted. Maggie didn't understand the words her mother was saying, but she felt she got the gist of it and she had faith in whatever her mother would do. Sarah Golding, her mother who helped at the school and was known as the island sage that others would quietly come to with a problem, dispute or illness that the doctor could not right, would do the right thing. That was a given.

It was small comfort though. While reminding herself of her mother's good reputation with the islanders, with the people, Maggie understood that she did not enjoy the same rapport with the island's authority: the likes of Mr Scriven, the priest, the doctor, the sheriff. They were envious of her standing and suspicious of her ways and intelligence. She was a woman after all and an intelligent, fine-looking one at that, but still a woman.

Sarah Golding had watched her daughter process what she'd said and watched the notions settle like silver dabs in shallow water in the lagoon, flashing like mirrors sliding from the surface sunlight to the shadows and rivulets on the sandy bottom, assimilated.

'Oh darling! I've got to go *now*. I don't know when I'll be back or how this will play out. This is a lot greater than we first thought. I may not get to school today. But try not to worry too much about me. Go and get some rest and then go to Old Sea Dog Cottage and have some breakfast with Billy. He'll be dying to see you. They'll have tea and smoked herring, knowing them. I'll be back as soon as I can. You've done a very brave thing tonight and now it's my turn. I love you.'

Gathering her coat to put on as she walked, Sarah Golding left, leaving her daughter alone in the stillness of the kitchen. Maggie tried to settle. She thought about going upstairs, but she knew sleep wouldn't come. Her nerves were too taut. Company was what she needed. And so, for the second time that night, Maggie Golding broke the curfew and made for Old Sea Dog Cottage.

Chapter 19
Probability in 1992

Captain Collins had eventually dozed off about an hour before the alarm went off. Why did that always happen? He wondered, rotating his ankles and wrists under the blanket to try and rid himself of the aches of his age. *Time waits for no man, Collins*, came a voice from the past, from the mists of time in the back of his mind. Captain Collins quizzed himself, perplexed as to why the voice was so familiar, but filled him with unease and by the time he had laced up his impeccably polished boots, he had it.

That acrid, ammonia stink, that livid purple scar on his face, that academic gown flapping in the gusts as Mr Scriven stood by the school house door, slapped the back of young Billy Collins' head for his tardiness, because he'd been up and fishing, helping his widowed mother before school with a practical task. The injustice of it caused twists of emotion in him and suspicious of authority to that day.

The memory of it caused the bile to rise even now. *And how that old bugger made my life a misery back then*, Captain Collins reflected as he straightened his collar in the mirror, checking his jumper and trousers for fluff and lint. He looked himself in the eye, squinted with concentration and questioned himself aloud.

'What would you do if you met him now, Captain Collins? I know what Corporal Collins would have done!' He murmured, noting the whiteness of his knuckles.

Hearing the reveille rap on the door and the familiar young voice of Sapper Mike, 'Time, sir!' The Captain opened the door, nodded with a curt smile and carefully closed and locked the door behind him. Then, vigorously clapped his hands and enthusiastically rubbed them dryly together.

'Breakfast then, lad! Army marches on its stomach!' Every morning the same phrase, every morning the hand clap. Had it been anyone else, it might have been tedious. Sapper Mike was just happy there was no weirdness, though the old boy couldn't have slept a wink by the look of him. Cream crackered. No masking that, though he hadn't had the best of nights himself.

'Sleep, sir?'

'Like a baby, Sapper, like a baby,' the Captain lied. Not a wink, save for a last fitful minutes, had the Captain slept, staring at the ceiling assailed by the past, his childhood on the isle, on Portland. Awkward sepia stills of family members and old cinema film projector celluloid, ticking and whirring sequences of jerky hi-jinks and horror, all spliced together, grainy and bitty.

Try as he might, the Captain couldn't banish the questions that flash flooded his insomnia. There seemed to be no possibility of gagging his interior monologue, locking down his feelings with his rationale or simply focus on the job at hand: to diffuse the half-century-old bomb. By the sounds of the intel, the bomb *was* a Satan. How could it be anything else?

How many times in the last 24 hours had he reprimanded himself that it was just another job like any of the hundreds of others in his career that nigh on spanned a half century. But he couldn't rid himself of the feeling that it had been waiting there for him all this time. This bomb had been was his destiny. Dormant, buried until now. *Get on with it, Collins*!

What he couldn't escape was the central recurring query, why, when he'd decided that whatever, wherever the next job is it's going to be the last, did it have to involve a return to Portland? In Central London in a two-mile square of the capital where there were 40,000 known unexploded Second World War bombs. Goodness only knows how much unexploded ordnance lay in wait beneath tarmac, concrete and clay at other strategic targets like Southampton, Portsmouth, Plymouth, Bristol, Cardiff, Swansea before you even got to thinking about the Midlands and the North of England. What were the odds? Potentially, hundreds to one.

And as a man who enjoyed an occasional flutter on the ponies and dogs, who had spent a fair bit of time calculating the odds, Captain Collins knew that the odds on it being on Portland were hundreds of thousands to one. Then when you factored in the number of serving BDOs in the country in the Royal Engineers, the odds became absurd.

And to his knowledge, Captain Collins was the only BDO to come from Portland. His mother's words came back to him: *There's no such thing as coincidences, Billy. Everything happens for a reason.* Although he had scant remembrance of his mother, Captain Collins' memories were for the most part warm, reassuring and welcome. But today was another case entirely. *Probability, jeefreemoses!* It had just gained a whole new meaning.

Sapper Mike led them on into the Officers' Mess. A few tables were occupied by other staff, but it seemed that the Mess was almost solidly occupied by his unit who had all arrived before him. The Captain was not at all impressed with himself. He was usually the first to breakfast to greet his unit, as his head of unit had done for him—lead by example.

'The works, sir?' Sapper Mike asked as he surveyed the full English with chipped potatoes at the server. Reminded him of a family holiday in Butlins. When the Captain didn't reply, he ventured gamely, 'Army marches on its stomach, eh sir?' But again the Captain didn't reply as he surveyed the trays of eggs, sausages, mushrooms… all the rest of the usual fare.

'Not for me today, I think, Sapper. Just some coffee. I need something to keep me alert.'

'Really?'

'Yes Mike. Sort yourself out. I'll be over there by the window. And hurry up, Mike. The others are finished up ready to go by the look of it. Did we oversleep?'

'Yes, sir. I must have knocked about every five minutes for a half hour before you answered the door.'

'Good grief, that's not good at all. Must be all the ozone, all that sea air and oxygen making me heavy-headed.'

'Yes sir, that must be it,' Sapper Mike replied in a lacklustre fashion that wasn't lost on the Captain. The lad was beginning to have his doubts, the Captain could see that. Too many unusual behaviours, out of character for the young Sapper to contend with, for him to be able to maintain his total confidence in his mentor.

The Captain hoped that the rest of the unit hadn't got wind of it. It was a matter of self-preservation as much as anything, else in this high stakes game in which there was no margin for error, no margin for doubt. The Captain felt he could kick himself for his apparent dip in confidence, but on the other hand was impressed by the vigilance of the young man which affirmed to him that, when his time came, he would make a good leader. You had to be able to focus 110% on the job, but also keep an eye on the unit to make sure that nerves weren't getting the better of anyone.

A unit was only as good as its weakest link and if one link went, if one man couldn't be relied on to do his job, his particular tasks, he could endanger the lives of the rest of the unit and a bad day at the office for a Royal Engineers bomb disposal unit officer meant a very different thing than for a bank clerk or plumber.

As he gazed out of the window, Captain Collins understood that he had always been hardwired to be a risk-taker, a lover of adrenalin, a seeker of the high stakes game. As he thought about it now, supping his coffee looking over the naval dockyard, he could see that even as a child running barefoot over the cliff paths of Portland, cheating death by a matter of inches; tomb stoning off Pulpit Rock; putting to sea in his skiff in a risky south squall, pitting his wits against Mr Scriven—he'd always loved danger.

The possibility of it all going horribly wrong in the most dramatic of ways was never a thing he'd thought through then, he'd just never be able to escape the gamble of the high stakes game. The deed was all and he'd thrived on it. That's what had brought him to Ordnance Disposal even if he tried to conceal the truth with the appearance of order, discipline and care. It was the ragged, unpredictable appearance of danger that excited him, drew him in 'like the weather and the coastal shifts on the island, of Portland,' he conceded to himself.

It felt right as a conclusion, but any more than that, what that meant he couldn't fathom anymore. He supposed he'd been lacking a sense of self-preservation that others had in spades and who saw his fearlessness as courage and he'd enjoyed that reputation. It had in fact encouraged him all the more. Small comfort now though when he'd reached an age where he really cared not a jot to be seen as courageous and when he prided himself on his meticulous planning and calmness in the face of calamity. This morning though, his focus and concentration was shot. He couldn't keep a train of thought in a straight line. He felt reckless with adrenalin. He felt like he was ten years old again. How could that be?

The Year, The Night before Operation Tiger: The Massacre

At 6.45 am now, a quarter of an hour before the lifting of the blackout curfew, the sun was bright in the east, a dazzling gold disc resting on the horizon. But it was not quite a true daylight, for the low morning cloud was a grey, blue, pewter with an earthy brown in the palette also. Sarah Collins took in the familiarity in a blink and then noted how much darker the scene up at Fortuneswell looked. With no-one around, the houses all closed up, blacked out, dawn seemed a way off yet. The lack of activity was eerie.

These observations took away from the immediacy so that she didn't have time to fully register that familiar, acrid odour. But then came the surge of shock and adrenalin rose in her stomach as Mr Scriven suddenly loomed before her and roughly took her wrist in a cold, unyielding grip. Mr Scriven had planted his feet and let her momentum and his weight spin Sarah Golding towards him.

'What are you doing out during curfew, Miss Golding?' His eyes were dark and expressionless even if there were the vestiges of a cruel smile around the corners of his mouth. The scar tissue on the left side of his face twitched a tick.

Gather yourself, Sarah. Wait till the moment passes! she inwardly counselled herself. She locked him in an unflinching stare. Then she let her gaze drop to her wrist in his grip. Her demeanour was one of anger and outrage. When she felt him relax, she whipped her wrist out of his grip and studied his expression again. She thought, *This man has no good intentions, no kindliness of spirit whatsoever. He may be a colleague and of good standing in the community, but he shared no common sense of purpose. His want was to be right at all costs. His motivations were of self-interest only.*

What happened next, her words surprised her to her core. Sarah Collins spat with uncharacteristic venom and lack of measure that days later would make her wonder what else was she had that was hidden within her. Her vitriol was so potent that for that instant she hadn't recognised herself.

'Ten minutes before curfew lifts? Is that what drives you, Mr Scriven? The arbitrary enforcement of rules? Oh, you are a small-minded and unimaginative man! Base at that.'

In that moment, she felt as if she were trapped in a mirror regarding herself, a dark shadow of herself. Mr Scriven's eyes had widened with surprise and he had taken an involuntarily step back.

Meekly he had replied, 'What is it, Sarah? What's happened? What's the matter?'

'Sarah, now is it?'

He gave her a curious look then stammered, injured in some way, 'I was just concerned for you.'

And then he surprised himself by taking a voluntary step backwards as he registered what he could only construe as hate in her eyes. Sarah Golding's jaw had set unflinchingly, her eyes unblinking and she seemed to have grown taller in those brief moments. Mr Scriven's arms dangled ineffectually by his sides, the purple livid scarred side of his face began to spasm and Sarah Golding picked up that acrid-foul ammonia stink of him.

Sensing the power dynamic shift between then, even if unfamiliar, Sarah Golding took the initiative and took a step forward so that they were only inches apart. She was looking up at him, directly in the eye and was very much in his personal space. Quietly she stated, 'We will never share anything, you and I, Paul Scriven. Not now, not next week, not ever! So, get out of my way, I have something important to do. And make very sure that you never cross those that I love again.' She'd said it so quietly that it was barely audible above the sound of the surf and the gulls and terns calling morning on the breeze. But Mr Scriven had heard and ingested every word and felt himself swallow, watery eyes with the resurgence of a long forgotten feeling.

'Do you understand what I am saying to you, Paul?' she added as if to drive the point home.

Eyes down, dumbly, he murmured his reply, 'Yes.'

With that Sarah Golding unnecessarily pushed past him, emphasising her sense of self and purpose. She picked up her coattails so as to more easily run and took off over the rough limestone path up to Fortuneswell. She had to get to the naval dockyard to speak to someone in high command. Time was very much of the essence. They had to be warned about the presence of the E-boats and the imminent threat they presented. Surely they wouldn't attack in daylight hours?

But more than that, Sarah Golding was under no illusion when the import of what she had said to Mr Scriven settled, his sense of hurt, injured pride and any other residual feelings he had had for her would soon turn to hate and she well knew that hell had no fury like Mr Scriven's scorn. She had seen Billy bear the brunt of it too many times. He was an adult and Billy was a child. Goodness only knew how the adult dynamics of the situation could fire the furnaces of his wrath. He certainly was going to just let her go about her business. His intrigue would be piqued and it wouldn't be long before he fathomed what her important business might be given her familial connections and her direction of travel. It was a race against time and there were now two clocks ticking.

Paul Scriven watched Sarah Golding hurry up the track through Fortuneswell. They too had grown up on Portland together. He had known her as a child and watched her change from a girl to a woman. He'd thought about her a lot when he was away during the war and she'd been there when he returned to Portland. She had even taught the island's children at the school in his absence until he resumed his duties. These were his thoughts as he watched her pass out of sight, evidently heading towards the Admiralty. And then his blood ran cold.

'Damned witch. Think you'll make a fool of me? You've got another thing coming,' he uttered as he drew his palm to the hot, livid scar tissue on his cheek, considering.

It must have taken a good fifteen minutes to get to the top of the island, to the top of Portland and then the same again to descend the snaking road down again. As she did so, Sarah Collins took in the eighteen-mile stretch of pebble beach, Chisel beach that opened out before her and the lagoon behind. She was surprised to see the hive of activity this morning after Maggie had told her that there had been none during the night, save for the *Schnellenboot*.

Hundreds of soldiers visible on the beach busying themselves about the vessels and more than three dozen landing craft in the water, the decks lined with servicemen. As she took it in, Sarah Golding came to the shuddering realisation that the combined British and American naval forces must be gearing up for something of consequence, maybe even a full-scale practice of the open secret that was Operation Tiger.

Galvanising her steel, Sarah Golding lifted her coattails higher so as to lengthen her stride and quicken her pace. As she did so, again she took in the scores of chugging diesels in the dockyard and lagoon. Even up in the rock, Sarah Golding could the low, brown mist of diesel fumes forming. The wind had dropped to nothing; the sea, like the lagoon, was a mill pond. It would have been unusually still and quiet at this time were it not for all the servicemen.

There were many more than she'd initially thought: all arms swinging crates and loads onto jeeps and trucks, the columns of soldiers now marching to the landing craft on Chesil Beach, the rows of soldiers in lines of a score or more passing boxes of rations, munitions, medical supplies and the thousand other essential logistics required to fuel and sustain an invading army. She was so engrossed in the long distance scene, overwhelmed and in awe of the organisation required to martial what now appeared to be thousands of troops that she didn't register the Amis jeep blister past her within inches. Sarah Golding didn't notice the very cramped tall figure of Mr Scriven in the back of the jeep. He, on the other hand, was very much aware that he had passed her by.

Chapter 20
Sarah Golding Heads to the Admiralty

Sarah Golding had noted that these Amis, when they arrived, seemed to have more than enough of everything in spades: good humour, manners and muscles to these pungent Lucky Strikes and Chesterfields they smoked that smelled like something dry-roasted-exotic-alluring rather than the cloying, old fug stench of tobacco the islanders smoked. And that was before you got the chocolates, tights and tins of food that were bright with sunshine when you opened them. It wasn't hard to see why these well-fed, tall, square-jawed, starched-presentable Americans seemed to have made the Portland men retreat further into sullenly into their scruffy-hermitic, salty ways.

Men who were naturally conservative and cautious as islanders usually are, suspicious of outsiders, would be particularly so of those from three and a half thousand miles away across the Atlantic, when those from across the Causeway were often enough of a challenge. But they were here to fend off the Nazis and without the Americans, all England could conceivably be taking hasty German lessons under duress.

Being the sort of person who naturally saw both binary sides of a black and white argument, as well as (and more importantly in her mind) the myriad shades of grey between, Sarah Golding knew that beneath their rough-stubble-weathered exteriors, you couldn't hope to meet a more courageous band of wizened souls than Portland men. They would give their all to help another islander in a crises, put their lives at risk and set sail in a maelstrom to assist a neighbour stranded on the sand banks, their skiff's rigging and canvas snapped and torn by natures violence. All disagreements and feuds could be suspended until an adversary was safely back on the rock. And then the discontent could happily continue. Take up where they left off. Curious bunch.

The array of activity before was nothing short of intimidating. Hundreds of men, all organised and set to purpose was quite beleaguering. How could you even begin to wonder how to organise such as thing as an invasion force? From afar up on the rock it was simply like watching a colony of ants at work. But as with ants, when you get up close and personal and see what they are up to, it's a different prospect. That's what it was for Sarah Golding although she was prepared to be halted by the impression. It just took a broad, general view and layer upon layer of delegation like any institution.

And as Chinese whispers took orders down the ranks, the messages changed and details were missed. Chinks in the armour, fissures in the diamond appeared. So busy were they all in their tasks and the threat across the water on the Continent, what was happening right in front of them had passed them by. With all the mesmerising organisation, activity, drills, manoeuvres and preparations, the combined Allied forces had taken their eye off the game and the threat had crept in undetected so that a vigilant thirteen-year-old's observations could well be the last paper-thin defence against the fires of disaster. Billy had spotted the E-boats, the Scimitar leaving and the entire navy was potentially vulnerable to attack. If there were a half dozen E-boats in the vicinity, what else could be mustered in a flash?

As she watched two young, muscular guards cheerfully hand turning the crank that raised the dockyard barrier to a 6x6 GMC cargo truck, known as a 'Jimmy', its engine grinding with a laboured arrhythmia as the barrier raised, Sarah Golding again remarked to herself that if Portlanders were naturally suspicious of mainlanders, no wonder the lot of them had issue with the Amis' apparent wealth of technology and power. It would have to be something to envy, covet, reject and grudgingly respect. The truck was a six-wheeled monster that looked like it meant business. And that was before they stood up with pearly, winning smiles when they noticed her.

As her mind seemed to settle, content with her observations, Sarah Golding began to wonder how she would play it with the naval commander/commodore. She knew her looks would get her past the various barriers, gates, guards and sentries. But how to play it with these men of authority—she'd never met one before—they still had to be human surely? 'He'll be just a man for goodness sake! As equally stupid as the rest of us,' she chided herself and she was there to deliver vital information or 'intel' as the Amis seemed to call it.

Would they take exception to being *upstaged* by a woman and some children that had spotted what they, with all their man power and technology, had missed? They were certainly clever and polite, but would they simply dismiss the testimony of a woman and two children? Would they revert to that exasperating, bovine maleness? Or would they carefully listen, all attention with ears, eyes and minds keenly focussed on expedient solutions as she herself was?

Well, what she could know was that it was going to take all her courage and that she had covered. She also understood it would be uncomfortable, but more than a lot less so than a Pearl Harbour repeat (or Peril Harbour as Billy had it) on her doorstep.

Her crowding thoughts had slowed her to a standstill and she became aware that the three American servicemen in their sandy uniforms, white T-shirts and the white MP pots on their heads were all three scrutinising her with both professional interest and something altogether more human. And then the one who, given the thick black hair and swarthy complexion, may have been Mediterranean North African somewhere along the line, looking up at her as she was tall by either genders standards at five nine, drawled, 'How can I help you, miss?'

With all the detail to take in and her strategy to be calculated, Sarah Golding had not noticed that in front of the 6X6 cargo truck she had watched go through the barrier was the Amis jeep that had sailed past her, kicking up dust and spray of gravel as it passed her at the top of Fortuneswell. She also missed Mr Scriven disentangling his tall frame from the back of the jeep and enter through a doorway, amicably ushered by two Amis MPs towards the American Commander and English Commodore that she also desperately needed to be taken to. Sarah Golding wasn't aware that she'd been pipped to the post and had missed what was right in front of her.

Chapter 21
Tick Tock 1992

Breakfasted fit, Captain Collins selected the young Sapper plus two for an initial inspection of the bomb site, the rest to make a last check of equipment. No point putting *all* at risk at that point. On the face of it, a final equipment check was a meritless task. Everything they would need was there in the vehicles without a shadow. But the familiarisation with the equipment and the method of the check served a purpose of its own while the Captain made his risk assessment.

The advances in technology were truly brilliant. All sorts of nifty gadgetry. All manner of cleverness learned from trial and error that took gall and caution beyond the nth degree—the cause for fear, exhilaration, joy or death in thousand pieces. And there was so much of it, too, tech. But the crew still marvelled at the Captain's old school ways. He always had his kit to hand stowed behind the seat in the Red Wing or in the back of his modest civvy car to be put under the bed wherever he slept. In a five star hotel or under a bivvy in the desert, it was always within arm's reach. A slightly larger than briefcase-sized mahogany box, oiled and gleaming-polished with a brass tag with his initials WMC (no rank) under the leather handle that he had evidently put together himself for purpose decades ago that simply contained his snips; brush; hand drill, bits and chuck key; a small hammer and chisel, screw drivers and, of course, the all-important brush.

'That box has to go in my box when I shuffle. Let's hope there's enough of me in it to stop it rattling because I don't want it slopping around in the cat food!' guffawed the Captain tirelessly, making the Sapper and anyone else who had heard the line down the years shudder and chuckle with equal measure. That is until it became the norm and as unusual as a 'good morning'.

True enough, the bomb really was under the centre spot of Portland United after all. The Captain had squatted down beside the 2,000 kilo bomb like he would his faithful greyhound and patted it as such too. Sapper Mike looked on, nerves unapparent, checked, but there in bundles all the same, while the old boy appeared to be admiring the Satan beside him. In fact, he seemed to be talking to it in a kindly way, though the words were lost on the wind and sound of the surf, 'Hello, sleeping beauty. You've lain here all this time, perhaps since the day I left, and we've not heard a peep from you. Surely, you're not going to give me gyp now are you, old girl? You haven't brought me back here to have us both give up the ghost? Well, *que sera sera*. At least there are no bloody rabbits around!'

'What was that, sir?'

Then, raising his voice above the wind to be heard, 'Your first Satan, lad, I believe?' Captain Collins had opened his BDO case to remove his brush to give the Satan's timer a quick dust off as if he were a make-up artist at the theatre giving an actress her final confidence boosting bit of attention and spruce up.

Sapper Mike had prepared for this so that there wasn't a trace of stammer-nerves when he replied, 'Happily, yes sir! And hopefully the first of many.'

Captain Collins squinted at him a moment, that avuncular gleam in his eye, before replying, 'That's the spirit, lad. You *will* go far!' Sapper Mike returned the broad smile. This was the Captain he knew. Again, what he didn't hear as the Captain turned, still squatting as he returned his brush to the mould in his case was the Captain mutter, 'Let's just hope I don't,' as he snapped the clasps shut on his box, stood up and squared his shoulders in an effort to distract himself from the aches in his back and knees.

Having calculated a safe distance for the operational command post and completed a preliminary dig with a trench tool for its footings, the other two BDOs returned and all four men folded their arms to have a look at 'Goering's deposit', as the Captain called it. Manly chuckles as they stood there as if appreciating a newly dug goldfish pond in the back garden. Sapper started off the football humour by repeating the Captain's joke about kick-offs potentially going off with a bang.

The Captain followed up with one about Goering's 'knuckle ball'. Someone said they thought that it was Hitler who only had one ball and the round was finished with one about it not being quite the day for thousand yard 'screamer'.

They drove back through Fortuneswell, down the s-bends of Portland to the naval yard. When they arrived, the rest of the unit was on point at the vehicles, ready. The last of the sandbags was being loaded onto the trailer of the seven and a half tonner. The fifty-kilo sacks were tossed down the line, past the parcel-

orderly-fashion and placed in the trailer. They'd make up a last added defence in front of the operational command post's steel bomb shield.

Only the Captain got out, left the engine running, door open and addressed the unit whose activity had ceased and were all now standing at ease, legs apart, planted like terriers, hands clasped behind backs, primed for instruction. Captain Collins reiterated that although the bomb posed no imminent threat as Cat C ordnance, that although there was no infrastructure in terms of public buildings, school, hospitals, police stations, etcetera: if the timer went and the bomb detonated and the island had (all but two) been entirely evacuated, there was still the risk that the explosive aftershock tremor could still cause buildings to collapse. And as many of the island cottages had been built more than a few centuries before, chances could not be taken.

All of this the Captain had delivered as deadpan instruction to be said once only and once only to then be thoroughly digested and implemented. Economy of words. Repetition was not a part of the programme. They listened intently, ears acute, eyes glistening, unblinking until they sensed the information had been imparted and the Captain paused. They all shifted foot to foot, rolled necks and shoulders having been perfectly still for the duration of the briefing.

'Right chaps! All looks pretty straightforward. Satan, just as reported. The locals have only had a preliminary scrape around it. Solid rock an inch down. Should take a good couple of hours prep. And some quick dry cement wouldn't go amiss for the footings of the OCP. Nothing left to chance, lads. Not today. Not never. The weather's changeable on the Rock so let's get this show on the road before we all get wet.' And then, almost as an afterthought, 'At the site, when we're all clear on what's what, Sapper Lapin and I will have to go at the last two stubborn buggers left on the island who *shall not be moved*. The stubborn old bird and the pigeon fancier who won't leave his flock. See if we can't prise them out!'

More chuckles.

'Ready?'

'Yes, sir!' chorused the unit.

Sapper Mike had rolled the window down to hear the brief and was watching the Captain march, head down, back to the Red Wing. When the Captain had slammed the door shut and enquired, 'Fit for purpose?' all three had affirmed with a silent, curt nod. Ready. The Captain was all steel and purpose. Vital. No vestiges, no shadows. Sapper Mike's relief was palpable if not visible. But he would have done well to have remembered his mother's frequent admonition that: *you can't judge a book by its cover.*

On arrival at the site, parked up at a safe enough distance so that the vibrations shouldn't disturb the bomb's timing mechanism, but close enough so that humping the kit wasn't overly laborious, Captain Collins' unit of BDOs got to it.

Well-drilled, well-practiced, the prep couldn't have gone smoother. One detail for the CCP: they'd dug the footings for the steel CCP, bolted it together and set it in the quick dry cement. Sand bags placed in front for an extra measure of safety to absorb the shrapnel. Next came the electricals: computers and monitors set up with the wiring reeled of a wheel to set up for the four cameras that would be placed strategically to film the process of drilling out the timing mechanism and the disarming of it.

The cameras were there to record the process in full so that it could be turned into a training video for future use or so that, if all hell fire was let loose and Captain Collins had an off day at the office, at least the next BDO would have learned from his last mistake. The Captain had dated the bomb from 1944 perhaps within weeks of the end of the Second World War. And that made it even more dangerous as the Captain was famous for saying in his tutorials, 'Desperation is the mother of all invention. And by God, was Jerry desperate by extra time. He was a wily old stoat at the beginning. By the end, you've got to give the Jerry boffins credit, they'd come up with all manner of delayed detonation booby traps, mercury timers and the like that make your head spin like a kid's puzzle.'

With one detail busy around the operational command post, the other detail prepared the area around the bomb itself. Division of labour, it wasn't. Far from it. Although each and every man in the unit had a specific job, each role was rota'd on a rolling rota so that every man knew everyone else's, kept his hand in and no-one got to sit pretty and safe more than their fair share. It was proper egalitarian in the Captain's unit and something of an overlooked idiosyncrasy in the Engineers. Every man knew his place and rank, but none felt more valued than the next. That way, there was always a man on hand who could take on another's role if it all went south.

As Captain Collins was fond of his football metaphors, he described it thus in his spiels, 'The best of players is the players' player. And that makes him the manager's player too. He's not a glory boy. He's got his head up, watching the game, always. He understands and can play every position in the team. That way, he makes the beautiful game happen—by keeping his hand in and his head up. That's the man you want to be.'

The other detail got to work on the bomb itself. Having brushed away the soil, earth and rock around the bomb to fully expose it without shifting it, the mechanism and timer were washed and brushed clean and clear of dust. Then they'd dug around it and put in the timber shafting around to prevent the walls of the pit collapsing in on the bomb. The Captain was fond of telling new recruits that the timber shafting process had been invented by the Romans and a better method was yet to be discovered.

No point reinventing the wheel. And if it ain't broke, don't fix it, son! Sapper Mike had noticed that the Captain had a curious way of putting an extra emphasis on his southeast accent whenever he said it, as he did with many of his favoured epithets and sayings. Mental note to quiz him on it.

Picture of timber shafting

As the unit busied itself with task, the Captain, his hands thrust deep in his pockets, stood peering at the protruding tail piece and fin of the bomb, scrutinising it, squinting as the sun pushed passed the cumulus clouds off over the horizon. After some while, the Captain turned his back on the bomb and ambled over to a nearby south-facing boundary wall. He stood there, hands still deep in the pockets, idly tapping the base of the wall with the steel toecap of his boot. His downturned mouth suggested that he was deep in thought. Having finished running the spool cables of wire to and from what was to be the bomb pit and the OCP and assisted with the last sandbag defence, Sapper Mike had spotted his mentor and gone to join him at the wall.

'Penny for them, sir?'

The Captain eyed his apprentice keenly, but did not reply and averted his gaze, south out across the Channel. Sapper Mike thought he'd just wait it out. Eventually, the Captain inhaled and exhaled deeply and appeared to be about to speak, but just shook his head and closed his mouth. Mike had a feeling that the Captain was observing more than he could see and so to chivvy things along, he ventured, 'What's it like being back after all these years, sir?'

The Captain took a few moments to surface and register. Taking him in, the Captain replied with his characteristic smiling eyes, 'It doesn't change, if that's what you mean. It's as if the last 40 years haven't happened. All that experience and I'm stood here as an old man, hours off retirement with a lad not that much older than I was when I was evacuated from the island after Operation Tiger. I learned a lot, experienced a lot. I've been busy all over the world and yet I'm still the same. My shell may have grown, weathered, aged. But, like this island, like that bomb, I've not changed. Like time standing still.'

Wistful again. Not good. Sapper Mike had listened very carefully to the old boot over the last eighteen months and knew full well that Captain couldn't afford the luxury of *pensive* to distract him with the job. Particularly today of all days, it being his last job. The last bomb he would diffuse in his career, in his life. So, the young man decided to wrong foot-distract him with humour.

'Oh, Dr Who! I get it. Time travelling again or not as the case may be. But less of time travelling, who are we visiting first, sir? The old bird or the pigeon fancier?'

'You cheeky young bugger!' It was a reprimand with warmth. But spot on, nevertheless.

'We'll go the for maid first, you can try out your boyish charms on her and I'll lead with the pigeon fancier. Don't want you getting in a flap, eh Sapper?' Saying it, the Captain had turned, heading back to the Red Wing. Over his shoulder, he shouted, 'Come on, lad, shake a tail feather!'

'On my way, sir! And I got the addresses and directions for those two. Didn't want both of us to go bird brain on the job, sir!' For a moment Sapper Mike wondered if he'd overstepped the mark. The Captain stopped in his tracks as he registered the humorous putdown, half turning in an exaggerated slow-mo. But he took the insubordination, calling a senior officer "bird brain" which could have earned the young Sapper a 28-day spell in the Glass House in Colchester, as it was intended—a wake-up joke between friends. And given that that was what they would be within 24 hours if he got through this last job when the Captain walked down civvy street, he thought he might as well start getting used to it now. On he carried, walking. Over his shoulder, he added, 'And you're driving, Mike.'

The young Sapper noted the omission of rank as he wiped his hands before pocketing his handkerchief and set off after his friend and mentor, aglow with optimism and the dawning light.

Chapter 22
Sarah Golding and Admirals

Getting past the barrier had been a whole load easier than anticipated. The young fellas appeared to be falling over themselves to help out this particular local. She'd not had to wait more than five minutes having informed the gate guards that she had *important information on matters of naval security.* What she hoped was the correct level of elevated language had hit the mark.

Coat open, her lapis blue print patterned dress aglow with cornflowers, Sarah Golding was very much aware that she was sailing solo, giving the austere, functional surroundings of British and American Naval Command a necessary bit of verve and colour—a reminder of life, perhaps even. She thought it a bit unnecessary to have to be flanked by two Amis MPs as well as being preceded and followed by another two along the parquet-floored corridors of power. It was an odd mix, she felt. Important and taken seriously on the one hand, but also as if she were a little dangerous as an unknown on the other.

There was something else there too, in abundance, that she could have let get her goat on any other occasion—those less than surreptitious, snatching glances. *Men! Didn't they ever switch off?* But now was not the time and place. Her focus was whittled to the sharpest of points, she'd air all that later when she'd done what she came to do. They could savour their impressions: dark horse, wild card or whatever—all they like. What needed to be done was more important than her private concerns.

With that thought she flexed, head up, shoulders back and saw that they were approaching two wide nine foot, heavy oak doors that were being silently opened by two white socked, white helmeted MPs to reveal fairly dazzlingly light from what seemed like a cathedral-sized window in front of which was a battleship sized oak desk. Behind sat a spindly, lithe old fellow with half-moon glasses balanced on his nose and gold braid all over his epaulettes enthroned on a carved oak and velvet chair that would have comfortably sat someone three foot taller. He was unmistakably British.

Leaning in front on the corner of the battleship, arms folded, a cigarette hanging from the corner of his mouth stood a much more casual in his sandy short-sleeved shirt with white vest beneath, she guessed was the old boy's American counterpart. Sarah Golding stood on the edge of the red carpet. To move further forward, even though there was a good twelve feet between them that was less than comfortable for a conversation didn't seem like an option. The office of naval high command seemed to operate its own magnetic fields of rank and file. And she quickly realised that this wasn't going to be a conversation, but an interview.

'Good morning, Miss,' boomed the American naval officer thrusting an enthusiastic, sweaty paw towards the attractive woman before him. The British Admiral, as Sarah Golding guessed him to be, barely moved. He may have flicked his eyes above the half-moons, but she couldn't be sure. He had to be seventy-five if he was a day. The American officer looked to be athletic in his mid-fifties, a generation between them at least. That had to present its difficulties, she mused, even before you got to the startling obvious cultural difference between the two, the one aged, silent and austere, the other younger, effusive and welcoming by comparison.

Whichever way Sarah Golding looked at it, it presented a problem of how to pitch her information. What might work for one would almost certainly graze against the other. Any preconceived ideas about how to convey her information about the E-boats, her "intelligence" as they called it, had sailed off over the horizon.

As she shook the American's hand, these fleeting impressions passing above these shifting thoughts, Sarah Golding reminded herself that either way, it was more than likely that neither was about to appreciate what she had to say and that they would do what they would do with the information regardless of how it was presented. Neither was going to admit a failure of vigilance on their part and no matter how she played it, to be outwitted by a woman and two children was never going to amount to anything but tarnished male pride somewhere along the line.

And as she settled at this conclusion, the tall doors closed behind her with a barely perceptible click. Sarah Golding grimaced as she caught that unmistakable acrid scent that, even after all these years, caught in her throat like a fishbone. Her shoulders began to tense, until she forced herself to breathe and gain command of herself, banishing the memory of his grip on her arm not an hour before. And then, though she needed no more confirmation, she heard a match strike behind her. The sulphurous odour and the cloying whiff of his pipe tobacco that made the children wince and cough with repulsion enveloped her. Evidently, quite deliberately.

Such was the concentration on the two naval officers before her and consternation about how to present what she knew, Sarah Golding had not sensed that he was there, that Mr Scriven could only be a few feet behind given the strength of the filthy odours and the volume of smoke.

I am not going to give you the satisfaction of turning around to acknowledge you, Sarah Golding silently counselled herself.

Bracing herself to begin, summoning an enormous effort of will to prevent herself from turning around, Sarah Golding resisted her rage for the time being and exhaling began her delivery with what, in retrospect she could only describe as what she thought was a martial manner.

'Gentlemen, I've come this morning with some important information. Intelligence that is vital to Operation Tiger, to all of your safety,' There was an audible vacuum of silence that hissed in the high-ceilinged room. To Sarah Golding, it seemed to go on for an age until it was cut through with a derisory snort from behind her. But before his pestilence could grow into anything more vocal, Mr Scriven was unequivocally silenced by a flash of attention from behind those authoritative half-moons behind the desk. And then, after more silence and squaring some papers and placing them aside, the British Admiral, as Sarah guessed him to be, continued in that upper-crust kind of voice that could give you papercuts.

'What would you know of Operation Tiger, Miss …?' He trailed off.

'*Mrs* Golding. *Mrs* Sarah Golding, sir!' she corrected him, maintaining eye contact. The Admiral might have raised an eyebrow; she couldn't be sure as he turned his head. There was definitely something bird like about his countenance in profile. But benign, it wasn't. He was sharp and defined like a kestrel.

'Again then, what would you know of Operation Tiger, *Mrs* Sarah Golding? That is classified information.'

She paused to try to find a register of language that wouldn't be deemed offensive to this man who wielded such power. Did she have to present herself as a submissive, little woman? 'So be it,' she thought if that's what it took for the information about the sighting of the E-boats was to be seriously and acted upon. God knew that it was an effort of will though to prevent her frustration giving edge to her voice.

'Sir, I know nothing specifically of Operation Tiger. I live in Portland and have vitally important information regarding the naval activity in the area.'

'But you somehow know the name of a classified naval operation, *Miss* Golding!' Sarah Golding ignored the belittling. The Admiral had either forgotten already that she was a *Mrs* or simply didn't care for affording her that respect. Who could know? But that wasn't important for the minute.

'Sir, I live in Portland and have seen all the shipping activity and I have information vital to its safety,' she repeated curtly, making an effort to keep the exasperation out of her voice.

The Admiral's ancient, hawkish visage registered what might have been a fleeting moment of amusement were it not for it disappearing into the wrinkles of his jowls before it could take a hold. 'But my question to you is how would you know the classified name of a military operation?' He had those inhibiting sort of eyes that conveyed no warmth, no anger and nothing in between, portholes to a void.

Sarah Golding wondered why such a detail could be so important to the Admiral in the face of the, as yet, unspoken information that was for the benefit of his men, his naval operation. His *reputation* when day was done. And then when she realised that she was getting caught up in whatever it was too, but not quick enough to have noticed his change in demeanour and she was caught off guard.

'So young lady! I ask you again. What do you know of Operation Tiger?' This time with more than a discernible tincture of vitriol permeating his words, eyes down. Like a pulse of electricity passing through the room, the atmosphere changed. The American naval officer gave his English counterpart a subtle glance of assessment. The line of questioning was clearly at odds with the affable manner he had presented. But this wasn't his show and he was a guest there.

Before she could think, Sarah Golding's words were out, 'I think that the propaganda phrase is *Loose lips sinks ships.* And it's not my lips that are loose. You'll have to look closer to home to find that battalion of culprits. The information I have may well prevent the sinking of *your* ships. Now, I would be grateful if you would let me say what I have to say and then I can be gone.'

All through, Sarah's eyes had been fixed on the carpet and now she felt the other six in the room piercing her like cold spears. You couldn't talk to an

Admiral like that. She knew her mistake. Behind her, Mr Scriven had removed the pipe from his mouth in amazement. From his point of view, the silly little woman had cooked her goose. There was no way she could get a fair hearing now. It couldn't have played out better even if he had had an input in the design. A sly grin of triumphant malice crossed his mouth and then he disguised his jubilation with a narrowing of the eyes and a return to the demeanour of an officer, the ever serious head of the Home Watch, appalled at the impropriety of the behaviour he had witnessed. He knew how to play this game.

Sarah Golding knew that she'd blown it, that whatever she said would now be obscured by her apparent lack of respect for the established order of things. But as nature abhors a vacuum and no-one else was about to punctuate the silence with anything pragmatic, she continued with what she had come to do, to add insult to injury or save lives, or both depending on your point of view. At least, if it was *out there,* they would have no choice but to act and investigate her claim. Then, all might not all be lost.

'There are German E-boats, short range fast attack vessels in the Channel, sir! Half a dozen of them, at least. The ships assembling for manoeuvres are in grave danger.'

Another proverbial pin drop, broken this time by a ghastly rasp of contempt from behind her. She didn't expect anything less from Paul Scriven. Somewhere over the last twenty-four hours, lines had been drawn in the sand. Consciously, decisions and conclusions had been made. Although it had always been a quiet war of glances between them, no terse words or expressions of emotion or anger, the rules of the game had irrevocably changed. And so, Sarah Golding, with an energy she had been storing for more than a long time, turned to Mr Scriven, turning her back on the Admirals, and appraised him before she began. He lost his smile.

'Mr Scriven? What have you been doing for the last five years? What has been your destination and how have you travelled there? What have you learned along the way? What have you noticed? Well?' She paused. He paused. They all paused. Perhaps the Admirals realised there was more going on here than met the eye. But maybe they didn't.

'Well, I can tell you, Mr Scriven. Very little. Very little indeed. You have great difficulty spotting what is under your nose or what is inside you for that matter. Let's not spell it all out. But it doesn't bode well for your public role if your private thoughts are ruined and charred.' She was talking in riddles, she chided herself, it wasn't doing her case any good. And she knew that she had to get back on track and speak only of things professional, not personal and to diffident to the unwritten social codes that the institutions around her were permeated with.

Taking advantage of the male perplexity stagnating around her. she continued, 'What you have failed to spot on your Home Front watches of reconnaissance are the half dozen German E-boats in the Channel. William Collins spotted them with my daughter two days ago and identified them. And my daughter confirmed the sightings again last night. As well as watching the departure of the destroyer, *HMS Scimitar,* leaving the flotilla wide open to attack.'

Paul Scriven pushed past his colleague to address the Admirals who were all ears now, stalking the exchange like terriers. Mr Scriven mustered the saliva to speak, 'That Collins boy is nothing but trouble with his overactive imagination!' He was trembling with rage, face puce. Quite clearly, he didn't have the self-control to get any more words out. Sarah Golding, now behind Mr Scriven making him the triangulation point of scrutiny, was quicker off the mark.

'That Collins boy, as you call him, is more observant than you by far. His excellent imagination isn't to be underestimated either. But that is not why we are here today. If you could get past your plethora of prejudices maybe you could, maybe you might just see what is right before you, which, in this case are a half dozen or more Jerry E-boats poised to open the gates of hell on our warships.'

Regaining her composure, Sarah Golding paused in the hope that her silence might allow some trust to permeate the minds about her. She searched the Admirals for a sign that she was getting through. Dust motes played in the penetrating shafts of morning light beaming through the window behind the British Admiral. Sarah Golding wondered who would break the silence. She was just beginning to allow herself the hope that she was getting through to them when the Amis Admiral took up the initiative and drawled in an accent that she placed in the Deep South of the United States, 'Look here, missy. Pretty as you are, you're out of line speaking to Captain Scriven here, in that tone. And, I think that this boy you are talking about is mistaken. The destroyer has left as you rightly say. But only because the threat assessed is negligible and repairs need to be done.'

'How can you say that the threat is negligible? There must be more than 100 ships in the flotilla. That has to be thousands of souls?' She had marched forward and was now gripping the corners of the high-backed chair before her, knuckles white with irritation.

'Now look here, little lady! The threat is assessed as negligible as there are no, repeat no, German E-boats in the Channel. Are you saying that the naval watches of the combined Allied task forces and intelligence have missed something that your Billy Collins has spotted in the Channel? You're out of your mind and damned impertinent if I may add, Madam!'

Madam? she thought, bewildered by this play of events. And then her mind alighted on a few other words and phrases that pushed their way through her chagrin. *Little Lady? Missy?* Quite clearly, they could only see before them a mother who would be better off at home making scones that worrying her pretty little head about affairs of security and the defence of the realm.

Waking from her thoughts, Sarah Golding took in the faces around her. The American was affronted and even worse, had an air of disappointment about him, too. Mr Scriven's scar was a vivid purple though his eyes betrayed something else she couldn't place for a moment and the English Admiral's quick, hawk-like eyes sparkled with a darkness that was unfathomable. Her eyes swept the room, the painting of another character that might have been Admiral Nelson or some other naval dignitary imperiously surveyed those before him. She took in the high-backed chairs and paused curiously, noting that those in front of the Admirals' frigate-sized desk were evidently lower than the Admirals.

The game was rigged. It was pointless. How could she have let herself begin to believe that in that day and age they would have taken her testimony seriously? A cold mantle of stoicism settled around her. Sarah Golding had more self-respect than to go flogging a dead horse. She mustered all the calm she possessed and in her most deferent, polite voice that was a touch higher pitched than she would have liked, Sarah Golding confounded them by stating, 'Well then, Sirs, if you'll kindly excuse me. I must have made a mistake. Those children surely do imagine all sorts of things. Maybe they have led me up the garden path and I have gotten all excited myself. I don't wish to waste any more of our time.'

The most expressive of the faces about her was the Ami's. His look was of complete bafflement. Foxed but safe, the Ami looked to the British Admiral as the confidence returned to his throat.

'Well, as Mrs Golding seems to have understood our situation, I think we can bring this meeting to a swift closure, Admiral Blithe?'

'Yes,' murmured Admiral Blithe, elongating the vowel and consonants as a series of unreadable impressions passed behind his eyes.

'That'll be all, Miss Golding. You can take your leave now.' And more pointedly, 'you've said enough, I should say.' Sarah Golding held the Admiral's gaze for what she hoped was just a mite too long before turning to begin to make her exit. With that the tall doors behind her opened soundlessly, creating a draught. When she looked up, the white-belted Amis MP who had opened the door from the outside, evidently aware the meeting had come to a close, inclined his head in a slight imperceptible, swift motion, advising her to depart.

Sarah Golding turned once more at the door to nod her goodbye to the Admirals. She couldn't help herself take in Mr Scriven. At some point during the brief exchange, he appeared to have moved soundlessly to the corner of the opulent room. *To regroup*, she thought. His damaged face was a picture of undisguised loathing and fury. She imagined her own look was pretty much reciprocal.

As she passed through the tall double doors, escorted by the Amis MP, another began to close them delicately as you would a child's bedroom door, a child that had finally gone to sleep. But before that world closed on her for good, she heard Admiral Blithe utter a few simple words that warmed her with a satisfaction she hadn't anticipated.

'Mr Scriven, you are to stay here. I think you'll agree that we have a matter to discuss.' His reply was a barely audible scraping as the doors clicked shut behind her. Sarah Golding let herself fall in step with the MP. Neither of them spoke. She felt a tangle of emotion knot within her. A personal minor victory maybe, but in the face of a visibly public defeat. And there was no way of knowing if they would act on her information. She knew instinctively how to explain it to Maggie and Billy. Not that it would make a lot of sense to a child's mind or an adult's for that matter.

The MP walked her through the corridors of naval command with the American Admiral following silently behind them; back out to the sand-bagged barrier. Another MP released it to let her through, the crank clicking furiously as another soldier turned the crank arm. Sarah Golding paused to look at all the activity again in the yard. Hundreds of men making preparation for war games. How would they feel if they knew what she knew? She shook away the notion and made to pass the barrier.

'Good morning, Ma'am,' chorused those assembled cheerily as she passed them. She gave a curt nod of uninterested dismissal, her mind temporarily quelled, quiet as the sun broke through, the cold warming her face and shoulders. Twenty yards off, she turned to see the sentry-guards, faces turned together conspiratorially to share a light, puffing cigs into life, following her progress with their eyes. The American Admiral was in the background watching her leave too. Sarah Golding let it pass and concentrated on the ascent back up to Portland, to Fortuneswell and home to her cottage and her daughter Maggie. *You can but try, Sarah, you can but try,* she consoled herself as she fell into a determined rhythm. She could rest when she got home.

Back behind closed doors of the Admiralty's inner sanctum, Mr Scriven had sighed his relief as that Golding fishwife had left. But he instantly froze again as the Admiral Blithe addressed him with his characteristically bone-dry delivery which might have seemed strange for a naval man.

'Mr Scriven,' he'd said quietly, pausing to remove his spectacles and press his fingertips into tired eyes before massaging his jaw. The Admiral then carefully replaced his glasses, rested his elbows on the desk and clasped his hands together.

'Yes, sir,' Mr Scriven replied, attempting to disguise the tremor clawing at his throat. The dust mites trapped in the shafts of morning light roared as he waited for the Admiral to continue.

'You'd better make damn sure that neither the Home Guard nor the Naval Watch has missed something that a woman and some children have. Damn sure! Yes?'

Emphatically, Mr Scriven replied, 'I would stake my life on it that there are no E-boats in the vicinity—' He was about to continue, but the Admiral cut him dead.

'I am not interested in your assertions and theatrics. What I want is complete assurance. Another Pearl Harbour is not, repeat not going to happen on my watch. This head is not going to roll. But yours might. And I could quite conceivably have you keel hauled for neglect on duty before that happens. Think on, Mr Scriven.' The delivery was so quiet that Mr Scriven had to lean forward and strain to hear it.

He paused again as Mr Scriven nodded his unblinking silent assent.

'Good, then I think we understand each other. You can leave now.'

Chapter 23
1992

Sapper Mike hauled himself up into the driver's seat of the Red Wing, drew the seat back and adjusted the mirrors to suit as the Captain had was of a smaller frame than him. Driving was also relatively new to him and therefore exciting and he was keen to get prepared so he didn't make any school boy errors on a debut drive with the Captain. The army had put him through his tests and he was legal to drive up to a seven and half tonner now.

As he was readying himself, Mike looked up to note the Captain hands on hips wistfully taking in the view again, reabsorbing the environment. Mike fired up the Land Rover as the Captain pulled himself up into the cab.

'All set, Sapper?' Enquiring.

'Yes sir, where to first? Stubborn old lady or the pigeon fancier?'

'Hardest first, in all things, Sapper. And then it's all downhill after that. Bull by the horns and all! I have a feeling this one'll be a tough nut to crack. Apparently, they're both islanders, born and bred. A Mrs Sansom, by all accounts. It's an old Portland name but I can't make any associations with it. The name's not ringing any bells. As an older Portlander, we'll have a hell of a job trying to shift her. Might never been off the island. Same with the pigeon fancier, Mr Gibbs, too.'

'What was that, sir? How'd do you mean?'

'Just what I say, Mike. There always were, and it sounds like there still are, some Portlanders who have never crossed the Causeway and set foot on the mainland. So evacuating off the island to safety will be a tall order.'

'You are joking? Surely, sir?' Astonished eyebrows.

'Nope! 'Fraid not, Sapper. Eight years off the millennium and there are still some folk on Portland who've never left the island, possibly for generations and whose lifestyles have barely changed. Fishing, quarrying, growing their own spuds.'

These last words hung in the air before sinking into the young man's take on the world. Mike thought that his view of the world came from a narrow frame of experience. He was from a stock of stonemasons and fishermen. Solitary occupations with insular, provincial perspectives. But this was just another level again. The Captain caught Mike's eye for signs of recognition.

'I know it's where you grew up, sir. But that's a very strange mentality. You're going to have a very different view of the world if you've never been off a tiny island.'

'Oh yes, young man! With bells on, for sure.'

'Jeez, you'll be telling me next that they don't have television here either.' Again, the Captain caught the young man's eye and the affirmation passed between them wordlessly.

'Unbelievable!' he said to himself as he shoved the Red Wing into gear and they juddered off, kangarooing embarrassingly as Mike fought to get the balance between clutch and accelerator. His cheeks reddened in embarrassment as he stalled the Land Rover.

'Oh cripes,' he remarked.

'No, no, Sapper. I don't think it's your fault. I noticed there was a problem with the timing as we came across the Causeway. Listen as you start her up again. There's an irregular thrum. When we get to the old lady's place, I'll take a look under the bonnet. You can cut your negotiation teeth on a stubborn Portlander. That'll be a challenge,' the Captain joked good-naturedly. He was smiling, but a sound somewhere between a ringing and white noise had started up in his ears. The Captain licked his lips, searching for moisture. His pulse was intermittently laboured and racing.

He just about managed, 'You've got the addresses, then?'

'Yep! Got 'em off the locals this morning.'

'Good lad,' murmured the Captain, 'good lad.'

Chapter 24
1942: Sarah Golding Breaks the News
at Old Sea Dog Cottage

By the time Sarah Golding arrived back home, she'd just about got her head around the disappointment of how things had gone with the Admirals and Mr Scriven. She'd got her head around it, but she knew that it would smart for a long time. What stung was the sense that she had been excluded from being a part of something important solely because she was a woman. That fact somehow alone meant that the information she had to deliver was null and void. That something potentially horrible and tragic could be allowed to happen simply because her word could be discounted by the Admirals solely because she was a woman and too emotional to be credible was a horrendous anathema to her. She just hoped that sense might prevail and that they'd at least take her seriously enough to investigate her claims. Surely, they would?

Opening the garden gate of the Collins' house, Old Sea Dog Cottage, Sarah Golding was as sure as night follows day that her distaste for Mr Scriven had been apparent and that the content of her information was therefore received as suspect. Her lack of cool would have called her objectivity into question. Had she failed, she wondered? Or was that always how it was going to play out? In spite of her self-doubt on that score, one thing was for certain, there was no way she'd be setting foot in that school house to work alongside Mr Scriven again. That door had finally and irrevocably closed shut.

What to do next? That was the question. But she wouldn't concern herself with that now. She had to tell Maggie and the Collins' what happened, but she was certain that an opportunity would present itself. It always did. After all, there was a war on and the war effort, the engines that powered all the destruction and evil would need stoking to keep the fires burning hot. There was a lot of work in the munitions factories around Plymouth. But that jarred with her feelings about the war.

She knew that if she had been born a fella that she'd have been a conscientious objector. No, that wouldn't work. But she was a practical woman with a good working knowledge of biology and understood what made people tick. They were crying out for nurses to take care of the casualties of war, especially the tens of thousands with shell shock. There were convalescence homes popping up all over, usually in the big country houses, to deal with these men who had been reduced to gibbering wrecks because of the horrors of war they had experienced and witnessed. Sarah Golding had a feeling that the mind can only take so much experience before it overfloweth. Maybe that was where he she could put herself to good use.

Sarah Golding lifted the latch of Old Sea Dog Cottage, noting that those creaky hinges could do with a drop of oil. She walked past the front room to the kitchen in the back knowing that her daughter Maggie wouldn't have been able to sleep and would have gone to join Billy and his mum.

As she entered the kitchen, the faces of Maggie, Billy and his mum lifted in unison—all query and expectation. Although she'd prepared her words in a number of ways, they failed her and all she could do was shake her head in negation and add, 'I'm sorry. I did my best.' Three heads dropped in dismay.

Hot-headed with incredulity, Billy asked, 'But why, Mrs Golding? How come they didn't believe you that the E-boats are out there?'

And with her self-disappointment weighing heavy on her, she delivered her two-word reply, 'Mr Scriven.' These two quiet words accompanied by a shake of the head. Mrs Collins had folded her arms, her eyes smouldering. The two children watched as a silent exchange took place between the two women. In spite of the potential implications, they all silently nodded their acquiescence, their Portland stoicism as hardened as the rock they lived on. They had played their part. *What'll be, will be.*

An impetuous yell in Billy's head had it reeling against the unfairness of it all: that he couldn't be taken seriously; because he was a child; because he was a Collins and that made him an outsider on an island of outsiders; because of an age old disagreement that his grandfather had had with Mr Scriven that have never been explained to him. Why should any of that discredit the fact that he had spotted that fast-attack German E-boats that could wreak an untold havoc and destruction on the navy? Where was the common sense in that?

Just because of who and what he was, his observation of fact could be discredited and ignored. But he knew that there was no way around Mr Scriven and that, whatever it was between them, could never be healed. He had tried. To continue would be tantamount to lack of self-respect. And so, with a half-hearted sincerity, he questioned, 'Is that that, then?'

No-one made eye contact, but there was a uniform sigh. The emotion dissipated from the room sliding out under doors and cracks and wherever else the drafts went. Perhaps his mother and the Goldings' had been worried about his reaction. They had expected Billy to be angry. But they were wrong. An eerie quiet and calm settled on him, over then over all of them. Sarah Golding set down at the table and began to butter herself a slice of bread while Billy's mother poured her some tea from the pot.

There was much more that could have been said but each of them tacitly understood that Sarah Golding's resignation signified that all could have been said and done had been. Their part in the play had come to an end. And from now on, they could only watch the drama unfold. The events and scenes they had tried to prevent now had a life of their own, a gathering momentum that they were powerless to stop. The hour glass had been set and the grains of sand had all but drained from top to bottom. And Billy imagined this, the sound of the sand passing through the waist of the hour glass. It turned into a roar.

Maggie noted the brief change in him and offered, 'We could watch tonight to see if they come, Bill?'

Billy Collins looked up and then down again to concentrate on buttering another slice of bread. 'Everyone will be looking tonight. Scriven, the navy, all of them. They are not that stupid. And neither is Jerry. We won't see hide nor hair of him tonight. They'll be satisfied it is just a hoax.'

Billy's mum and Sarah Golding exchanged a look. Maggie watched all of them. She was searching furiously for a solution.

Chapter 25
The Dreadful Inevitability of It All:
You Could Make It Up

Before he could ask where they were going, Captain Collins knew. The knowledge had risen from his stomach to his mind, leadening his legs. Even if he'd wanted to, he couldn't have opened the passenger door of the Red Wing. For the moment, he was stupefied with the knowledge and he didn't have to ask Sapper Mike, the address of where the stubborn lady, Mrs Sansom, lived.

The events of the last 48 hours, his decision that when the phone rang for the next job it would be his last; the fact that it had him returning to Portland to his place of birth was just all too contrived to be coincidence. He understood that the weight of fate was upon him and he knew better than to try and beat his luck. It was as if it had been scripted, inescapably written in the stars. There was a dreadful inevitability to it all.

And so, Captain Collins knew that he was returning to Old Sea Dog Cottage; the house he had grown up in for nearly eleven years before he left the island. Of course, the stubborn old lady who wouldn't leave the island in spite of the 2,000 kilo Second World War bomb on her doorstep lived in his childhood home in Old Sea Dog Cottage. With the way things had played out so far, how could it have been anywhere else?

'Well, here we are, sir!' Sapper Mike informed as his mentor surveyed the old place that had hardly changed. The woodwork had been painted up fresh and the small garden out front looked like it had had some scrupulous attention, but other than that, time appeared to have stood still. He never thought he would see it again. After he'd had word that his mother had died, there seemed little point in returning to the cottage, to Portland. It had been sold in his absentia. He had paid no mind to the buyer. Sansom was just another old Portland name. He thought that he had finished with the old place and Portland altogether and then out loud, he said, 'But it obviously isn't finished with me.'

'You what, sir?' enquired Sapper Mike.

'Eh?' The Captain returned, thundering back into the present.

'We're here, sir, I said!'

'Right you are, Sapper, I can see that!'

The Captain had that *here but not here* look in his eye that had arrived soon after they'd got the call about the bomb, that prior to that, Sapper Mike had not seen. Now was not the time to wonder what was going on with Captain. There was work to be done.

They exchanged a look, both gripping their respective door handles of the Red Wing.

'Better get in there and see if that charm of yours can shift the old lady! I'm going to have a quick look under the bonnet. See if I can't work out what the problem with this diesel is. Fire her up again, lad.'

'You're not coming in then?' Sapper Mike was ever so slightly put out, but refused to be daunted.

'Oh, yes. I'll be in shortly. Just want to see what's up with the timing on this old girl.'

'Okey doke, sir. Don't want to miss out on this lady, though. Bit of a looker, by all accounts. Tall and dark. Green eyes. Well preserved was how she was described,' the young man added with a wink.

But the Captain was ignoring the bonhomie. In fact, he looked as if he'd seen a ghost. Resisting the urge to shake his head in frustration with his mentor, Sapper Mike hopped out of the Red Wing to focus on the matter at hand. He'd be damned if was about to try and fathom his mentor anymore. Now was not the time or place. And this was the first 'negotiation' he'd been assigned. He wanted to get his thoughts straight, get it all straight in his mind what he had to say: to finely tune that mixture of fact and projection of potential damage if the bomb were to go off.

In short, he didn't have time to worry about his mentor who was now, to all intents and purposes, peering under the bonnet of the Red Wing as he looked back, knuckles posed to rap the front door of Old Sea Dog Cottage. But why would the description of the lady—tall, dark and green-eyed make the old boy swallow his tongue like that? And he'd paled like a corpse, for goodness sake!

'Dunno and don't need to know,' he said aloud as he knocked the door.

The front door opened so quickly she had to have been right behind it, waiting in readiness, Sapper Mike reasoned. He stepped back off the step to give them a bit of space.

'Come in!' she commanded quickly, standing aside as part of the instruction. 'Aren't you a bit young to be doing this?' She added with a finality that told Sapper Mike that the question didn't require a response. He barely had time to take her in. But a glance confirmed to him what he had been told about her—she was well preserved. Tall, dark-haired with what might have been a chestnut glow in the sunlight, clear-skinned and with arresting green cat eyes that took him in an instant and made him reassess his assumption about an 'old lady'. Evidently, she was to be no pushover. There was too much of a steely confidence about that. Charm alone was never going to convince.

'Follow the hall through to the back and sit down.' The second instruction came from behind him. Sapper Mike turned to see the 'old lady' about to close the stable front door of the cottage when she paused, eyes creasing to scrutinise. Must have been the Captain she'd spotted, Sapper Mike noted, and then turned into the kitchen. He guessed that it probably hadn't changed in fifty years, antiquated and simple it was with a rough oak table and chairs with an enamel mug and plate atop.

It looked to all the world that the old lady boiled her kettle above the driftwood fire in the hearth that crackled and spat with salt crystals. The uneven purple and mauve earthenware, chequered tiles clinked unsteadily underfoot. Seemed like the kettle was about to come to the boil given the hiss. It was as if she'd been expecting him, them, timing eerily spot on.

'I've left the front door open for Mr Collins,' the old lady stated matter-of-factly.

'Yes, he'll be in shortly no doubt,' the young man turned to meet her gaze and then he checked himself. 'Mr Collins? You mean *Captain* Collins? You know him?'

'You could say that. But that's not for now, not for you, young man.'

And there it was again, that 'young man' description almost as if it were retaliation for his references for his various 'old lady' references. But he hadn't said that out loud or to her. She was definitely no pushover. And how could she know the Captain?

Outside, Captain William Collins had got out tools that now sat on the battery of the Red Wing, his head cocked all the better to listen to that irregular thrum of the diesel engine. The thing was, he couldn't concentrate whatsoever and could only hear that infernal ringing in his ears that had started with the phone call about this Portland job. He'd just have to leave it for the time being.

More than that, he was now utterly spooked. What were the chances of his having to return not only to Portland for his last job, but back to Old Sea Dog Cottage? The house of his birth. Every last iota of logic and rationalism of career spanning had left him the moment the Red Wing had turned into the lane and the unrelenting inevitability of it all had hit home. But that wasn't to be Captain Collins' final disconcerting surprise of the day. No, far from it.

With that numbing sense of apprehension and with the gait of a man walking in his sleep, Captain Collins closed the Red Wing bonnet, forgot to turn off the Land Rover's engine and stumbled up the garden path of Old Sea Dog Cottage, fifty years nearly to the day since, if the truth be known, he had left as a boy of ten. Operation Tiger had been the twenty-eighth of April. Now, it was the thirtieth and spring was well on its way. Obviously the island, Portland and his family home were not done with him yet.

And he'd lost years of calm, focussed thinking, evaporated in an instant. He hoped that that was all that would be evaporating before the day was out. For the time being though, it was all he could do to man the floodgates of his memory to prevent the intense feelings of his first ten years, the luminous Technicolour events of childhood, returning.

Chapter 26
Operation Tiger: 28 April 1944 and 1992

It was the tolling of the church bell, that ominous, lonely chime that woke both Billy Collins and Maggie Golding from their sleep that night probably within seconds of each other. It was that night, that full-mooned night that would change their lives irrevocably; the night that they had tried so hard to avoid. But as we know, the march of time waits for no-one.

For one thing, the church bell of St George's hadn't tolled since the outbreak of war in 1939. That it should have echoed across the quarries and bluffs of the Portland every thirty seconds for the last ten minutes at 1 am was more than enough to let the islanders know that something of terrible importance was afoot.

Gingerly, Billy had turned back a fraction of the blackout blind of his bedroom window, to see terrible bright orange flowers blooming in the sky out past Pulpit Rock on Chesil Beach. He whipped back the curtain completely, something that was utterly forbidden in wartime blackout, but he did it anyway, throwing caution to the wind.

Across the way, in her home, Zennor Cottage, Billy could see that Maggie had also wakened, her face framed in her bedroom window, her mouth open in an 'O' of silent fear, her pulse beating out a tattoo. And then the chime of church bell of St George's filtered out and the thunder and report of a multitude of explosions echoed like the contact of tidal waves breaking across the shores of their shared sensibility, the agonised shouts of terrified men in their confusion blistering across the wrenching groans and screams of tearing metal rose up.

That dreadful cacophony drew each and every one of the remaining islanders down their garden paths towards Pulpit Rock for the clearest view of the slaughter. They lined the headland, hundreds of glowing lanterns, Davey lamps, congregated to see the spectacle.

As predicted, the previous night, there had been no sign of the *Schnellenboot*. With the moon twenty-four hours off full, visibility had been good for Mr Scriven and the combined Navies' watch. There hadn't been even a breath of wind. The sea was calm—a gentle, reassuring lap punctuating the night sound scape was all that was heard. Manoeuvres had been suspended for 24 hours. Nothing had stirred, convincing all that no threat was imminent.

However, that was not to be way on 28 April 1944. Instinctively, Billy and Maggie knew the E-boats were back, their worst fears confirmed by the horror of noise erupting from the bay. All were drawn to it and this was what Captain Collins remembered walking up the garden path of Old Sea Dog Cottage nigh on fifty years later, the memories as clear as the dew on the rose bushes his grandfather had planted in the front garden as pungent, briny as the scent of kelp in his nostrils and salt on his lips.

As he gingerly stepped over the threshold, Captain Collins paused to run his thumb over the latch and lock, feeling the familiarity of the rough-hewed metal. He took in the orange quarry stone tiles in the short hall that led to the kitchen in the back. He nodded involuntarily at the open door to the front room on the left briefly glimpsing his grandfather in his rocking chair, tired after a back breaking day of hard labour in the quarries. Memories and faces crowded around him in an ominous-friendly greeting.

All those years in the Royal Engineers focussing on the here and now on the details of the job at hand, poised to make safe a deadly oblivion. All that concentration and focus slid away as he picked up where he left off 50 years beforehand. The power of the past, of memory overpowering the present he pushed open the kitchen door, the talk trailing off and saw Sapper Mike with a questioning look of expectancy across the eyes.

Captain Collins gently pushed open the kitchen door further to see her, same as him 50 years older but there wasn't even the briefest moment of hesitation in his recognition, the years rolling away like breakers on the shore.

'Billy Collins, hello,' said the lady as she took him in. 'Fifty years later, almost to the day too. You always had a sense of timing, Billy. A little late, perhaps, as always. But always a presence, eh?'

Captain Collins was swallowing hard to get a little moisture in his mouth in order to speak. After an exercise of frowns and shuffles, he managed to stammer, 'Maggie Golding, you haven't aged a day!' He instantly clammed up with the stupidity of his statement. The embarrassment quelled the Captain's tongue.

Quite clearly, given the crimson bloom in his cheeks, he wasn't going to recover without some assistance. *Golding?*

'Mrs *Sansom,*' Sapper Mike ventured with emphasis, 'has said that she can't leave the cottage and is not setting foot off Portland no matter who does the asking.'

Captain Collins found his tongue, 'Well, if that's what she's said, we've done all we can do. I know better than to undo this girl's resolve.'

'I haven't been a girl for a long time, Billy. Not that you'd know that, my friend,' added Mrs Sansom with a hint of cattiness, followed by a smile.

Sapper Mike was trying his best to conceal his bewilderment as he looked from one to the other. A lot they had in common, that much was plain to see. And feel too, as the room crackled with the static between them. He was just a little surprised that in all the talk of Portland over the last 23 hours the Captain hadn't mentioned anyone specific and certainly no-one as close as this lady seemed. There was certainly more than a fleeting connection there and when he checked the Captain again, gone was any hint of consternation.

In fact, his gait and whole demeanour had transformed. Gone was the tired frame with tensed shoulders, a brow lined with worry and fatigued, puffy eyes. To his utter amazement, there stood before him a man with his arms outstretched for an embrace, relaxed open and eyes shining, expectant. Warm the Captain could be after he'd worked you out and was at ease with your presence. Tactile, never. Mike had received the odd congratulatory, thudding slap on the back that nearly sent him into next week when he'd got something right. But that was the long and the short of it.

No, the Captain had always been a self-contained unit, not one for talk about himself or for displays of feeling. The man was an island attached but distant at the same time.

'This job seems to have no end of surprises,' Sapper Mike murmured to himself and then he noticed the old lady. The years had slipped away from her too in a radical thaw. The worry lines and crow's feet around her now glowing eyes gave off an energy and light you might see on a cloudless equinox night. And what he'd assumed were her tired, arthritic movements were fluid and quick. And then they were hugging each other, all affection as if two long-separated siblings had been reunited. As the moment passed with the hug and they appraised each other, a shimmer of awkward embarrassment returned as they became aware of company, of Sapper Mike squinting at them with a barrel full of questions, hope for an answer or two.

'Uh Mike. This old lady as you've been referring to her,' for which the Captain received a playful jab in the ribs that he was obviously expecting, 'is Maggie Golding.' He then paused as he turned to hold her gaze. 'Still my oldest and dearest friend, it seems, even after all these years.' Time stretched for a while that was probably, in fact, only a few moments but felt a while longer for Sapper Mike as the old fella gushed like a schoolgirl. The young man's embarrassment felt about as complete as complete could be with all that emotion flying about the room.

'We really ought to go now, sir,' he gulped silently to himself, rocking on the balls of his feet.

Drinking in the Captain's profile, Mrs Sansom, or rather Maggie Golding, said with her commanding manner, 'Off you go then. You'd better do as the young man says, Captain Collins. I believe you have a job to do. That bomb isn't going to diffuse itself. Go now and be lucky, Bill.'

The Captain turned to his old friend and after a moment of silent searching replied, 'I certainly hope to be, Maggie. Certainly hope to be.' Sapper Mike led the way out, trying his best to shake off the doubt implied in the Captain's tone.

Having started up the Red Wing, Sapper Mike asked of his mentor, 'What was that all about, sir?' Captain Collins was staring at Mrs Sansom or Maggie who was framed in the doorway of Old Sea Dog Cottage, watching them leave.

'What? Oh nothing, Sapper. I'll tell you about it another time, maybe.'

'Right you are, sir,' replied the young man, shoving the Land Rover into reverse, unconvinced by his own words.

Chapter 27

Captain Collins and Sapper Mike had had more luck shifting the pigeon fancier who had taken only a little persuasion after he had recognised the Captain.

'Well, I never! Billy Collins. Come home to roost after all this time, eh? Who'd have thought it would be you who'd come back to save the day.'

The Captain hadn't characteristically come back with a quip or self-effacing comment. He'd just shook his head and walked back to the Red Wing leaving the pigeon fancier shrugging with indifference. It seemed to Sapper Mike that the Captain's return to Portland was to be full of surprises. Like Mrs Sansom, the pigeon fancier would not leave the island but had agreed to be moved to the bunkers in the naval yard. They'd been bored into the rock to keep Naval First Command safe from the Luftwaffe in 1941. With a hundred metres of Portland stone above them, no-one could have been safer anywhere in England. But that was not to be for the Captain.

'Right then, let's get to it. No more procrastinating.'

'Thief of time and all that, sir!'

'Dunno about that, lad.'

'You okay to do this, sir? I mean, I could make this one mine. I've had plenty enough practice runs. What say I take this one, sir? You don't seem quite yourself about it.'

'No lad. This one's got my name on it. I've said I will, so I must.'

On hearing these words, Sapper Mike remembered a story about soldiers inscribing their own names on a bullet and keeping it about their person as a good luck charm in the hope that the enemy would never possess it. It seemed that there was to be no dissuading the Captain from his final mission.

The old boy and his apprentice left for the bomb site. Sapper Mike broke the silence that was weighing heavy on them, 'Seems hard to believe that the bomb could have lain under the centre spot of a football pitch for all these years and never went off. How many games do you recall kicked off over the bomb, Captain?'

'More than plenty, I'd imagine. I do know that Portland was hit by more than 500 bombs through the course of the Second World War, over the six years, roughly one every few days when you even it out. I guess much of that was after I left though in the latter part of the ward when the fighting was fiercer.'

'When did you leave, sir?'

'When did I leave Portland? Oh, that must have been the day after of the Operation Tiger massacre. Maggie and I were evacuated out after the disaster. I guess they didn't want the story getting out. I was in Yorkshire until 1947. Two years after the war ended. I had no idea up on the moors that it had ended.'

Rainwater hissed under the tyres of the Red Wing as it ascended the hairpin bends of the rock up to Fortuneswell. The Captain hushed again in thought. Sapper Mike, however, wasn't about to abandon his mentor to his memories.

'Where did you say were you evacuated to, sir? Did you go with Mrs Golding?'

As he glanced across, Sapper Mike couldn't help but notice that the Captain seemed to have aged over the last twenty-four hours. Now he looked his age. No doubt he was still as strong as an ox, quick witted and thick-wristed-powerful with a grip like a bull terrier. There was that powerful barrel chest, too. Physically, he was all there. But he looked exhausted, looked his age. He had that vulnerable look in the eyes and a sense of distraction. Most of all, he seemed to have lost that irrepressible edge, like all the fight had gone out of him. Sapper Mike wondered if the old boy really was a liability to himself? He'd tried to tell Colonel Wildblood. Who could he confide in now? Should he mention it to the unit? No, he couldn't possibly do that. It was his last job and there was a lot of pride at stake. But what was it about pride going before a fool?

'Evacuated, yes, up to Harrogate up in the North of England. But not with Mrs Golding. Two days after the slaughter that was Operation Tiger, all us children were evacuated. Maggie and I were the first though. Deemed it too dangerous to stay on Portland and we had no school teacher by then.' That look again and the Captain quietened. Sapper Mike was hunched over the Red Wing steering wheel in concentration as the tarmac gave way to a potholed track which required care to navigate. He didn't want to go upsetting all that plastic explosive in the back.

The Captain's last statement begged the question, 'What happened to the school teacher? Evil old sod, I remember you saying. What was his name? Mr Scribber?'

'Scriven. Paul Scriven. Captain Paul Scriven,' the Captain replied with a weighty sigh. Still waters running deep there, Sapper Mike noted. And with another deep exhalation, the Captain righted himself. 'That's another story and not for now. Right, let's get this done!' A customary steel returned to his tone, a keen animal flash of alertness returning to his eye. They were there now.

'Back up behind the seven and half tonner. Best to have it between this lot in the back and the bomb. Don't want all that going up as well if I have a bad day at the office.'

He was already halfway out of the Red Wing cab as he said it, all sprightly again as if he'd just asked someone to put the kettle on. He was pretty much used to the Captain's ways by now, though the last twenty-four hours had been a test. He was more than glad of this return to his characteristic 'all business manner' which still had the power to stun the young man.

'I may get like that in time, all business and calm in the face of it.' Sapper Mike shuddered a moment as he switched off the ignition and carefully shut the Red Wing door. He didn't want any of his vibrations disturbing that bomb.

'Come on, laddie', the Captain shouted over his shoulder, 'get to it, then,' he added as he strode to the bombsite as cool as if he were approaching the bar in the Officer's Mess to buy a round rather than to potentially unstable Second War Ordinance. It made him wonder if the Captain wasn't a bit unhinged, the way he seemed to be able to switch off his fear.

Sapper Mike rounded the 7.5 tonner to see that the Captain was stood at ease, legs apart, one elbow in the palm of his other hand, addressing the unit at the operational command post that was a sand-bagged horseshoe shape enough for four men and the recording equipment. From inside trailed the lines of wire that led some seventy-five metres off to the bomb which now lay exposed, uncovered all 2 metres in length of the 2,000 kilo legacy of the Luftwaffe.

Since the Captain and Sapper Mike had left to visit Maggie Golding and the pigeon fancier to encourage them to a distance, the remainder of the unit had been busy. With a cautious efficiency, they had removed the earth and stone from around the bomb. Three metres square, a metre deep around it. As they had dug down around the Satan, they had reinforced the edge of the pit with timber shafting every six inches. The team, with force and caution enough to not disturb the sleeping menace of explosive, drove in the four cover posts to create an enclosure similar to a wooden animal pen. Each and every strike of the shovel and pick axe could potentially have triggered the bomb's timer.

At the centre of the pit, on an altar of Portland stone that the bomb had lain dormant on for nearly fifty years, its tarnished, cast iron shell a dull pewter colour, it almost looked harmless, prone-vulnerable even. Now a serial number and the double lightning strike symbol of the Luftwaffe were clearly visible. For Sapper Mike, there was something definitely ominous about the numbers, the arbitrary cataloguing of something with so much destructive potential. He dispelled the thought, consigned it to the 'unhelpful' pile in his mind and focussed on his task of double sand bagging the lip of the pit as protocol dictated to contain the blast and shrapnel should the damn thing go off. He'd been on sand bagging duty for most of the year. He hadn't been permitted yet to go down into 'the pit'. The Captain had said that he preferred him sand bagging to get him used to being in the locus of unstable explosive.

By now, the other members of the unit were out of harm's way behind the OCP. Bothe the Captain and the Sapper had inserted their ear pieces and clipped on their mics so that those in the OCP could keep tabs on progress and respond to practical requests. All had suited up with their body armour. The Kevlar plating for Mike was part reassurance, part fear inducing: it might save you from shrapnel and flying debris if you were a reasonable distance away, but wasn't going to stop you from being vaporised if you were in the immediate vicinity.

'So that is what a Satan looks like, sir?' Get the conversation going again. Banish the thoughts.

'Seen plenty in my time. Two thousand kilos of potential hellfire with an M-class detonator,' he replied matter-of-factly.

And then, almost as if posed as a question, 'Should be a piece of cake.' But he'd trailed off completely and appeared to be staring intently at the bomb's serial number. Without due care and attention, the Captain jumped down into the pit and with his brush in hand was crouched down, cleaning the accumulated dust off the numbers. When the numbers were completely revealed, he stood up quickly and took a step back to a safe distance as if he had been crouched in front of a driftwood fire that had begun to crackle and spit, or as if he had uncovered a serpent from beneath a rock. Sapper Mike's first thought was out of his mouth before he could get the brain in gear.

'Is it the timer, sir? Get out now!' he yelled, the panic in his voice clear as day, an animal look of fear in his eye. He could have kicked himself. Schoolboy error. An urgent voice in his ear demanded a status report immediately.

It couldn't have been the timer for the Captain had remained where he was, staring intently. And then he gathered himself and was massaging his eyes with the heels of his hands.

The voice in their ears from the OCP insistent, 'Status report!'

'Nothing to report. Over. Just lost my footing. Over,' lied the Captain.

'Well, with respect, get those bloody cameras switched on, sir. We're blind over here.'

'Roger that.'

The Captain had removed his mic and switched it off. Stood at the lip of the pit, Sapper Mike glared fiercely at his Captain. Things just didn't feel right at all. On previous jobs, it had been pretty much banter all the way apart from at the crucial moments that required quiet, no distraction. This job had had a runaway feel to it right from the start. It was making the young man feel like sacking the whole thing and getting out of harm's way. Without his mentor firing on all cylinders, without his mentor's absolute confidence, flaws in the glass ceiling of Sapper Mike's confidence were appearing. In a team where there was no place for weakness, shadows of doubt were creeping in. Despite the clear spring sunshine, Mike felt cold. He could feel the goose bumps when he should not. It was making him angry and there was no place for that either, here.

More than a little tersely, Sapper Mike demanded, 'What is it, sir?'

The Captain had his back to him, his fingers holding up his chin to the sunlight after massaging his cheeks and jowls. Without turning around, he responded automatically, 'It's the serial number. That's all.'

'What about the serial number, sir?'

'30.03.30.'

'And?'

'That's my birth date, Sapper.'

The world around him raced into sharp focus. He felt a sharp pop in his ears followed by a ringing that faded to nothing. The sound of the nearby surf reasserted itself. Words failed him. Thoughts failed him.

'Now, what are the chances of that, young man?' stated the Captain. Once again, an authority and calm, mixed with resignation had returned to the tenor of his voice. There was nothing to say to that. Sapper Mike was utterly flummoxed.

The chances of that were infinitesimal. He couldn't begin to think about it. So, he wouldn't. In an ultra-determined fashioned, Sapper Mike finished stacking the sand bags, paying scrupulous attention to getting them straight, placed perfectly, overlapping like brick work, no gaps. For several minutes, neither exchanged a word or a look, their focus complete. Eventually, Sapper Mike stood to his full height, hands on hips to rest.

'Piece of cake this is going to be, sir! Routine job. Except it's your last one! You've been saying that this is your last job. You decided that well before the call came in that it was to be on Portland your last job, a final farewell testament to experience before retirement. I think were your exact words.' The Captain intently searched his young apprentice's eyes, reading him.

For the life of him, Sapper Mike couldn't work out how the Captain was about to respond. Over the last twenty-four hours he had appeared furious, vulnerable and also his affable self. Now, he seemed to be all three. A twitch at the corner of the Captain's eye broke the spell and the affirmative boom to Captain's voice returned.

'Right you are, Sapper! Let's get going. Carpe diem and all that!'

'Carpet what, sir?'

'Eh, carpe diem, Sapper! Seize the day, eh! Don't you know your Latin, young man? Amo, amass, am at it again!' The Captain stated, beaming expectant for something and then the eyes flattened as the head shook, 'Never mind, never mind. Generation gap,' he replied as he climbed out of the pit.

'Let's do a last check on the kit. Gotta make sure the Mic Steth is perfect. I don't want to be hearing anything other than silence, no extra ringing in my ears, I'll need to know exactly if Satan starts the old tick tock. I'll only have 12 seconds to get the hell out of there and behind your beautiful sand bags before she pops. Good job, lad.' The Captain was smiling contentedly to himself. In the years to come, Sapper Mike would always remember how the Captain could understate potential death, being blown to smithereens, and couch it in friendly, everyday language. A beautiful enigma perhaps.

Now having opened his personalised kit box, the Captain was paying particular attention to the mic-steth or microphone-stethoscope. Like everything else in the Captain's possession, it was pristine-clean, polished to within an inch of its life. And being the most important piece of kit in a Royal Engineers ordinance disposal officer's toolbox, so it should be.

Exactly the same idea as a doctor's stethoscope except it was used for detecting the rhythm of life in a bomb rather than a human heart.

'Funny, really when you think about it,' chuckled the Captain.

'Hilarious, sir,' replied the young Sapper who was having something of a sense of humour failure. The Captain eyed him and continued with his explanation of the kit.

The mic-steth had two primary functions. Firstly, it amplified the sound of the commencement of the ticking of the timing mechanism of the bomb, if in the process of disarming the bomb the timing pin is accidently engaged or disturbed by the movement of the process. Then in the event of this unfortunate circumstance, the unlucky bomb disposal has roughly twelve seconds to run like fury to put as much distance between himself and sleeping Satan before literally, all hell breaks loose and he has, as the Captain put it his famous 'bad day at the office'. Sapper Mike had heard the spiel countless times before but the meter and delivery of it served its calming purpose. Familiarisation of the kit so that it was an extension of his being.

The second purpose, and the order of importance depends on your point of view or experience, whether you are sat on top of the bomb when it goes off, is that the micro-steth is also a recording device so that the rest of the unit can hear and understand the event preceding an untimely demise. By hearing the unlucky officer's description as that's what it is, a step by step talk through of his actions in his disposal of the bomb, they can work out what and what not to do the next time they have to dispose this or that type of bomb.

'And people being people, there is always going to be another bomb.' It's what the Captain quaintly referred to as *research for the next chap*. This was what went through Sapper Mike's mind as he watched Captain Collins, his friend and mentor, explain all the gubbins.

There were other sayings of the Captain's that he would remember that would take a while, sometimes years in fact to filter through. And the Captain was fond of pausing in whatever sort of work he was focussing to look up and deliver up a grain of information that would grow into a pearl in the oyster mind of his apprentice. In the Captain's book, all information was to be shared. No secrets between friends. At least, that was what he professed, though the young Sapper was beginning to get the feeling that the Captain might have more than a few skeletons in his closet. He just didn't want to be around when they came home to roost.

As he was finishing up and as if on cue, he added cryptically, 'You know what, Sapper, the most capable of men can appear in the most unlikely of packages. And people are frequently not what they seem.'

'Getting that impression, sir,' replied the Sapper. The Captain didn't respond. He'd said something similar on the trip down. *Didn't it sound like he was summing up, though?*

Happy with his tests, Captain Collins set the mic-steth back in its case and turned to address the unit, who had assembled for the last talk before the nitty-gritty of the job was undertaken. 9 am was the projected time for kick off and here they all were at 8.50 am sharp. To all intents and purposes, it was all going as regular as clockwork.

'It's time then, gentlemen. The last job for this old man and I want to thank you all.'

Why was he talking about himself in the third person? Strange. But there was no interrupting the fellow now.

'I'll keep it short and sweet. You've all been a pleasure to work with.' He surveyed each of the men in the unit, making sure he made eye contact.

'Each and every one of you. There's not a man here that I don't have one hundred per cent confidence in. You've all got what it takes. A diligent, hardworking, talented bunch, if there ever was one. Not a shirker among you, apart from Lieutenant Billington, but we'll give him a pass on account of his excellent tea-making!' Hearty chuckles and then the Captain's face clouded with a severity.

'Lastly, diligence and talent will get you so far. Luck is the other ingredient. You can shorten the odds with hard work and ability, but you can never know the odds. You can never beat your luck. So, don't give it a thought. When it's your time, it's your time.' The last words hung silent in the air as if after a detonation.

'Right! Let's get to it, then!' he said to himself as much as the assembled. As he turned his back, many exchanged an enquiring look. It wasn't the done thing to explain and thank with such a finality in case you felt they were tempting fate, sinking the job at hand. It just didn't ring right for the unit, but they buried it with business rather than talk about it or give it any more air time. But that wasn't the only thing that wasn't ringing right. Just as they set off for the relative safety of the OCP, that disconcerting ringing in the Captain's ears was like an alarm for him only.

Sapper Mike blinked at his mentor, his mouth open a fraction, but words failed him.

'Go on! Don't just stand there. Get!' cajoled the Captain avuncularly. There was nothing more for it. Sapper Mike followed the unquestionable order.

Chapter 28
1944 Remembered

As he walked the ground between the operational command post and the bomb, Captain Collins remembered the last time he had seen his childhood friend Maggie Golding. It was the day after the disastrous events of Operation Tiger, the day before they were to be evacuated, removed from Portland and all that they had known of life.

The day after the event was the quietest that Billy had experienced then or since. There was little or no breeze and the sea was flat calm, lacklustre. Eerily quiet, none of the regular rhythm of activity. But a great deal of activity there was. The whispered word quickly spread from the dockyard up the hairpins and then all over the island—more than eight hundred souls, mostly Amis, missing from the base, presumed drowned, killed in the slaughter. Their bodies and parts were washing up all over the island and Chesil Beach and they would all the way some thirty miles southwest as far as Slapton Sands in their scores, in their hundreds.

Probably because of the numbers of corpses that were taken by the current west to Slapton Sands, the Admiralty happened upon the decision to have official records state that the attack had occurred there rather than in the deep waters around Portland, a pebble's throw from the Admiralty dockyard. There was too much of the Singeing of the King of Spain's Beard about it. Cadiz 1516. Or Pearl Harbour 1941. What could be written up and deemed daring, cunning and guile was a different proposition altogether when it landed on your own doorstep, it seemed to Maggie and Bill.

The Admiralty's shock and fear and embarrassment that the German Navy, in tiny numbers of less than half a dozen small craft, could pretty much waltz undetected (save for a couple of kids and a woman), unchallenged and slaughter the preparation force for the D-day landings had predictably turned from an acute, trembling fury to cold pragmatism. Despite the Official Secrets Act, the story would undoubtedly get out. The scale of the evidence was such that that couldn't be helped.

But what could be controlled was the official story of the losses: reduce the figures, the numbers of dead, the loss of equipment, unarmed landing craft, troop carriers and other vessels, of all the logistics required to send an invasion force to Normandy to challenge the grip Nazis had over Europe and try to prevent an invasion of Britain itself. The navy's jeopardy had been the Kreigsmarine's opportunity.

Bottom line was the story couldn't get out. If it became common knowledge, it could potentially have a devastating effect on morale and the British War effort. The only way of dealing with the fierce heat of that violence was with swift, stone-cold pragmatism. And so, it would not have been a surprise to an informed observer to see the two MP jeeps arrive separately and simultaneously at Old Sea Dog and Zennor Cottages within twenty-four hours of the clatter and boom of the last searing shots and shells fired on Operation Tiger, when the dark shapes of the now very much apparent Schnellenboot disappeared over the horizon.

News of the destruction and loss and the part played by the Collins and Golding families had sped through the telecommunication wires from the Admiralty in Portland, to Whitehall, the Ministry of Defence and the bunker under 10 Downing Street. Important men spoke in hushed, serious tones in high-ceilinged, wood panelled rooms lined with leather bound volumes and tomes—the appropriate setting for deciding fates. Gold-braided epaulettes and pinstriped suits made definite, gravelly voiced decisions for the two families on Portland. The news was delivered in each case by an English man in a suit accompanied by two American MPs whose arrival in their fume-belching jeeps had been observed by the two children from the upstairs windows of the cottages.

The two mothers could remain on the island (*as soon as they had signed the appropriate documentation*) while the two children, Billy Collins and Maggie Golding, would be collected that morning by the Royal Women's Voluntary Service and escorted, Billy to Harrogate in Yorkshire, Maggie to the far tip of Cornwall to live out the rest of the Second World War in safety, as it was put.

And so it was, still numb from visions of destruction and feeling more than a tremendous weight of responsibility, separately and simultaneously, forbidden to communicate, Billy Collins and Maggie Golding packed their few belongings and clothes and were removed from their homes and taken to board an angry, impatient huffing steam locomotive bound for opposite ends of the country.

No phones, no letters, no contact. For Billy, just the one telegram read and passed to him over breakfast, one square piece of card typed informing that his mother had died and with her his reason to return to the island, as he saw it as a boy, until now when the echoes of yesteryear and fate had conspired to draw him back to his home and his childhood friend, Maggie Golding, to Portland. And more than that: to diffuse an unexploded memory of the very reason, the war, that had banished him from Portland.

'Oh my days, what a life,' the Captain murmured to himself as he quickened his step and straightened his beret as he covered the last few yards to commence the job at hand.

'What'll be, will be,' he told himself as he climbed down into the pit and squatted down to place and open his kit box. Captain Collins ran an appreciative thumb over the high-polished dovetails of the box. And in that moment, he remembered his last walk with Maggie, first and only time hand in hand, fifty years previous thereabouts. Not knowing what mutilation or severed horror they might find on the beaches, the two children had kept to the bluff paths, eyes averted from the near, fixed on the far.

They had been close to Red Rock when Maggie spotted them. First it was the shoes, she spotted, unlaced placed neatly, incongruously atop a scruffy clump of grass, toes pointing seawards. They had paused to question each other silently. Then they had noticed the rough, green cloth of the military uniform folded neatly beside the shoes. They squatted down to inspect them. Oxford brogues. Highly polished. As big as barges. Socks pushed into the toes. Maggie picked up the tunic. It had that acrid scent about it that they recognised immediately. She dropped the tunic and they both stood up and instinctively scanned the shoreline, but there was nothing unusual to be seen, no sign of their teacher, Mr Scriven. Wordlessly, they had returned home and made no mention of their find.

Chapter 29

Back in the Real World, Something Doesn't Feel Right in the OCP / Doesn't Look Right in the Pit

'What's he doing?'

From behind the binoculars, 'He's just squatting there. Hasn't even connected up the mic-steth yet.'

Sapper Mike, 'Shall I go out?'

'No! Breach of protocol! Don't even think about it. Stay exactly where you are.'

Sapper Mike grabbed a set of binoculars to see for himself what was going on. The Captain had stood up and was standing stock-still, rigid, his back to the OCP. He wasn't looking at the bomb. He appeared to be staring intently at Pulpit Rock.

Captain Collins had raised himself up to his full height to gaze at the Rock. Mr Scriven was leaning over Pulpit Rock, a massive aberration of what should be.

'You're back, I see, Collins. Didn't think you were going to get away with it that easily, did you? Time to take on your responsibility.'

Captain Collins carefully laid down his equipment at the edge of the dugout, the bomb site that was to be the theatre of events of his last job—the final act in the play of a life, if you like. He shrugged away the monstrous notion and image before him.

And then he sat down on the edge and admired the construction of the timber shafting, running a palm of approval over the snug fit of the corner port nearest him. The 'Satan' was so shallow in the dugout that in all likelihood the walls of the pit wouldn't collapse. But digging in was the method and there was a comfort in that, in the protocol. Treat all unexploded ordinance the same and it's just another job, the job. The Captain nodded at the neatness of the preparations his unit had done.

For a good few minutes, the Captain remained immobile, going over in his mind what needed to be done to diffuse the bomb. He'd done scores of 'Satans' in and around London. Two thousand kilos of explosive. A real street flattener, as it was known in the Blitz. But in spite of his experience, the Captain knew better than to allow any sort of complacency to dull his concentration. A' Satan' could be a tricky customer and the M-class detonator was a puzzle to be deciphered. The German boffins might have installed all manner of trickery to undo a BDO.

'Yes, the boys have done a fine job for me. Made a fitting stage for my last act,' murmured the Captain aloud.

The pit or dugout was constructed to channel the explosive energy upwards. And if Satan popped, that's where the BDO's bad day at the office would end, in a misty vapour. Hope was something impractical not to be factored into the equation. However, hope and a belief in luck did linger in the mind with reference to unusual tales of the experiences of some Londoners in the Blitz who may have been but a few metres from the detonation point of bomb who had somehow survived. The blast may have removed every last stitch, every last item of clothing from their bodies, but aside from that, they remained intact, unscathed, alive if a little wide-eyed with shock with something of a perpetual hum in their ears and with a sense that reality was somewhere off to the left.

And with that thought, the tinnitus ring in the Captain's ears tuned in, alerting him to the tools of his job and the cast iron casing of the Satan with its dormant, destructive energies.

'Right! On with the show, Collins!' he instructed himself, clapping and rubbing his hands together with customary vigour.

Carefully, the Captain drew the headset of the mic-steth over his head and connected up the lead that linked him up with his unit safely behind the sand bagged Operational Command Point. It crackled and rasped breathily in to life.

'Ah, there you are, sir! Everything ok?'

'All fine, Sapper! Just having a little think, lad.'

'Having a little think? Isn't that a little dangerous, sir?'

'Shut it, Lapin,' the Captain shot back with a warmth and mirth.

Usually, a more experienced BDO would have been communicating over the mic-steth but Sapper Mike had requested that although familiar with an M-class detonator, this was the first Satan he'd come across and so he'd wanted to hear, first-hand, the explanation of the defusal. He'd come across a few 'Hermans' in his time, the smaller but fatter cousin of the Satan named after the rotund Reichsfuhrer, Herman Goering, the figurehead of the German Air Force, the Luftwaffe.

It was a little unusual to have the least experience member of the unit on the other end of the mic-steth line. But as the Captain had diffused scores of Satans, it was reasoned in the unit that it should just be a routine job for him. And what the Captain didn't know about his trade really wasn't worth knowing. That was the common knowledge that came with the respect also.

From the Operational Command Point, the unit could see Captain's head bobbing about as he busied himself methodically with his preparations.

'Old boys taking his time!' Someone said.

'Leave him be,' said another. 'He's just making sure. It's a big thing, your last job.'

So, it seemed that Sapper Mike wasn't the only one who knew that it was the Captain's last job. A hunch had kept him quiet on that point. It didn't feel right to share the info. But it seemed that that cat was out of the bag.

'Wonder what he'll do when he retires?' Another asked idly from behind the binocs again.

'He'll be busier than he is now, no doubt. He'll have all sorts or projects planned, things to build, things to fix, places to go. Can't see those hands being idle for a moment.'

'That's true,' came a chorused response. They were confident, but Sapper Mike wasn't sharing their optimism. *That* feeling was washing over him.

And then, right on cue, with an exclamation of caution, another asked, 'What's he up to now?' Hands clamped on suddenly impatient hips, wonderment as all eyes watched with growing incredulity as the Captain clambered out of the pit, turned his back on the job and headed calmly off in a south-westerly direction.

'What the heck?'

'He's not done that before!'

'No-one's ever done that before.'

251

'You can't just leave the site once you've started a job. That's rule one in the rule book!'

'Not without explanation of what's already been done. If anything?' another added.

'Hasn't even switched on the cameras yet,' observed another, flicking the equipment on and off experimentally, illustrating the absence of a connection. So, they watched in silence as the silhouetting figure of the Captain disappeared over an incline.

'What now?' came the enquiry. As no-one seemed about to venture a solution, Sapper Mike filled the gap.

'We wait till he gets back, till he's ready. That's what we do.' More than a modicum of arched eye-browed surprise as the directive came from the Captain's apprentice, from the least experienced of the unit. There was a bit of foot shuffling while some of the more seasoned fellas in the unit considered nipping this in the bud, pulling rank, putting the whippersnapper in his place. But, all silently acquiesced, And then the most senior, Lieutenant Billington, claimed it for his own and repeated, 'Yes, we wait till he gets back from whatever he's up to. We wait till he's ready.' Comforted by the order of senior officer, the unit quietly nodded.

'Tea on then, chaps. Chop-Chop. I'm dying of thirst over here!'

Sapper Mike was not about to share his consternation.

Mindful of his protocol, Captain Collins thought he better be quick. It was only a short yomp, ten minutes if he was quick, to Pulpit Rock. He thought as he sat surveying the bomb that he'd felt a twinge of cramp in his leg. 'Best walk it off,' he mused. Last thing he needed on his last job was the distraction of a useless, cramping leg. And a bit of movement might rid him of that infernal ringing in his ears too.

His other motivation was to have a look at Pulpit Rock. He couldn't explain it, but he felt he had to look at it. Damn silly, it wouldn't have changed in the intervening years. But it had been pressing on him to visit Pulpit ever since he'd got the call. Sure enough, it was of massive personal significance to him as a boy. It was from there that Maggie had confirmed the presence and dark intention of the enemy that had set off a chain of events that had separated him from his home and family and friends. There was that. But there was other stuff too.

'Yes, there were a lot of happy memories too!' the Captain exclaimed out loud, sounding like an effort to convince himself. Having arrived, he stared up at Pulpit Rock hearing that familiar restless crash and mumbles of the waves at the base of Pulpit Rock, Chisel Bay opening out in that welcoming arc behind; that salt, dense wind also blasting away at the rock. He knew he wasn't going to climb the rock now, quick and nimble as a rat of boy, he might have been. But not now. Getting on for sixty now, that would take a careful methodical ascent.

'But there were a heap of happy memories associated with the rock too! Oh Lord, yes there were.' And the Captain remembered the giant Wrasse he'd caught from atop the rock.

The Wrasse were huge in the kelp beds and channels and caves at the bottom of Pulpit Rock. Standing there, Captain Collins could feel that snap and jerk, sometimes unbalancing him over 100 feet up above the water atop Pulpit Rock, he heard his exhilarant boyish whoops of joy, that surge and clutch of adrenalin that beat its way through him, bending his rod double at times with the weight of the monster that'd gone for the rag worm. He remembered being breathless with excitement as he steadily drew it up 100 feet out of the water, through the air, glistening, iridescent but unseen till the last few feet until it'd land flapping, a confused eye questioning at his feet. But to Billy Collins, the victory made him feel as if he could levitate.

With a fingertip, he'd trace the glowing turquoise or Halloween orange veins of colour that camouflaged the body of the fish, browns, yellows and greens and blacks amongst the kelp. And after admiring the colours and strength of the Wrasse, there was always a moment of sadness, of the waste of the life as it coughed up its last breathe from between those pouting, fat lips and teeth. But the sentiment evaporated in the sea spray as he placed it in the hessian carrying sack with seaweed in to keep the fish moist. Off to the pub or home they'd then go, to make fish cakes, Wrasse being too bony by half to be served otherwise.

Captain Collins sighed at the memory, his mop of unruly, dark hair flapping about his eyes up there in the wind atop the rock. And he found himself patting down the thinned out, grey wisps that were left before replacing his beret. Thumbing the Royal Engineers insignia bought him back to the here and now, and the certainty of his determination to return to the job that needed to be done.

'Jeez, the unit will be wondering what you're up to, you silly old fool. Put a shake on it!' he chided himself as he about-faced and made for the dugout, back up the bluff, up and over. He got into his stride, got a march on which invigorated his sense of purpose.

Arriving back at the bombsite, Captain Collins signalled his re-arrival to the unit with the flat of his hand. Heads bobbed busily above the blast barrier of the operational command post. Somebody waved back the affirmation of contact. Gingerly, the Captain got down into the dugout and laid out the kit he'd need so that it was all within arm's reach when he straddled the bomb to begin the defusal. He made the connection with the cameras and put the mic-steth headset on. Crackles, then, 'Ah, there you are, sir. Had us a bit concerned there for a mo.'

'All's well, tickety boo, Sapper.'

Captain Collins noted the unusual presence of his apprentice being on the other end of the wire. Now that was irregular. But with all the other unforeseen advents and coincidences of the last twenty-four, he wasn't about to start questioning now.

'All good, Sapper. All good!'

With Sapper Mike on the other end of mic-steth, Captain Collins reasoned that Lieutenant Billington who'd usually be listening would be busy planning next steps such as where to take the bomb to a safe place for disposal, supposing all went well. Then there was the movement of lifting gear to lift old 'Satan' out of the dugout. That had to be transported over. No point doing it prior, risking destroying good equipment if the office went up—that'd be a waste. The Captain paused for a moment to decide where he'd go for a safe demolition away from infrastructure, away from habitation.

The Captain arranged his kit in order of use, most important first: his flask of tea, the faithful old bike pump (as he called it), the bottles of acid, the requisite spanners and the hessian sacks.

'All present and correct,' to himself and then, 'Right you are there then, Sapper,' over the mic-steth. 'Let's see what Jerry's got up his sleeve for us here. The war goes on, eh!'

Sapper Mike couldn't quite get this concept straight in his head: the Captain really and truly believed that the Second World War had, to all intents and purposes, never ended and nor was it likely to. For the Captain, it had all started in 1939 and in 1992, it was still going strong. There was no emotion about it. It was just a matter of fact.

'Fact was I'm still diffusing the bombs, so the war goes on.' The young Sapper had initially quizzed other members of the unit about it. But the closest he got was Lieutenant Billington's perfunctory explanation, 'He lived through it, 39-45. Different time. No point digging any deeper on that one.'

'So, let's get to it, lad!' boomed the Captain over the mic-steth intercom. 'We've got a 2,000 kilo Satan M-class Type 17 clockwork delay fuse, proper old street flattener but simple enough to make safe. Not half as wily as the mercury anti-handling technology come 45 when the Jerry boffins really got sneaky.'

'Yes, sir,' the Sapper replied uncertainly. This was an aside in the bomb disposal lectures, as he'd come to think of them, that he'd later follow up on a mercury timer. That was a new one. Another detail in the Captain's encyclopaedic knowledge of his subject.

The Captain was referring to the fact that a detonation delay came as an evil after thought in the Second World War dropping of bombs. Initially they'd have exploded on impact but some didn't and the courageous British army response was to create the world's first bomb disposal officers out of the Royal Engineers that were at first billeted with civilians in the highly populated areas that the Luftwaffe had in their crosshairs. Who'd have volunteered for that job—all civic purpose these days—having no intel on what it was there were up against!

So cunning old Jerry cottoned onto the 'BDOs' and so, to effect the maximum damage to the infrastructure, they started fitting their 'Hermans' and 'Satans' with timer-delays. Reason being, it would give the BDOs, wardens and civvies time to gather around the bomb in stunned wonder before the timer went and the thing blew. Maximum loss of life and injury plus one less BDO in the world to confound the Luftwaffe's work.

'The war within a war, son. God, those Jerry boffins are a wily lot. You have to give them credit.' It was a recurring sentiment, that curious co-mingling of respect and hate.

The Captain knelt by the bomb, pretty much as supple as a cat now the cramp had left him. And the ringing in his ears had abated.

'TEFT,' he murmured into the mic-steth, Sapper Mike noting the only acronym the Captain allowed himself. '1/8th of an inch drill bit in place, and the power's good too,' the Captain remarked, experimentally pulling the drill trigger.

'Now then, I'm going to make two holes, 2 inches deep, either side of the nut. Steady as she goes. I'm not in a hurry to heaven!' he spluttered into the mic-steth, amusing himself.

On the other end of the mic-steth, Sapper Mike noticeably visibly winced and involuntarily shook his head. Goodness only knew how the old boy could make jokes sat on nearly 2K of German explosive. But joke he did. He wasn't wired up right.

The whine of the drill went on for some minutes which extended, it seemed, over hours. Sheer purgatory. Worse in the listening than the doing, by all accounts. The young Sapper noted how time could stretch or stand still at critical times when they were on a job. And this was certainly proving to be one of them. He had to keep reprimanding himself to focus on the sound and sight of the whirring drill bit on the monitor to prevent his mind coasting off in comfortable directions, on the Captain's changes in mood and behaviour on the trip down here to Portland that had so disconcerted him.

After what felt like an age, 'Come on then, lad! You haven't gone to sleep over there, have you?' cajoled the Captain over the connection.

As if! The Sapper's shirt was drenched with adrenalin-sweat and he had to keep wiping his palms on his trousers.

'No, sir. I'm with you, Captain,' the Sapper responded, clearing his throat as he did so.

The Captain carefully removed the bit from the drill and replaced both and the chuck key in the drill case, snapping shut the clasps of the handmade case. He laid it flat and wiped away dust that had settled on it.

'OK, young man. Now let's have a listen,' he whispered across the line. On the other end, Sapper Mike was wide eyes boring into the listening kit's sensitive dials with an intensity as if his life were flashing before him. He hoped his steely focus would disguise how he really felt.

Sapper Mike searched the four dials for the merest of flickers of movement. He'd flipped the switch from a vocal audio to sensitive in order that they might hear that dreaded ticking that signified a disturbed timer. Literally, you could have heard a pin drop. Even the ever present Portland wind had stilled. The unit stood poised, immobile. Involuntarily, the young Sapper held his breath. Nothing moved save for a bead of sweat that was making its cautious descent down the young man's temple like a field mouse alerted to the presence of a predator. Bile started to churn and claw in the Sapper's stomach. And then he heard the Captain's whispered rasp. 'Oh Christmas, here we go! Tick, tock!'

It was the tone that put a jolt through the Captain's apprentice. Gone was the jocular, hearty confident old boy. The sound was young, raw—the delicate timbre of fear. In the CCP, the hackles went up, nostrils flared, eyes flattened. A crackle of fear overloaded the audio on the mic-steth, sending the dials smashing back and forth. Sapper Mike nearly lost his balance completely as his consciousness shunted back and forth in his skull.

'Update, Sapper!' boomed Lieutenant Billington. Sapper Mike shook the emotion from himself and locked eyes into his superior. And with all the calm and perfunctory he could muster, ashen-faced, 'Timer's gone, sir. I think.' The look in the Lieutenant's glare was nothing short of livid.

'You think? What in the hell is that supposed to mean? You bloody fool! We don't deal in thoughts! We deal in facts! Now what do you bloody know, boy?'

Sapper Mike looked blank and for the first time in a while felt his mere nineteen years. He squinted and replied, all eyes on him now, save for the Lieutenant who was behind the binoculars scanning the bomb dugout trying to get a visual handle on what had happened.

'Only what the Captain said, sir! Oh Christmas, here we go!'

In the deafening quiet, Sapper Mike looked up above to see a half dozen gulls wheeling and duelling on the updrafts over the bluffs, scanning below for movement, some poised unmoving on the wind.

Chapter 30
Yorkshire

Billy Collins stood transfixed in front of the grandfather clock on the black and white chequered tile floor in the hall of Black Gate Farm. All that dark wood, tables and settees, blue and white plates, porcelain King Charles spaniels and the musty cloying odour of beeswax and dust, that austere, reserved air you could sculpt with a knife. Someone other than the government man had lived there before him and left their mark. The place just didn't marry up with Billy's guardian, the tall, sallow wordless man.

Hypnotised by the pendulum movement, back and forth, Billy had never seen such a clock before. Things on Portland had been basic to say the least. And there had never been time to contemplate time. But up here on the moors, he had little else. Never had the passage of time been so audible, so visual and so painstakingly slow. Each click of the mechanism denoting moments lost forever. The ponderous, onerous passage of time, the second hand tapping minute to minute, marking time slipping away as he saw it, sand through the glass neck of the hour glass. Truth be known, it frightened him the precision of it all, a far cry from the gradual changes of the tides, winds, the morning and evening weather of Portland, the imperceptible shift of light to dark and the lengthening of shadows on Portland. Something in his spirit baulked at the measuring and setting of time in this way.

That inescapable click of the swing of the pendulum pierced him to his core. Nevertheless, as if magnetised, Billy Collins was drawn to the clock. He relished turning the key to open the wooden front panel for glimpses of the internal workings of the thing, the interlocking, shining brass cogs of various sizes that drove the mechanism of the clock. Sure enough, he couldn't deny his admiration for the precision of the thing.

For Captain Collins, as the boy Billy in his dreams, the clock was an object of terrible beauty that over the course of the next three years, of what he thought was of the rest of the war, became his most enduring remembrance of his time there. As a boy, he withdrew into himself, his jaw set with silence, an oppressive blanket of quiet covered his unsettled mind, his spirit disturbed. He often dreamt of giant clocks spinning through azure-blue sea light, himself as a mouse slipping across brassy surfaces desperate to avoid being crushed by the cogs, the mechanism, by the blade of the pendulum.

As BDO Captain William Michael Collins, he would remember that clock in hall of Black Gate Farm as he tinkered with the brass clogs of the Luftwaffe boffin's timing mechanisms.

Billy Collins stood before the grandfather clock watching that second hand, the door of the clock open like a coffin lid, as he watched the cog movements as he tried to marry up the cog workings with the hands of the clock face, the swing of the pendulum cutting its swathe through time. After some time, Billy became aware of another rhythm, distant to the clock, like a tapping, sometimes on the beat, sometimes before, sometimes after. But insistent and growing louder undoubtedly.

Slowly, he turned registering that it came from the heavy dark oak front door. Someone was knocking on the door, synchronised with the clock tick, the volume increasing. Involuntarily, he turned and proceeded to the door, drawn to the sound. Billy squinted to focus to see the latch. He was about to lift the latch, when he paused as he picked up a series of familiar sounds that took him home to Portland. What lay behind the door was not that barren, still moorland landscape. Wheels spun in his mind as he placed the memory and then he felt it, could taste the salt. It was the buffeting comfort of the wind around Pulpit Rock.

Billy Collins flipped the latch in his excitement and flung open the door. The salt blast of a beautiful howl of wind, lifting his hair off his face, weaving around him like so many cats into the hall, filling the house. Billy's face creased into a smile as he was infused with the warmth of the memory of home. And then, as abruptly as it had arrived, the wind died, vanished and the listless silence quelled his spirit too.

Billy struggled to see as his eyes adjusted to the bright light reflected off the vision of the sea before him and he recognised the outline of Pulpit Rock, the silhouette that was burned into him as his most familiar point of reference in memory. He caught the sound of the shrieks of gulls that whirled above the rock, duelling and hovering on the up draughts. Billy stood forward in the doorway gazing in awe at the displaced scene before him: where had the tree lined lane leading up to the gate, that he passed only twice in his three years in Yorkshire— on the way in and the way out, gone. Unnerved and intrigued in equal measure.

Billy Collins' attention refocussed as he tuned into the sound of the grandfather clock marking the passage of time once more. He turned to hear the sound growing louder and louder until the clock struck the midnight hour. Each chime pierced and reverberated in him as sure as the blade of the pendulum swing. As it did so, Billy felt an old shadow cast over his turned head—goose bumps registering. Something had changed outside, diminishing the light around Pulpit Rock. Billy turned to face it.

Again, his vision took a few moments to adjust to the change in light from the dark interior of the hallway. Billy forced himself to stare at Pulpit Rock and the horribly familiar outline that was forming above and around the rock. Shaking with terror, Billy admitted to himself that the gaseous form developing before him was the monstrous semblance of the only person he had ever loathed, Mr Scriven. The air was filled with that acrid, ammoniac reek of the man. Billy noted that the mustard gas scar on the left side of his face teemed with activity. It took him a few moments to see that it was in fact made of schooling, long black fish. Thousands of them. The sight repelled him. They weren't fish. They were eels.

'Even as a man, you're just a frightened little boy, Collins,' boomed the voice of the spectre before him. The words were followed by a disappearing, sucking sound. A derisory laugh?

Billy Collins did not reply, squinting with incredulity and fear at the scale of the apparition before him. After a few extended moments without reply, the furious apparition continued, 'In the final analysis, Collins, it matters not. You are guilty of my demise and you're coming with me now. It's your time, boy.'

'But I'm not guilty of anything, Mr Scriven! We found your shoes and uniform above the Red Pool. That's all. I never knew what happened to you. I was sent away!'

'Of course, you're responsible!' Thundered the apparition of Scriven. 'You and the Goldings, all of you.'

The apparition's visage shimmered with a terrible velocity, its eyes boring into the boy before it. The livid scar came alive with a slithering movement, a repulsive, black bait ball of teaming eels causing the apparition to claw at itself.

That acrid ammonia stench engulfed the boy, causing him to retch. Sweat trickled between his shoulder blades. He had to close his eyes and swallow to try to control the nausea. The apparition grew more livid still, each word delivered as a thunderous swell and detonation.

'You are guilty and it's your time, now!'

Billy Collins, the boy, squared his shoulders and with a sanguine defiance replied, 'No, Mr Scriven. I am going nowhere with you. Not now, not then, never.' The apparition's face contorted in irritation and anger sending the black fish into a frenzy of lashing, black activity.

'What?'

'I said I'm not coming with you. It's not my time and I'm not leaving this life with you. *You have to leave now*. Leave this rock, this place. You don't belong here. I tried to help you. I tried to warn you about the E-boats. I knew, we knew the havoc they'd wreak. You wouldn't listen. Your vanity deafened you to us. You couldn't listen to us because you hated us for whatever reason. We even tried to warn the Admiralty. But you scuppered that too!'

Billy Collins delivered these words without a quiver, fearfully calm. He couldn't prevent the words escaping his mouth. Spoken as a boy, meant as a man. As he did so, behind Pulpit Rock, behind the apparition of Mr Scriven, on the waters of Chesil Bay, the terrible events of the slaughter of Operation Tiger began to play out, causing the apparition to whirl around, turning its back on Billy.

Billy could see through the thousands of tonnes of solid rock, through the apparition as, caught off-guard, unawares as shells boomed, exploded and bloomed like poisonous, orangey-red flowers over the midnight waters, pewter silver in the moonlight. Shouts of anguished despair and tearing metal travelled across the water, as souls weighted down with rucksacks of equipment leapt, slow motion to watery bubble-surrounded graves in an effort to escape the searing heat of super-heated metals. It was carnage exactly and Billy felt that powerlessness, that constricting weight of responsibility pressuring him.

Very quietly, he continued, 'We tried to warn you, Mr Scriven. That's the end of it. What you did was up to you. You did that on your own. You should have listened to Mrs Golding. You met her outside the cottage and then at the Admiralty. You had the chance to listen and act and warn them about the E-boats. But you didn't and that's down to you, alone.'

The last words left him breathless, the enormity of speaking up to the apparition of the man who had hung so heavy on him all his life who was still trying to burden him with the weight of responsibility. But Billy also felt a lessening of that weight. He was lighter of mind, exhausted by it too. He had more to say, other questions to ask.

Billy's jaw was set in anger, his back teeth grinding, muscles visibly working, the crow's feet of a man who had spent his life outdoors squinting at the light, exacerbated by the rising of frustration and fury within him. He was fight or flight, alright. However, the apparition remained oblivious with its back to him, transfixed by the destruction of Operation Tiger, the same scene that had haunted both the boy, Billy Collins and the old man Captain Collins in the vivid bright light of pre-dawn dreams. Billy knew the scene only all too well and then understood that he had no need of watching it all again, reliving it all again.

With that thought, Billy noticed that the white noise of panic and fury that always accompanied this looping play of events began to fade. The Halloween oranges and reds of rose bloom explosions lessened and dimmed in the night light. The sound and fury were tuning out. As it did so, the apparition turned to him. The piercing anger in its eyes was replaced with something else as its form, too, began to fade. And that was when he heard that familiar voice. Billy turned in the doorway of Black Gate Farm. There in front of the grandfather clock was his oldest friend. Maggie Golding. She closed and locked the front panel of the clock and pocketed the key and instructed him, 'He's gone now, Billy. He can do you no more harm. It's time for you to come home, friend.'

An impression pushed its way to the front of Billy's mind, one last time. The cries of anguished men and tearing metal quelled and the ever present sound of the surf's reassuring pulses reasserted itself, the soundscape and the vision of destruction faded to a pin point and then nothing. A thought came to Billy, 'I'll never know Mr Scriven's motivations or the reasons for his hatred and meanness. And that doesn't matter. I don't need to know. I don't need to understand everything. No need to dig deeper in that. It's none of my business. That's for him alone. They don't have to affect me. I don't want or need them. They can be gone from me.'

That thought was a realisation, an awakening of sorts that the man, Captain Collins, understood.

Backwards through time, Mr Scriven's apparitional face faded through his decades, each movement a year flickering by until the face was barely recognisable. Paul Scriven, a boy of age comparable to Billy Collins, about ten years old when the transformation paused as the realisation passed across the eyes that this retrograde travel wasn't about to stop there and the years stripped away and the apparition shrunk to nothing, disappearing in a baby's initial cry of anguish until there was nothing.

Billy Collins stood squinting at Pulpit Rock, at the memory of what he had just seen. Immobile, the sea breeze, iodine and salt cleansing, enveloping around him, the endless wash of waves below. And then Billy Collins smiled a quiet smile, an unfettered contentment he hadn't felt in a very long time. A sense of atonement and connection with the moment, not before or after the beat, but within.

And that was how a breathless Sapper Mike found the old boy, Captain Collins, crouching beside 2,000 kilos of the Luftwaffe's finest explosive grinning wildly, eyes as clear and bright as a summer tide pool alive with quick, shrimp movement. Sapper Mike 'broke ground', as they say, flaunted protocol amid a hail of yelled commands (you can imagine the language of fear) from his seniors behind the operational command post as he scrambled over the grit and gravel to assist his mentor Captain Collins when he thought he'd heard Satan's timing mechanism trigger over the mic-steth. The Captain, who'd fallen silent, immobile after his initial, 'Oh Christmas, here we go!'

Sapper Mike had skidded, jumped, fallen into the pit to see his crouching grinning mentor who then filled the screaming silent void between them.

'Hello lad, what brings you here in such a hurry?'

Stunned by the incongruity of the language and the scene, Sapper Mike managed only the merest of replies, 'sir, are you alright?'

'Tip top actually, Sapper!' Replied a rejuvenated old man looking down at the removed, disabled and now safe timing detonation mechanism for the bomb.

'Is it safe, sir?'

'It would seem so. We still appear to be here, lad,' replied the Captain, rising gingerly to his feet in the way you do after a short, deep sleep. He surveyed his apparatus, the bomb, the disarmed detonator and finally Sapper Mike, fixing him with a look of scrutiny and intent. 'What the blazes are you doing here, lad? Why aren't you at the OCP? You could have got yourself killed,' he stated, musing over his blithe statement of the obvious.

In the quiet, Captain Collins noted that the mic-steth was all a-twitter, where he had placed it carefully on the now benign bomb. The explosive still needed removing, another delicate task, but much the less dangerous with the detonator removed. Running through the protocol at what needed to be done next, Captain Collins put the mic-steth on. Lieutenant Billington was mid-sentence.

'Will you send that stupid bugger back over here, Captain? God, is he going to get a dressing down for this! Wantonly disobeying orders, endangering life, leaving his post! He could have got himself killed! Distracting a senior office in the execution of duty—you don't need to be worrying about a team member when you're—'

'Slow down, Lieutenant,' the Captain interjected, hoping to derail the Lieutenant's protective fury. 'Lieutenant! Listen to me! I'm not sending him back. He is staying right here.'

'I'll give him such a … what, Captain?' replied the Lieutenant with incredulity.

'I said that I'm not sending him back to the CCP, not until the job's done. The lad's got to learn.'

'But sir, for such flagrant disregard for the rules, he should be—'

'Yes, I'm quite aware of the protocols and what constitutes a breach of practice. I fully understand that his actions are a disciplinary matter. But that's not going to happen. Not here, not today. It never happened and you can make sure the rest of the unit understands that. What has happened on Portland today stays in Portland, never to be mentioned again. Colonel Wildblood is not to get wind of it. Got it, Lieutenant?'

'No, sir! I don't … got it?'

'Uh, Lieutenant, the Sapper's actions are not to be spoken of or discussed off this island.'

'Uh, I don't understand, sir?'

'You don't have to understand, you just have to do as I've said. Comprendez?'

'Uh, yes sir!'

'Right, that's settled then. And as he's here, I'll make use of him. Make the most of the opportunity. Detonator removed. The explosive still needs to be dissolved, removed. I'll be getting him to assist. A live lesson, if you like. Got it, now?'

After a pause, Lieutenant Billington replied, 'Yes sir. Excellent idea, sir.'

'Good, I'm quite pleased to be here myself.'

The Lieutenant was more than a little confused by the Captain's last comment as well as the breach of process and protocol. There should never be more than one officer on site to reduce the risk of potential loss of life. But the Captain must have had his reasons. The whole job had had an irregular feel to it that he wasn't comfortable with. It was the old boy's last job though. *An order is an order*, he reflected to himself, and he paused to take in the rest of the unit who had been watching him carefully, wondering about the bafflement on the Lieutenant's face as he received his orders.

The Lieutenant took in the unit who were eagerly awaiting the update, the orders, he gathered himself, squared his shoulders and tone of voice and informed the unit of the unusual instructions, making it as plain and definite them as the Captain had made it to him.

The unit then waited for the all clear when they could make their way to the dugout for debrief and orders for the next phase of the job. They stood to attention, assembled around the pit, the Captain and his apprentice still in it. The Captain delivered his final instructions crisply, succinctly in an effort to conceal the happy fatigue that seemed to have settled on him. Each man in the unit nodded his affirmation. There was no need for any more than was necessary, an economy of words was fitting.

As such Captain Collins conveyed his final words, in his official capacity without drama or show of emotion. 'Chaps, you know what needs to be done. Quick, quiet and efficient, does it. As per! I'm not going to drone on. You know this was my last job. I could say a lot but there's no need. You know me, I know you and it's been a pleasure working with you as a unit. I couldn't have asked for more and you've certainly been no less. You are a credit to the Royal Engineers.

'You know the drill. Winch her up and put her in the trailer with the sandbags. I have a feeling that the powers that be might want to keep hold of this visitor for posterity's sake. The Sapper and I are heading back to the Admiralty. That's been quite enough excitement for one day.'

Sapper Mike and the Captain clambered out of the dugout and made their way to the Red Wing. Captain Collins chucked him the keys which Sapper Mike caught them left-handed, a hand raised to the sky, all instinct.

'You're driving,' the Captain added. Though that was obvious—a given. Reassuring though. They got in the Red Wing and pulled off carefully. The unit paused to watch them depart for a moment before they got busy to finish the job.

In the Red Wing, neither spoke—content in amicable silence, stilling the minds, taking in the detail, the here and now, alive.

Back at the dugout, Lieutenant was giving orders, allocating tasks. They'd got the winch in place to remove the body of the bomb now rendered harmless with chains around it as it swung gently in the breeze, halfway out of the pit when he stopped mid instruction, 'Will you look at that, lads?'

Each member of the unit paused their actions to follow his gaze. Not twenty feet from the dugout were about a dozen rabbits, grazing, playing. Someone said, 'Brazen little buggers here, aren't they?'

Another said, 'Don't they have some weird ideas about rabbits here?'

'Yairs, funny old lot, these Portlanders,' came the reply.

'Too true,' replied Lieutenant Billington, absentmindedly thinking of their Captain.

Final Chapter / Epilogue

Back at the Admiralty, Sapper Mike and the Captain got their heads down for an hour or so before getting shaved, showered and changed, as the powers that be had decided that, in the event the job went off alright, they'd put on a bit of a spread for the Captain and his unit to for making the island safe again. Word must have got out that the Captain was a son of the island who'd returned to Portland to execute his last job. Evidently, someone had noted the poetry in it, oblivious to the fact that the Hairy Hand of God and the Fates had got together and given the Captain the fright of his life.

The Captain had been informed that the great and good would be attending. As he shaved, the Captain prepared himself by running through the scene of the 'spread' to come, the inevitable tray of egg sandwiches, cocktail sausages and all the usual fare. Then there'd be the parquet-floored hall emanating its beeswaxed, polished odour mixed with the scents of the food. The red, white and blue bunting and the hubbub, murmurs and guffaws of the mostly male crowd, politely munching sandwiches off paper plates in circles of congregation. He'd play it like he always did. Flitting between groups so as not to get too drawn into conversation. Truth be known and true to type, the Captain had never much cared for large social gatherings, small talk or crowds for that matter.

'Nothing much extrovert about you, Billy Collins,' Maggie's mother, Sarah, had said at some point in time, many, many moons ago.

No, he'd be polite and stick around for half an hour, making sure he gave due attention to the chief of staff, local bigwigs and the great and good. Apparently, the sheriff of the island and the mayor in his robes and chains would be in attendance. He hoped to God there would be no ceremony where some sort of speech was expected; he sighed heavily at the thought.

The Captain checked the shine in the toecaps of his boots. Immaculate— could practically see his face in them. He checked his uniform for fluff, stray hairs, lint and nodded to himself in the mirror, content with his presentation. He went to pass a last comb through his thick, greying short back and sides but replaced the tortoiseshell in his wet bag, safe. No need. He'd had the comb since he was a boy—a gift from the lady of the sallow government man at Black Gate Farm.

As he remembered that tall, wordless man, Captain Collins smiled and spoke to his reflection in the mirror, 'Will I pay such attention to personal presentation and detail in retirement?'

'Of course you will, old boy! Can't let the standards slip. Method and care in all things!'

And with that, there came a familiar rap at the door.

'Ready, sir?' As if it needed asking! The Captain opened the door quick smart, causing the young Sapper to take a step back as he saw the keen gleam in his mentor's eye, the wry smile.

'Last act, lad, let's get to it! Any word from the unit? They should be back by now.'

'Not a dicky bird yet, sir. You think all's well?' The Captain had turned his back on his apprenticeship who was leaning in to lock up his room.

'Of course, it is, lad. Have a bit of confidence!'

The young man shrugged his assent. If the Captain was fine with it, it was fine. No need to delve further on that one.

'Come on, lad, let's eat cake,' the Captain instructed over his shoulder.

'Now you're talking, sir.'

The gathering of the great and good in the Officer's Mess was much as the Captain had imagined—congenial atmosphere with the ubiquitous sandwiches to get the calories up. The hubbub and chuckle of polite conversation echoed off the wood panel walls and muffled off the mostly male bodies. Red, white and blue triangles of bunting and Union Jacks availed. Sapper Mike grabbed a plate and sandwiches, famished, and joined the Captain who was talking to one of the bigwigs.

'Tell me, Commodore,' the Captain asked between sips of tea gone orange, too strong in the urn. 'The bunting? Planning for a party?'

'Well, yes, as it happens, Captain. The evacuated islanders have been having a whale of a time at their quarters at the holiday camp in Weymouth. It seems that finding that bomb appears to have awoken something of the sterling British spirit of the Second World War. Thought we'd get on the bandwagon and invite them here this afternoon. Make the most of the wave of patriotism and nostalgia and all that goes with it.'

'Yes, Commodore. And all that goes with it,' the Captain added wistfully.

'What was that?' replied the Commodore, quizzically, searching.

'Oh nothing, Commodore! Something my grandfather said came back to me when you said all that goes with it.'

'I'm sorry, I don't follow?'

'All that goes with it. One of the last things he said to me. *It's just a uniform.* That was what he said.'

Sapper Mike noted that the Captain was away in his memories as he had frequently been in the last twenty-four hours. And then he looked to the Commodore and observed the visage of camaraderie clouded with a momentary suspicion. The young man guessed that he hadn't taken kindly to the Captain's reference to 'just a uniform'—given where they were, what they did, and the various components of the 'service machine'—uniform was all. The essence of all their being.

But something had shifted, changed in the Captain. Clearly, it was no longer *his all*. Maybe it was his impending retirement. Who could know? Sapper Mike shrugged to himself. The Captain would let him know in good time if he needed to know. No need to mind on that unnecessarily. If the Captain was going to share that confidence, he would, and something told the young man that it wouldn't be now, within the Commodore's earshot. It seemed that the Commodore had also sensed this, but chose to ignore it and his demeanour returned to the avuncular camaraderie required of the occasion.

'A wave of good old-fashioned patriotism!' He declared and paused for a moment for the three to shift their feet to assume a position to concentrate on the import of what he had to say next.

'The history teacher at the local school has turned their 'evacuation' into a sort of living history experience. Period costumes, ration books, needs of the time. Powdered eggs too, by Jove! They even had a Vera Lynn 'We shall not be moved party' in the clubhouse last night.'

'That's the spirit. Turn a potential problem into something positive. Solution focussed!'

'I have to say, Captain, I do marvel at the way you Royal Engineers in bomb disposal underplay your language.'

The Captain looked baffled. 'Come again, sir?'

The Commodore squinted and cocked his head to reply, 'A potential problem, Captain?'

'I don't think I quite understand, Commodore.'

'Really, Captain? There are very few of us who'd have the presence of mind and courage to sit on top of 2,000 kilos of German explosive with the possible consequences of being blown to kingdom come and refer to it merely as a 'potential problem'!' The Commodore guffawed at his observations and was shaking his head in merriment as he slapped the Captain on the back.

'Oh I see. I'd not thought of it like that,' replied the Captain, nodding slowly as he processed the information and salted it away to examine at a later date.

Feeling emboldened by his observations, the Commodore straightened himself into a composure befitting of his station and nodded to the Mess hall doors to alert the attention of the Captain and his apprentice, who both turned to see what he had noticed. They turned to see the first of the islander guests and the Commodore murmur, 'By gosh, it's that stubborn old bird who wouldn't leave her home until the last minute. The gall of these people who just can't listen to reason and be told what to do. Putting their lives in danger!'

'That's because some people don't live by reason alone, sir. They live by something older, wiser, like instinct—the intuition that there were wolves in the forest even if you couldn't see, hear or smell them,' interjected the Captain who was striding to meet his oldest friend, Maggie Golding, who, all dolled up in forget-me-not print dress and cream cardigan and shoes, had a similar look of intent about her. Sapper Mike was glad of the interruption. He didn't want to hear the Captain going off-piste for the time being.

A baffled Commodore and savvy Sapper watched, saucers held, cups poised at lips as the Captain and the lady momentarily grasped each other's outstretched hands and exchanged the briefest of looks that told the Sapper that some sort of exchange and agreement had been made. As the Commodore took in the scene and looked away as the couple turned to make their way back to him and the young Sapper, he murmured, 'Life in the old dog yet.'

At the risk of contradicting his elders and betters, Sapper Mike corrected his Commodore, 'No, sir! That's the friendship of a lifetime in the waiting and making,' he stated as he grinned at his mentor.

The Commodore shrugged, aware that there was possibly more going on there than met the eye and that he wasn't about to be brought up to speed with the lady present at any rate. And besides it was a social occasion, a party, so why not keep it light?

In a relaxed manner that the young Sapper hadn't seen in days, perhaps ever, Captain Collins introduced Maggie to the Commodore, 'Maggie Golding, Commodore.'

Maggie extended her hand to greet the Commodore and then corrected the Captain, 'Maggie Sansom, actually. I took on my mother's maiden name.'

'Oh, I see,' replied the Captain when clearly he didn't.

'But I may be due for a change,' Maggie added.

Captain Collins looked baffled, but shook it away as the Commodore took up the initiative, 'So, Captain. I hear you are about to retire? This return to your birthplace also marks the end of your service. What are you going to do with yourself?' enquired the Commodore, puffing himself up.

'A spot of fishing, sir, I believe,' the Captain replied.

'When did you last fish, Billy?' Maggie asked.

'About 50 years ago, if the truth be known, Maggie.'

They exchanged a look that neither the Commodore nor the Sapper deciphered, as Maggie observed, 'I think you've been fishing all that time, Billy Collins.'

'That I might, Maggie, that I might,' he responded with an exhalation.

'But first, it so happens that I have a spare ticket to go whale watching in the Pacific Northwest next month. In Oregon.'

'Oh, splendid, splendid!' interjected the Commodore. 'No finer sight than to see those majestic creatures in their natural habitat.'

The Captain had a glint of shy happiness in his eyes.

'Oregon, you say?' offered the Captain's apprentice.

'That's right, Oregon,' replied Maggie.

'Would that be Portland, Oregon, by any chance?'

'Where else,' replied Captain Collins' oldest, dearest friend.

THE END